The Three Miss Kings

An Australian Story

by

Ada Cambridge

Double 9
BOOKS

The Three Miss Kings
An Australian Story
by Ada Cambridge

Copyright © 2024

All Rights reserved.

ISBN: 978-93-69071-18-0

Published by

DOUBLE 9 BOOKS

2/13-B, Ansari Road
Daryaganj, New Delhi – 110002
info@double9books.com
www.double9books.com
Tel. 011-40042856

This book is under public domain

ABOUT THE AUTHOR

Ada Cambridge was an English-born Australian writer, born on November 21, 1844, in Saint Germans, United Kingdom. She immigrated to Australia, where she became a significant literary figure, producing over 25 works of fiction, three volumes of poetry, and two autobiographical works. Many of her novels were serialised in Australian newspapers but were never published as standalone books. Her literary career spanned decades, reflecting both her personal experiences and her observations of societal dynamics. Cambridge married Rev. George Frederick Cross in 1870, and they had five children, one of whom was Dr. K. Stuart Cross. She spent much of her life in Melbourne, where she passed away on July 19, 1926, at the age of 81. Her work remains an important part of the literary history of Australia, contributing significantly to the cultural and social landscape of the time. While her fame was largely confined to Australia during her lifetime, her writing offers valuable insight into the experiences of women and the challenges they faced in the 19th and early 20th centuries.

CONTENTS

CHAPTER I
A DISTANT VIEW 9

CHAPTER II
A LONELY EYRIE 14

CHAPTER III
PREPARATIONS FOR FLIGHT 19

CHAPTER IV
DEPARTURE 25

CHAPTER V
ROCKED IN THE CRADLE OF THE
DEEP 29

CHAPTER VI
PAUL 33

CHAPTER VII
A MORNING WALK 40

CHAPTER VIII
AN INTRODUCTION TO MRS.
GRUNDY 45

CHAPTER IX
MRS. AARONS 51

CHAPTER X
THE FIRST INVITATION 59

CHAPTER XI
DISAPPOINTMENT 63

CHAPTER XII
TRIUMPH 69

CHAPTER XIII
PATTY IN UNDRESS 75

CHAPTER XIV
IN THE WOMB OF FATE 81

CHAPTER XV
ELIZABETH FINDS A FRIEND 86

CHAPTER XVI
"WE WERE NOT STRANGERS, AS TO
US AND ALL IT SEEMED" 90

CHAPTER XVII
AFTERNOON TEA 95

CHAPTER XVIII
THE FAIRY GODMOTHER 101

CHAPTER XIX
A MORNING AT THE EXHIBITION 106

CHAPTER XX
CHINA V. THE CAUSE OF HUMANITY 111

CHAPTER XXI
THE "CUP" 117

CHAPTER XXII
CROSS PURPOSES 125

CHAPTER XXIII
MR. YELVERTON'S MISSION 128

CHAPTER XXIV
AN OLD STORY 134

CHAPTER XXV
OUT IN THE COLD 140

CHAPTER XXVI
WHAT PAUL COULD NOT KNOW 146

CHAPTER XXVII
SLIGHTED 152

CHAPTER XXVIII
"WRITE ME AS ONE WHO LOVES
HIS FELLOW MEN" 158

CHAPTER XXIX
PATTY CONFESSES...164

CHAPTER XXX
THE OLD AND THE NEW 170

CHAPTER XXXI
IN RETREAT 177

CHAPTER XXXII
HISTORY REPEATS ITSELF 184

CHAPTER XXXIII
THE DRIVE HOME 190

CHAPTER XXXIV
SUSPENSE 197

CHAPTER XXXV
HOW ELIZABETH MADE UP
HER MIND 203

CHAPTER XXXVI
INVESTIGATION 208

CHAPTER XXXVII
DISCOVERY 215

CHAPTER XXXVIII
THE TIME FOR ACTION 221

CHAPTER XXXIX
AN ASSIGNATION...229

CHAPTER XL
MRS. DUFF-SCOTT HAS TO BE
RECKONED WITH..239

CHAPTER XLI
MR. YELVERTON STATES HIS
INTENTIONS 243

CHAPTER XLII
HER LORD AND MASTER..250

CHAPTER XLIII
THE EVENING BEFORE THE
WEDDING...258

CHAPTER XLIV
THE WEDDING DAY 266

CHAPTER XLV
  IN SILK ATTIRE 273

CHAPTER XLVI
  PATTY CHOOSES HER CAREER 281

CHAPTER XLVII
  A FAIR FIELD AND NO FAVOUR.. 287

CHAPTER XLVIII
  PROBATION 293

CHAPTER XLIX
  YELVERTON.. 298

CHAPTER L
  "THY PEOPLE SHALL BE MY
  PEOPLE" 306

CHAPTER LI
  PATIENCE REWARDED.. 310

CHAPTER LII
  CONCLUSION 315

CHAPTER I
A DISTANT VIEW

On the second of January, in the year 1880, three newly-orphaned sisters, finding themselves left to their own devices, with an income of exactly one hundred pounds a year a-piece, sat down to consult together as to the use they should make of their independence.

The place where they sat was a grassy cliff overlooking a wide bay of the Southern Ocean—a lonely spot, whence no sign of human life was visible, except in the sail of a little fishing boat far away. The low sun, that blazed at the back of their heads, and threw their shadows and the shadow of every blade of grass into relief, touched that distant sail and made it shine like bridal satin; while a certain island rock, the home of sea-birds, blushed like a rose in the same necromantic light. As they sat, they could hear the waves breaking and seething on the sands and stones beneath them, but could only see the level plain of blue and purple water stretching from the toes of their boots to the indistinct horizon. That particular Friday was a terribly hot day for the colony, as weather records testify, but in this favoured spot it had been merely a little too warm for comfort, and, the sea-breeze coming up fresher and stronger as the sun went down, it was the perfection of an Australian summer evening at the hour of which I am writing.

"What I want," said Patty King (Patty was the middle one), "is to make a dash—a straight-out plunge into the world, Elizabeth—no shilly-shallying and dawdling about, frittering our money away before we begin. Suppose we go to London—we shall have enough to cover our travelling expenses, and our income to start fair with—surely we could live anywhere on three hundred a year, in the greatest comfort—and take rooms near the British Museum?—or in South Kensington?—or suppose we go to one of those intellectual German towns, and study music and languages? What do you think, Nell? I am sure we could do it easily if we tried."

"Oh," said Eleanor, the youngest of the trio, "I don't care so long as we go *somewhere*, and do *something*."

"What do you think, Elizabeth?" pursued the enterprising Patty, alert and earnest. "Life is short, and there is so much for us to see and learn—all these years and years we have been out of it so utterly! Oh, I wonder how we have borne it! How *have* we borne it—to hear about things and never to know or do them, like other people! Let us get into the thick of it at once, and recover lost time. Once in Europe, everything would be to our hand—everything would be possible. What do you think?"

"My dear," said Elizabeth, with characteristic caution, "I think we are too young and ignorant to go so far afield just yet."

"We are all over twenty-one," replied Patty quickly, "and though we have lived the lives of hermits, we are not more stupid than other people. We can speak French and German, and we are quite sharp enough to know when we are being cheated. We should travel in perfect safety, finding our way as we went along. And we *do* know something of those places—of Melbourne we know nothing."

"We should never get to the places mother knew—the sort of life we have heard of. And Mr. Brion and Paul are with us here—they will tell us all we want to know. No, Patty, we must not be reckless. We might go to Europe by-and-bye, but for the present let Melbourne content us. It will be as much of the world as we shall want to begin with, and we ought to get some experience before we spend our money—the little capital we have to spend."

"You don't call two hundred and thirty-five pounds a little, do you?" interposed Eleanor. This was the price that a well-to-do storekeeper in the neighbouring township had offered them for the little house which had been their home since she was born, and to her it seemed a fortune.

"Well, dear, we don't quite know yet whether it is little or much, for, you see, we don't know what it costs to live as other people do. We must not be reckless, Patty—we must take care of what we have, for we have only ourselves in the wide world to depend on, and this is all our fortune. I should think no girls were ever so utterly without belongings as we are now," she added, with a little break in her gentle voice.

She was half lying on the grass, leaning on her elbow and propping her head in her hand. The light behind her was growing momentarily less fierce, and the breeze from the quiet ocean more cool and delicious; and she had taken off her hat in order to see and breathe in freedom. A noble figure she was, tall, strong, perfect in proportion, fine in texture, full of natural dignity and grace—the product of several generations of healthy and cultured people, and therefore a truly well-bred woman. Her face was a little too grave and thoughtful for her years, perhaps—she was not quite eight-and-twenty—and it was not at all handsome, in the vulgar sense of the word. But a sweeter, truer, kinder face, with its wide, firm mouth and its open brows, and its candid grey eyes, one could not wish to see. She had smooth brown hair of excessive fineness and brightness (a peculiarity of good blood shared by all the sisters), and it was closely coiled in a knot of braids at the back of her head, without any of those curls and fringes about the temples that have since become the prevailing fashion. And she was dressed in a very common, loosely-made, black print gown, with a little frill of crape at her throat, and a leather belt round her by no means slender waist. Her feet were encased in large and clumsy boots, and her shapely hands, fine-skinned and muscular, were not encased at all, but were brown with constant exposure to sun and wind, and the wear and tear of miscellaneous housework. The impetuous Patty, who sat bolt upright clasping her knees, was like her, but with marked differences. She was smaller and slighter in make, though she had the same look of abundant health and vigour. Her figure, though it had never worn stays, was more after the pattern of modern womanhood than Elizabeth's, and her brilliant little face was exquisite in outline, in colour, in all the charms of bright and wholesome youth. Patty's eyes were dark and keen, and her lips were delicate and red, and her hair had two or three ripples in it, and was the colour of a half-ripe chestnut. And altogether, she was a very striking and unmistakeably handsome girl. She, too, wore a black print gown, and a straw sailor hat, with a black ribbon, tilted back on her bead, and the same country-made boots, and the same brown and gloveless hands. Eleanor, again, with the general family qualities of physical health and refinement, had her own characteristics. She was slim and tall—as slim as Patty, and nearly as tall as Elizabeth, as was shown in her attitude as she lay full length on the grass, with her feet on the edge of the cliff, and her head on her elder sister's knee. She had a pure white skin, and sentimental blue eyes, and lovely yellow hair, just tinged with red; and her voice was low and sweet, and her manners gentle and graceful, and altogether she was one of the most pleasing young women that ever blushed unseen like a wild flower in the savage solitudes of the bush. This young person was not in black—because, she said, the weather was too hot for black. She wore an old blue gingham that had faded to a faint lavender in course of numerous washings, and she had a linen handkerchief loosely tied round her neck, and cotton gloves on her hands. She was the only one of the sisters to whom it had occurred that, having a good complexion, it was worth while to preserve it.

The parents of these three girls had been a mysterious couple, about whose circumstances and antecedents people knew just as much as they liked to conjecture, and no more. Mr. King had been on the diggings in the old days—that much was a fact, to which he had himself been known to testify; but where and what he had been before, and why he had lived like a pelican in the wilderness ever since, nobody knew, though everybody was at liberty to guess. Years and years ago, he came to this lone coast—a region of hopeless sand and scrub, which no squatter or free selector with a grain of sense would look at—and here on a bleak headland he built his rude house, piece by piece, in great part with his own hands, and fenced his little paddock, and made his little garden; and here he had lived till the other day, a morose recluse, who shunned his neighbours as they shunned him, and never was known to have either business or pleasure, or commerce of any kind with his fellow-men. It was supposed that he had made some money at the diggings, for he took up no land (there was none fit to take up, indeed, within a dozen miles of him), and he kept no stock—except a few cows and pigs for the larder; and at the same time there was never any sign of actual poverty in his little establishment, simple and humble as it was. And it was also supposed—nay, it was confidently believed—that he was not, so to speak, "all there." No man who was not "touched" would conduct himself with such preposterous eccentricity as that which had marked his long career in their midst—so the neighbours argued, not without a show of reason. But the greatest mystery in connection with Mr. King was Mrs. King. He was obviously a gentleman, in the conventional sense of the word, but she was, in every sense, the most beautiful and accomplished lady that ever was seen, according to the judgment of those who knew her—the women who had nursed her in her confinements, and washed and scrubbed for her, and the tradesmen of the town to whom she had gone in her little buggy for occasional stores, and the doctor and the parson, and the children whom she had brought up in such a wonderful manner to be copies (though, it was thought, poor ones) of herself. And yet she had borne to live all the best years of her life, at once a captive and an exile, on that desolate sea-shore— and had loved that harsh and melancholy man with the most faithful and entire devotion—and had suffered her solitude and privations, the lack of everything to which she *must* have been once accustomed, and the fret and trouble of her husband's bitter moods—without a murmur that anybody had ever heard.

Both of them were gone now from the cottage on the cliff where they had lived so long together. The idolised mother had been dead for several years, and the harsh, and therefore not much loved nor much mourned, father had lain but a few weeks in his grave beside her; and they had left their children, as Elizabeth described it, more utterly without belongings than ever girls were before. It was a curious position altogether. As far as they knew, they had no relations, and they had never had a friend. Not one of them had left their home for a night since Eleanor was born, and not one invited guest had slept there during the whole of that period. They had never been to school, or had any governess but their mother, or any experience of life and the ways of the world save what they gained in their association with her, and from the books that she and their father selected for them. According to all precedent, they ought to have been dull and rustic and stupid (it was supposed that they were, because they dressed themselves so badly), but they were only simple and truthful in an extraordinary degree. They had no idea what was the "correct thing" in costume or manners, and they knew little or nothing of the value of money; but they were well and widely read, and highly accomplished in all the household arts, from playing the piano to making bread and butter, and as full of spiritual and intellectual aspirations as the most advanced amongst us.

CHAPTER II
A LONELY EYRIE

"Then we will say Melbourne to begin with. Not for a permanence, but until we have gained a little more experience," said Patty, with something of regret and reluctance in her voice. By this time the sun had set and drawn off all the glow and colour from sea and shore. The island rock was an enchanted castle no longer, and the sails of the fishing-boats had ceased to shine. The girls had been discussing their schemes for a couple of hours, and had come to several conclusions.

"I think so, Patty. It would be unwise to hurry ourselves in making our choice of a home. We will go to Melbourne and look about us. Paul Brion is there. He will see after lodgings for us and put us in the way of things generally. That will be a great advantage. And then the Exhibition will be coming—it would be a pity to miss that. And we shall feel more as if we belonged to the people here than elsewhere, don't you think? They are more likely to be kind to our ignorance and help us."

"Oh, we don't want anyone to help us."

"Someone must teach us what we don't know, directly or indirectly—and we are not above being taught."

"But," insisted Patty, "there is no reason why we should be beholden to anybody. Paul Brion may look for some lodgings for us, if he likes—just a place to sleep in for a night or two—and tell us where we can find a house—that's all we shall want to ask of him or of anybody. We will have a house of our own, won't we?—so as not to be overlooked or interfered with."

"Oh, of course!" said Eleanor promptly. "A landlady on the premises is not to be thought of for a moment. Whatever we do, we don't want to be interfered with, Elizabeth."

"No, my dear—you can't desire to be free from interference—unpleasant interference—more than I do. Only I don't think we shall be able to be so independent as Patty thinks. I fancy, too, that we shall not care to be, when we begin to live in the world with other people. It will be so charming to have friends!"

"Oh—friends!" Patty exclaimed, with a little toss of the head. "It is too soon to think about friends—when we have so much else to think about! We must have some lessons in Melbourne, Elizabeth. We will go to that library every day and read. We will make our stay there a preparation for England and Germany and Italy. Oh, Nell, Nell! think of seeing the great Alps and the Doge's Palace before we die!"

"Ah!" responded Eleanor, drawing a long breath.

They all rose from the grass and stood still an instant, side by side, for a last look at the calm ocean which had been the background of their simple lives. Each was sensible that it was a solemn moment, in view of the changes to come, but not a word was spoken to imply regret. Like all the rest of us, they were ungrateful for the good things of the present and the past, and were not likely to understand how much they loved the sea, that, like the nurse of Rorie Mhor, had lulled them to sleep every night since they were born, while the sound of its many waters was still in their ears.

"Sam Dunn is out late," said Eleanor, pointing to a dark dot far away, that was a glittering sail a little while ago.

"It is a good night for fishing," said Patty.

And then they turned their faces landward, and set forth on their road home. Climbing to the top of the cliff on the slope of which they had been sitting, they stood upon a wide and desolate heath covered in all directions with a short, stiff scrub, full of wonderful wild-flowers (even at this barren season of the year), but without a tree of any sort; a picturesque desert, but still a desert, though with fertile country lying all around it—as utterly waste as the irreclaimable Sahara. Through this the girls wended their way by devious tracks amongst the bushes, ankle deep in the loose sand; and then again striking the cliff, reached a high point from which they had a distant view of human habitations—a little township, fringing a little bay; a lighthouse beyond it, with its little star shining steadily through the twilight; a little pier, running like a black thread through the silvery surf; and even a little steamer from Melbourne lying at the pier-head, veiling the rock-island, that now frowned like a fortress behind it, in a thin film of grey smoke from its invisible little funnels. But they did not go anywhere near these haunts of their fellow-men. Hugging the cliff, which was here of a great height, and honeycombed with caves in which the green sea-water rumbled and thundered like a great drum in the calm weather, and like a furious bombardment in a storm, they followed a slender track worn in the scant grass by their own light feet, until they came to a little depression in the line of the coast—a hollow scooped out of the great headland as if some Titanic monster of a prehistoric period had risen up out of the waves and bitten it—where, sheltered and hidden on three sides by grassy banks, sloping gently upward until they overtopped the chimneys, and with all the great plain of the sea outspread beneath the front verandah, stood the house which had been, but was to be no more, their home.

It was well worth the money that the storekeeper had offered for it. It was a really charming house, though people had not been accustomed to look at it in that light—though it was built of roughest weatherboard that had never known a paint-brush, and heavily roofed with great sheets of bark that were an offence to the provincial eye, accustomed to the chaste elegance of corrugated zinc. A strong, and sturdy, and genuine little house—as, indeed, it had to be to hold its own against the stormy blasts that buffeted it; mellowed and tanned with time and weather, and with all its honest, rugged features softened under a tender drapery of hardy English ivy and climbing plants that patient skill and care had induced to grow, and even to thrive in that unfriendly air. The verandah, supported on squat posts, was a continuation of the roof; and that roof, with green leaves curling upward over it, was so conspicuously solid, and so widely overspread and over-shadowed the low walls, that it was about all that could be seen of the house from the ridges of the high land around it. But lower down, the windows—nearly all set in rude but substantial door frames—opened like shy eyes in the shadow of the deep eaves of the verandah, like eyes that had expression in them; and the retiring walls bore on numerous nails and shelves a miscellaneous but orderly collection of bird-cages, flower boxes, boating and fishing apparatus, and odds and ends of various kinds, that gave a charming homely picturesqueness to the quaint aspect of the place. The comparatively spacious verandah, running along the front of the house (which had been made all front, as far as possible), was the drawing-room and general living room of the family during the greater part of the year. Its floor, of unplaned hardwood, dark with age and wear, but as exquisitely clean as sweeping and scrubbing could make it, was one of the loveliest terraces in the country for the view that it afforded—so our girls will maintain, at any rate, to their dying day. Now that they see it no more, they have passionate memories of their beloved bay, seen through a frame of rustling leaves from that lofty platform—how it looked in the dawn and sunrise, in the intensely blue noon, in the moonlight nights, and when gales and tempests were abroad, and how it sounded in the hushed darkness when they woke out of their sleep to listen to it—the rhythmic fall of breaking waves on the rocks below, the tremulous boom that filled the air and seemed to shake the foundations of the solid earth. They have no wish to get back to their early home and their hermit life there now—they have tasted a new wine that is better than the old; but, all the same, they think and say that from the lonely eyrie where they were nursed and reared they looked out upon such a scene as the wide world would never show them any more. In the foreground, immediately below the verandah, a little grass, a few sturdy shrubs, and such flowers as could keep their footing in so exposed a place, clothed the short slope of the edge of the cliff, down the steep face of which a breakneck path zig-zagged to the beach, where only a narrow strip of white sand, scarcely more than a couple of yards wide, was uncovered when the tide was out. Behind the house was a well-kept, if rather sterile, kitchen garden; and higher up the cliff, but still partly sheltered in the hollow, a very small farm-yard and one barren little paddock.

Through a back gate, by way of the farm-yard and kitchen garden, the sisters entered their domain when it was late enough to be called night, though the twilight lingered, and were welcomed with effusion by an ugly but worthy little terrier which had been bidden to keep house, and had faithfully discharged that duty during their absence. As they approached the house, a pet opossum sprang from the dairy roof to Eleanor's shoulder, and a number of tame magpies woke up with a sleepy scuffle and gathered round her. A little monkey-bear came cautiously down from the only gum tree that grew on the premises, grunting and whimpering, and crawled up Patty's skirts; and any quantity of cats and kittens appealed to Elizabeth for recognition. The girls spoke to them all by name, as if they had been so many children, cuffed them playfully for their forward manners, and ordered them to bed or to whatever avocations were proper to the hour. When a match was struck and the back-door opened, the opossum took a few flying leaps round the kitchen, had his ears boxed, and was flung back again upon the dairy roof. The little bear clung whining to his mistress, but was also put outside with a firm hand; and the cats and magpies were swept over the threshold with a broom. "*Brats!*" cried Patty with ferocious vehemence, as she closed the kitchen door sharply, at the risk of cutting off some of their noses; "what *are* we to do with them? They seem as if they *knew* we were going away, the aggravating little wretches. There, there" — raising the most caressing voice in answer to the whine of the monkey-bear — "don't cry, my pet! Get up your tree, darling, and have a nice supper and go to sleep."

Then, having listened for a few seconds at the closed door, she followed Elizabeth through the kitchen to the sitting-room, and, while her sister lit the lamp, stepped through the French window to sniff the salt sea air. For some time the humble members of the family were heard prowling disconsolately about the house, but none of them, except the terrier, appeared upon the verandah, where the ghost of their evil genius still sat in his old armchair with his stick by his side. They had been driven thence so often and with such memorable indignities that it would never occur to them to go there any more. And so the sisters were left in peace. Eleanor busied herself in the kitchen for awhile, setting her little batch of bread by the embers of the hearth, in view of a hot loaf for their early breakfast, while she sang some German ballads to herself with an ear for the refinements of both language and music that testified to the thoroughness of her mother's culture, and of the methods by which it had been imparted. Patty went to the dairy for a jug of milk for supper, which frugal meal was otherwise prepared by Elizabeth's hands; and at nine o'clock the trio gathered round the sitting-room table to refresh themselves with thick slices of bread and jam, and half-an-hour's gossip before they went to bed.

A pretty and pathetic picture they made as they sat round that table, with the dim light of one kerosene lamp on their strikingly fair faces—alone in the little house that was no longer theirs, and in the wide world, but so full of faith and hope in the unknown future—discussing ways and means for getting their furniture to Melbourne. That time-honoured furniture, and their immediate surroundings generally, made a poor setting for such a group—a long, low, canvas-lined room, papered with prints from the *Illustrated London News* (a pictorial European "history of our own times"), from the ceiling to the floor, the floor being without a carpet, and the glass doors furnished only with a red baize curtain to draw against the sea winds of winter nights. The tables and chairs were of the same order of architecture as the house; the old mahogany bureau, with its brass mounting and multitudinous internal ramifications, was ridiculously out of date and out of fashion (as fashion was understood in that part of the world); the ancient chintz sofa, though as easy as a feather bed, and of a capacity equal to the accommodation of Giant Blunderbore, was obviously home-made and not meant to be too closely criticised; and even the piano, which was a modern and beautiful instrument in itself, hid its music in a stained deal case than which no plain egg of a nightingale could be plainer. And yet this odd environment for three beautiful and cultured women had a certain dignity and harmoniousness about it—often lacking in later and more luxurious surroundings. It was in tune with those simple lives, and with the majestic solitude of the great headland and the sea.

CHAPTER III
PREPARATIONS FOR FLIGHT

Melbourne people, when they go to bed, chain up their doors carefully, and bar all their windows, lest the casual burglar should molest them. Bush people, no more afraid of the night than of the day, are often quite unable to tell you whether there is such a thing as an effective lock upon the premises. So our girls, in their lonely dwelling on the cliff, slept in perfect peace and security, with the wind from the sea blowing over their faces through the open door-windows at the foot of their little beds. Dan Tucker, the terrier, walked softly to and fro over their thresholds at intervals in the course of the night, and kept away any stray kitten that had not yet learned its proper place; that was all the watch and ward that he or they considered necessary.

At five o'clock in the morning, Elizabeth King, who had a little slip of a room to herself, just wide enough to allow the leaves of the French window at the end of it to be held back, when open, by buttons attached to the side walls, stirred in her sleep, stretched herself, yawned, and then springing up into a sitting posture, propped herself on her pillows to see the new day begin. It was a sight to see, indeed, from that point of view; but it was not often that any of them woke from their sound and healthy slumber at this time of the year, until the sun was high enough to shoot a level ray into their eyes. At five o'clock the surface of the great deep had not begun to shine, but it was light enough to see the black posts and eaves of the verandah, and the stems and leaves that twined about them, outlined sharply upon the dim expanse. Elizabeth's bed had no footrail, and there was no chair or dressing-table in the way to impede a clear view of sea and sky. As she lay, the line of the horizon was drawn straight across the doorway, about three feet above the edge of the verandah floor; and there a faint pink streak, with fainter flushes on a bank of clouds above it, showed where the sun was about to rise. The waves splashed heavily on the beach, and boomed in the great caves of the rocks below; the sea-gulls called to each other with their queer little cry, at once soft and shrill; and the magpies piped and chattered all around the house, and more cocks than could anyhow be accounted for crowed a mutual defiance far and near. And yet, oh, how still—how solemnly still—it was! I am not going to describe that sunrise, though I saw one exactly like it only this very morning. I have seen people take out their tubes and brushes, and sit down with placid confidence to paint sun-kissed hills, and rocks, and seas; and, if you woke them up early enough, they would "sketch" the pink and golden fire of this flaming dawn without a moment's hesitation. But I know better.

Ere the many-coloured transformation scene had melted in dazzle of daylight, Elizabeth was dressing herself by her still open window—throwing long shadows as she moved to and fro about the now sun-flooded room. Patty was busy in her dairy churning, with a number of her pets round the door, hustling each other to get at the milk dish set down for their breakfast—the magpies tugging at the cats and kittens by ears and tail, and the cats and kittens cuffing the magpies smartly. Eleanor, singing her German ballads still, was hard at work in the kitchen, baking delicate loaves for breakfast, and attending to kitchen matters generally. The elder sister's office on this occasion was to let out and feed the fowls, to sweep and dust, and to prepare the table for their morning meal. Never since they had grown out of childhood had they known the sensation of being waited upon by a servant, and as yet their system of education had been such that they did not know what the word "menial" meant. To be together with no one to interfere with them, and independent of everybody but themselves, was a habit whose origin was too remote for inquiry, and that had become a second nature and a settled theory of life—a sort of instinct of pride and modesty, moreover, though an instinct too natural to be aware of its own existence.

When the little loaves were done and the big ones put in the oven, Eleanor fetched a towel, donned a broad hat, and, passing out at the front of the house, ran lightly down the steep track on the face of the cliff to their bath-house on the beach—a little closet of rough slabs built in the rock above high water; whence she presently emerged in a scanty flannel garment, with her slender white limbs bare, and flung herself like a mermaid into the sea. There were sharks in that bay sometimes, and there were devil-fish too (Sam Dunn had spread one out, star-wise, on a big boulder close by, and it lay there still, with its horrible arms dangling from its hideous bag of a body, to be a warning to these venturesome young ladies, who, he fully expected, would be "et up" some day like little flies by a spider); but they found their safety in the perfect transparency of the water, coming in from the great pure ocean to the unsullied rocks, and kept a wary watch for danger. While Eleanor was disporting herself, Patty joined her, and after Patty, Elizabeth; and one by one they came up, glowing and dripping, like—no, I *won't* be tempted to make that familiar classical comparison—like nothing better than themselves for artistic purposes. As Elizabeth, who was the last to leave the water, walked up the short flight of steps to her little dressing closet, straight and stately, with her full throat and bust and her nobly shaped limbs, she was the very model that sculptors dream of and hunt for (as many more might be, if brought up as she had been), but seldom are fortunate enough to find. In her gown and leather belt, her beauty of figure, of course, was not so obvious: the raiment of civilisation, however simple, levelled it from the standard of Greek art to that of conventional comparison with other dressed-up women—by which, it must be confessed, she suffered.

Having assumed this raiment, she followed her sisters up the cliff path to the house; and there she found them talking volubly with Mrs. Dunn, who had brought them, with Sam's best respects, a freshly caught schnapper for their breakfast. Mrs. Dunn was their nearest neighbour, their only help in domestic emergencies, and of late days their devoted and confidential friend. Sam, her husband, had for some years been a ministering angel in the back yard, a purveyor of firewood and mutton, a killer of pigs, and so on; and he also had taken the orphan girls under his protection, so far as he could, since they had been "left."

"Look at this!" cried Eleanor, holding it up—it took both hands to hold it, for it weighed about a dozen pounds; "did you ever see such a fish, Elizabeth? Breakfast indeed! Yes, we'll have it to breakfast to-day and to-morrow too, and for dinner and tea and supper. Oh, how stupid Sam is! Why didn't he send it to market? Why didn't he take it down to the steamer? He's not a man of business a bit, Mrs. Dunn—he'll never make his fortune this way. Get the pan for me, Patty, and set the fat boiling. We'll fry a bit this very minute, and you shall stay and help us to eat it, Mrs. Dunn."

"Oh, my dear Miss Nelly—"

"Elizabeth, take charge of her, and don't let her go. Don't listen to her. We have not seen her for three whole days, and we want her to tell us about the furniture. Keep her safe, and Patty and I will have breakfast ready in a minute."

And in a short time the slice of schnapper was steaming on the table—a most simply appointed breakfast table, but very clean and dainty in its simplicity—and Mrs. Dunn sat down with her young *protégées,* and sipped her tea and gave them matronly advice, with much enjoyment of the situation.

Her advice was excellent, and amounted to this—"Don't you go for to take a stick o' that there furniture out o' the place." They were to have an auction, she said; and go to Melbourne with the proceeds in their pockets. Hawkins would be glad o' the beds, perhaps, with his large family; as Mrs. Hawkins had a lovely suite in green rep, she wouldn't look at the rest o' the things, which, though very comf'able, no doubt—very nice indeed, my dears—were not what *ladies and gentlemen* had in their houses *now-a-days*. "As for that there bureau"—pointing to it with her teaspoon—"if you set that up in a Melbourne parlour, why, you'd just have all your friends laughing at you."

The girls looked around the room with quick eyes, and then looked at each other with half-grave and half amused dismay. Patty spoke up with her usual promptness.

"It doesn't matter in the least to us what other people like to have in their houses," said she. "And that bureau, as it happens, is very valuable, Mrs. Dunn: it belonged to one of the governors before we had it, and Mr. Brion says there is no such cabinet work in these days. He says it was made in France more than a hundred years ago."

"Yes, my dear. So you might say that there was no such stuff now-a-days as what them old gowns was made of, that your poor ma wore when she was a girl. But you wouldn't go for to wear them old gowns now. I daresay the bureau was a grand piece o' furniture once, but it's out o' fashion now, and when a thing is out o' fashion it isn't worth anything. Sell it to Mr. Brion if you can; it would be a fine thing for a lawyer's office, with all them little shelves and drawers. He might give you a five-pound note for it, as he's a friend like, and you could buy a handsome new cedar chiffonnier for that."

"Mrs. Dunn," said Eleanor, rising to replenish the worthy matron's plate, with Patty's new butter and her own new bread, "we are not going to sell that bureau—no, not to anybody. It has associations, don't you understand?—and also a set of locks that no burglar could pick if he tried ever so. We are not going to sell our bureau—nor our piano—"

"Oh, but, my dear Miss Nelly—"

"My dear Mrs. Dunn, it cost ninety guineas, I do assure you, only five years ago, and it is as modern and fashionable as heart could wish."

"Fashionable! why, it might as well be a cupboard bedstead, in that there common wood. Mrs. Hawkins gave only fifty pounds for hers, and it is real walnut and carved beautiful."

"We are not going to sell that piano, my dear woman." Though Nelly appeared to wait meekly upon her elder sisters' judgment, it often happened that she decided a question that was put before them in this prompt way. "And I'll tell you for why," she continued playfully. "You shut your eyes for five minutes—wait, I'll tie my handkerchief over them"—and she deftly blindfolded the old woman, whose stout frame shook with honest giggles of enjoyment at this manifestation of Miss Nelly's fun. "Now," said Nelly, "don't laugh—don't remember that you are here with us, or that there is such a thing as a cupboard bedstead in the world. Imagine that you are floating down the Rhine on a moonlight night—no, by the way, imagine that you are in a drawing-room in Melbourne, furnished with a lovely green rep suite, and a handsome new cedar chiffonnier, and a carved walnut piano—and that a beautiful, fashionable lady, with scent on her pocket-handkerchief, is sitting at that piano. And—and listen for a minute."

Whereupon, lifting her hands from the old woman's shoulders, she crossed the room, opened the piano noiselessly, and began to play her favourite German airs—the songs of the people, that seem so much sweeter and more pathetic and poetic than the songs of any other people—mixing two or three of them together and rendering them with a touch and expression that worked like a spell of enchantment upon them all. Elizabeth sat back in her chair and lost herself in the visions that appeared to her on the ceiling. Patty spread her arms over the table and leaned towards the piano, breathing a soft accompaniment of German words in tender, sighing undertones, while her warm pulses throbbed and her eyes brightened with the unconscious passion that was stirred in her fervent soul. Even the weather-beaten old charwoman fell into a reverent attitude as of a devotee in church.

"There," said Eleanor, taking her hands from the keys and shutting up the instrument, with a suddenness that made them jump. "Now I ask you, Mrs. Dunn, as an honest and truthful woman—*can* you say that that is a piano to be *sold?*"

"Beautiful, my dear, beautiful—it's like being in heaven to hear the like o' that," the old woman responded warmly, pulling the bandage from her eyes. "But you'd draw music from an old packing case, I do believe." And it was found that Mrs. Dunn was unshaken in her conviction that pianos were valuable in proportion to their external splendour, and their tone sweet and powerful by virtue solely of the skill of the fingers that played upon them. If Mr. King had given ninety guineas for "that there"—about which she thought there must be some mistake—she could only conclude that his rural innocence had been imposed upon by wily city tradesmen.

"Well," said Nelly, who was now busy collecting the crockery on the breakfast table, "we must see if we can't furbish it up, Mrs. Dunn. We can paint a landscape on the front, perhaps, and tie some pink satin ribbons on the handles. Or we might set it behind a curtain, or in a dark corner, where it will be heard and not seen. But keep it we must—both that and the bureau. You would not part with those two things, Elizabeth?"

"My dear," said Elizabeth, "it would grieve me to part with anything."

"But I think," said Patty, "Mrs. Dunn may be right about the other furniture. What would it cost to take all our things to Melbourne, Mrs. Dunn?"

"Twice as much as they are worth, Miss Patty—three times as much. Carriage is awful, whether by sea or land."

"It is a great distance," said Patty, thoughtfully, "and it would be very awkward. We cannot take them with us, for we shall want first to find a place to put them in, and we could not come back to fetch them. I think we had better speak to Mr. Hawkins, Elizabeth, and, if he doesn't want them, have a little auction. We must keep some things, of course; but I am sure Mr. Hawkins would let them stay till we could send for them, or Mr. Brion would house them for us."

"We should feel very free that way, and it would be nice to buy new things," said Eleanor.

"Or we might not have to buy—we might put this money to the other," said Patty. "We might find that we did not like Melbourne, and then we could go to Europe at once without any trouble."

"And take the pianner to Europe along with you?" inquired Mrs. Dunn. "And that there bureau?"

CHAPTER IV
DEPARTURE

They decided to sell their furniture—with the exception of the piano and the bureau, and sundry treasures that could bestowed away in the latter capacious receptacle; and, on being made acquainted with the fact, the obliging Mr. Hawkins offered to take it as it stood for a lump sum of £50, and his offer was gratefully accepted. Sam Dunn was very wroth over this transaction, for he knew the value of the dairy and kitchen utensils and farm-yard appliances, which went to the new tenant along with the household furniture that Mrs. Dunn, as a candid friend, had disparaged and despised; and he reproached Elizabeth, tenderly, but with tears in his eyes, for having allowed herself to be "done" by not taking Mr. Brion's advice upon the matter, and shook his head over the imminent fate of these three innocent and helpless lambs about to fling themselves into the jaws of the commercial wolves of Melbourne. Elizabeth told him that she did not like to be always teasing Mr. Brion, who had already done all the legal business necessary to put them in possession of their little property, and had refused to take any fee for his trouble; that, as they had nothing more to sell, no buyer could "do" them again; and that, finally, they all thought fifty pounds a great deal of money, and were quite satisfied with their bargain. But Sam, as a practical man, continued to shake his head, and bade her remember him when she was in trouble and in need of a faithful friend—assuring her, with a few strong seafaring oaths (which did not shock her in the least, for they were meant to emphasise the sincerity of his protestations), that she and her sisters should never want, if he knew it, while he had a crust of bread and a breath in his body.

And so they began to pack up. And the fuss and confusion of that occupation—which becomes so irksome when the charm of novelty is past—was full of enjoyment for them all. It would have done the travel-worn cynic good to see them scampering about the house, as lightly as the kittens that frisked after them, carrying armfuls of house linen and other precious chattels to and fro, and prattling the while of their glorious future like so many school children about to pay a first visit to the pantomime. It was almost heartless, Mrs. Dunn thought—dropping in occasionally to see how they were getting on—considering what cause had broken up their home, and that their father had been so recently taken from them that she (Mrs. Dunn) could not bring herself to walk without hesitation into the house, still fancying she should see him sitting in his arm-chair and looking at her with those hard, unsmiling eyes, as if to ask her what business she had there. But Mr. King had been a harsh father, and this is what harsh fathers must expect of children who have never learned how to dissemble for the sake of appearances. They reverenced his memory and held it dear, but he had left them no associations that could sadden them like the sight of their mother's clothes folded away in the long unopened drawers of the wardrobe in her room—the room in which he had slept and died only a few weeks ago.

These precious garments, smelling of lavender, camphor, and sandalwood, were all taken out and looked at, and tenderly smoothed afresh, and laid in a deep drawer of the bureau. There were treasures amongst them of a value that the girls had no idea of—old gowns of faded brocade and embroidered muslin, a yellow-white Indian shawl so soft that it could be drawn through a wedding ring, yellower lace of still more wonderful texture, and fans, and scarfs, and veils, and odds and ends of ancient finery, that would have been worth considerably more than their weight in gold to a modern art collector. But these reminiscences of their mother's far-off girlhood, carefully laid in the bottom of the drawer, were of no account to them compared with the half-worn gowns of cheap stuff and cotton—still showing the print of her throat and arms—that were spread so reverently on the top of them; and compared with the numerous other memorials of her last days—her workbox, with its unfinished bit of needlework, and scissors and thimble, and tapes and cottons, just as she had left it—her Prayer-Book and Bible—her favourite cup, from which she drank her morning tea—her shabby velvet slippers, her stiff-fingered gardening gloves—all the relics that her children had cherished of the daily, homely life that they had been privileged to share with her; the bestowal of which was carried on in silence, or with tearful whispers, while all the pets were locked out of the room, as if it had been a religious function. When this drawer was closed, and they had refreshed their saddened spirits with a long walk, they set themselves with light hearts to fill the remainder of the many shelves and niches of the bureau with piles of books and music, painting materials, collections of wild flowers and shells and seaweeds, fragments of silver plate that had lain there always, as far as they knew, along with some old miniatures and daguerreotypes in rusty leather cases, and old bundles of papers that Mr. Brion had warned them to take care of—and with their own portfolios of sketches and little personal treasures of various kinds, their father's watch, and stick, and spurs, and spectacles—and so on, and so on.

After this, they had only to pack up their bed and table linen and knives and forks, which were to go with them to Melbourne, and to arrange their own scanty wardrobes to the best advantage.

"We shall certainly want some clothes," said Eleanor, surveying their united stock of available wearing apparel on Elizabeth's bedroom floor. "I propose that we appropriate—say £5—no, that might not be enough; say £10—from the furniture money to settle ourselves up each with a nice costume—dress, jacket, and bonnet complete—so that we may look like other people when we get to Melbourne."

"We'll get there first," said Patty, "and see what is worn, and the price of things. Our black prints are very nice for everyday, and we can wear our brown homespuns as soon as we get away from Mrs. Dunn. She said it was disrespectful to poor father's memory to put on anything but black when she saw you in your blue gingham, Nelly. Poor old soul! one would think we were a set of superstitious heathen pagans. I wonder where she got all those queer ideas from?"

"She knows a great deal more than we do, Patty," said wise Elizabeth, from her kneeling posture on the floor.

They packed all their clothes into two small but weighty brass-bound trunks, leaving out their blue ginghams, their well-worn water-proofs, and their black-ribboned sailor hats to travel in. Then they turned their attention to the animals, and suffered grievous trouble in their efforts to secure a comfortable provision for them after their own departure. The monkey-bear, the object of their fondest solicitude, was entrusted to Sam Dunn, who swore with picturesque energy that he would cherish it as his own child. It was put into a large cage with about a bushel of fresh gum leaves, and Sam was adjured to restore it to liberty as soon as he had induced it to grow fond of him. Then Patty and Eleanor took the long walk to the township to call on Mrs. Hawkins, in order to entreat her good offices for the rest of their pets. But Mrs. Hawkins seized the precious opportunity that they offered her for getting the detailed information, such as only women could give, concerning the interior construction and capabilities of her newly-acquired residence, and she had no attention to spare for anything else. The girls left, after sitting on two green rep chairs for nearly an hour, with the depressing knowledge that their house was to be painted inside and out, and roofed with zinc, and verandahed with green trellis-work; and that there was to be a nice road made to it, so that the family could drive to and from their place of business; and that it was to have "Sea View Villa" painted on the garden gate posts. But whether their pets were to be allowed to roam over the transformed premises (supposing they had the heart to do so) was more than they could tell. So they had an anxious consultation with Elizabeth, all the parties concerned being present, cuddled and fondled on arms and knees; and the result was a determination *not* to leave the precious darlings to the tender mercies of the Hawkins family. Sam Dunn was to take the opossum in a basket to some place where there were trees, a river, and other opossums, and there turn him out to unlearn his civilisation and acquire the habits and customs of his unsophisticated kinsfolk—a course of study to which your pet opossum submits himself very readily as a rule. The magpies were also to be left to shift for themselves, for they were in the habit of consorting with other magpies in a desultory manner, and they could "find" themselves in board and lodging. But the cats—O, the poor, dear, confiding old cats! O, the sweet little playful kitties!—the girls were distracted to know what to do for *them*. There were so many of them, and they would never be induced to leave the place—that rocky platform so barren of little birds, and those ancient buildings where no mouse had been allowed so much as to come into the world for years past. They would not be fed, of course, when their mistresses were gone. They would get into the dairy and the pantry, and steal Mrs. Hawkins's milk and meat—and it was easy to conjecture what would happen *then*. Mrs. Hawkins had boys moreover—rough boys who went to the State school, and looked capable of all the fiendish atrocities that young animals of their age and sex were supposed to delight in. Could they leave their beloved ones to the mercy of *boys?* They consulted Sam Dunn, and Sam's advice was— —

Never mind. Cats and kittens disappeared. And then only Dan Tucker was left. Him, at any rate, they declared they would never part with, while he had a breath in his faithful body. He should go with them to Melbourne, bless his precious heart!—-or, if need were, to the ends of the earth.

And so, at last, all their preparations were made, and the day came when, with unexpected regrets and fears, they walked out of the old house which had been their only home into the wide world, where they were utter strangers. Sam Dunn came with his wood-cart to carry their luggage to the steamer (the conveyance they had selected, in preference to coach and railway, because it was cheaper, and they were more familiar with it); and then they shut up doors and windows, sobbing as they went from room to room; stood on the verandah in front of the sea to solemnly kiss each other, and walked quietly down to the township, hand in hand, and with the terrier at their heels, to have tea with Mr. Brion and his old housekeeper before they went on board.

CHAPTER V
ROCKED IN THE CRADLE OF THE DEEP

Late in the evening when the sea was lit up with a young moon, Mr. Brion, having given them a great deal of serious advice concerning their money and other business affairs, escorted our three girls to the little jetty where the steamer that called in once a week lay at her moorings, ready to start for Melbourne and intermediate ports at five o'clock next morning. The old lawyer was a spare, grave, gentlemanly-looking old man, and as much a gentleman as he looked, with the kindest heart in the world when you could get at it: a man who was esteemed and respected, to use the language of the local paper, by all his fellow-townsmen, whether friends or foes. They Anglicised his name in speaking it, and they wrote it "Bryan" far more often than not, though nothing enraged him more than to have his precious vowels tampered with; but they liked him so much that they never cast it up to him that he was a Frenchman.

This good old man, chivalrous as any paladin, in his shy and secret way, always anxious to hide his generous emotions, as the traditional Frenchman is anxious to display them, had done a father's part by our young orphans since their own father had left them so strangely desolate. Sam Dunn had compassed them with sweet observances, as we have seen; but Sam was powerless to unravel the web of difficulties, legal and otherwise, in which Mr. King's death had plunged them. Mr. Brion had done all this, and a great deal more that nobody knew of, to protect the girls and their interests at a critical juncture, and to give them a fair and clear start on their own account. And in the process of thus serving them he had become very much attached to them in his old-fashioned, reticent way; and he did not at all like having to let them go away alone in this lonely-looking night.

"But Paul will be there to meet you," he said, for the twentieth time, laying his hand over Elizabeth's, which rested on his arm. "You may trust to Paul—as soon as the boat is telegraphed he will come to meet you—he will see to everything that is necessary—you will have no bother at all. And, my dear, remember what I say—let the boy advise you for a little while. Let him take care of you, and imagine it is I. You may trust him as absolutely as you trust me, and he will not presume upon your confidence, believe me. He is not like the young men of the country," added Paul's father, putting a little extra stiffness into his upright figure. "No, no—he is quite different."

"I think you have instructed us so fully, dear Mr. Brion, that we shall get along very well without having to trouble Mr. Paul," interposed Patty, in her clear, quick way, speaking from a little distance.

The steamer, with her lamps lit, was all in a clatter and bustle, taking in passengers and cargo. Sam Dunn was on board, having seen the boxes stowed away safely; and he came forward to say good-bye to his young ladies before driving his cart home.

"I'll miss ye," said the brawny fisherman, with savage tenderness; "and the missus'll miss ye. Darned if we shall know the place with you gone out of it. Many's the dark night the light o' your winders has been better'n the lighthouse to show me the way home."

He pointed to the great headland lying, it seemed now, so far, far off, ghostly as a cloud. And presently he went away; and they could hear him, as he drove back along the jetty, cursing his old horse—to which he was as much attached as if it had been a human friend—with blood-curdling ferocity.

Mr. Brion stayed with them until it seemed improper to stay any longer—until all the passengers that were to come on board had housed themselves for the night, and all the baggage had been snugly stowed away—and then bade them good-bye, with less outward emotion than Sam had displayed, but with almost as keen a pang.

"God bless you, my dears," said he, with paternal solemnity. "Take care of yourselves, and let Paul do what he can for you. I will send you your money every quarter, and you must keep accounts—keep accounts strictly. And ask Paul what you want to know. Then you will get along all right, please God."

"O yes, we shall get along all right," repeated Patty, whose sturdy optimism never failed her in the most trying moments.

But when the old man was gone, and they stood on the tiny slip of deck that was available to stand on, feeling no necessity to cling to the railings as the little vessel heaved up and down in the wash of the tide that swirled amongst the piers of the jetty—when they looked at the lights of the town sprinkled round the shore and up the hillsides, at their own distant headland, unlighted, except by the white haze of the moon, at the now deserted jetty, and the apparently illimitable sea—when they realised for the first time that they were alone in this great and unknown world—even Patty's bold heart was inclined to sink a little.

"Elizabeth," she said, "we *must* not cry—it is absurd. What is there to cry for? Now, all the things we have been dreaming and longing for are going to happen—the story is beginning. Let us go to bed and get a good sleep before the steamer starts so that we are fresh in the morning—so that we don't lose anything. Come, Nelly, let us see if poor Dan is comfortable, and have some supper and go to bed."

They cheered themselves with the sandwiches and the gooseberry wine that Mr. Brion's housekeeper had put up for them, paid a visit to Dan, who was in charge of an amiable cook (whom the old lawyer had tipped handsomely), and then faced the dangers and difficulties of getting to bed. Descending the brass-bound staircase to the lower regions, they paused, their faces flushed up, and they looked at each other as if the scene before them was something unfit for the eyes of modest girls. They were shocked, as by some specific impropriety, at the noise and confusion, the rough jostling and the impure atmosphere, in the morsel of a ladies' cabin, from which the tiny slips of bunks prepared for them were divided only by a scanty curtain. This was their first contact with the world, so to speak, and they fled from it. To spend a night in that suffocating hole, with those loud women their fellow passengers, was a too appalling prospect. So Elizabeth went to the captain, who knew their story, and admired their faces, and was inclined to be very kind to them, and asked his permission to occupy a retired corner of the deck. On his seeming to hesitate—they being desperately anxious not to give anybody any trouble—they assured him that the place above all others where they would like to make their bed was on the wedge-shaped platform in the bows, where they would be out of everybody's way.

"But, my dear young lady, there is no railing there," said the captain, laughing at the proposal as a joke.

"A good eight inches—ten inches," said Elizabeth. "Quite enough for anybody in the roughest sea."

"For a sailor perhaps, but not for young ladies who get giddy and frightened and seasick. Supposing you tumbled off in the dark, and I found you gone when I came to look for you in the morning."

"*We* tumble off!" cried Eleanor. "We never tumbled off anything in our lives. We have lived on the cliffs like the goats and the gulls—nothing makes us giddy. And I don't think anything will make us seasick—or frightened either."

"Certainly not frightened," said Patty.

He let them have their way—taking a great many (as they thought) perfectly unnecessary precautions in fixing up their quarters in case of a rough sea—and himself carried out their old opossum rug and an armful of pillows to make their nest comfortable. So, in this quiet and breezy bedchamber, roofed over by the moonlit sky, they lay down with much satisfaction in each other's arms, unwatched and unmolested, as they loved to be, save by the faithful Dan Tucker, who found his way to their feet in the course of the night. And the steamer left her moorings and worked out of the bay into the open ocean, puffing and clattering, and danced up and down over the long waves, and they knew nothing about it. In the fresh air, with the familiar voice of the sea around them, they slept soundly under the opossum rug until the sun was high.

CHAPTER VI
PAUL

They slept for two nights on the tip of the steamer's nose, and they did not roll off. They had a long, delightful day at sea, no more troubled with seasickness than were the gulls to which they had compared themselves, and full of inquiring interest for each of the ports they touched at, and for all the little novelties of a first voyage. They became great friends with the captain and crew, and with some children who were amongst the passengers (the ladies of the party were indisposed to fraternise with them, not being able to reconcile themselves to the cut and quality of the faded blue gingham gowns, or to those eccentric sleeping arrangements, both of which seemed to point to impecuniosity—which is so closely allied to impropriety, as everybody knows). They sat down to their meals in the little cabin with wonderful appetites; they walked the deck in the fine salt wind with feet that were light and firm, and hearts that were high and hopeful and full of courage and enterprise. Altogether, they felt that the story was beginning pleasantly, and they were eager to turn over the pages.

And then, on the brightest of bright summer mornings, they came to Melbourne.

They did not quite know what they had expected to see, but what they did see astonished them. The wild things caught in the bush, and carried in cages to the Eastern market, could not have felt more surprised or dismayed by the novelty of the situation than did these intrepid damsels when they found themselves fairly launched into the world they were so anxious to know. For a few minutes after their arrival they stood together silent, breathless, taking it all in; and then Patty—yes, it *was* Patty—exclaimed:

"Oh, *where* is Paul Brion?"

Paul Brion was there, and the words had no sooner escaped her lips than he appeared before them. "How do you do, Miss King?" he said, not holding out his hand, but taking off his hat with one of his father's formal salutations, including them all. "I hope you have had a pleasant passage. If you will kindly tell me what luggage you have, I will take you to your cab; it is waiting for you just here. Three boxes? All right. I will see after them."

He was a small, slight, wiry little man, with decidedly brusque, though perfectly polite manners; active and self-possessed, and, in a certain way of his own, dignified, notwithstanding his low stature. He was not handsome, but he had a keen and clever face—rather fierce as to the eyes and mouth, which latter was adorned with a fierce little moustache curling up at the corners—but pleasant to look at, and one that inspired trust.

"He is not a bit like his father," said Patty, following him with Eleanor, as he led Elizabeth to the cab. Patty was angry with him for overhearing that "Where is Paul Brion?"—as she was convinced he had done—and her tone was disparaging.

"As the mother duck said of the ugly duckling, if he is not pretty he has a good disposition," said Eleanor. "He is like his father in that. It was very kind of him to come and help us. A press man must always be terribly busy."

"I don't see why we couldn't have managed for ourselves. It is nothing but to call a cab," said Patty with irritation.

"And where could we have gone to?" asked her sister, reproachfully.

"For the matter of that, where are we going now? We haven't the least idea. I think it was very stupid to leave ourselves in the hands of a chance young man whom we have hardly ever seen. We make ourselves look like a set of helpless infants—as if we couldn't do without him."

"Well, we can't," said Eleanor.

"Nonsense. We don't try. But," added Patty, after a pause, "we must begin to try—we must begin at once."

They arrived at the cab, in which Elizabeth had seated herself, with the bewildered Dan in her arms, her sweet, open face all smiles and sunshine. Paul Brion held the door open, and, as the younger sisters passed him, looked at them intently with searching eyes. This was a fresh offence to Patty, at whom he certainly looked most. Impressions new and strange were crowding upon her brain this morning thick and fast. "Elizabeth," she said, unconscious that her brilliant little countenance, with that flush of excitement upon it, was enough to fascinate the gaze of the dullest man; "Elizabeth, he looks at us as if we were curiosities—he thinks we are dowdy and countryfied and it amuses him."

"My dear," interposed Eleanor, who, like Elizabeth, was (as she herself expressed it) reeking with contentment, "you could not have seen his face if you think that. He was as grave as a judge."

"Then he pities us, Nelly, and that is worse. He thinks we are queer outlandish creatures—*frights*. So we are. Look at those women on the other side of the street, how differently they are dressed! We ought not to have come in these old clothes, Elizabeth."

"But, my darling, we are travelling, and anything does to travel in. We will put on our black frocks when we get home, and we will buy ourselves some new ones. Don't trouble about such a trifle *now*, Patty—it is not like you. Oh, see what a perfect day it is! And think of our being in Melbourne at last! I am trying to realise it, but it almost stuns me. What a place it is! But Mr. Paul says our lodgings are in a quiet, airy street—not in this noisy part. Ah, here he is! And there are the three boxes all safe. Thank you so much," she said warmly, looking at the young man of the world, who was some five years older than herself, with frankest friendliness, as a benevolent grandmamma might have looked at an obliging schoolboy. "You are very good—we are very grateful to you."

"And very sorry to have given you so much trouble," added Patty, with the air of a young duchess.

He looked at her quickly, and made a slight bow. He did not say that what he had done had been no trouble at all, but a pleasure—he did not say a word, indeed; and his silence made her little heart swell with mortification. He turned to Elizabeth, and, resting his hands on the door-frame, began to explain the nature of the arrangements that he had made for them, with business-like brevity.

"Your lodgings are in Myrtle Street, Miss King. That is in East Melbourne, you know—quite close to the gardens—quite quiet and retired, and yet within a short walk of Collins Street, and handy for all the places you want to see. You have two bedrooms and a small sitting-room of your own, but take your meals with the other people of the house; you won't mind that, I hope—it made a difference of about thirty shillings a week, and it is the most usual arrangement. Of course you can alter anything you don't like when you get there. The landlady is a Scotchwoman—I know her very well, and can recommend her highly—I think you will like her."

"But won't you come with us?" interposed Elizabeth, putting out her hand. "Come and introduce us to her, and see that the cabman takes us to the right place. Or perhaps you are too busy to spare the time?"

"I—I will call on you this afternoon, if you will permit me—when you have had your lunch and are rested a little. Oh, I know the cabman quite well, and can answer for his taking you safely. This is your address"— hastily scribbling it on an envelope he drew from his pocket—"and the landlady is Mrs. M'Intyre. Good morning. I will do myself the pleasure of calling on you at four or five o'clock."

He thereupon bowed and departed, and the cab rattled away in an opposite direction. Patty deeply resented his not coming with them, and wondered and wondered why he had refused. Was he too proud, or too shy, or too busy, or too indifferent? Did he feel that it was a trouble to him to have to look after them? Poor Paul! He would have liked to come, to see them comfortably housed and settled; but the simple difficulty was that he was afraid to risk giving them offence by paying the cab fare, and would not ride with them, a man in charge of three ladies, without paying it. And Patty was not educated to the point of appreciating that scruple. His desertion of them in the open street was a grievance to her. She could not help thinking of it, though there was so much else to think of.

The cab turned into Collins Street and rattled merrily up that busy thoroughfare in the bright sunshine. They looked at the brilliant shop windows, at the gay crowd streaming up and down the pavements, and the fine equipages flashing along the road-way at the Town Hall, and the churches, and the statues of Burke and Wills—and were filled with admiration and wonder. Then they turned into quieter roads, and there was the Exhibition in its web of airy scaffolding, destined to be the theatre of great events, in which they would have their share—an inspiring sight. And they went round a few corners, catching refreshing glimpses of green trees and shady alleys, and presently arrived at Myrtle Street—quietest of suburban thoroughfares, with its rows of trim little houses, half-a-dozen in a block, each with its tiny patch of garden in front of it—where for the present they were to dwell.

Mrs. M'Intyre's maid came out to take the parcels, and the landlady herself appeared on the doorstep to welcome the new-comers. They whispered to themselves hurriedly, "Oh, she has a nice face!"—and then Patty and Elizabeth addressed themselves to the responsible business of settling with the cabman.

"How much have we to pay you?" asked Patty with dignity.

"Twelve shillings, please, miss," the man gaily replied.

Elizabeth looked at her energetic sister, who had boasted that they were quite sharp enough to know when they were being cheated. Upon which Patty, with her feathers up, appealed to the landlady. Mrs. M'Intyre said the proper sum due to him was just half what he had asked. The cabman said that was for one passenger, and not for three. Mrs. M'Intyre then represented that eighteen-pence apiece was as much as he could claim for the remaining two, that the luggage was a mere nothing, and that if he didn't mind what he was about, &c. So the sum was reduced to nine shillings, which Elizabeth paid, looking very grave over it, for it was still far beyond what she had reckoned on.

Then they went into the house—the middle house of a smart little terrace, with a few ragged fern trees in the front garden—and Mrs. M'Intyre took them up to their rooms, and showed them drawers and cupboards, in a motherly and hospitable manner.

"This is the large bedroom, with the two beds, and the small one opens off it; so that you will all be close together," said she, displaying the neat chambers, one of which was properly but a dressing-closet; and our girls, who knew no luxury but absolute cleanliness, took note of the whiteness of the floors and bedclothes, and were more than satisfied. "And this is your sitting-room," she proceeded, leading the way to an adjoining apartment pleasantly lighted by a French window, which opened upon a stone (or, rather, what looked like a stone) balcony. It had a little "suite" in green rep like Mrs. Hawkins's, and Mrs. Dunn's ideal cedar-wood chiffonnier; it had also a comfortable solid table with a crimson cloth, and a print of the ubiquitous Cenci over the mantelpiece. The carpet was a bed of blooming roses and lilies, the effect of which was much improved by the crumb cloth that was nailed all over it. It was a tiny room, but it had a cosy look, and the new lodgers agreed at once that it was all that could be desired. "And I hope you will be comfortable," concluded the amiable landlady, "and let me know whenever you want anything. There's a bathroom down that passage, and this is your bell, and those drawers have got keys, you see, and lunch will be ready in half-an-hour. The dining-room is the first door at the bottom of the stairs, and—phew! that tobacco smoke hangs about the place still, in spite of all my cleaning and airing. I never allow smoking in the house, Miss King—not in the general way; but a man who has to be up o' nights writing for the newspapers, and never getting his proper sleep, it's hard to grudge him the comfort of his pipe—now isn't it? And I have had no ladies here to be annoyed by it—in general I don't take ladies, for gentlemen are so much the most comfortable to do for; and Mr. Brion is so considerate, and gives so little trouble—"

"What! Is Mr. Paul Brion lodging here?" broke in Patty impetuously, with her face aflame.

"Not now," Mrs. M'Intyre replied. "He left me last week. These rooms that you have got were his—he has had them for over three years. He wanted you to come here, because he thought you would be comfortable with me"—smiling benignly. "He said a man could put up anywhere."

She left them, presently; and as soon as the girls found themselves alone, they hurriedly assured each other that nothing should induce them to submit to this. It was not to be thought of for a moment. Paul Brion must be made to remove the mountainous obligation that he had put them under, and return to his rooms instantly. They would not put so much as a pocket handkerchief in the drawers and cupboards until this point had been settled with him.

At four o'clock, when they had visited the bathroom, arranged their pretty hair afresh, and put on the black print gowns—when they had had a quiet lunch with Mrs. M'Intyre (whose other boarders being gentlemen in business, did not appear at the mid-day meal), prattling cheerfully with the landlady the while, and thinking that the cold beef and salads of Melbourne were the most delicious viands ever tasted—when they had examined their rooms minutely, and tried the sofas and easy-chairs, and stood for a long while on the balcony looking at the other houses in the quiet street—at four o'clock Paul Brion came; and the maid brought up his card, while he gossiped with Mrs. M'Intyre in the hall. He had no sooner entered the girls' sitting-room than Elizabeth hastened to unburden herself. Patty was burning to be the spokeswoman for the occasion, but she knew her place, and she remembered the small effect she had produced on him in the morning, and proudly held aloof. In her sweet and graceful way, but with as much gravity and earnestness as if it were a matter of life and death, Elizabeth explained her view of the situation. "Of course we cannot consent to such an arrangement," she said gently; "you must have known we could never consent to allow you to turn out of your own rooms to accommodate us. You must please come back again, Mr. Brion, and let us go elsewhere. There seem to be plenty of other lodgings to be had—even in this street."

Paul Brion's face wore a pleasant smile as he listened. "Oh, thank you," he replied lightly. "But I am very comfortable where I am—quite as much so as I was here—rather more, indeed. For the people at No. 6 have set up a piano on the other side of that wall"—pointing to the cedar chiffonnier— "and it bothered me dreadfully when I wanted to write. It was the piano drove me out—not you. Perhaps it will drive you out too. It is a horrible nuisance, for it is always out of tune; and you know the sort of playing that people indulge in who use pianos that are out of tune."

So their little demonstration collapsed. Paul had gone away to please himself. "And has left *us* to endure the agonies of a piano out of tune," commented Patty.

As the day wore on, reaction from the mood of excitement and exaltation with which it began set in. Their spirits flagged. They felt tired and desolate in this new world. The unaccustomed hot dinner in the evening, at which they sat for nearly an hour in company with strange men who asked them questions, and pressed them to eat what they didn't want, was very uncongenial to them. And when, as soon as they could, they escaped to their own quarters, their little sitting-room, lighted with gas and full of hot upstairs air, struck them with its unsympathetic and unhomelike aspect. The next door piano was jingling its music-hall ditties faintly on the other side of the wall, and poor Dan, who had been banished to the back yard, was yelping so piteously that their hearts bled to hear him. "We must get a house of our own at once, Elizabeth—at *once*," exclaimed Eleanor—"if only for Dan's sake."

"We will never have pets again—never!" said Patty, with something like an incipient sob in her voice, as she paced restlessly about the room. "Then we shall not have to ill-treat them and to part from them." She was thinking of her little bear, and the opossum, and the magpies, who were worse off than Dan.

And Elizabeth sat down at the table, and took out pencil and notebook with a careworn face. She was going to keep accounts strictly, as Mr. Brion had advised her, and they not only meant to live within their income, as a matter of course, but to save a large part of it for future European contingencies. And, totting up the items of their expenditure for three days—cost of passage by steamer, cost of provisions on board, cab fare, and the sum paid for a week's board and lodging in advance—she found that they had been living for that period at the rate of about a thousand a year.

So that, upon the whole, they were not quite so happy as they had expected to be, when they went to bed.

CHAPTER VII
A MORNING WALK

But they slept well in their strange beds, and by morning all their little troubles had disappeared. It was impossible not to suppose that the pets "at home" were making themselves happy, seeing how the sun shone and the sea breezes blew; and Dan, who had reached years of discretion, was evidently disposed to submit himself to circumstances. Having a good view of the back yard, they could see him lolling luxuriously on the warm asphalte, as if he had been accustomed to be chained up, and liked it. Concerning their most pressing anxiety—the rapid manner in which money seemed to melt away, leaving so little to show for it—it was pointed out that at least half the sum expended was for a special purpose, and chargeable to the reserve fund and not to their regular income, from which at present only five pounds had been taken, which was to provide all their living for a week to come.

So they went downstairs in serene and hopeful spirits, and gladdened the eyes of the gentlemen boarders who were standing about the dining-room, devouring the morning's papers while they waited for breakfast. There were three of them, and each placed a chair promptly, and each offered handsomely to resign his newspaper. Elizabeth took an *Argus* to see what advertisements there were of houses to let; and then Mrs. M'Intyre came in with her coffee-pot and her cheerful face, and they sat down to breakfast. Mrs. M'Intyre was that rare exception to the rule, a boarding-house keeper who had private means as well as the liberal disposition of which the poorest have their share, and so her breakfast was a good breakfast. And the presence of strangers at table was not so unpleasant to our girls on this occasion as the last.

After breakfast they had a solemn consultation, the result being that the forenoon was dedicated to the important business of buying their clothes and finding their way to and from the shops.

"For we must have *bonnets*," said Patty, "and that immediately. Bonnets, I perceive, are the essential tokens of respectability. And we must never ride in a cab again."

They set off at ten o'clock, escorted by Mrs. M'Intyre, who chanced to be going to the city to do some marketing. The landlady, being a very fat woman, to whom time was precious, took the omnibus, according to custom; but her companions with one consent refused to squander unnecessary threepences by accompanying her in that vehicle. They had a straight road before them all the way from the corner of Myrtle Street to the Fishmarket, where she had business; and there they joined her when she had completed her purchases, and she gave them a fair start at the foot of Collins Street before she left them.

In Collins Street they spent the morning—a bewildering, exciting, anxious morning—going from shop to shop, and everywhere finding that the sum they had brought to spend was utterly inadequate for the purpose to which they had dedicated it. They saw any quantity of pretty soft stuffs, that were admirably adapted alike to their taste and means, but to get them fashioned into gowns seemed to treble their price at once; and, as Patty represented, they must have one, at any rate, that was made in the mode before they could feel it safe to manufacture for themselves. They ended by choosing—as a measure of comparative safety, for thus only could they know what they were doing, as Patty said—three ready-made costumes that took their fancy, the combined cost of which was a few shillings over the ten pounds. They were merely morning dresses of black woollen stuff; lady-like, and with a captivating style of "the world" about them, but in the lowest class of goods of that kind dispensed in those magnificent shops. Of course that was the end of their purchases for the day; the selection of mantles, bonnets, gloves, boots, and all the other little odds and ends on Elizabeth's list was reserved for a future occasion. For the idea of buying anything on twenty-four hours' credit was never entertained for a moment. To be sure, they did ask about the bonnets, and were shown a great number, in spite of their polite anxiety not to give unprofitable trouble; and not one that they liked was less than several pounds in price. Dismayed and disheartened, they "left it" (Patty's suggestion again); and they gave the rest of their morning to the dressmaker, who undertook to remodel the bodices of the new gowns and make them fit properly. This fitting was not altogether a satisfactory business, either; for the dressmaker insisted that a well-shaped corset was indispensable—especially in these days, when fit was everything—and they had no corsets and did not wish for any. She was, however, a dressmaker of decision and resource, and she sent her assistant for a bundle of corsets, in which she encased her helpless victims before she would begin the ripping and snipping and pulling and pinning process. When they saw their figures in the glass, with their fashionable tight skirts and unwrinkled waists, they did not know themselves; and I am afraid that Patty and Eleanor, at any rate, were disposed to regard corsets favourably and to make light of the discomfort they were sensibly conscious of in wearing them. Elizabeth, whose natural shape was so beautiful—albeit she is destined, if the truth must be told, to be immensely stout and heavy some day—was not seduced by this specious appearance. She ordered the dressmaker, with a quiet peremptoriness that would have become a carriage customer, to make the waists of the three gowns "free" and to leave the turnings on; and she took off the borrowed corset, and drew a long breath, inwardly determining never to wear such a thing again, even to have a dress fitted—fashion or no fashion.

It was half-past twelve by this time, and at one o'clock Mrs. M'Intyre would expect them in to lunch. They wanted to go home by way of those green enclosures that Paul Brion had told them of, and of which they had had a glimpse yesterday—which the landlady had assured them was the easiest thing possible. They had but to walk right up to the top of Collins Street, turn to the right, where they would see a gate leading into gardens, pass straight through those gardens, cross a road and go straight through other gardens, which would bring them within a few steps of Myrtle Street—a way so plain that they couldn't miss it if they tried. Ways always do seem so to people who know them. Our three girls were self-reliant young women, and kept their wits about them very creditably amid their novel and distracting surroundings. Nevertheless they were at some loss with respect to this obvious route. Because, in the first place, they didn't know which was the top of Collins Street and which the bottom.

"Dear me! we shall be reduced to the ignominious necessity of asking our way," exclaimed Eleanor, as they stood forlornly on the pavement, jostled by the human tide that flowed up and down. "If only we had Paul Brion here."

It was very provoking to Patty, but he *was* there. Being a small man, he did not come into view till he was within a couple of yards of them, and that was just in time to overhear this invocation. His ordinarily fierce aspect, which she had disrespectfully likened to that of Dan when another terrier had insulted him, had for the moment disappeared. The little man showed all over him the pleased surprise with which he had caught the sound of his own name.

"Have you got so far already?" he exclaimed, speaking in his sharp and rapid way, while his little moustache bristled with such a smile as they had not thought him capable of. "And—and can I assist you in any way?"

Elizabeth explained their dilemma; upon which he declared he was himself going to East Melbourne (whence he had just come, after his morning sleep and noontide breakfast), and asked leave to escort them thither. "How fortunate we are!" Elizabeth said, turning to walk up the street by his side; and Eleanor told him he was like his father in the opportuneness of his friendly services. But Patty was silent, and raged inwardly.

When they had traversed the length of the street, and were come to the open space before the Government offices, where they could fall again into one group, she made an effort to get rid of him and the burden of obligation that he was heaping upon them.

"Mr. Brion," she began impetuously, "we know where we are now quite well—"

"I don't think you do," he interrupted her, "seeing that you were never here before."

"Our landlady gave us directions—she made it quite plain to us. There is no necessity for you to trouble yourself any further. You were not going this way when we met you, but exactly in the opposite direction."

"I am going this way now, at any rate," he said, with decision. "I am going to show your sisters their way through the gardens. There are a good many paths, and they don't all lead to Myrtle Street."

"But we know the points of the compass—we have our general directions," she insisted angrily, as she followed him helplessly through the gates. "We are not quite idiots, though we do come from the country."

"Patty," interposed Elizabeth, surprised, "I am glad of Mr. Brion's kind help, if you are not."

"Patty," echoed Eleanor in an undertone, "that haughty spirit of yours will have a fall some day."

Patty felt that it was having a fall now. "I know it is very kind of Mr. Brion," she said tremulously, "but how are we to get on and do for ourselves if we are treated like children—I mean if we allow ourselves to hang on to other people? We should make our own way, as others have to do. I don't suppose *you* had anyone to lead you about when *you* first came to Melbourne"—addressing Paul.

"I was a man," he replied. "It is a man's business to take care of himself."

"Of course. And equally it is a woman's business to take care of herself—if she has no man in her family."

"Pardon me. In that case it is the business of all the men with whom she comes in contact to take care of her—each as he can."

"Oh, what nonsense! You talk as if we lived in the time of the Troubadours—as if you didn't *know* that all that stuff about women has had its day and been laughed out of existence long ago."

"What stuff?"

"That we are helpless imbeciles—a sort of angelic wax baby, good for nothing but to look pretty. As if we were not made of the same substance as you, with brains and hands—not so strong as yours, perhaps, but quite strong enough to rely upon when necessary. Oh!" exclaimed Patty, with a fierce gesture, "I do so *hate* that man's cant about women—I have no patience with it!"

"You must have been severely tried," murmured Paul (he was beginning to think the middle Miss King a disagreeable person, and to feel vindictive towards her). And Eleanor laughed cruelly, and said, "Oh, no, she's got it all out of books."

"A great mistake to go by books," said he, with the air of a father. "Experience first—books afterwards, Miss Patty." And he smiled coolly into the girl's flaming face.

CHAPTER VIII
AN INTRODUCTION TO MRS. GRUNDY

Patty and her sisters very nearly had their first quarrel over Paul Brion. Patty said he was impertinent and patronising, that he presumed upon their friendless position to pay them insulting attentions—that, in short, he was a detestable young man whom she, for one, would have nothing more to do with. And she warned Elizabeth, in an hysterical, high-pitched voice, never to invite him into their house unless she wished to see her (Patty) walk out of it. Elizabeth, supported by Eleanor, took up the cudgels in his defence, and assured Patty, kindly, but with much firmness, that he had behaved with dignity and courtesy under great provocation to do otherwise. They also pointed out that he was his father's representative; that it would be ungracious and unladylike to reject the little services that it was certainly a pleasure to him to render, and unworthy of them to assume an independence that at present they were unable to support. Which was coming as near to "words" as was possible for them to come, and much nearer than any of them desired. Patty burst into tears at last, which was the signal for everything in the shape of discord and division to vanish. Her sisters kissed and fondled her, and assured her that they sympathised with her anxiety to be under obligations to nobody from the bottom of their hearts; and Patty owned that she had been captious and unreasonable, and consented to forgive her enemy for what he hadn't done and to be civil to him in future.

And, as the days wore on, even she grew to be thankful for Paul Brion, though, of course, she would never own to it. Their troubles were many and various, and their helpless ignorance more profound and humiliating than they could have believed possible. I will not weary the reader by tracing the details of the process by which they became acquainted with the mode and cost of living "as other people do," and with the ways of the world in general; it would be too long a story. How Patty discovered that the cleverest fingers cannot copy a London bonnet without some previous knowledge of the science of millinery; how she and her sisters, after supplying themselves grudgingly with the mere necessaries of a modern outfit, found that the remainder of their "furniture money," to the last pound note, was spent;

how, after weary trampings to and fro in search of a habitable house in a wholesome neighbourhood, they learned the ruinous rates of rent and taxes and (after much shopping and many consultations with Mrs. M'Intyre) the alarming prices of furniture and provisions; how they were driven to admit, in spite of Patty, that that landlady on the premises, whom Eleanor had declared was not to be thought of, might be a necessary safeguard against worse evils; and how they were brought to ask each other, in surprise and dismay, "Is it possible that we are poor people after all, and not rich, as we supposed?"—all these things can be better imagined than described. Suffice it to say, they passed through much tribulation and many bitter and humbling experiences during the early months of their sojourn in Melbourne; but when at last they reached a comparatively safe haven, and found themselves once more secure under their own control, able to regulate their needs and their expenditure, and generally to understand the conditions and possibilities of their position, Elizabeth and Eleanor made a solemn declaration that they were indebted for this happy issue to the good offices and faithful friendship of Paul Brion alone, and Patty—though she turned up her nose and said "Pooh!"—though she hated to be indebted to him, or to anybody—agreed with them.

They settled down to their housekeeping by very slow degrees. For some time they stayed with Mrs. M'Intyre, because there really seemed nothing else to do that was at all within their means; and from this base of operations they made all those expeditions of inquiry into city habits and customs, commercial and domestic, which were such conspicuous and ignominious failures. As the sense of their helplessness grew upon them, they grudgingly admitted the young man (who was always at hand, and yet never intruded upon or pestered them) to their counsels, and accepted, without seeming to accept, his advice; and the more they condescended in this way the better they got on. Gradually they fell into the habit of depending on him, by tacit consent—which was the more easy to do because, as his father had promised, he did not presume upon their confidence in him. He was sharp and brusque, and even inclined to domineer—to be impertinent, as Patty called it—when they did submit their affairs to his judgment; but not the smallest suspicion of an unauthorised motive for his evident devotion to their interests appeared in his face, or voice, or manner, which were those of the man of business, slightly suggesting occasionally the imperious and impartial "nearest male relative." They grew to trust him—for his father's sake, they said, but there was nothing vicarious about it; and that they had the rare fortune to be justified in doing so, under such unlikely circumstances, made up to them for whatever ill luck they might otherwise have seemed to encounter in these days. It was he who finally found them their home, after their many futile searches—half a house in their own street and terrace, vacated by the marriage and departure to another colony of the lady who played the piano that was out of tune. No. 6, it appeared, had been divided into flats; the ground floor was occupied by the proprietor, his wife, and servant; and the upper, which had a gas stove and other kitchen appliances in a back room, was let unfurnished for £60 a year. Paul, always poking about in quest of opportunities, heard of this one and pounced upon it. He made immediate inquiries into the character and antecedents of the landlord of No. 6, the state of the drains and chimneys, and paint and paper, of the house; and, having satisfied himself that it was as nearly being what our girls wanted as anything they would be likely to find, called upon Elizabeth, and advised her to secure it forthwith. The sisters were just then adding up their accounts—taking stock of their affairs generally—and coming to desperate resolutions that something must be done; so the suggested arrangement, which would deliver them from bondage and from many of their worst difficulties, had quite a providential opportuneness about it. They took the rooms at once—four small rooms, including the improvised kitchen—and went into them, in defiance of Mrs. M'Intyre's protestations, before they had so much as a bedstead to sleep upon; and once more they were happy in the consciousness that they had recovered possession of themselves, and could call their souls their own. Slowly, bit by bit, the furniture came in—the barest necessaries first, and then odds and ends of comfort and prettiness (not a few of them discovered by Paul Brion in out-of-the-way places, where he "happened" to be), until the new little home grew to look as homelike as the old one. They sent for the bureau and the piano, which went a long way towards furnishing the sitting-room; and they bought a comfortable second-hand table and some capacious, cheap, wickerwork chairs; and they laid a square of matting on the floor, and made some chintz curtains for the window, and turned a deal packing-case into an ottoman, and another into a set of shelves for their books; and over all these little arrangements threw such an air of taste, such a complexion of spotless cleanliness and fastidious neatness, as are only seen in the homes of "nice" women, that it takes nice people to understand the charm of.

One day, when their preparations for regular domestic life were fairly completed, Patty, tired after a long spell of amateur carpentering, sat down to the piano to rest and refresh herself. The piano had been tuned on its arrival in Melbourne; and the man who tuned it had stared at her when she told him that it had been made to her mother's order, and showed him the famous name above the key-board. He would have stared still more had he heard what kind of magic life she could summon into the exquisite mechanism boxed up in that poor-looking deal case. All the sisters were musicians, strange to say; taught by their mother in the noble and simple spirit of the German school, and inheriting from her the sensitive ear and heart to understand the dignity and mystery, if not the message (which nobody understands) of that wonderful language which begins where words leave off. To "play the piano" was no mere conventional drawing-room performance with them, as they themselves were no conventional drawing-room misses; a "piece" of the ordinary pattern would have shocked their sense of art and harmony almost as much as it might have shocked Mozart and Mendelssohn, and Schubert and Schumann, and the other great masters whose pupils they were; while to talk and laugh, either when playing or listening, would have been to them like talking and laughing over their prayers. But, of the three, Patty was the most truly musical, in the serious meaning of the word, inasmuch as her temperament was warmer than those of her sisters, her imagination more vivid, her senses generally more susceptible to delicate impressions than theirs. The "spirits of the air" had all their supernatural power over her receptive and responsive soul, and she thrilled like an Æolian harp to the west wind under the spell of those emotions that have no name or shape, and for which no imagery supplies a comparison, which belong to the ideal world, into which those magic spirits summon us, and where the sacred hours of our lives—the sweetest, the saddest, the happiest—are spent.

To-day she sat down, suddenly prompted by the feeling that she was fagged and tired, and began to play mechanically a favourite Beethoven sonata; but in five minutes she had played her nerves to rest, and was as steeped in dreams as the great master himself must have been when he conceived the tender passages that only his spiritual ears could hear. Eleanor, who had been sewing industriously, by degrees let her fingers falter and her work fall into her lap; and Elizabeth, who had been arranging the books in the new book-shelves, presently put down her duster to come and stand behind the music-stool, and laid her large, cool hands on Patty's head. None of them spoke for some time, reverencing the Presence in their quiet room; but the touch of her sister's palms upon her hair brought the young musician out of her abstractions to a sense of her immediate surroundings again. She laid her head back on Elizabeth's breast and drew a long sigh, and left off playing. The gesture said, as plainly as words could have said it, that she was relieved and revived—that the spirit of peace and charity had descended upon her.

"Elizabeth," she said presently, still keeping her seat on the music-stool, and stroking her cheek with one of her sister's hands while she held the other round her neck, "I begin to think that Paul Brion has been a very good friend to us. Don't you?"

"I am not beginning," replied Elizabeth. "I have thought it every day since we have known him. And I have wondered often how you could dislike him so much."

"I don't dislike him," said Patty, quite amiably.

"I have taken particular notice," remarked Eleanor from the hearthrug, "and it is exactly three weeks since you spoke to him, and three weeks and five days since you shook hands."

Patty smiled, not changing her position or ceasing to caress her cheek with Elizabeth's hand. "Well," she said, "don't you think it would be a graceful thing to ask him to come and have tea with us some night? We have made our room pretty"—looking round with contentment—"and we have all we want now. We might get our silver things out of the bureau, and make a couple of little dishes, and put some candles about, and buy a bunch of flowers—for once—what do you say, Nelly? He has *never* been here since we came in—never farther than the downstairs passage—and wouldn't it be pleasant to have a little house warming, and show him our things, and give him some music, and—and try to make him enjoy himself? It would be some return for what he has done for us, and his father would be pleased."

That she should make the proposition—she who, from the first, had not only never "got on" with him, but had seemed to regard him with active dislike—surprised both her sisters not a little; but the proposition itself appeared to them, as to her, to have every good reason to recommend it. They thought it a most happy idea, and adopted it with enthusiasm. That very evening they made their plans. They designed the simple decorations for their little room, and the appropriate dishes for their modest feast. And, when these details had been settled, they remembered that on the following night no Parliament would be sitting, which meant that Paul would probably come home early (they knew his times of coming and going, for he was back at his old quarters now, having returned in consequence of the departure of the discordant piano, and to oblige Mrs. M'Intyre, he said); and that decided them to send him his invitation at once. Patty, while her complaisant mood was on her, wrote it herself before she went to bed, and gave it over the garden railing to Mrs. M'Intyre's maid.

In the morning, as they were asking which of them should go to town to fetch certain materials for their little *fête*, they heard the door bang and the gate rattle at No. 7, and a quick step that they knew. And the slavey of No. 6 came upstairs with Paul Brion's answer, which he had left as he passed on his way to his office. The note was addressed to "Miss King," whose amanuensis Patty had carefully explained herself to be when writing her invitation.

"MY DEAR MISS KING,—You are indeed very kind, but I fear I must deny myself the pleasure you propose—than which, I assure you, I could have none greater. If you will allow me, I will come in some day with Mrs. M'Intyre, who is very anxious to see your new menage. And when I come, I hope you will let me hear that new piano, which is such an amazing contrast to the old one.—Believe me, yours very truly,

"PAUL BRION."

This was Paul Brion's note. When the girls had read it, they stood still and looked at each other in a long, dead silence. Eleanor was the first to speak. Half laughing, but with her delicate face dyed in blushes, she whispered under her breath, "Oh—oh, don't you see what he means?"

"He is quite right—we must thank him," said Elizabeth, gentle as ever, but grave and proud. "We ought not to have wanted it—that is all I am sorry for."

But Patty stood in the middle of the room, white to the lips, and beside herself with passion. "That we should have made such a mistake!—and for *him* to rebuke us!" she cried, as if it were more than she could bear. "That *I* should have been the one to write that letter! Elizabeth, I suppose he is not to blame—"

"No, my dear—quite the contrary."

"But, all the same, I will never forgive him," said poor Patty in the bitterness of her soul.

CHAPTER IX
MRS. AARONS

There was no room for doubt as to what Paul Brion had meant. When the evening of the next day came—on which there was no Parliament sitting—he returned to No. 7 to dinner, and after dinner it was apparent that neither professional nor other engagements would have prevented him from enjoying the society of his fair neighbours if he had had a mind for it. His sitting-room opened upon the balcony—so did theirs; there was but a thin partition between them, and the girls knew not only when he was at home, but to a great extent what he was doing, by the presence and pungency of the odour from his pipe. When only faint whiffs stole into their open window from time to time, he was in his room, engaged—it was supposed—upon those wonderful leading articles which were, to them, the great feature of the paper to whose staff he belonged. At such times—for the houses in Myrtle Street were of a very lath-and-plastery order—they were careful to make no noise, and especially not to open their piano, that he might pursue his arduous labours undisturbed. But sometimes on these "off" nights he sat outside his window or strolled up and down the few feet of space allotted to him; and they would hear the rustle of the leaves of books on the other side of the partition, and the smell of his pipe would be very strong. This indicated that he had come home to rest and relax himself; on which occasions, prompted by some subtle feminine impulse, they would now and then indulge themselves with some of their best music— tacitly agreeing to select the very finest movements from the works of those best-beloved old masters whose majestic chimes rang out the dark evening of the eighteenth century and rang in the new age of art and liberty whose morning light we see—so as not to suggest, except by extreme comparison, the departed lady who played conventional rubbish on the instrument that was out of tune. That Paul Brion did not know Bach and Spohr, even by name and fame (as he did not), never for a moment occurred to them. How were they to know that the science and literature of music, in which they had been so well instructed, were not the usual study of educated people? They heard that he ceased to walk up and down his enclosure when they began to play and sing, and they smelt that his pipe was as near their window as it could get until they left off. That was enough.

To-night, then, he was strolling and sitting about his section of the balcony. They heard him tramping to and fro for a full hour after dinner, in a fidgetty manner; and then they heard him drag a chair through his window, and sit down on it heavily. It occurred to them all that he was doing nothing—except, perhaps, waiting for a chance to see and speak to them. A little intercourse had taken place of late in this way—a very little. One night, when Elizabeth had gone out to remonstrate with Dan for barking at inoffensive dogs that went by in the street below, Paul, who had been leaning meditatively on his balustrade, bent his head a little forward to ask her if she found the smell of his tobacco unpleasant. She assured him that none of them minded it at all, and remarked that the weather was warm. Upon which he replied that the thermometer was so and so, and suggested that she must miss the sea breezes very much. She said they missed them very much indeed, and inquired if he had heard from his father lately, and whether he was well. He was glad to inform her that his father, from whom he had just heard, was in excellent health, and further, that he had made many inquiries after her and her sisters. She thanked Mr. Brion sincerely, and hoped he (Mr. Paul) would give him their kindest regards when he wrote again and tell him they were getting on admirably. Mr. Paul said he would certainly not forget it. And they bade each other a polite good-night. Since then, both Elizabeth and Eleanor had had a word to say to him occasionally, when he and they simultaneously took the air after the day was over, and simultaneously happened to lean over the balustrade. Patty saw no harm in their doing so, but was very careful not to do it herself or to let him suppose that she was conscious of his near neighbourhood. She played to him sometimes with singular pleasure in her performance, but did not once put herself in the way of seeing or speaking to him.

To-night, not only she, but all of them, made a stern though unspoken vow that they would never—that they *could* never—so much as say good-night to him on the balcony any more. The lesson that he had taught them was sinking deeply into their hearts; they would never forget it again while they lived. They sat at their needlework in the bright gaslight, with the window open and the venetian blind down, and listened to the sound of his footstep and the dragging of his chair, and clearly realised the certainty that it was not because he was too busy that he had refused to spend the evening with them, but because he had felt obliged to show them that they had asked him to do a thing that was improper. Patty's head was bent down over her sewing; her face was flushed, her eyes restless, her quick fingers moving with nervous vehemence. Breaking her needle suddenly, she looked up and exclaimed, "Why are we sitting here so dull and stupid, all silent, like three scolded children? Play something, Nellie. Put away that horrid skirt, and play something bright and stirring—a good rousing march, or something of that sort."

"The Bridal March from 'Lohengrin,'" suggested Elizabeth, softly.

"No," said Patty; "something that will brace us up, and not make us feel small and humble and sat upon." What she meant was "something that will make Paul Brion understand that we don't feel small and humble and sat upon."

Eleanor rose, and laid her long fingers on the keyboard. She was not in the habit of taking things much to heart herself, and she did not quite understand her sister's frame of mind. The spirit of mischief prompted her to choose the saddest thing in the way of a march that she could recall on the spur of the moment—that funeral march of Beethoven's that Patty had always said was capable of reducing her to dust and ashes in her most exuberant moments. She threw the most heartbreaking expression that art allowed into the stately solemnity of her always perfectly balanced execution, partly because she could never render such a theme otherwise than reverently, but chiefly for the playful purpose of working upon Patty's feelings. Poor Patty had "kept up" and maintained a superficial command of herself until now, but this unexpected touch of pathos broke her down completely. She laid her arm on the table, and her pretty head upon her arm, and broke into a brief but passionate fit of weeping, such as she had never indulged in in all her life before. At the sound of the first sob Eleanor jumped up from the music-stool, contrite and frightened—Elizabeth in another moment had her darling in her arms; and both sisters were seized with the fear that Patty was sickening for some illness, caught, probably, in the vitiated atmosphere of city streets, to which she had never been accustomed.

In the stillness of the night, Paul Brion, leaning over the balustrade of the verandah, and whitening his coat against the partition that divided his portion of it from theirs, heard the opening bars of the funeral march, the gradually swelling sound and thrill of its impassioned harmonies, as of a procession tramping towards him along the street, and the sudden lapse into untimely silence. And then he heard, very faintly, a low cry and a few hurried sobs, and it was as if a lash had struck him. He felt sure that it was Patty who had been playing (he thought it must always be Patty who made that beautiful music), and Patty who had fallen a victim to the spirit of melancholy that she had invoked—simply because she always *did* seem to him to represent the action of the little drama of the sisters' lives, and Elizabeth and Eleanor to be the chorus merely; and he had a clear conviction, in the midst of much vague surmise, that he was involved in the causes that had made her unhappy. For a little while he stood still, fixing his eyes upon a neighbouring street lamp and scowling frightfully. He heard the girls' open window go down with a sharp rattle, and presently heard it open again hastily to admit Dan, who had been left outside. Then he himself went back, on tiptoe, to his own apartment, with an expression of more than his usual alert determination on his face.

Entering his room, he looked at his watch, shut his window and bolted it, walked into the adjoining bedchamber, and there, with the gas flaring noisily so as to give him as much light as possible, made a rapid toilet, exchanging his loose tweeds for evening dress. In less than ten minutes he was down in the hall, with his latch key in his pocket, shaking himself hurriedly into a light overcoat; and in less than half an hour he was standing at the door of a good-sized and rather imposing-looking house in the neighbouring suburb, banging it in his peremptory fashion with a particularly loud knocker.

Within this house its mistress was receiving, and she was a friend of his, as might have been seen by the manner of their greeting when the servant announced him, as also by the expression of certain faces amongst the guests when they heard his name—as they could not well help hearing it. "Mr.—*Paul*—BRION," the footman shouted, with three distinct and well-accentuated shouts, as if his lady were entertaining in the Town Hall. It gave Mrs. Aarons great pleasure when her domestic, who was a late acquisition, exercised his functions in this impressive manner.

She came sailing across the room in a very long-tailed and brilliant gown—a tall, fair, yellow-haired woman, carefully got up in the best style of conventional art (as a lady who had her clothes from Paris regardless of expense was bound to be)—flirting her fan coquettishly, and smiling an unmistakeable welcome. She was not young, but she looked young, and she was not pretty, but she was full of sprightly confidence and self-possession, which answered just as well. Least of all was she clever, as the two or three of her circle, who were, unwillingly recognised; but she was quick-witted and vivacious, accomplished in the art of small talk, and ready to lay down the law upon any subject, and somehow cleverness was assumed by herself and her world in general to be her most remarkable and distinguishing characteristic. And, finally, she had no pretensions to hereditary distinction—very much the contrary, indeed; but her husband was rich (he was standing in a retired corner, a long-nosed man with dark eyes rather close together, amongst a group of her admirers, admiring her as much as any of them), and she had known the social equivalent for money obtainable by good management in a community that must necessarily make a table of precedence for itself; and she had obtained it. She was a woman of fashion in her sphere, and her friends were polite enough to have no recollection of her antecedents, and no knowledge of the family connections whose existence she found it expedient to ignore. It must be said of her that her reputation, subject to the usual attacks of scandal-loving gossips who were jealous of her success, was perfectly untarnished; she was too cold and self-contained to be subject to the dangers that might have beset a less worldly woman in her position (for that Mr. Aarons was anything more than the minister to her ambitions and conveniences nobody for a moment supposed). Nevertheless, to have a little court of male admirers always hanging about her was the chief pleasure, and the attracting and retaining of their admiration the most absorbing pursuit of her life. Paul Brion was the latest, and at present the most interesting, of her victims. He had a good position in the press world, and had recently been talked of "in society" in connection with a particularly striking paper signed "P. B.," which had appeared in the literary columns of his journal. Wherefore, in the character of a clever woman, Mrs. Aarons had sought him out and added him to the attractions of her *salon* and the number of sympathetic friends. And, in spite of his hawk eyes, and his keen discernment generally, our young man had the ordinary man's belief that he stood on a pedestal among his rivals, and thought her the kindest and most discriminating and most charming of women.

At least he had thought so until this moment. Suddenly, as she came across the room to meet him, with her long train rustling over the carpet in a queenly manner, and a gracious welcome in her pale blue eyes, he found himself looking at her critically—comparing her complacent demeanour with the simple dignity of Elizabeth King, and her artificial elegance with the wild-flower grace of Eleanor, who was also tall and fair—and her studied sprightliness with Patty's inspired vigour—and her countenance, that was wont to be so attractive, with Patty's beautiful and intellectual face.

"Ah!" said Mrs. Aarons, shaking hands with him impressively, "you have remembered my existence, then, *at last!* Do you know how many weeks it is since you honoured me with your company?—*five*. And I wonder you can stand there and look me in the face."

He said it had been his misfortune and not his fault—that he had been so immersed in business that he had had no time to indulge in pleasure.

"Don't tell me. You don't have business on Friday evenings," said Mrs. Aarons promptly.

"Oh, don't I?" retorted Mr. Brion (the fact being that he had spent several Friday evenings on his balcony, smoking and listening to his neighbours' music, in the most absolute and voluptuous idleness). "You ladies don't know what a press-man's life is—his nose to the grindstone at all hours of the night and day."

"Poor man! Well, now you are here, come and sit down and tell me what you have been doing."

She took a quick glance round the room, saw that her guests were in a fair way to support the general intercourse by voluntary contributions, set the piano and a thin-voiced young lady and some "Claribel" ditties going, and then retired with Paul to a corner sofa for a chat. She was inclined to make much of him after his long absence, and he was in a mood to be more effusive than his wont. Nevertheless, the young man did not advance, as suspicious observers supposed him to be doing, in the good graces of his charming friend—ready as she was to meet him half-way.

"Of course I wanted very much to see you—it seems an awful time since I was here—but I had another reason for coming to-night," said Paul, when they had comfortably settled themselves (he was the descendant of countless gentlefolk and she had not even a father that she could conveniently call her own, yet was she constrained to blush for his bad manners and his brutal deficiency in delicacy and tact). "I want to ask a favour of you—you are always so kind and good—and I think you will not mind doing it. It is not much—at least to you—but it would be very much to them—"

"To whom?" inquired Mrs. Aarons, with a little chill of disappointment and disapproval already in her voice and face. This was not what she felt she had a right to expect under the present combination of circumstances.

"Three girls—three sisters, who are orphans—in a kind of way, wards of my father's," explained Paul, showing a disposition to stammer for the first time. "Their name is King, and they have come to live in Melbourne, where they don't know anyone—not a single friend. I thought, perhaps, you would just call in and see them some day—it would be so awfully kind of you, if you would. A little notice from a woman like *you* would be just everything to them."

"Are they nice?—that is to say, are they the sort of people whom one would—a—care to be responsible for—you know what I mean? Are they *ladies?*" inquired Mrs. Aarons, who, by virtue of her own extraction, was bound to be select and exclusive in her choice of acquaintances.

"Most certainly," replied Paul, with imprudent warmth. "There can be no manner of doubt about that. *Born* ladies."

"I don't ask what they were born," she said quickly, with a toss of the head. "What are they *now?* Who are their connections? What do they live on?"

Paul Brion gave a succinct and graphic sketch of the superficial history and circumstances of his father's "wards," omitting various details that instinct warned him might be accounted "low"—such, for instance, as the fact that the single maidservant of the house they lived in was nothing more to them than their medium of communication with the front door. He dwelt (like the straightforward blunderer that he was) on their personal refinement and their high culture and accomplishments, how they studied every day at the Public Library, taking their frugal lunch at the pastry-cook's—how they could talk French and German like "natives"—how they played the piano in a way that made all the blood in one's veins tingle—how, in short, they were in all things certain to do honour and credit to whoever would spread the wing of the matron and chaperon over them. It seemed to him a very interesting story, told by himself, and he was quite convinced that it must touch the tender woman's heart beating under that pretty dress beside him.

"You are a mother yourself," he said (as indeed she was—the mother of four disappointing little Aaronses, who were *all* long-nosed and narrow-eyed and dark, each successive infant more the image of its father than the last), "and so you can understand their position—you know how to feel for them." He thought this an irresistible plea, and was unprepared for the dead silence with which it was received. Glancing up quickly, he saw that she was by no means in the melting mood that he had looked for.

"Of course, if you don't wish it—if it will be troubling you too much—" he began, with his old fierce abruptness, drawing himself together.

"It is not that," said she, looking at her fan. "But now I know why you have stayed away for five weeks."

"Why *I* have stayed away—oh! I understand. But I told you they were living *alone*, did I not? Therefore I have never been into their house—it is quite impossible for me to have the pleasure of their society."

"Then you want me to take them up, so that you can have it here? Is that it?"

The little man was looking so ferocious, and his departure from her side appeared so imminent, that she changed her tone quickly after putting this question. "Never mind," she said, laying her jewelled fingers on his coat sleeve for a moment, "I will not be jealous—at least I will try not to be. I will go and call on them to-morrow, and as soon as they have called on me I will ask them to one of my Fridays. Will that do?"

"I don't wish you for a moment to do what would be at all unpleasant to yourself," he said, still in a hurt, blunt tone, but visibly softening.

"It won't be unpleasant to me," she said sentimentally, "if it will please you."

And Paul went home at midnight, well satisfied with what he had done, believing that a woman so "awfully kind" as Mrs. Aarons would be a shield and buckler to those defenceless girls.

CHAPTER X
THE FIRST INVITATION

Mrs. Aarons kept her promise, and called upon the Kings on Saturday. Mrs. M'Intyre saw her get down at the gate of No. 6, at about four o'clock in the afternoon, watched the brougham which had brought her trundling slowly up and down the street for half-an-hour, and then saw her get into it and drive off; which facts, communicated to Paul Brion, gave him the greatest satisfaction.

He did not see his neighbours for several days after. He heard their piano, and their footsteps and voices on the verandah; but, whenever he essayed to go outside his own room for a breath of fresh air, they were sure to retire into theirs immediately, like mice into a hole when the cat has frightened them. At last he came across them in an alley of the Fitzroy Gardens, as he and they were converging upon Myrtle Street from different points. They were all together as usual—the majestic Elizabeth in the middle, with her younger sisters on either side of her; and they were walking home from an organ recital in the Town Hall to their tea, and a cosy evening over a new book, having spent most of the morning at the Public Library, and had their mid-day dinner at Gunsler's. As he caught sight of them, he was struck by the change in their outward appearance that a few weeks of Melbourne experience had brought about, and pleased himself with thinking how much their distinguished aspect must have impressed that discerning woman of the world, who had so kindly condescended to take them up. They were dressed in their new gowns, and bonneted, booted, and gloved, in the neatest manner; a little air of the mode pervaded them now, while the primitive purity of their taste was still unadulterated. They had never looked more charming, more obviously "born ladies" than to-day, as he saw them after so long an interval.

The three black figures stood the shock of the unexpected meeting with admirable fortitude. They came on towards him with no faltering of that free and graceful gait that was so noticeable in a city full of starched and whale-boned women, and, as he lifted his hat, bowed gravely—Elizabeth only giving him a dignified smile, and wishing him a good evening as she went by. He let them pass him, as they seemed to wish to pass him; then he turned sharply and followed them. It was a chance he might not get again for months, perhaps, and he could not afford to let it slip.

"Miss King," he called in his imperative brusque way; and at the sound of his voice Elizabeth looked back and waited for him to join her, while her younger sisters, at a sign from Patty, walked on at a brisk pace, leaving her in command of the situation. "Miss King," said Paul earnestly, "I am so glad to have an opportunity of speaking to you—I have been wanting all the week to see you, that I might thank you for your kindness in asking me to tea."

"Oh," said Elizabeth, whose face was scarlet, "don't mention it, Mr. Brion. We thought of it merely as a—a little attention—a sort of acknowledgment—to your father; that it might please him, perhaps, for you to see that we had settled ourselves, as he could not do so himself."

"It would have pleased *me*, beyond everything in the world, Miss King. Only—only—"

"Yes, I know. We forgot that it was not quite *de rigueur*—or, rather, we had not learned about those things. We have been so out of the world, you see. We were dreadfully ashamed of ourselves," she added candidly, with a little embarrassed laugh, "but you must set it down to our ignorance of the laws of propriety, and not suppose that we consciously disregarded them."

"The laws of propriety!" repeated Paul hotly, his own face red and fierce. "It is Schiller, I think, who says that it is the experience of corruption which originated them. I hate to hear you speak of impropriety, as if you could even conceive the idea of it!"

"Well, we are not in Arcadia now, and we must behave ourselves accordingly," said Elizabeth, who was beginning to feel glad in her gentle heart that she had been able to make this explanation. "I think we are getting corrupted with wonderful rapidity. We have even been *called upon*, quite as if we were people of fashion and consequence, by a lady who was dressed in the most magnificent manner, and who came in her carriage. Her name was Aarons—Mrs. Aarons. She said she had heard of of our being here, and thought she would like to make our acquaintance."

"Did she?" responded Paul warmly, thinking how nice and delicate it was of Mrs. Aarons to respect his anxious wish that his name and interposition should not be mentioned, which was certainly more than he had expected of her. "And were you all at home when she called?"

"As it happened—yes. It was on Saturday afternoon, when we are generally rather busy."

"And have you returned her call yet?"

"No. We don't mean to return it," said Elizabeth composedly; "we did not like her enough to wish to make an acquaintance of her. It is no good to put ourselves out, and waste our own time and theirs, for people whom we are sure not to care about, and who would not care about us, is it?"

"But I think you would like her if you knew her, Miss King," pleaded Paul, much disturbed by this threatened downfall of his schemes. "I am sure—at least, I have always heard, and I can speak a little from personal knowledge—that she is a particularly nice woman; thoroughly kind and amiable, and, at the same time, having a good position in society, and a remarkably pleasant house, where you might meet interesting people whom you *would* like. Oh, don't condemn her at first sight in that way! First impressions are so seldom to be trusted. Go and call, at any rate—indeed, you know, you ought to do that, if only for form's sake."

"For politeness, do you mean? Would it be rude not to return her call?"

"It would be thought so, of course."

"Ah, I was not sure—I will call then. I don't *mind* calling in the least. If she has done us a kindness, it is right to acknowledge it in whatever is the proper way. It was my sisters—especially Patty—who took a dislike to her, and particularly wished not to see her again. Patty thought she asked too many questions, and that she came from some motive of curiosity to pry into our affairs. She was certainly a little impertinent, I thought. But then, perhaps, ladies in 'the world' don't look at these things as we have been accustomed to do," added Elizabeth humbly.

"I don't think they do," said Paul.

By this time they had reached the gate through which Patty and Eleanor had passed before them out of the gardens. As they silently emerged into the road, they saw the pair flitting along the pavement a considerable distance ahead of them, and when they turned the corner into Myrtle Street both the slender black figures had disappeared. Paul wondered to see himself so irritated by this trifling and inevitable circumstance. He felt that it would have done him good to speak to Patty, if it were only to quarrel with her.

Elizabeth bade him good-night when she reached the gate of No. 6, where the hall door stood open—putting her warm, strong hand with motherly benevolence into his.

"Good-night, Miss King. I am so glad to have seen you," he responded, glaring fiercely at the balcony and the blank window overhead. "And—and you will return that call, won't you?"

"O yes—of course. We will walk there on Monday, as we come home from the Library. We are able to find our way about in Melbourne very well now, with the help of the map you were so kind as to give us when we first came. I can't tell you how useful that has been."

So, with mutual friendship and goodwill, they parted—Elizabeth to join her sisters upstairs, where one was already setting the tea-kettle to boil on the gas stove, and the other spreading a snow-white cloth on the sitting-room table—Paul Brion to get half-an-hour's work and a hasty dinner before repairing to the reporters' gallery of "the House."

He did not see them again for a long time, and the first news he heard of them was from Mrs. Aarons, whom he chanced to meet when she was shopping one fine morning in Collins Street.

"You see, I remembered my promise," she said, when matters of more personal moment had been disposed of; "I went to see those extraordinary *protégées* of yours."

"Extraordinary—how extraordinary?" he inquired stiffly.

"Well, I put it to you—*are* they not extraordinary?"

He was silent for a few seconds, and the points of his moustache went up a little. "Perhaps so—now you mention it," he said. "Perhaps they *are* unlike the—the usual girl of the period with whom we are familiar. But I hope you were favourably impressed with your visit. Were you?"

"No, I wasn't. I will be frank with you—I wasn't. I never expected to find people living in that manner—and dressing in that manner. It is not what I am used to."

"But they are very lady-like—if I am any judge—and that is the chief thing. Very pretty too. Don't you think so?"

"O *dear* no! The middle one has rather nice eyes perhaps—though she gives herself great airs, I think, considering her position. And the youngest is not bad looking. *Miss* King is *plain*, decidedly. However, I told you I would do something for them, and I have kept my word. They are coming to my next Friday. And I do *hope*," proceeded Mrs. Aarons, with an anxious face, "that they will dress themselves respectably for the reputation of my house. Do you know anyone who could speak to them about it? Could you give them a hint, do you think?"

"*I!*—good gracious! I should like to see myself at it," said Paul, grimly. "But I don't think," he added, with a fatuity really pitiable in a man of his years and experience, "that there is any danger of their not looking nice. They must have had their old frocks on when you saw them."

CHAPTER XI
DISAPPOINTMENT

How they should dress themselves for Mrs. Aarons's Friday was a question as full of interest for our girls as if they had been brought up in the lap of wealth and fashion. They were not so ignorant of the habits and customs of "the world" as not to know that evening dress was required of them on this occasion, and they had not seen so many shop windows and showrooms without learning something of its general features as applied to their sex and to the period. Great were the discussions that went on over the momentous subject. Even their studies at the Public Library lost their interest and importance, it is to be feared, for a day or two, while they were anxiously hesitating, first, whether they should accept the invitation, and, secondly, in what costume they should make their first appearance in polite society. The former of these questions was settled without much trouble. Elizabeth's yearning for "friends," the chance of discovering whom might be missed by missing this unusual opportunity; Patty's thirst for knowledge and experience in all available fields, and Eleanor's habit of peaceably falling in with her sisters' views, overcame the repugnance that all of them entertained to the idea of being patronised by, or beholden for attentions that they could not reciprocate to, Mrs. Aarons, against whom they had conceived a prejudice on the first day of contact with her which a further acquaintance had not tended to lessen. But the latter question was, as I have said, a matter of much debate. Could they afford themselves new frocks?—say, black grenadines that would do for the summer afterwards. This suggestion was inquired into at several shops and of several dressmakers, and then relinquished, but not without a struggle. "We are just recovering ourselves," said Elizabeth, with her note-book before her and her pencil in her hand; "and if we go on as we are doing now we shall be able to save enough to take us to Europe next year without meddling with our house-money. But if we break our rules—well, it will throw us back. And it will be a bad precedent, Patty."

"Then we won't break them," said Patty valiantly. "We will go in our black frocks. Perhaps," she added, with some hesitation, "we can find something amongst our mother's things to trim us up a little."

"She would like to see us making ourselves look pretty with her things," said Eleanor.

"Yes, Nelly. That is what I think. Come along and let us look at that bundle of lace that we put in the bottom drawer of the bureau. Elizabeth, does lace so fine as that *go* with woollen frocks, do you think? We must not have any incongruities if we can help it."

Elizabeth thought that plain white ruffles would, perhaps, be best, as there was so much danger of incongruities if they trusted to their untrained invention. Whereupon Patty pointed out that they would have to buy ruffles, while the lace would cost nothing, which consideration, added to their secret wish for a little special decoration, now that the occasion for it had arisen—the love of adornment being, though refined and chastened, an ingredient of their nature as of every other woman's—carried the day in favour of "mother's things."

"And I think," said Patty, with dignity, when at last Friday came and they had spread the selected finery on their little beds, "I think that ladies ought to know how to dress themselves better than shop-people can tell them. When they want to make themselves smart, they should think, first, what they can afford and what will be suitable to their position and the occasion, and then they should think what would look pretty in a picture. And they should put on *that*."

Patty, I think, was well aware that she would look pretty in a picture, when she had arrayed herself for the evening. Round the neck of her black frock she had loosely knotted a length of fine, yellow-white Brussels lace, the value of which, enhanced by several darns that were almost as invisibly woven as the texture itself, neither she nor her sisters had any idea of. Of course it did not "go" with the black frock, even though the latter was not what mourning was expected to be, but its delicacy was wonderfully thrown up by its contrast with that background, and it was a most becoming setting for the wearer's brilliant face. Patty had more of the priceless flounce sewn on her black sleeves (the little Vandal had cut it into lengths on purpose), half of it tucked in at the wrists out of sight; and the ends that hung over her breast were loosely fastened down with a quaint old silver brooch, in which a few little bits of topaz sparkled. Elizabeth was not quite so magnificent. She wore a fichu of black lace over her shoulders—old Spanish, that happened just then to be the desire and despair of women of fashion, who could not get it for love or money; it was big enough to be called a shawl, and in putting it on Patty had to fold and tack it here and there with her needle, to keep it well up in its proper place. This was fastened down at the waist with a shawl-pin shaped like a gold arrow, that her grandmother had used to pin her Paisley over her chest; and, as the eldest daughter, Elizabeth wore her mother's slender watch-chain wound round and round her neck, and, depending from it, an ancient locket of old red gold, containing on its outward face a miniature of that beautiful mother as a girl, with a beading of little pearls all round it. Eleanor was dressed up in frills of soft, thick Valenciennes, taken from the bodice of one of the brocaded gowns; which lace, not being too fragile to handle, Elizabeth, ignorant as yet of the artistic excellence of the genuine coffee-colour of age, had contrived to wash to a respectable whiteness. And to Eleanor was given, from the little stock of family trinkets, a string of pearls, fastened with an emerald clasp—pearls the size of small peas, and dingy and yellow from never having been laid out on the grass, as, according to a high authority, pearls should be. Upon the whole, their finery, turned into money, would probably have bought up three of the most magnificent costumes worn in Melbourne that night; yet it can scarcely be said to have been effective. Neither Mrs. Aarons nor her lady friends had the requisite experience to detect its quality and understand what we may call its moral value. Only one person amongst the company discovered that Eleanor's pearls were real, and perhaps only that one had been educated in lace, save rudimentally, in the Melbourne shops. And amongst the *nouveaux riches*, as poor gentlefolks well know, to have no claims to distinction but such as are out of date is practically to have none.

Late in the evening, Paul Brion, who had not intended to go to this particular Friday, lest his presence should betray to the sisters what he was so anxious to conceal from them, found that he could not resist the temptation to see with his own eyes how they were getting on; and when he had entered the room, which was unusually crowded, and had prowled about for a few minutes amongst the unpleasantly tall men who obstructed his view in all directions, he was surprised and enraged to see the three girls sitting side by side in a corner, looking neglected and lonely, and to see insolent women in long-tailed satin gowns sweeping past them as if they had not been there. One glance was enough to satisfy *him* that there had been no fear of their not looking "nice." Patty's bright and flushed but (just now) severe little face, rising so proudly from the soft lace about her throat and bosom, seemed to him to stand out clear in a surrounding mist, apart and distinct from all the faces in the room—or in the world, for that matter. Elizabeth's dignified serenity in an uncomfortable position was the perfection of good breeding, and made a telling contrast to the effusive manners of those about her; and fair Eleanor, sitting so modestly at Elizabeth's side, with her hands, in a pair of white silk mittens, folded in her lap, was as charming to look at as heart of man could desire. Other men seemed to be of his opinion, for he saw several hovering around them and looking at them with undisguised interest; but the ladies, who, he thought, ought to have felt privileged to take them up, appeared to regard them coldly, or to turn their backs upon them altogether, literally as well as metaphorically. It was plain that Mrs. Aarons had introduced them to nobody, probably wishing (as was indeed the case—people of her class being morbidly sensitive to the disgrace of unfashionable connections) not to own to them more than she could help.

He withdrew from their neighbourhood before they saw him, and went to seek his hostess, swelling with remonstrant wrath. He found her on a sofa at the other end of the room, talking volubly (she was always voluble, but now she was breathless in her volubility) to a lady who had never before honoured her Fridays, and who, by doing so to-night, had gratified an ambition that had long been paramount amongst the many ambitions which, enclosed in a narrow circle as they were, served to make the interest and occupation of Mrs. Aarons's life. She looked up at Paul as he approached her, and gave him a quick nod and smile, as if to say, "I see you, but you must be perfectly aware that I am unable to attend to you just now." Paul understood her, and, not having the honour of Mrs. Duff-Scott's acquaintance himself, fell back a little behind the sofa and waited for his opportunity. As he waited, he could not help overhearing the conversation of the two ladies, and deriving a little cynical amusement therefrom.

"And, as soon as I heard of it, I *begged* my husband to go and see if it was *really* a genuine example of Derby-Chelsea; and, you see, it *was*," said Mrs. Aarons, with subdued enthusiasm—almost with tears of emotion.

"It was, indeed," assented Mrs. Duff-Scott earnestly. "There was the true mark—the capital D, with the anchor in the middle of it. It is extremely rare, and I had no hope of ever possessing a specimen."

"I *knew* you would like to have it. I said to Ben. 'Do go and snatch it up at once for Mrs. Duff-Scott's collection.' And he was so pleased to find he was in time. We were so afraid someone might have been before us. But the fact is, people are so ignorant that they have no idea of the value of things of that sort—fortunately."

"I don't call it fortunate at all," the other lady retorted, a little brusquely. "I don't like to see people ignorant—I am quite ready to share and share." Then she added, with a smile, "I am sure I can never be sufficiently obliged to Mr. Aarons for taking so much trouble on my account. I must get him into a corner presently, and find out how much I am in his debt—though, of course, no money can represent the true worth of such a treasure, and I shall always feel that I have robbed him."

"Oh, pray, pray don't talk of *payment*," the hostess implored, with a gesture of her heavily-ringed hands. "You will hurt him *dreadfully* if you think of such a thing. He feels himself richly paid, I assure you, by having a chance to do you a little service. And such a mere *trifle* as it is!"

"No, indeed, it is not a trifle, Mrs. Aarons—very far from it. The thing is much too valuable for me to—to"—Mrs. Duff-Scott hesitated, and her face was rather red—"to deprive you of it in that way. I don't feel that I can take it as a present—a bit of *real* Derby-Chelsea that you might never find a specimen of again—really I don't."

"Oh, *please*"—and Mrs. Aarons's voice was at once reproachful and persuasive—"*please!* I know you wouldn't wish to hurt us."

A little more discussion ensued, which Paul watched with an amused smile; and Mrs. Duff-Scott gave in.

"Well, if you insist—but you are really too good. It makes me quite uncomfortable to take such a treasure from you. However, perhaps, some day I may be able to contribute to *your* collection."

Like her famous model, Mrs. Ponsonby de Tompkins, Mrs. Aarons stalked her big game with all kinds of stratagems, and china was the lure with which she had caught Mrs. Duff-Scott. This was a lady who possessed not only that most essential and valuable qualification of a lady, riches, but had also a history that was an open page to all men. It had not much heraldic emblazonment about it, but it showed a fair and honourable record of domestic and public circumstances that no self-respecting woman could fail to take social credit for. By virtue of these advantages, and of a somewhat imperious, though generous and unselfish, nature, she certainly did exercise that right to be "proud" which, in such a case, the most democratic of communities will cheerfully concede. She had been quite inaccessible to Mrs. Aarons, whom she was wont to designate a "person," long after that accomplished woman had carried the out-works of the social citadel in which she dwelt, and no doubt she would have been inaccessible to the last. Only she had a weakness—she had a hobby (to change the metaphor a little) that ran away with her, as hobbies will, even in the case of the most circumspect of women; and that hobby, exposed to the seductions of a kindred hobby, broke down and trampled upon the barriers of caste. It was the Derby-Chelsea specimen that had brought Mrs. Duff-Scott to occupy a sofa in Mrs. Aarons's drawing-room—to their mutual surprise, when they happened to think of it.

She rose from that sofa now, slightly perturbed, saying she must go and find Mr. Aarons and acknowledge the obligation under which he had placed her, while all the time she was cudgelling her brains to think by what means and how soon she could discharge it—regretting very keenly for the moment that she had put herself in the way of people who did not understand the fine manners which would have made such a dilemma impossible. Her hostess jumped up immediately, and the two ladies passed slowly down the room in the direction of the corner where our neglected girls were sitting. Paul followed at a respectful distance, and was gratified to see Mrs. Duff-Scott stop at the piano, in place of hunting for her host (who was never a conspicuous feature of these entertainments), and shake hands cordially with a tall German in spectacles who had just risen from the music-stool. He had come to Mrs. Aarons's Friday in a professional capacity, but he was a sufficiently great artist for a great lady to make an equal of him.

"Ah, my dear Herr Wüllner," she said, in a very distinct voice, "I was listening, and I thought I could not be mistaken in your touch. Heller's *Wanderstunden*, wasn't it?" And they plunged head first into musical talk such as musical people (who never care in the least how much unmusical people may be bored by it) love to indulge in whenever an occasion offers, while Mrs. Aarons stood by, smiling vaguely, and not understanding a word of it. Paul Brion listened to them for a few minutes, and a bright idea came into his head.

CHAPTER XII
TRIUMPH

Our girls still sat in their corner, but a change had come over them within the last few minutes. A stout man sitting near them was talking to Elizabeth across Eleanor's lap—Eleanor lying back in her seat, and smiling amiably as she listened to them; and Miss King was looking animated and interested, and showed some signs of enjoying herself at last. Patty also had lost her air of angry dignity, and was leaning a little forward, with her hands clasped on her knees, gazing at Herr Wüllner's venerable face with rapt enthusiasm. Paul, regarding her for a moment, felt himself possessed of sufficient courage to declare his presence, and, waiting until he could catch her eye, bowed pleasantly. She looked across at him with no recognition at first, then gave a little start, bent her head stiffly, and resumed her attentive perusal of Herr Wüllner's person. "Ah," thought Paul, "the old fellow has woke her up. And she wants him to play again." Mrs. Duff-Scott had dropped into a chair by the piano, and sat there contentedly, talking to the delighted musician, who had been as a fish out of water since he came into the room, and was now swimming at large in his native element again. She was a distinguished looking matron of fifty or thereabouts, with a handsome, vivacious, intelligent face and an imposing presence generally; and she had an active and well-cultivated mind which concerned itself with many other things than china. Having no necessity to work, no children on whom to expend her exuberant energies, and being incapable of finding the ordinary woman's satisfaction in the ordinary routine of society pleasures, she made ardent pursuits for herself in several special directions. Music was one. Herr Wüllner thought she was the most enlightened being in female shape that he had ever known, because she "understood" music—what was really music and what was not (according to his well-trained theories). She had, in the first place, the wonderful good sense to know that she could not play herself, and she held the opinion that people in general had no business to set themselves up to play, but only those who had been "called" by Divine permission and then properly instructed in the science of their art. "We won't look at bad pictures, nor read trashy books," she would say. "Why should our artistic sense be depraved and demoralised through our ears any more than through our eyes? Mothers should know better, my dear Herr Wüllner, and keep the incapables in the background. All girls should learn, if they *like* learning—in which case it does them good, and delights the domestic circle; but if at sixteen they can't play—what *we* call play—after having had every chance given them, they should leave off, so as to use the time better, or confine their performances to a family audience." And Mrs. Duff-Scott had the courage of her convictions, and crushed unrelentingly those presumptuous amateurs (together with their infatuated mammas) who thought they could play when they couldn't, and who regarded music as a mere frivolous drawing-room amusement for the encouragement of company conversation. Herr Wüllner delighted in her. The two sat talking by the piano, temporarily indifferent to what was going on around them, turning over a roll of music sheets that had had a great deal of wear and tear, apparently. Mrs. Aarons sat beside them, fanning herself and smiling, casting about her for more entertaining converse. And Paul Brion stood near his hostess, listening and watching for his opportunity. Presently it came.

Mrs. Duff-Scott lifted up a sheet of crabbed manuscript as yellowed by time as Patty's Brussels lace, and said: "This is not quite the thing for a mixed audience, is it?"

"Ah, no, you are right; it is the study of Haydn that a friend of mine asked of me yesterday, and that I propose to read to him to-night," said Herr Wüllner, in that precise English and with that delicate pronunciation with which the cultivated foreigner so often puts us to shame. "It is, you perceive, an arrangement for one violin and a piano only—done by a very distinguished person for a lady who was for a short time my pupil, when I was a young man. You have heard it with the four-stringed instruments at your house; that was bad—bad! Ach! that second violin squeaked like the squeaking of a pig, and it was always in the wrong place. But in good hands it is sublime. This"—and he sighed as he added more sheets to the one she held and was steadily perusing—"this is but a crippled thing, perhaps; the piano, which should have none of it, has it all—and no one can properly translate that piano part—not one in ten thousand. But it is well done. Yes, it is very well done. And I have long been wanting my friend to try it with me."

"And what about the young lady for whom it was written?—which part did she take?"

"The piano—the piano. But then she had a wonderful execution and sympathy—it was truly wonderful for a lady, and she so young. Women play much better now, as a rule, but I never hear one who is an amateur play as she did. And so quick—so quick! It was an inspiration with her. Yes, this was written on purpose for that lady—I have had it ever since—it has never been published. The manuscript is in her own hand. She wrote out much of her music in her own hand. It was many, many years ago, and I was a young man then. We were fellow-pupils before I became her master, and she was my pupil only for a few weeks. It was a farce—a farce. She did not play the violin, but in everything else she was better than I. Ah, she was a great genius, that young lady. She was a great loss to the world of art."

"Did she die, Herr Wüllner?"

"She eloped," he said softly, "she ran away with a scapegrace. And the ship she sailed in was lost at sea."

"Dear me! How very sad. Well, you must make your friend try it over, and, if you manage it all right, bring him with you to my house on Monday evening and let me hear it."

"That shall give me great pleasure," said the old man, bowing low.

"You have your violin with you, I suppose?" she asked.

"It is in the hall, under my cloak. I do not bring it into this room," he replied.

"Why not?" she persisted. "Go and fetch it, Herr Wüllner, and let Mrs. Aarons hear you play it"—suddenly bethinking herself of her hostess and smiling upon that lady—"if she has never had that treat before."

Mrs. Aarons was eager to hear the violin, and Herr Wüllner went himself, though reluctantly, to fetch his treasure from the old case that he had hidden away below. When he had tuned up his strings a little, and had tucked the instrument lovingly under his chin, he looked at Mrs. Duff-Scott and said softly, "What?"

"Oh," cried Mrs. Aarons, striking in, "play that—you know—what you were talking of just now—what Mrs. Duff-Scott wanted so much to hear. I want to hear it too."

"Impossible—impossible," he said quickly, almost with a shudder. "It has a piano part, and there is no one here to take that."

Then Paul Brion broke in, conscious that he was running heavy risks of all sorts, but resolved to seize his chance.

"I think there *is* someone who could play it," he said to Mrs. Aarons, speaking with elaborate distinctness. "The Miss Kings—one of them, at any rate—"

"Nonsense," interrupted Mrs. Aarons, sharply, but under her breath. "Not at all likely." She was annoyed by the suggestion, and wished to treat it as if unheard (it was unreasonable, on the face of it, of course); but Mrs. Duff-Scott caught at it in her direct way. "Who are they? Which are the Miss Kings?" she asked of Paul, putting up her eye-glass to see what manner of man had taken upon himself to interfere.

"My dear lady," sighed Herr Wüllner, dropping his bow dejectedly, "it is out of the question, absolutely. It is not normal music at its best—and I have it only in manuscript. It is impossible that any lady can attempt it."

"She will not attempt it if she cannot do it, Herr Wüllner," said Paul. "But you might ask her."

Mrs. Duff-Scott had followed the direction of his eyes, and her attention was violently arrested by the figures of the three girls sitting together, who were so remarkably unlike the majority of Mrs. Aarons's guests. She took note of all their superficial peculiarities in a moment, and the conviction that the lace and the pearls were real flashed across her like an inspiration. "Is it the young lady with the bright eyes?" she inquired. "What a charming face! Yes, Herr Wüllner, we *will* ask her. Introduce her to me, Mrs. Aarons, will you?"

She rose as she spoke and sailed towards Patty, Mrs. Aarons following; and Paul Brion held his breath while he waited to see how his reckless enterprise would turn out. In a few minutes Patty came towards the piano, with her head up and her face flushed, looking a little defiant, but as self-possessed as the great lady who convoyed her across the room. The events of the evening had roused her spirit, and strung up her nerves like Herr Wüllner's fiddle-strings, and she, too, was in a daring and audacious mood.

"This is it," said the old musician, looking at her critically as he gave a sheet of manuscript into her hand. It was a wonderful chance, of course, but Patty had seen the facsimile of that manuscript many times before, and had played from it. It is true she had never played with the violin accompaniment—had never so much as seen a violin until she came to Melbourne; but her mother had contrived to make her understand how the more delicate and sensitive instrument ought to be deferred to in the execution of the piano part, and what the whole should sound like, by singing the missing air in her flexible trilling voice; and just now she was in that peculiar mood of exaltation that she felt inspired to dare anything and assured that she should succeed. "You will not be able to read it?" Herr Wüllner suggested persuasively, drawing hope from her momentary silence.

"Oh, yes," she said, looking up bravely: "I think so. You will stop me, please, if I do not play it right." And she seated herself at the piano with a quiet air of knowing what she was doing that confounded the two ladies who were watching her and deeply interested Mrs. Duff-Scott. Paul Brion's heart was beating high with anticipated triumph. Herr Wüllner's heart, on the contrary, sank with a mild despair.

"Well, we will have a few bars," he sighed. "And pray, my dear young lady, don't bang the piano—I mean don't play over me. And try to keep time. But you will never do it—with the best intentions, my dear, you will never be able to read it from such a manuscript as that."

Patty looked up at him with a sort of radiant calmness, and said gently, "Go on. You see you have an opening movement to yourself."

Bewildered, the old man dropped his bow upon the strings, and set forth on his hopeless task. And at exactly the right moment the piano glided in, so lightly, so tenderly, and yet with such admirable precision and delicate clearness, that it justified, for once, its trespass upon ground that belonged to more aerial instruments. It was just what Paul Brion had counted on— though Paul Brion had not the least idea what a wild chance had brought about the fulfilment of his expectations. Patty was able to display her chief accomplishment to the very best advantage, and the sisters were thereby promoted to honour. The cold shade of neglect and obscurity was to chill them no more from this happy moment. It was a much greater triumph than Patty herself had any idea of, or than anybody had had the least reason to expect. *She* knew that piles of music, all in this self-same handwriting (she had never seen any other and supposed that all manuscript music was alike), were stowed away in the old bureau at home, and in the ottoman which she had constructed out of a packing-case, and that long familiarity had made it as easy to her to read as print; but Herr Wüllner was not in a position to make the faintest guess at such a circumstance. When Elizabeth moved her seat nearer to the piano, as if to support her sister, though he was close enough to see it, he did not recognise in the miniature round her neck the face of that young lady of genius who eloped with a scapegrace, and was supposed to have been drowned at sea with her husband. And yet it was that lady's face. Such wonderful coincidences are continually happening in our small world. It was not more wonderful than that Herr Wüllner, Mrs. Duff-Scott, Paul Brion, and Patty King should have been gathered together round one piano, and that piano Mrs. Aarons's.

The guests were laughing and talking and flirting, as they were wont to do under cover of the music that generally prevailed at these Friday receptions, when an angry "Hush!" from the violinist, repeated by Mrs.

Duff-Scott, made a little circle of silence round the performers. And in this silence Patty carried through her responsible undertaking with perfect accuracy and the finest taste—save for a shadowy mistake or two, which, glancing over them as if they were mere phantoms of mistakes, and recovering herself instantly, only served to show more clearly the finished quality of her execution, and the thoroughness of her musical experience. She was conscious herself of being in her very best form.

"Ah!" said Herr Wüllner, drawing a long breath as he uttered the exclamation, and softly laying down his violin, "I was mistaken. My dear young lady, allow me to beg your pardon, and to thank you." And he bowed before Patty until his nose nearly touched his knees.

Mrs. Duff-Scott, who was a woman of impulses, as most nice women are, was enthusiastic. Not only had she listened to Patty's performance with all her intelligent ears, but she had at the same time investigated and appraised the various details of her personal appearance, and been particularly interested in that bit of lace about her neck.

"My dear," she said, putting out her hand as the girl rose from the music-stool, "come here and sit by me and tell me where you learned to play like that."

Patty went over to her readily, won by the kind voice and motherly gesture. And, in a very few minutes, Paul had the pleasure of seeing the great lady sitting on a sofa with all three sisters around her, talking to them, and they to her, as if they had known one another for years.

Leaving them thus safe and cared for, he bade good-night to his hostess, and went home to his work, in a mood of high contentment.

CHAPTER XIII
PATTY IN UNDRESS

When Paul Brion bade Mrs. Aarons good-night, he perceived that she was a little cold to him, and rather wondered at himself that he did not feel inclined either to resent or to grieve over that unprecedented circumstance.

"I am going to steal away," he said in an airy whisper, coming across her in the middle of the room as he made his way to the door. "I have a good couple of hours' work to get through to-night."

He was accustomed to speak to her in this familiar and confidential fashion, though she was but a recent acquaintance, and she had always responded in a highly gratifying way. But now she looked at him listlessly, with no change of face, and merely said, "Indeed."

"Yes," he repeated; "I have a lot to do before I can go to bed. It is delightful to be here; but I must not indulge myself any longer. Good-night."

"Good-night," she said, still unsmiling, as she gave him her hand. "I am sorry you must go so soon." But she did not look as if she were sorry; she looked as if she didn't care a straw whether he went or stayed. However, he pressed her hand with the wonted friendly pressure, and slipped out of the room, unabashed by her assumed indifference and real change of manner, which he was at no great trouble to interpret; and he took a cab to his office—now a humming hive of busy bees improving the shining hours of the gaslit night—and walked back from the city through the shadowy gardens to his lodgings, singing a tuneless air to himself, which, if devoid of music, was a pleasant expression of his frame of mind.

When he reached Myrtle Street the town clocks were striking twelve. He looked up at his neighbours' windows as he passed the gate of No. 6, and saw no light, and supposed they had returned from their revels and gone peaceably to bed. He opened his own door softly, as if afraid of waking them, and went upstairs to his sitting-room, where Mrs. M'Intyre, who loved to make him comfortable, had left him a bit of supper, and a speck of gas about the size of a pea in the burner at the head of his arm-chair; and he pulled off his dress coat, and kicked away his boots, and got his slippers and his dressing-gown, and his tobacco and his pipe, and took measures generally for making himself at home. But before he had quite settled himself the idea occurred to him that his neighbours might *not* have returned from Mrs. Aarons's, but might, indeed (for he knew their frugal and unconventional habits), be even then out in the streets, alone and unprotected, walking home by night as they walked home by day, unconscious of the perils and dangers that beset them. He had not presumed to offer his escort—he had not even spoken to them during the evening, lest he should seem to take those liberties that Miss Patty resented so much; but now he angrily reproached himself for not having stayed at Mrs. Aarons's until their departure, so that he could, at least, have followed and watched over them. He put down his pipe hastily, and, opening the window, stepped out on the balcony. It was a dark night, and a cold wind was blowing, and the quarter-hour after midnight was chiming from the tower of the Post Office. He was about to go in for his boots and his overcoat, when he was relieved to hear a cab approaching at a smart pace, and to see it draw up at the gate of No. 6. Standing still in the shadow of the partition that divided his enclosure from theirs, he watched the girls descend upon the footpath, one by one, fitfully illuminated from the interior of the vehicle. First Eleanor, then Elizabeth, then Patty—who entered the gate and tapped softly at her street door. He expected to see the driver dismissed, with probably double the fare to which he was entitled; but to his surprise, the cab lingered, and Elizabeth stood at the step and began to talk to someone inside. "Thank you so much for your kindness," she said, in her gentle but clear tones, which were perfectly audible on the balcony. A voice from the cab answered, "Don't mention it, my dear. I am very glad to see as much of you as possible, for I want to know you. May I come and have a little gossip to-morrow afternoon?" It was the voice of Mrs. Duff-Scott, who, after keeping them late at Mrs. Aarons's, talking to them, had frustrated their intention of making their own way home. That powerful woman had "taken them up," literally and figuratively, and she was not one to drop them again—as fine ladies commonly drop interesting impecunious *protégées* when the novelty of their acquaintance has worn off—save for causes in their own conduct and circumstances that were never likely to arise. Paul Brion, thoroughly realising that his little schemes had been crowned with the most gratifying success, stole back to his rooms, shut the window softly, and sat down to his pipe and his manuscripts. And he wrote such a maliciously bitter article that, when he took it to the office, his editor refused to print it without modifications, on the ground that it would land the paper in an action for libel.

Meanwhile our girls parted from their new friend with affectionate good-nights, and were let into their house by the landlady, who had herself been entertaining company to a late hour. They went upstairs with light feet, too excited to feel tired, and all assembled in Elizabeth's meagrelyappointed bedchamber to take off their finery and to have a little happy gossip before they went to rest. Elizabeth herself, who was not a gushing person, had the most to say at first, pouring out her ingenuous heart in grateful reminiscences of the unparalleled kindness of Mrs. Duff-Scott. "What a dear, dear woman!" she murmured, with soft rapture, as she unwound the watch-chain and locket from her neck and disembarrassed herself of her voluminous fichu. "You can *see* that what she does and says is real and truthful—I am certain you can trust her. I do not trust Mrs. Aarons—I do not understand her ways. She wanted us to go and see her, and when we went she was unkind to us; at least, she was not polite. I was very sorry we had gone to her house—until Mrs. Duff-Scott came to our sofa to speak to us. But now I feel so glad! For it has given us *her*. And she is just the kind of friend I have so often pictured to myself—so often longed to know."

"I think it was Patty's playing that gave us Mrs. Duff-Scott," said Eleanor, who was sitting by the dressing table with her frock unbuttoned. "She is fond of music, and really there was no one who could play at all except Herr Wüllner—which was a very strange thing, don't you think? And the singing was worse—such sickly, silly sort of songs, with such eccentric accompaniments. I could not understand it, unless the fashion has changed since mother was a girl. I suppose it has. But when Patty and Herr Wüllner got together it was like another atmosphere in the room. How did you come to play so well, Patty?—to be so collected and quiet when there was so much to frighten you? I was so nervous that my hands shook, and I had to squeeze them to keep myself still."

"I was nervous, too, at first," said Patty, who, divested of her dress and laces, was lying all along on Elizabeth's bed, with her pretty bare arms flung up over the pillows, and her hands clasped one over the other at the back of her head. "When we got there, that impudent maid in the room where we took our things off upset me; she looked at our old hats and water-proofs as if she had never seen such things before—and they *did* seem very shabby amongst all the pretty cloaks and hoods that the other ladies were taking off. And then it was so ignominious to have to find our way to the drawing-room by following other people, and to have our names bawled out as if to call everybody's attention to us, and then not to *have* attentions. When we trailed about the room, so lost and lonely, with all those fine people watching us and staring at us, my knees were shaking under me, and I felt hot and cold—I don't know how I felt. The only comfort I had was seeing how calm Elizabeth was. She seemed to stand up for us all, and to carry us through it. *I* felt—I hate to think I could be such an idiot—so nervous and so unhinged, and so miserable altogether, that I should have liked to go away somewhere and have a good cry. But," added Patty, suddenly sitting up in the bed, and removing her hands from the back of her head to her knees, "but after a little while it got *too* horrid. And then I got angry, and that made me feel much better. And by-and-bye, when they began to play and sing, and I saw how ridiculous they made themselves, I brightened up, and was not nervous any more—for I saw that they were rather ignorant people, in spite of their airs and their fine clothes. When the girl in that beautiful creamy satin dress sang her whining little song about parting and dying half a note flat, while she dashed her hands up and down the keyboard, and they all hung round her when she had done and said how charming it was, I felt that *really*—" Patty paused, and stared into the obscurity of the room with brilliant, humorous, disdainful eyes, which expressed her sentiments with a distinctness that made further words unnecessary.

"But, you see, if people don't *know* that you are superior to them—" suggested Eleanor, folding up Elizabeth's best gloves, and wrapping them in tissue paper, with a reflective air.

"Who would care about their knowing?" interposed Elizabeth. "We should not be very much superior to anyone if we could indulge in a poor ambition to seem so. That is not one of Patty's feelings, I think."

"But it is, then," Patty confessed, with honest promptness. "I found it out to-night, Elizabeth. When I saw those conceited people sweeping about in their splendid trains and looking as if all Melbourne belonged to them— when I heard that girl singing that preposterous twaddle, and herself and all her friends thinking she was a perfect genius—I felt that I would give anything, *anything*, just to rise up and be very grand and magnificent for a little while and crush them all into vulgarity and insignificance."

"Patty!" murmured Elizabeth.

"Yes, my dear, it shocks you, I know. But you wouldn't have me disguise the truth from you, would you? I wanted to pay them out. I saw they were turning up their noses at us, and I longed—I *raged*—to be in a position to turn up my nose at them, if only for five minutes. I thought to myself, oh, if the door should suddenly open and that big footman shout out, 'His Grace the Duke of So and So;' and they should all be ready to drop on their knees before such a grand person—as you know they would be, Elizabeth; they would *grovel*, simply—and he should look with a sort of gracious, ducal haughtiness over their heads and say to Mrs. Aarons, 'I am told that I shall find here the daughters of my brother, who disappeared from home when he was young, along with his wife, the Princess So and So.' You know, Elizabeth, our father, who never would talk about his family to anybody, *might* have been a duke or an earl in disguise, for anything we know, and our mother was the very image of what a princess *ought* to be—"

"We should have been found out before this, if we had been such illustrious persons," said Elizabeth, calmly.

"Yes, of course—of course. But one needn't be so practical. You are free to think what you like, however improbable it may be. And that is what I thought of. Then I thought, suppose a telegram should be brought in, saying that some enormously wealthy squatter, with several millions of money and no children, had left us all his fortune—"

"I should think that kind of news would come by post," suggested Eleanor.

"It might and it mightn't, Nelly. The old squatter might have been that queer old man who comes to the Library sometimes, and seems to take such interest in seeing us reading so hard. He might have thought that girls who were so studious would have serious views of life and the value of money. Or he might have overheard us castle-building about Europe, and determined to help us to realise our dreams. Or he might have fallen in love with Elizabeth—at a distance, you know, and in a humble, old-fashioned, hopeless way."

"But that doesn't account for the telegram, Patty."

"And have felt himself dying, perhaps," continued Patty, quite solemnly, with her bright eyes fixed on her invisible drama, "and have thought he would like to see us—to speak to Elizabeth—to give some directions and last wishes to us—before he went. No," she added, checking herself with a laugh and shaking herself up, "I don't think it was that. I think the lawyer came himself to tell us. The lawyer had opened the will, and he was a friend of Mrs. Aarons's, and he came to tell her of the wonderful thing that had happened. 'Everyone has been wondering whom he would leave his money to,' he says to her, 'but no one ever expected this. He has left it to three poor girls whom no one has ever heard of, and whom he never spoke to in his life. I am now going to find them out, for they are living somewhere in Melbourne. Their name is King, and they are sisters, without father or mother, or friends or fortune—mere nobodies, in fact. But now they will be the richest women in Australia.' And Mrs. Aarons suddenly remembers us, away there in the corner of the room, and it flashes across her that *we* are the great heiresses. And she tells the other ladies, and they all flock round us, and—and—"

"And you find yourself in the position to turn up your nose at them," laughed Eleanor. "No one would have guessed your thoughts, Patty, seeing you sitting on that sofa, looking so severe and dignified."

"But I had other thoughts," said Patty, quickly. "These were just passing ideas, of course. What really *did* take hold of me was an intense desire to be asked to play, so that I might show them how much better we could play than they could. Especially after I heard Herr Wüllner. I knew he, at least, would appreciate the difference—and I thought Mrs. Duff-Scott looked like a person who would, also. And perhaps—perhaps—Paul Brion."

"Oh, Patty!" exclaimed Elizabeth, smiling, but reproachful. "Did you really want to go to the piano for the sake of showing off your skill—to mortify those poor women who had not been taught as well as you had?"

"Yes," said Patty, hardily. "I really did. When Mrs. Duff-Scott came and asked me to join Herr Wüllner in that duet, I felt that, failing the duke and the lawyer, it was just the opportunity that I had been looking and longing for. And it was because I felt that I was going to do so much better than they could that I was in such good spirits, and got on—as I flatter myself I did—so splendidly."

"Well, I don't believe you," said Elizabeth. "You could never have rendered that beautiful music as you did simply from pure vindictiveness. It is not in you."

"No," said Patty, throwing herself back on the bed and flinging up her arms again, "no—when I come to think of it—I was not vindictive all the time. At first I was *savage*—O yes, there is no doubt about it. Then Herr Wüllner's fears and frights were so charming that I got amused a little; I felt jocose and mischievous. Then I felt Mrs. Duff-Scott looking at me— *studying* me—and that made me serious again, and also quieted me down and steadied me. Then I was a little afraid that I *might* blunder over the music—it was a long time since I had played that thing, and the manuscript was pale and smudged—and so I had to brace myself up and forget about the outside people. And as soon as Herr Wüllner reached me, and I began safely and found that we were making it, oh, so sweet! between us—then I lost sight of lots of things. I mean I began to see and think of lots of other things. I remembered playing it with mother—it was like the echo of her voice, that violin!—and the sun shining through a bit of the red curtain into our sitting-room at home, and flickering on the wall over the piano, where it used to stand; and the sound of the sea under the cliffs—*whish-sh-sh-sh*—in the still afternoon—" Patty broke off abruptly, with a little laugh that was half a sob, and flung herself from the bed with vehemence. "But it won't do to go on chattering like this—we shall have daylight here directly," she said, gathering up her frock and shoes.

CHAPTER XIV
IN THE WOMB OF FATE

Mrs. Duff-Scott came for her gossip on Saturday afternoon, and it was a long one, and deeply interesting to all concerned. The girls took her to their trustful hearts, and told her their past history and present circumstances in such a way that she understood them even better than they did themselves. They introduced her to their entire suite of rooms, including the infinitesimal kitchen and its gas stove; they unlocked the drawers and cupboards of the old bureau to show her their own and their mother's sketches, and the family miniatures, and even the jewels they had worn the night before, about which she was frankly curious, and which she examined with the same discriminating intelligence that she brought to bear upon old china. They chattered to her, they played to her, they set the kettle on the gas-stove and made tea for her, with a familiar and yet modest friendliness that was a pleasant contrast to the attitude in which feminine attentions were too often offered to her. In return, she put off that armour of self-defence in which she usually performed her social duties, fearing no danger to pride or principle from an unreserved intercourse with such unsophisticated and yet singularly well-bred young women; and she revelled in unguarded and unlimited gossip as freely as if they had been her own sisters or her grown-up children. She gave them a great deal of very plain, but very wholesome, advice as to the necessity that lay upon them to walk circumspectly in the new life they had entered upon; and they accepted it in a spirit of meek gratitude that would have astonished Paul Brion beyond measure. All sorts of delicate difficulties were touched upon in connection with the non-existent chaperon and the omnipotent and omnipresent Mrs. Grundy, and not only touched upon, but frankly discussed, between the kindly woman of the world who wished to serve them and the proud but modest girls who were but too anxious to learn of one who they felt was authorised to teach them. In short, they sat together for more than two hours, and learned in that one interview to know and trust each other better than some of us will do after living for two years under the same roof. When at last the lady called her coachman, who had been mooning up and down Myrtle Street, half asleep upon his box, to the gate of No. 6, she had made a compact with herself to "look after" the three sweet and pretty sisters who had so oddly fallen in her way with systematic vigilance; and they were unconsciously of one mind, that to be looked after by Mrs. Duff-Scott was the most delightful experience, by far, that Melbourne had yet given them.

On the following Monday they went to her house, and spent a ravishing evening in a beautiful, cosy, stately, deeply-coloured, softly-lighted room, that was full of wonderful and historical bric-à-brac such as they had never seen before, listening to Herr Wüllner and three brother artists playing violins and a violoncello in a way that brought tears to their eyes and unspeakable emotions into their responsive hearts. Never had they had such a time as this. There was no Mr. Duff-Scott—he was away from home just now, looking after property in Queensland; and no Mrs. Aarons—she was not privileged to join any but large and comprehensive parties in this select "set." There were no conceited women to stare at and to snub them, and no girls to sing sickly ballads, half a note flat. Only two or three unpretentious music-loving ladies, who smiled on them and were kind to them, and two or three quiet men who paid them charmingly delicate attentions; nothing that was unpleasant or unharmonious—nothing to jar with the exquisite music of a well-trained quartette, which was like a new revelation to them of the possibilities of art and life. They went home that night in a cab, escorted by one of the quiet men, whose provincial rank was such that the landlady curtsied like an English rustic, when she opened the door to him, and paid her young lodgers marked attentions for days afterwards in honour of their acquaintance with such a distinguished individual. And Paul Brion, who was carefully informed by Mrs. M'Intyre of their rise and progress in the world that was not his world, said how glad he was that they had been recognised and appreciated for what they were, and went on writing smart literary and political and social criticisms for his paper, that were continually proving too smart for prudent journalism.

Then Mrs. Duff-Scott left Melbourne for a visit to some relations in Brisbane, and to join her husband on his homeward journey, and the girls fell back into their old quiet life for a while. It was an exceedingly simple and homely life. They rose early every morning—not much after the hour at which their neighbour on the other side of the wall was accustomed to go to bed—and aired, and swept, and scrubbed their little rooms, and made their beds, and polished their furniture, and generally set their dwelling in an exquisite order that is not at all universal with housewives in these days, but must always be the instinct of really well-bred women. They breakfasted frugally after the most of this was done, and took a corresponding meal in the evening, the staple of both being bread and butter; and at mid-day they saved "messing" and the smell of cooking about their rooms, and saved also the precious hours of the morning for their studies, by dining at a restaurant in the city, where they enjoyed a comfortable and abundant repast for a shilling apiece. Every day at about ten o'clock they walked through the leafy Fitzroy and Treasury Gardens, and the bright and busy streets that never lost their charm of novelty, to the Public Library, where with pencils and note-books on the table before them, they read and studied upon a systematic principle until the clock struck one; at which hour they closed their books and set off with never-failing appetites in search of dinner. After dinner, if it was Thursday, they stayed in town for the organ recital at the Town Hall; but on other days they generally sauntered quietly home, with a new novel from Mullen's (they were very fond of novels), and made up their fire, and had a cup of tea, and sat down to rest and chat over their needlework, while one read aloud or practised her music, until the time came to lay the cloth for the unfashionable tea-supper at night-fall. And these countrified young people invariably began to yawn at eight o'clock, and might have been found in bed and asleep, five nights out of six, at half-past nine.

So the days wore on, one very much like another, and all very gentle and peaceful, though not without the small annoyances that beset the most flowery paths of this mortal life, until October came—until the gardens through which they passed to and from the city, morning and afternoon (though there were other and shorter routes to choose from), were thick with young green leaves and odorous with innumerable blossoms—until the winter was over, and the loveliest month of the Australian year, when the brief spring hurries to meet the voluptuous summer, made even Melbourne delightful. And in October the great event that was recorded in the annals of the colony inaugurated a new departure in their career.

On the Thursday immediately preceding the opening of the Exhibition they did not go to the Library as usual, nor to Gunsler's for their lunch. Like a number of other people, their habits were deranged and themselves demoralised by anticipations of the impending festival. They stayed at home to make themselves new bonnets for the occasion, and took a cold dinner while at their work, and two of them did not stir outside their rooms from morn till dewy eve for so much as a glance into Myrtle Street from the balcony.

But in the afternoon it was found that half a yard more of ribbon was required to complete the last of the bonnets, and Patty volunteered to "run into town" to fetch it. At about four o'clock she set off alone by way of an adjoining road which was an omnibus route, intending to expend threepence, for once, in the purchase of a little precious time, but every omnibus was full, and she had to walk the whole way. The pavements were crowded with hurrying folk, who jostled and obstructed her. Collins Street, when she turned into it, seemed riotous with abnormal life, and she went from shop to shop and could not get waited on until the usual closing hour was past, and the evening beginning to grow dark. Then she got what she wanted, and set off home by way of the Gardens, feeling a little daunted by the noise and bustle of the streets, and fancying she would be secure when once those green alleys, always so peaceful, were reached. But to-night even the gardens were infested by the spirit of unrest and enterprise that pervaded the city. The quiet walks were not quiet now, and the sense of her belated isolation in the growing dusk seemed more formidable here instead of less. For hardly had she passed through the gates into the Treasury enclosure than she was conscious of being watched and peered at by strange men, who appeared to swarm all over the place; and by the time she had reached the Gardens nearer home the appalling fact was forced upon her that a tobacco-scented individual was dogging her steps, as if with an intention of accosting her. She was bold, but her imagination was easily wrought upon; and the formless danger, of a kind in which she was totally inexperienced, gave a shock to her nerves. So that when presently, as she hurriedly pattered on, hearing the heavier tread and an occasional artificial cough behind her, she suddenly saw a still more expeditious pedestrian hastening by, and recognised Paul's light figure and active gait, the words seemed to utter themselves without conscious effort of hers—"Mr. Brion!—oh, Mr. Brion, is that you?"

He stopped at the first sound of her voice, looked back and saw her, saw the man behind her, and comprehended the situation immediately. Without speaking, he stepped to her side and offered his arm, which she took for one happy moment when the delightful sense of his protection was too strong for her, and then—reacting violently from that mood—released. "I—I am *mortified* with myself for being such a fool," she said angrily; "but really that person did frighten me. I don't know what is the matter with Melbourne to-night—I suppose it is the Exhibition." And she went on to explain how she came to be abroad alone at that hour, and to explain away, as she hoped, her apparent satisfaction in meeting him. "It seems to promise for a fine day, does it not?" she concluded airily, looking up at the sky.

Paul Brion put his hands in his pockets. He was mortified, too. When he spoke, it was with icy composure.

"Are you going to the opening?"

"Yes," said Patty. "Of course we are."

"With your swell friends, I suppose?"

"Whom do you mean by our swell friends? Mrs. Duff-Scott is not in Melbourne, I believe—if you allude to her. But she is not swell. The only swell person we know is Mrs. Aarons, and she is not our friend."

He allowed the allusion to Mrs. Aarons to pass. "Well, I hope you will have good seats," he said, moodily. "It will be a disgusting crush and scramble, I expect."

"Seats? Oh, we are not going to have seats," said Patty. "We are going to mingle with the common herd, and look on at the civic functions, humbly, from the outside. *We* are not swell"—dwelling upon the adjective with a malicious enjoyment of the suspicion that he had not meant to use it—"and we like to be independent."

"O yes, I know you do. But you'll find the Rights of Woman not much good to you to-morrow in the Melbourne streets, I fancy, if you go there on foot without an escort. May I ask how you propose to take care of yourselves?"

"We are going," said Patty, "to start very early indeed, and to take up a certain advantageous position that we have already selected before the streets fill. We shall have a little elevation above the heads of the crowd, and a wall at our backs, and—the three of us together—we shall see the procession beautifully, and be quite safe and comfortable."

"Well, I hope you won't find yourself mistaken," he replied.

A few minutes later Patty burst into the room where her sisters were sitting, placidly occupied with their bonnet-making, her eyes shining with excitement. "Elizabeth, Elizabeth," she cried breathlessly, "Paul Brion is going to ask you to let him be our escort to-morrow. But you won't—oh, you *won't*—have him, will you?"

"No, dear," said Elizabeth, serenely; "not if you would rather not. Why should we? It will be broad daylight, when there can be no harm in our being out without an escort. We shall be much happier by ourselves."

"Much happier than with *him*," added Patty, sharply.

And they went on with their preparations for the great day that had been so long desired, little thinking what it was to bring forth.

CHAPTER XV
ELIZABETH FINDS A FRIEND

They had an early breakfast, dressed themselves with great care in their best frocks and the new bonnets, and, each carrying an umbrella, set forth with a cheerful resolve to see what was to be seen of the ceremonies of the day, blissfully ignorant of the nature of their undertaking. Paul Brion, out of bed betimes, heard their voices and the click of their gate, and stepped into his balcony to see them start. He took note of the pretty costumes, that had a gala air about them, and of the fresh and striking beauty of at least two of the three sweet faces; and he groaned to think of such women being hustled and battered, helplessly, in the fierce crush of a solid street crowd. But they had no fear whatever for themselves.

However, they had not gone far before they perceived that the idea of securing a good position early in the day had occurred to a great many people besides themselves. Even sleepy Myrtle Street was awake and active, and the adjoining road, when they turned into it, was teeming with holiday life. They took their favourite route through the Fitzroy and Treasury Gardens, and found those sylvan glades alive with traffic: and, by the time they got into Spring Street, the crowd had thickened to an extent that embarrassed their progress and made it devious and slow. And they had scarcely passed the Treasury buildings when Eleanor, who had been suffering from a slight sore throat, began to cough and shiver, and aroused the maternal anxiety of her careful elder sister. "O, my dear," said Elizabeth, coming to an abrupt standstill on the pavement, "have you nothing but that wisp of muslin round your neck? And the day so cold—and looking so like rain! It will never do for you to stand about for hours in this wind, with the chance of getting wet, unless you are wrapped up better. We must run home again and fix you up. And I think it would be wiser if we were all to change our things and put on our old bonnets."

"Now, look here, Elizabeth," said Patty, with strong emphasis; "you see that street, don't you?"—and she pointed down the main thoroughfare of the city, which was already gorged with people throughout its length. "You see that, and that"—and she indicated the swarming road ahead of them and the populous valley in the opposite direction. "If there is such a crowd now, what will there be in half-an-hour's time? And we couldn't do it in half-an-hour. Let us make Nelly tie up her throat in our three pocket-handkerchiefs, and push on and get our places. Otherwise we shall be out of it altogether—we shall see *nothing*."

But the gentle Elizabeth was obdurate on some occasions, and this was one of them. Eleanor was chilled with the cold, and it was not to be thought of that she should run the risk of an illness from imprudent exposure—no, not for all the exhibitions in the world. So they compromised the case by deciding that Patty and Eleanor should "run" home together, while the elder sister awaited their return, keeping possession of a little post of vantage on the Treasury steps—where they would be able to see the procession, if not the Exhibition—in case the crowd should be too great by-and-bye to allow of their getting farther.

"Well, make yourself as big as you can," said Patty, resignedly.

"And, whatever you do," implored Eleanor, "don't stir an inch from where you are until we come back, lest we should lose you."

Upon which they set off in hot haste to Myrtle Street.

Elizabeth, when they were gone, saw with alarm the rapid growth of the crowd around her. It filled up the street in all directions, and condensed into a solid mass on the Treasury steps, very soon absorbing the modest amount of space that she had hoped to reserve for her sisters. In much less than half-an-hour she was so hopelessly wedged in her place that, tall and strong as she was, she was almost lifted off her feet; and there was no prospect of restoring communications with Patty and Eleanor until the show was over. In a fever of anxiety, bitterly regretting that she had consented to part from them, she kept her eyes turned towards the gate of the Gardens, whence she expected them to emerge; and then she saw, presently, the figure of their good genius and deliverer from all dilemmas, Paul Brion, fighting his way towards her. The little man pursued an energetic course through the crowd, which almost covered him, hurling himself along with a velocity that was out of all proportion to his bulk; and from time to time she saw his quick eyes flashing over other people's shoulders, and that he was looking eagerly in all directions. It seemed hopeless to expect him to distinguish her in the sea of faces around him, but he did. Sunk in the human tide that rose in the street above the level of his head, he made desperately for a footing on a higher plane, and in so doing caught sight of her and battled his way to her side. "Oh, *here* you are!" he exclaimed, in a tone of relief. "I have been so anxious about you. But where is Miss Patty? Where are your sisters?"

"Oh, Mr. Brion," she responded, "you always seem to turn up to help us as soon as we get into trouble, and I am *so* thankful to see you! The girls had to go home for something, and were to meet me here, and I don't know what will become of them in this crowd."

"Which way were they to come?" he inquired eagerly.

"By the Gardens. But the gates are completely blocked."

"I will go and find them," he said. "Don't be anxious about them. They will be in there—they will be all right. You will come too, won't you? I think I can manage to get you through."

"I can't," she replied. "I promised I would not stir from this place, and I must not, in case they should be in the street, or we should miss them."

"'The boy stood on the burning deck,'" he quoted, with a laugh. He could afford a little jest, though she was so serious, for he was happy in the conviction that the girls had been unable to reach the street, that he should find them disconsolate in the gardens, and compel Miss Patty to feel, if not to acknowledge, that he was of some use and comfort to her, after all. "But I hate to leave you here," he added, glaring upon her uncomfortable but inoffensive neighbours, "all alone by yourself."

"Oh, don't mind me," said Elizabeth, cheerfully. "If you can only find Patty and Nelly, and be so good as to take care of them, *I* shall be all right."

And so, with apparent reluctance, but the utmost real alacrity, he left her, flinging himself from the steps into the crowd like a swimmer diving into the sea, and she saw him disappear with an easy mind.

Then began the tramp of the procession, first in sections, then in imposing columns, with bands playing, and flags flying, and horses prancing, and the people shouting and cheering as it went by. There were the smart men of the Naval Reserve and the sailors of the warships—English and French, German and Italian, eight or nine hundred strong—with their merry buglers in the midst of them; and there were the troops of the military, with their music and accoutrements; and all the long procession of the trades' associations, and the fire brigades, with the drubbing of drums and the blare of trumpets and the shrill whistle of innumerable fifes accompanying their triumphal progress. And by-and-bye the boom of the saluting guns from the Prince's Bridge battery, and the seven carriages from Government House rolling slowly up the street and round the corner, with their dashing cavalry escort, amid the lusty cheers of Her Majesty's loyal subjects on the line of route assembled.

But long before the Queen's representative made his appearance upon the scene, Elizabeth had ceased to see or care for the great spectacle that she had been so anxious to witness. Moment by moment the crowd about her grew more dense and dogged, more pitilessly indifferent to the comfort of one another, more evidently minded that the fittest should survive in the fight for existence on the Treasury steps. Rough men pushed her forward and backward, and from side to side, treading on her feet, and tearing the stitches of her gown, and knocking her bonnet awry, until she felt bruised and sick with the buffetings that she got, and the keen consciousness of the indignity of her position. She could scarcely breathe for the pressure around her, though the breath of all sorts of unpleasant people was freely poured into her face. She would have struggled away and gone home—convinced of the comforting fact that Patty and Eleanor were safely out of it in Paul Brion's protection—but she could not stir an inch by her own volition. When she did stir it was by some violent propelling power in another person, and this was exercised presently in such a way as to completely overbalance her. A sudden wave of movement broke against a stout woman standing immediately behind her, and the stout woman, quite unintentionally, pushed her to the edge of the step, and flung her upon the shoulder of a brawny larrikin who had fought his way backwards and upwards into a position whence he could see the pageant of the street to his satisfaction. The larrikin half turned, struck her savagely in the breast with his elbow, demanding, with a roar and an oath, where she was a-shoving to; and between her two assailants, faint and frightened, she lost her footing, and all but fell headlong into the seething mass beneath her.

But as she was falling—a moment so agonising at the time, and so delightful to remember afterwards—some one caught her round the waist with a strong grip, and lifted her up, and set her safely on her feet again. It was a man who had been standing within a little distance of her, tall enough to overtop the crowd, and strong enough to maintain an upright position in it; she had noticed him for some time, and that he had seemed not seriously incommoded by the bustling and scuffling that rendered her so helpless; but she had not noticed his gradual approach to her side. Now, looking up with a little sob of relief, her instant recognition of him as a gentleman was followed by an instinctive identification of him as a sort of Cinderella's prince.

In short, there is no need to make a mystery of the matter. At half-past ten o'clock in the morning of the first of October in the year 1880, when she was plunged into the most wretched and terrifying circumstances of her life—at the instant when she was struck by the larrikin's elbow and felt herself about to be crushed under the feet of the crowd—Elizabeth King met her happy fate. She found that friend for whom, hungrily if unconsciously, her tender heart had longed.

CHAPTER XVI
"WE WERE NOT STRANGERS, AS TO US AND ALL IT SEEMED"

"Stand here, and I can shelter you a little," he said, in a quiet tone that contrasted refreshingly with the hoarse excitement around them. He drew her close to his side by the same grip of her waist that had lifted her bodily when she was off her feet, and, immediately releasing her, stretched a strong left arm between her exposed shoulder and the crush of the crowd. The arm was irresistibly pressed upon her own arm, and bent across her in a curve that was neither more nor less than a vehement embrace, and so she stood in a condition of delicious astonishment, one tingling blush from head to foot. It would have been horrible had it been anyone else.

"I am so sorry," he said, "but I cannot help it. If you don't mind standing as you are for a few minutes, you will be all right directly. As soon as the procession has passed the crowd will scatter to follow it."

They looked at each other across a space of half-a-dozen inches or so, and in that momentary glance, upon which everything that mutually concerned them depended, were severally relieved and satisfied. He was not handsome—he had even a reputation for ugliness; but there are some kinds of ugliness that are practically handsomer than many kinds of beauty, and his was of that sort. He had a leathery, sun-dried, weather-beaten, whiskerless, red moustached face, and he had a roughly-moulded, broad-based, ostentatious nose; his mouth was large, and his light grey eyes deeply set and small. Yet it was a strikingly distinguished and attractive face, and Elizabeth fell in love with it there and then. Similarly, her face, at once modest and candid, was an open book to his experienced glance, and provisionally delighted him. He was as glad as she was that fate had selected him to deliver her in her moment of peril, out of the many who might have held out a helping hand to her and did not.

"I am afraid you cannot see very well," he remarked presently. There were sounds in the distance that indicated the approach of the vice-regal carriages, and people were craning their necks over each other's shoulders and standing on tiptoe to catch the first glimpse of them. Just in front of her the exuberant larrikin was making himself as tall as possible.

"Oh, thank you—I don't want to see," she replied hastily.

"But that was what you came here for—like the rest of us—wasn't it?"

"I did not know what I was coming for," she said, desperately, determined to set herself right in his eyes. "I never saw anything like this before—I was never in a crowd—I did not know what it was like."

"Some one should have told you, then."

"We have not any one belonging to us to tell us things."

"Indeed?"

"My sisters and I have lived in the bush always, until now. We have no parents. We have not seen much yet. We came out this morning, thinking we could stand together in a corner and look on quietly—we did not expect this."

"And your sisters—?"

"They went home again. They are all right, I hope."

"And left you here alone?"

Elizabeth explained the state of the case more fully, and by the time she had done so the Governors' carriages were in sight. The people were shouting and cheering; the larrikin was dancing up and down in his hob-nailed boots, and bumping heavily upon the arm that shielded her. Shrinking from him, she drew her feet back another inch or two; upon which the right arm as well as the left was firmly folded round her. And the pressure of those two arms, stretched like iron bars to defend her from harm, the throbbing of his heart upon her shoulder, the sound of his deep-chested breathing in her ear—no consideration of the involuntary and unromantic necessity of the situation could calm the tremulous excitement communicated to her by these things. Oh, how hideous, how simply insupportable it would have been, had she been thus cast upon another breast and into other arms than HIS! As it was, it was all right. He said he feared she was terribly uncomfortable, but, though she did not contradict him, she felt in the secret depths of her primitive soul that she had never been more comfortable. To be cared for and protected was a new sensation, and, though she had had to bear anxious responsibilities for herself and others, she had no natural vocation for independence. Many a time since have they spoken of this first half hour with pride, boasting of how they trusted each other at sight, needing no proofs from experience like other people—a foolish boast, for they were but a man and woman, and not gods. "I took you to my heart the first moment I saw you," he says. "And I knew, even as soon as that, that it was my own place," she calmly replies. Whereas good luck, and not their own wisdom, justified them.

He spoke to her with studied coldness while necessarily holding her embraced, as it were, to protect her from the crowd; at the same time he put himself to some trouble to make conversation, which was less embarrassing to her than silence. He remarked that he was fond of crowds himself—found them intensely interesting—and spoke of Thackeray's paper on the crowd that went to see the man hanged (which she had never read) as illustrating the kind of interest he meant. He had lately seen the crowd at the opening of the Trocadero Palace, and that which celebrated the completion of Cologne Cathedral; facts which proclaimed him a "globe-trotter" and new arrival in Melbourne. The few words in which he described the festival at Cologne fired her imagination, fed so long upon dreams of foreign travel, and made her forget for the moment that he was not an old acquaintance.

"It was at about this hour of the day," he said, "and I stood with the throng in the streets, as I am doing now. They put the last stone on the top of the cross on one of the towers more than six hundred years after the foundation stone was laid. The people were wild with joy, and hung out their flags all over the place. One old fellow came up to me and wanted to kiss me—he thought I must be as overcome as he was."

"And were you not impressed?"

"Of course I was. It was very pathetic," he replied, gently. And she thought "pathetic" an odd word to use. Why pathetic? She did not like to ask him. Then he made the further curious statement that this crowd was the tamest he had ever seen.

"*I* don't call it tame," she said, with a laugh, as the yells of the larrikin and his fellows rent the air around them.

He responded to her laugh with a pleasant smile, and his voice was friendlier when he spoke again. "But I am quite delighted with it, unimpressive as it is. It is composed of people who are not *wanting anything*. I don't know that I was ever in a crowd of that sort before. I feel, for once, that I can breathe in peace."

"Oh, I wish I could feel so!" she cried. The carriages, in their slow progress, were now turning at the top of Collins Street, and the hubbub around them had reached its height.

"It will soon be over now," he murmured encouragingly.

"Yes," she replied. In a few minutes the crush would lessen, and he and she would part. That was what they thought, to the exclusion of all interest in the passing spectacle. Even as she spoke, the noise and confusion that had made a solitude for their quiet intercourse sensibly subsided. The tail of the procession was well in sight; the heaving crowd on the Treasury steps was swaying and breaking like a huge wave upon the street; the larrikin was gone. It was time for the unknown gentleman to resume the conventional attitude, and for Elizabeth to remember that he was a total stranger to her.

"You had better take my arm," he said, as she hastily disengaged herself before it was safe to do so, and was immediately caught in the eddy that was setting strongly in the direction of the Exhibition. "If you don't mind waiting here for a few minutes longer, you will be able to get home comfortably."

She struggled back to his side, and took his arm, and waited; but they did not talk any more. They watched the disintegration and dispersion of the great mass that had hemmed them in together, until at last they stood in ease and freedom almost alone upon that coign of vantage which had been won with so much difficulty—two rather imposing figures, if anyone had cared to notice them. Then she withdrew her hand, and said, with a little stiff bow and a bright and becoming colour in her face—"*Thank* you."

"Don't mention it," he replied, with perfect gravity. "I am very happy to have been of any service to you."

Still they did not move from where they stood.

"Don't you want to see the rest of it?" she asked timidly.

"Do you?" he responded, looking at her with a smile.

"O dear no, thank you! I have had quite enough, and I am very anxious to find my sisters."

"Then allow me to be your escort until you are clear of the streets." He did not put it as a request, and he began to descend the steps before she could make up her mind how to answer him. So she found herself walking beside him along the footpath and through the Gardens, wondering who he was, and how she could politely dismiss him—or how soon he would dismiss her. Now and then she snatched a sidelong glance at him, and noted his great stature and the easy dignity with which he carried himself, and transferred one by one the striking features of his countenance to her faithful memory. He made a powerful impression upon her. Thinking of him, she had almost forgotten how anxious she was to find her sisters until, with a start, she suddenly caught sight of them sitting comfortably on a bench in an alley of the Fitzroy Gardens, Eleanor and Patty side by side, and Paul Brion on the other side of Eleanor. The three sprang up as soon as they saw her coming, with gestures of eager welcome.

"Ah!" said Elizabeth, her face flaming with an entirely unnecessary blush, "there are my sisters. I—I am all right now. I need not trouble you any further. Thank you very much."

She paused, and so did he. She bent her head without lifting her eyes, and he took off his hat to her with profound respect. And so they parted—for a little while.

CHAPTER XVII
AFTERNOON TEA

When he had turned and left her, Elizabeth faced her sisters with that vivid blush still on her cheeks, and a general appearance of embarrassment that was too novel to escape notice. Patty and Eleanor stared for a moment, and Eleanor laughed.

"Who is he?" she inquired saucily.

"I don't know," said Elizabeth. "Where have you been, dears? How have you got on? I have been so anxious about you."

"But who is he?" persisted Eleanor.

"I have not the least idea, I tell you. Perhaps Mr. Brion knows."

"No," said Mr. Brion. "He is a perfect stranger to me."

"He is a new arrival, I suppose," said Elizabeth, stealing a backward glance at her hero, whom the others were watching intently as he walked away. "Yes, he can have but just arrived, for he saw the last stone put to the building of Cologne Cathedral, and that was not more than six or seven weeks ago. He has come out to see the Exhibition, probably. He seems to be a great traveller."

"Oh," said Eleanor, turning with a grimace to Patty, "here have we been mooning about in the gardens, and she has been seeing everything, and having adventures into the bargain!"

"It is very little I have seen," her elder sister remarked, "and this will tell you the nature of my adventures"—and she showed them a rent in her gown. "I was nearly torn to pieces by the crowd after you left. I am only too thankful you were out of it."

"But we are not at all thankful," pouted Eleanor. "Are we, Patty?" (Patty was silent, but apparently amiable.) "It is only the stitching that is undone—you can mend it in five minutes. We wouldn't have minded little trifles of that sort—not in the least—to have seen the procession, and made the acquaintance of distinguished travellers. Were there many more of them about, do you suppose?"

"O no," replied Elizabeth, promptly. "Only he."

✦ "And you managed to find him! Why shouldn't we have found him too—Patty and I? Do tell us his name, Elizabeth, and how you happened on him, and what he has been saying and doing."

"He took care of me, dear—that's all. I was crushed almost into a pulp, and he allowed me to—to stand beside him until the worst of it was over."

"How interesting!" ejaculated Eleanor. "And then he talked to you about Cologne Cathedral?"

"Yes. But never mind about him. Tell me where Mr. Brion found you, and what you have been doing."

"Oh, *we* have not been doing anything—far from it. I *wish* you knew his name, Elizabeth."

"But, my dear, I don't. So leave off asking silly questions. I daresay we shall never see or hear of him again."

"Oh, don't you believe it! I'm *certain* we shall see him again. He will be at the Exhibition some day when we go there—to-morrow, very likely."

"Well, well, never mind. What are we going to do now?"

They consulted with Paul for a few minutes, and he took them where they could get a distant view of the crowds swarming around the Exhibition, and hear the confused clamour of the bands—which seemed to gratify the two younger sisters very much, in the absence of more pronounced excitement. They walked about until they saw the Royal Standard hoisted over the great dome, and heard the saluting guns proclaim that the Exhibition was open; and then they returned to Myrtle Street, with a sense of having had breakfast in the remote past, and of having spent an enormously long morning not unpleasantly, upon the whole.

Mrs. M'Intyre was standing at her gate when they reached home, and stopped them to ask what they had seen, and how they had enjoyed themselves. *She* had stayed quietly in the house, and busied herself in the manufacture of meringues and lemon cheese-cakes—having, she explained, superfluous eggs in the larder, and a new lodger coming in; and she evidently prided herself upon her well-spent time. "And if you'll stay, you shall have some," she said, and she opened the gate hospitably. "Now, don't say no, Miss King—don't, Miss Nelly. It's past one, and I've got a nice cutlet and mashed potatoes just coming on the table. Bring them along, Mr. Brion. I'm sure they'll come if *you* ask them."

"We'll come without that," said Eleanor, walking boldly in. "At least, I will. *I* couldn't resist cutlets and mashed potatoes under present circumstances—not to speak of lemon cheese-cakes and meringues—and your society, Mrs. M'Intyre."

Paul held the gate open, and Elizabeth followed Eleanor, and Patty followed Elizabeth. Patty did not look at him, but she was in a peaceable disposition; seeing which, he felt happier than he had been for months. They lunched together, with much enjoyment of the viands placed before them, and of each other's company, feeling distinctly that, however small had been their share in the demonstrations of the day, the festival spirit was with them; and when they rose from the table there was an obvious reluctance to separate.

"Now, I'll tell you what," said Eleanor; "we have had dinner with you, Mrs. M'Intyre, and now you ought to come and have afternoon tea with us. You have not been in to see us for *years*."

She looked at Elizabeth, who hastened to endorse the invitation, and Mrs. M'Intyre consented to think about it.

"And may not I come too?" pleaded Paul, not daring to glance at his little mistress, but appealing fervently to Elizabeth. "Mayn't I come with Mrs. M'Intyre for a cup of tea, too?"

"Of course you may," said Elizabeth, and Eleanor nodded acquiescence, and Patty gazed serenely out of the window. "Go and have your smoke comfortably, and come in in about an hour."

With which the sisters left, and, as soon as they reached their own quarters, set to work with something like enthusiasm to make preparations for their expected guests. Before the hour was up, a bright fire was blazing in their sitting-room, and a little table beside it was spread comfortably with a snow-white cloth, and twinkling crockery and spoons. The kettle was singing on the hearth, and a plate of buttered muffins reposed under a napkin in the fender. The window was open; so was the piano. Patty was flying from place to place, with a duster in her hand, changing the position of the chairs, and polishing the spotless surfaces of the furniture generally, with anxious industry. *She* had not asked Paul Brion to come to see them, but since he was coming they might as well have the place decent, she said.

When he came at last meekly creeping upstairs at Mrs. M'Intyre's heels, Patty was nowhere to be seen. He looked all round as he crossed the threshold, and took in the delicate air of cheerfulness, the almost austere simplicity and orderliness that characterised the little room, and made it quite different from any room he had ever seen; and then his heart sank, and a cloud of disappointment fell over his eager face. He braced himself to bear it. He made up his mind at once that he had had his share of luck for that day, and must not expect anything more. However, some minutes later, when Mrs. M'Intyre had made herself comfortable by unhooking her jacket, and untying her bonnet strings, and when Elizabeth was preparing to pour out the tea, Patty sauntered in with some needlework in her hand—stitching as she walked—and took a retired seat by the window. He seized upon a cup of tea and carried it to her, and stood there as if to secure her before she could escape again. As he approached she bent her head lower over her work, and a little colour stole into her face; and then she lifted herself up defiantly.

"Here is your tea, Miss Patty," he said, humbly.

"Thanks. Just put it down there, will you?"

She nodded towards a chair near her, and he set the cup down on it carefully. But he did not go.

"You are very busy," he remarked.

"Yes," she replied, shortly. "I have wasted all the morning. Now I must try to make up for it."

"Are you too busy to play something—presently, I mean, when you have had your tea? I must go and work too, directly. I should so enjoy to hear you play before I go."

She laid her sewing on her knee, reached for her cup, and began to sip it with a relenting face. She asked him what kind of music he preferred, and he said he didn't care, but he thought he liked "soft things" best. "There was a thing you played last Sunday night," he suggested; "quite late, just before you went to bed. It has been running in my head ever since."

She balanced her teaspoon in her hand, and puckered her brows thoughtfully. "Let me think—what was I playing on Sunday night?" she murmured to herself. "It must have been one of the *Lieder* surely—or, perhaps, a Beethoven sonata? Or Batiste's andante in G perhaps?"

"Oh, I don't know the name of anything. I only remember that it was very lovely and sad."

"But we shouldn't play sad things in the broad daylight, when people want to gossip over their tea," she said, glancing at Mrs. M'Intyre, who was energetically describing to Elizabeth the only proper way of making tomato sauce. But she got up, all the same, and went over to the piano, and began to play the andante just above a whisper, caressing the soft pedal with her foot.

"Was that it?" she asked gently, smiling at him as he drew up a low wicker chair and sat down at her elbow to listen.

"Go on," he murmured gratefully. "It was *like* that."

And she went on—while Mrs. M'Intyre, having concluded her remarks upon tomato sauce, detailed the results of her wide experience in orange marmalade and quince jelly, and Elizabeth and Eleanor did their best to profit by her wisdom—playing to him alone. It did not last very long—a quarter of an hour perhaps—but every moment was an ecstasy to Paul Brion. Even more than the music, delicious as it was, Patty's gentle and approachable mood enchanted him. She had never been like that to him before. He sat on his low chair, and looked up at her tender profile as she drooped a little over the keys, throbbing with a new sense of her sweetness and beauty, and learning more about his own heart in those few minutes than all the previous weeks and months of their acquaintance had taught him. And then the spell that had been weaving and winding them together, as it seemed to him, was suddenly and rudely broken. There was a clatter of wheels and hoofs along the street, a swinging gate and a jangling door bell; and Eleanor, running to the window, uttered an exclamation that effectually wakened him from his dreams.

"Oh, *Elizabeth—Patty*—it is Mrs. Duff-Scott!"

In another minute the great lady herself stood amongst them, rustling over the matting in her splendid gown, almost filling the little room with her presence. Mrs. M'Intyre gave way before her, and edged towards the door with modest, deprecatory movements, but Paul stood where he had risen, as stiff as a poker, and glared at her with murderous ferocity.

"You see I have come back, my dears," she exclaimed, cordially, kissing the girls one after the other. "And I am so sorry I could not get to you in time to make arrangements for taking you with me to see the opening—I quite intended to take you. But I only returned last night."

"Oh, thank you," responded Elizabeth, with warm gratitude, "it is treat enough for us to see you again." And then, hesitating a little as she wondered whether it was or was not a proper thing to do, she looked at her other guests and murmured their names. Upon which Mrs. M'Intyre made a servile curtsey, unworthy of a daughter of a free country, and Paul a most reluctant inclination of the head. To which again Mrs. Duff-Scott responded by a slight nod and a glance of good-humoured curiosity at them both.

"I'll say good afternoon, Miss King," said Mr. Brion haughtily.

"Oh, *good* afternoon," replied Elizabeth, smiling sweetly. And she and her sisters shook hands with him and with his landlady, and the pair departed in some haste, Paul in a worse temper than he had ever known himself to indulge in; and he was not much mollified by the sudden appearance of

Elizabeth, as he was fumbling with the handle of the front door, bearing her evident if unspoken apologies for having seemed to turn him out.

"You will come with Mrs. M'Intyre another time," she suggested kindly, "and have some more music? I would have asked you to stay longer to-day, but we haven't seen Mrs. Duff-Scott for such a long time—"

"Oh, pray don't mention it," he interrupted stiffly. "I should have had to leave in any case, for my work is all behind-hand."

"Ah, that is because we have been wasting your time!"

"Not at all. I am only too happy to be of use—in the absence of your other friends."

She would not notice this little sneer, but said good-bye and turned to walk upstairs. Paul, ashamed of himself, made an effort to detain her. "Is there anything I can do for you, Miss King?" he asked, gruffly indeed, but with an appeal for forbearance in his eyes. "Do you want your books changed or anything?"

She stood on the bottom step of the stairs, and thought for a moment; and then she said, dropping her eyes, "I—I think *you* have a book that I should like to borrow—if I might."

"Most happy. What book is it?"

"It is one of Thackeray's. I think you told us you had a complete edition of Thackeray that some one gave you for a birthday present. I scarcely know which volume it is, but it has something in it about a man being hanged— and a crowd—" She broke off with an embarrassed laugh, hearing how oddly it sounded.

"You must mean the 'Sketches,'" he said. "There is a paper entitled 'Going to See a Man Hanged' in the 'London Sketches'—"

"That is the book I mean."

"All right—I'll get it and send it in to you at once—with pleasure."

"Oh, *thank* you. I'm *so* much obliged to you. I'll take the greatest care of it," she assured him fervently.

CHAPTER XVIII
THE FAIRY GODMOTHER

Elizabeth went upstairs at a run, and found Patty and Eleanor trying to make Mrs. Duff-Scott understand who Paul Brion was, what his father was, and his profession, and his character; how he had never been inside their doors until that afternoon, and how he had at last by mere accident come to be admitted and entertained. And Mrs. Duff-Scott, serene but imperious, was delivering some of her point-blank opinions upon the subject.

"Don't encourage him, my dears—don't encourage him to come again," she was saying as Elizabeth entered the room. "He and his father are two very different people, whatever they may think."

"We cannot help being grateful to him," said Patty sturdily. "He has done so much for us."

"Dear child, that's nonsense. Girls *can't* be grateful to young men—don't you see? It is out of the question. And now you have got *me* to do things for you."

"But he helped us when we had no one else."

"Yes, that's all right, of course. No doubt it was a pleasure to him—a privilege—for *him* to be grateful for rather than you. But—well, Elizabeth knows what I mean"—turning an expressive glance towards the discreet elder sister. Patty's eyes went in the same direction, and Elizabeth answered both of them at once.

"You must not ask us to give up Paul Brion," she said, promptly.

"I don't," said Mrs. Duff-Scott. "I only ask you to keep him in his place. He is not the kind of person to indulge with tea and music, you know—that is what I mean."

"You speak as if you knew something against him," murmured Patty, with heightened colour.

"I know this much, my dear," replied the elder woman, gravely; "he is *a friend of Mrs. Aarons's.*"

"And is not Mrs. Aarons—"

"She is very well, in her way. But she likes to have men dangling about her. She means no harm, I am sure," added Mrs. Duff-Scott, who, in the matter of scandal, prided herself on being a non-conductor, "but still it is not nice, you know. And I don't think that her men friends are the kind of friends for you. You don't mind my speaking frankly, my love? I am an old woman, you know, and I have had a great deal of experience."

She was assured that they did not mind it, but were, on the contrary, indebted to her for her good advice. And the subject of Paul Brion was dropped. Patty was effectually silenced by that unexpected reference to Mrs. Aarons, and by the rush of recollections, embracing him and her together, which suddenly gave form and colour to the horrible idea of him as a victim to a married woman's fascinations. She turned away abruptly, with a painful blush that not only crimsoned her from throat to temples, but seemed to make her tingle to her toes; and, like the headlong and pitiless young zealot that she was, determined to thrust him out for ever from the sacred precincts of her regard. Mrs. Duff-Scott was satisfied too. She was always sure of her own power to speak plainly without giving offence, and she found it absolutely necessary to protect these ingenuous maidens from their own ignorance. Needless to say that, since she had adopted them into her social circle, she had laid plans for their ultimate settlement therein. In her impulsive benevolence she had even gone the length of marking down the three husbands whom she considered respectively appropriate to the requirements of the case, and promised herself a great deal of interest and pleasure in the vicarious pursuit of them through the ensuing season. Wherefore she was much relieved to have come across this obscure writer for the press, and to have had the good chance, at the outset of her campaign, to counteract his possibly antagonistic influence. She knew her girls quite well enough to make sure that her hint would take its full effect.

She leaned back in her chair comfortably, and drew off her gloves, while they put fresh tea in the teapot, and cut her thin shavings of bread and butter; and she sat with them until six o'clock, gossiping pleasantly. After giving them a history of the morning's ceremonies, as witnessed by the Government's invited guests inside the Exhibition building, she launched into hospitable schemes for their enjoyment of the gay time that had set in. "Now that I am come back," she said, "I shall take care that you shall go out and see everything there is to be seen. You have never had such a chance to learn something of the world, and I can't allow you to neglect it."

"Dear Mrs. Duff-Scott," said Elizabeth, "we have already been indulging ourselves too much, I am afraid. We have done no reading—at least none worth doing—for days. We are getting all behind-hand. The whole of yesterday and all this morning—"

"What did you do this morning?" Mrs. Duff-Scott interrupted quickly.

They gave her a sketch of their adventures, merely suppressing the incident of the elder sister's encounter with the mysterious person whom the younger ones had begun to style "Elizabeth's young man"—though why they suppressed that none of them could have explained.

"Very well," was her comment upon the little narrative, which told her far more than it told them. "That shows you that I am right. There are a great many things for you to learn that all the books in the Public Library could not teach you. Take my advice, and give up literary studies for a little while. Give them up altogether, and come and learn what the world and your fellow-creatures are made of. Make a school of the Exhibition while it lasts, and let me give you lessons in—a—what shall I call it—social science?—the study of human nature?"

Nothing could be more charming than to have lessons from her, they told her; and they had intended to go to school to the Exhibition as often as they could. But—but their literary studies were their equipment for the larger and fuller life that they looked forward to in the great world beyond the seas. Perhaps she did not understand that?

"I understand this, my dears," the matron replied, with energy. "There is no greater mistake in life than to sacrifice the substance of the present for the shadow of the future. We most of us do it—until we get old—and then we look back to see how foolish and wasteful we have been, and that is not much comfort to us. What we've got, we've got; what we are going to have nobody can tell. Lay in all the store you can, of course—take all reasonable precautions to insure as satisfactory a future as possible—but don't forget that the Present is the great time, the most important stage of your existence, no matter what your circumstances may be."

The girls listened to her thoughtfully, allowing that she might be right, but suspending their judgment in the matter. They were all too young to be convinced by another person's experience.

"You let Europe take care of itself for a bit," their friend proceeded, "and come out and see what Australia in holiday time is like, and what the fleeting hour will give you. I will fetch you to-morrow for a long day at the

Exhibition to begin with, and then I'll—I'll—" She broke off and looked from one to another with an unwonted and surprising embarrassment, and then went on impetuously.

"My dears, I don't know how to put it so as not to hurt or burden you, but you won't misunderstand me if I express myself awkwardly—you won't have any of that absurd conventional pride about not being under obligations—it is a selfish feeling, a want of trust and true generosity, when it is the case of a friend who—" She stammered and hesitated, this self-possessed empress of a woman, and was obviously at a loss for words wherein to give her meaning. Elizabeth, seeing what it was that she wanted to say, sank on her knees before her, and took her hands and kissed them. But over her sister's bent head Patty stood up stiffly, with a burning colour in her face. Mrs. Duff-Scott, absently fondling Elizabeth, addressed herself to Patty when she spoke again.

"As an ordinary rule," she said, "one should not accept things from another who is not a relation—I know that. *Not* because it is improper—it ought to be the most proper thing in the world for people to help each other—but because in so many cases it can never happen without bitter mortifications afterwards. People are so—so superficial? But I—Patty, dear, I am an old woman, and I have a great deal of money, and I have no children; and I have never been able to fill the great gap where the children should be with music and china, or any interest of that sort. And you are alone in the world, and I have taken a fancy to you—I have grown *fond* of you—and I have made a little plan for having you about me, to be a sort of adopted daughters for whom I could feel free to do little motherly things in return for your love and confidence in me. You will indulge me, and let me have my way, won't you? It will be doing more for me, I am sure, than I could do for you."

"O no—no—*no!*" said Patty, with a deep breath, but stretching her hands with deprecating tenderness towards their guest. "You would do everything for us, and we *could* do nothing for you. You would overwhelm us! And not only that; perhaps—perhaps, by-and-bye, you would not care about us so much as you do now—we might want to do something that you didn't like, something we felt ourselves *obliged* to do, however much you disliked it—and if you got vexed with us, or tired of us—oh, think what that would be! Think how you would regret that you had—had—made us seem to belong to you. And how we should hate ourselves."

She looked at Mrs. Duff-Scott with a world of ardent apology in her eyes, before which the matron's fell, discouraged and displeased.

"You make me feel that I am an impulsive and romantic girl, and that *you* are the wise old woman of the world," she said with a proud sigh.

But at this, Patty, pierced to the heart, flung her arms round Mrs. Duff-Scott's neck, and crushed the most beautiful bonnet in Melbourne remorselessly out of shape against her young breast. That settled the question, for all practical purposes. Mrs. Duff-Scott went home at six o'clock, feeling that she had achieved her purpose, and entered into some of the dear privileges of maternity. It was more delightful than any "find" of old china. She did not go to sleep until she had talked both her husband and herself into a headache with her numerous plans for the welfare of her *protégées*, and until she had designed down to the smallest detail the most becoming costumes she could think of for them to wear, when she took them with her to the Cup.

CHAPTER XIX
A MORNING AT THE EXHIBITION

Paul Brion was wakened from his sleep next morning by the sound of Mrs. Duff-Scott's carriage wheels and prancing horses, and sauntering to his sitting-room window about ten minutes later, had the satisfaction of seeing his young neighbours step into the distinguished vehicle and drive away. There was Elizabeth reposing by her chaperon's side, as serene as a princess who had never set foot on common earth; and there were Patty and Eleanor, smiling and animated, lovelier than their wont, if that could be, nestling under the shadow of two tall men-servants in irreproachable liveries, with cockades upon their hats. It was a pretty sight, but it spoiled his appetite for his breakfast. He could no longer pretend that he was thankful for the fruition of his desires on their behalf. He could only feel that they were gone, and that he was left behind—that a great gulf had suddenly opened between them and him and the humble and happy circumstances of yesterday, with no bridge across it that he could walk over.

The girls, for their part, practically forgot him, and enjoyed the difference between to-day and yesterday in the most worldly and womanly manner. The sensation of bowling along the streets in a perfectly-appointed carriage was as delicious to them as it is to most of us who are too poor to indulge in it as a habit; for the time being it answered all the purposes of happiness as thoroughly as if they had never had any higher ambition than to cut a dash. They went shopping with the fairy godmother before they went to the Exhibition, and that, too, was absorbingly delightful—both to Elizabeth, who went in with Mrs. Duff-Scott to assist her in her purchases, and to the younger sisters, who reposed majestically in the carriage at the door. Patty's quick eyes caught sight of Mrs. Aarons and a pair of her long-nosed children walking on the pavement, and she cheerfully owned herself a snob and gloried in it. It gave her unspeakable satisfaction, she said, to sit there and look down upon Mrs. Aarons.

As they passed the Melbourne Club on their way to the Exhibition, the coachman was hailed by the elder of two gentlemen who were sauntering down the steps, and they were introduced for the first time to the fairy godmother's husband. Major Duff-Scott, an ex-officer of dragoons and a late prominent public man of his colony (he was prominent still, but for his social, and not his official qualifications), was a well-dressed and well-preserved old gentleman, who, having sown a large and miscellaneous crop of wild oats in the course of a long career, had been rewarded with great wealth and all the privileges of the highest respectability. He had been a prodigal, but he had enjoyed it—never knowing the bitterness of either hunger or husks. He had tasted dry bread at times, as a matter of course, but only just enough of it to give a proper relish to the abundant cakes and ale that were his portion; and the proverb which says you cannot eat your cake and have it was a perfectly dead letter in his case. He had been eating his all his life, and he had got it still. In person he was the most gentle-looking little man imaginable—about half the size of his imposing wife, thin and spare, and with a little stoop in his shoulders; but there was an alertness in his step and a brightness in his eye, twinkling remotely between the shadow of his hat brim and a bulging mass of white moustache that covered all the lower part of his small face, which had suggestions of youth and vigour about them that were lacking in the figure and physiognomy of the young man at his side. When he came up to the carriage door to be introduced to his wife's *protégées*, whom he greeted with as much cordiality as Mrs. Duff-Scott could have desired, they did not know why it was that they so immediately lost the sense of awe with which they had contemplated the approach of a person destined to have so formidable a relation to themselves. They shook hands with him, they made modest replies to his polite inquiries, they looked beyond his ostensible person to the eyes that looked at them; and then their three grave faces relaxed, and in half a minute were brimming over with smiles. They felt at home with Major Duff-Scott at once.

"Come, come," said the fairy godmother rather impatiently, when something like a fine aroma of badinage was beginning to perfume the conversation, "you must not stop us now. We want to have a long morning. You can join us at the Exhibition presently, if you like, and bring Mr. Westmoreland." She indicated the young man who had been talking to her while her spouse made the acquaintance of her companions, and who happened to be one of the three husbands whom she had selected for those young ladies. He was the richest of them all, and the most stupid, and therefore he seemed to be cut out for Patty, who, being so intellectual and so enterprising, would not only make a good use of his money, but would make the best that was to be made of *him*. "My dears," she said, turning towards the girls, "let me introduce Mr. Westmoreland to you. Mr. Westmoreland, Miss King—Miss Eleanor King—Miss *Patty* King."

The heavy young man made a heavy bow to each, and then stared straight at Eleanor, and studied her with calm attention until the carriage bore her from his sight. She, with her tender blue eyes and her yellow hair, and her skin like the petals of a blush rose, was what he was pleased to call, in speaking of her a little later to a confidential friend, the "girl for him." Of Patty he took no notice whatever.

Mrs. Duff-Scott, on her way to Carlton, stopped to speak to an acquaintance who was driving in an opposite direction, and by the time she reached the Exhibition, she found that her husband's hansom had arrived before her, and that he and Mr. Westmoreland were waiting at the entrance to offer their services as escort to the party. The major was the best of husbands, but he was not in the habit of paying her these small attentions; and Mr. Westmoreland had never been known, within her memory of him, to put himself to so much trouble for a lady's convenience. Wherefore the fairy godmother smiled upon them both, and felt that the Fates were altogether propitious to her little schemes. They walked up the pathway in a group, fell necessarily into single file in the narrow passage where they received and returned their tickets, and collected in a group again under the great dome, where they stood to look round on the twenty acres of covered space heaped with the treasures of those nations which Victoria welcomed in great letters on the walls. Mrs. Duff-Scott hooked her gold-rimmed glasses over her nose, and pointed out to her husband wherein the building was deficient, and wherein superfluous, in its internal arrangements and decorations. In her opinion—which placed the matter beyond discussion—the symbolical groups over the arches were all out of drawing, the colouring of the whole place vulgar to a degree, and the painted clouds inside the cupola enough to make one sick. The major endorsed her criticisms, perfunctorily, with amused little nods, glancing hither and thither in the directions she desired. "Ah, my dear," said he, "you mustn't expect everybody to have such good taste as yours." Mr. Westmoreland seemed to have exhausted the Exhibition, for his part; he had seen it all the day before, he explained, and he did not see what there was to make a fuss about. With the exception of some mysteries in the basement, into which he darkly hinted a desire to initiate the major presently, it had nothing about it to interest a man who, like him, had just returned from Europe and had seen the Paris affair. But to our girls it was an enchanted palace of delights—far exceeding their most extravagant anticipations. They gave no verbal expression to their sentiments, but they looked at each other with faces full of exalted emotion, and tacitly agreed that they were perfectly satisfied. The fascination of the place, as a storehouse of genuine samples of the treasures of that great world which they had never seen, laid hold of them with a grip that left a lasting impression. Even the *rococo* magnificence of the architecture and its adornments, which Mrs. Duff-Scott, enlightened by a large experience, despised, affected their untrained imaginations with all the force of the highest artistic sublimity. A longing took possession of them all at the same moment to steal back to-morrow—next day—as soon as they were free again to follow their own devices—and wander about the great and wonderful labyrinth by themselves and revel unobserved in their secret enthusiasms.

However, they enjoyed themselves to-day beyond all expectation. After skimming the cream of the many sensations offered to them, sauntering up and down and round and round through the larger thoroughfares in a straggling group, the little party, fixing upon their place of rendezvous and lunching arrangements, paired themselves for a closer inspection of such works of art as they were severally inclined to. Mrs. Duff-Scott kept Patty by her side, partly because Mr. Westmoreland did not seem to want her, and partly because the girl was such an interesting companion, being wholly absorbed in what she had come to see, and full of intelligent appreciation of everything that was pointed out to her; and this pair went a-hunting in the wildernesses of miscellaneous pottery for such unique and precious "bits" as might be secured, on the early bird principle, for Mrs. Duff-Scott's collection. Very soon that lady's card was hanging round the necks of all sorts of quaint vessels that she had greedily pounced upon (and which further researches proved to be relatively unworthy of notice) in her anxiety to outwit and frustrate the birds that would come round presently; while Patty was having her first lesson in china, and showing herself a delightfully precocious pupil. Mr. Westmoreland confined his attentions exclusively to Eleanor, who by-and-bye found herself interested in being made so much of, and even inclined to be a little frivolous. She did not know whether to take him as a joke or in earnest, but either way he was amusing. He strolled heavily along by her side for awhile in the wake of Mrs. Duff-Scott and Patty, paying no attention to the dazzling wares around him, but a great deal to his companion. He kept turning his head to gaze at her, with solemn, ruminating eyes, until at last, tired of pretending she did not notice it, she looked back at him and laughed. This seemed to put him at his ease with her at once.

"What are you laughing at?" he asked, with more animation than she thought him capable of.

"Nothing," said she.

"Oh, but you were laughing at something. What was it? Was it because I was staring at you?"

"Well, you *do* stare," she admitted.

"I can't help it. No one could help staring at you."

"Why? Am I such a curiosity?"

"You know why. Don't pretend you don't."

She blushed at this, making herself look prettier than ever; it was not in her to pretend she didn't know—nor yet to pretend that his crude flattery displeased her.

"A cat may look at a king," he remarked, his heavy face quite lit up with his enjoyment of his own delicate raillery.

"O yes, certainly," she retorted. "But you see I am not a king, and you are not a cat."

"'Pon my word, you're awfully sharp," he rejoined, admiringly. And he laughed over this little joke at intervals for several minutes. Then by degrees they dropped away from their party, and went straying up and down the nave *tête-à-tête* amongst the crowd, looking at the exhibits and not much understanding what they looked at; and they carried on their conversation in much the same style as they began it, with, I grieve to say, considerable mutual enjoyment. By-and-bye Mr. Westmoreland took his young companion to the German tent, where the Hanau jewels were, by way of giving her the greatest treat he could think of. He betted her sixpence that he could tell her which necklace she liked the best, and he showed her the several articles (worth some thousands of pounds) which he should have selected for his wife, had he had a wife—declaring in the same breath that they were very poor things in comparison with such and such other things that he had seen elsewhere. Then they strolled along the gallery, glancing at the pictures as they went, Eleanor making mental notes for future study, but finding herself unable to study anything in Mr. Westmoreland's company. And then suddenly came a tall figure towards them—a gentlemanly man with a brown face and a red moustache—at sight of whom she gave a a little start of delighted recognition.

"Hullo!" cried Mr. Westmoreland, "there's old Yelverton, I do declare. He *said* he'd come over to have a look at the Exhibition."

Old Yelverton was no other than "Elizabeth's young man."

CHAPTER XX
CHINA V. THE CAUSE OF HUMANITY

Meanwhile, Major Duff-Scott took charge of Elizabeth, and he was very well satisfied with the arrangement that left her to his care. He always preferred a mature woman to a young girl, as being a more interesting and intelligent companion, and he admired her when on a generous scale, as is the wont of small men. Elizabeth's frank face and simple manners and majestic physical proportions struck him as an admirable combination. "A fine woman," he called her, speaking of her later to his wife: "reminds me of what you were when I married you, my dear." And when he got to know her better he called her "a fine creature" — which meant that he recognised other good qualities in her besides that of a lofty stature.

As soon as Mrs. Duff-Scott stated her intention of going to see "what she could pick up," the major waved his hand and begged that he might be allowed to resign all his responsibilities on her behalf. "Buy what you like, my dear, buy what you like," he said plaintively, "but don't ask me to come and look on while you do it. Take Westmoreland — I'm sure he would enjoy it immensely."

"Don't flatter yourselves that I shall ask either of you," retorted his wife. "You would be rather in the way than otherwise. I've got Patty."

"Oh, she's got Patty!" he repeated, looking with gentle mournfulness at the young lady in question, while his far-off eyes twinkled under his hat brim. "I trust you are fond of china, Miss Patty."

"I am fond of *everything*," Patty fervently replied.

"Oh, that's right. You and Mrs. Duff-Scott will get on together admirably, I foresee. Come, Miss King" — turning to Elizabeth — "let us go and see what *we* can discover in the way of desirable bric-à-brac. We'll have a look at the Murano ware for you, my dear, if you like" — again addressing his wife softly — "and come back and tell you if there is anything particularly choice. I know they have a lovely bonnet there, all made of the sweetest Venetian glass and trimmed with blue velvet. But you could take the velvet off, you know, and trim it with a mirror. Those wreaths of leaves and flowers, and beautiful pink braids —"

"Oh, go along!" she interrupted impatiently. "Elizabeth, take care of him, and don't let him buy anything, but see what is there and tell me. I'm not going to put any of that modern stuff with my sixteenth century cup and bottle," she added, looking at nobody in particular, with a sudden brightening of her eyes; "but if there is anything pretty that will do for my new cabinet in the morning room—or for the table—I should like to have the first choice."

"Very well," assented her husband, meekly. "Come along, Miss King. We'll promise not to buy anything." He and Elizabeth then set off on their own account, and Elizabeth found herself led straight to the foot of a staircase, where the little major offered his arm to assist her in the ascent.

"But the Murano Court is not upstairs, is it?" she asked, hesitating.

"O no," he replied; "it is over there," giving a little backward nod.

"And are we not going to look at the glass?"

"Not at present," he said, softly. "That will keep. We'll look at it by-and-bye. First, I am going to show you the pictures. You are fond of pictures, are you not?"

"I am, indeed."

"Yes, I was certain of it. Come along, then, I can show you a few tolerably good ones. Won't you take my arm?"

She took his arm, as he seemed to expect it, though it would have been more reasonable if he had taken hers; and they marched upstairs, slowly, in face of the crowd that was coming down.

"My wife," said the major, sententiously, "is one of the best women that ever breathed."

"I am *sure* she is," assented Elizabeth, with warmth.

"No," he said, "*you* can't be sure; that is why I tell you. I have known her a long time, and experience has proved it to me. She is one of the best women that ever lived. But she has her faults. I think I ought to warn you, Miss King, that she has her faults."

"I think you ought not," said Elizabeth, with instinctive propriety.

"Yes," he went on, "it is a point of honour. I owe it to you, as the head of my house—the nominal head, you understand—the responsible head—not to let you labour under any delusion respecting us. It is best that you should know the truth at once. Mrs. Duff-Scott is *energetic*. She is fearfully, I may say abnormally, energetic."

"I think," replied Elizabeth, with decision, "that that is one of the finest qualities in the world."

"Ah, do you?" he rejoined sadly. "That is because you are young. I used to think so, too, when I was young. But I don't now—experience has taught me better. What I object to in my wife is that experience doesn't teach her anything. She *won't* learn. She persists in keeping all her youthful illusions, in the most obstinate and unjustifiable manner."

Here they reached the gallery and the pictures, but the major saw two empty chairs, and, sitting down on one of them, bade his companion rest herself on the other until she had recovered from the fatigue of getting upstairs.

"There is no hurry," he said wearily; "we have plenty of time." And then he looked at her with that twinkle in his eye, and said gently, "Miss King, you are very musical, I hear. Is that a fact?"

"We are very, very fond of music," she said, smiling. "It is rather a hobby with us, I think."

"A hobby! Ah, that's delightful. I'm so glad it is a hobby. You don't, by happy chance, play the violin, do you?"

"No. We only know the piano."

"You all play the piano?—old masters, and that sort of thing?"

"Yes. My sister Patty plays best. Her touch and expression are beautiful."

"Ah!" he exclaimed again, softly, as if with much inward satisfaction. He was sitting languidly on his chair, nursing his knee, and gazing through the balustrade of the gallery upon the crowd below. Elizabeth was on the point of suggesting that they might now go and look at the pictures, when he began upon a fresh topic.

"And about china, Miss King? Tell me, do you know anything about china?"

"I'm afraid not," said Elizabeth.

"You don't know the difference between Chelsea and Derby-Chelsea, for instance?"

"No."

"Nor between old Majolica and modern?"

"No."

"Nor between a Limoges enamel of the sixteenth century—everything *good* belongs to the sixteenth century, you must remember—and what they call Limoges now-a-days?"

"No."

"Ah, well, I think very few people do," said the major, resignedly. "But, at any rate"—speaking in a tone of encouragement—"you *do* know Sèvres and Dresden when you see them?—you could tell one of *them* from the other?"

"Really," Elizabeth replied, beginning to blush for her surpassing ignorance, "I am very sorry to have to confess it, but I don't believe I could."

The major softly unclasped his knees and leaned back in his chair, and sighed.

"But I could learn," suggested Elizabeth.

"Ah, so you can," he responded, brightening. "You can learn, of course. *Will* you learn? You can't think what a favour it would be to me if you would learn. Do promise me that you will."

"No, I will not promise. I should do it to please myself—and, of course, because it is a thing that Mrs. Duff-Scott takes an interest in," said Elizabeth.

"That is just what I mean. It is *because* Mrs. Duff-Scott takes such an interest in china that I want you to cultivate a taste for it. You see it is this way," he proceeded argumentatively, again, still clasping his knees, and looking up at her with a quaint smile from under his hat brim. "I will be frank with you, Miss King—it is this way. I want to induce you to enter into an alliance with me, offensive and defensive, against that terrible energy which, as I said, is my wife's alarming characteristic. For her own good, you understand—for my comfort incidentally, but for her own good in the first place, I want you to help me to keep her energy within bounds. As long as she is happy with music and china we shall be all right, but if she goes beyond things of that sort—well, I tremble for the consequences. They would be fatal—fatal!"

"Where are you afraid she should go to?" asked Elizabeth.

"I am afraid she should go into *philanthropy*," the major solemnly rejoined. "That is the bug-bear—the spectre—the haunting terror of my life. I never see a seedy man in a black frock coat, nor an elderly female in spectacles, about the house or speaking to my wife in the street, that I don't shake in my shoes—literally shake in my shoes, I do assure you. I can't think how it is that she has never taken up the Cause of Humanity," he proceeded reflectively. "If we had not settled down in Australia, she *must* have done it—she could not have helped herself. But even here she is beset with temptations. *I* can see them in every direction. I can't think how it is that she doesn't see them too."

"No doubt she sees them," said Elizabeth.

"O no, she does not. The moment she sees them—the moment she casts a serious eye upon them—that moment she will be a lost woman, and I shall be a desperate man."

The major shuddered visibly, and Elizabeth laughed at his distress. "Whenever it happens that Mrs. Duff-Scott goes into philanthropy," she said, a little in joke and a great deal in earnest, "I shall certainly be proud to accompany her, if she will have me." And, as she spoke, there flashed into her mind some idea of the meaning of certain little sentences that were breathed into her ear yesterday. The major talked on as before, and she tried to attend to what he said, but she found herself thinking less of him now than of her unknown friend—less occupied with the substantial figures upon the stage of action around her than with the delusive scene-painting in the background of her own imagination. Beyond the crowd that flowed up and down the gallery, she saw a dim panorama of other crowds—phantom crowds—that gradually absorbed her attention. They were in the streets of Cologne, looking up at those mighty walls and towers that had been six centuries a-building, shouting and shaking hands with each other; and in the midst of them *he* was standing, grave and critical, observing their excitement and finding it "pathetic"—nothing more. They were in London streets in the early daylight—daylight at half-past three in the morning! that was a strange thing to think of—a "gentle and good-humoured" mob, yet full of tragic interest for the philosopher watching its movements, listening to its talk, speculating upon its potential value in the sum of humankind. It was the typical crowd that he was in the habit of studying—not like the people who thronged the Treasury steps this time yesterday. Surely it was the *Cause of Humanity* that had laid hold of *him*. That was the explanation of the interest he took in some crowds, and of the delight that he found in the uninterestingness of others. That was what he meant when he told her she ought to read Thackeray's paper to help her to understand him.

Pondering over this thought, fitfully, amid the distractions of the conversation, she raised her head and saw Eleanor coming towards her.

"There's Westmoreland and your sister," said the major. "And one of those strangers who are swarming all about the place just now, and crowding us out of our club. It's Yelverton. Kingscote Yelverton he calls himself. He is rather a swell when he's at home, they tell me; but Westmoreland has no business to foist his acquaintance on your sister. He'll have my wife about him if he is not more careful than that."

Elizabeth saw them approaching, and forgot all about the crowd under Cologne Cathedral and the crowd that went to see the man hanged. She remembered only the crowd of yesterday, and how that stately gentleman— could it be possible?—had stood with her amid the crush and clamour, holding her in his arms. For the first time she was able to look at him fairly and see what he was like; and it seemed to her that she had never seen a man of such a noble presence. His eyes were fixed upon her as she raised hers to his face, regarding her steadily, but with inscrutable gravity and absolute respect. The major rose to salute him in response to Mr. Westmoreland's rather imperious demand. "My old friend, whom I met in Paris," said Mr. Westmoreland; "come over to have a look at us. Want you to know him, major. We must do our best to make him enjoy himself, you know."

"Didn't I tell you?" whispered Eleanor, creeping round the back of her sister's chair. "Didn't I tell you he would be here?"

And at the same moment Elizabeth heard some one murmur over her head, "Miss King, allow me to introduce Mr. Yelverton—my friend, whom I knew in Paris—"

And so he and she not only met again, but received Mrs. Grundy's gracious permission to make each other's acquaintance.

CHAPTER XXI
THE "CUP"

Out of the many Cup Days that have gladdened the hearts of countless holiday-makers on the Flemington course assembled, perhaps that of 1880 was the most "all round" satisfactory and delightful to everybody concerned—except the bookmakers, and nobody grieves much over their disasters (though there are several legitimate and highly respected lines of business that are conducted on precisely the same system as governs their nefarious practices). It was, indeed, considered that the discomfiture of the bookmakers was a part of the brilliant success of the occasion. In the capricious spring-time of the year, when cold winds, or hot winds, or storms of rain, or clouds of dust, might any of them have been expected, this second of November displayed a perfect pattern of the boasted Australian climate to the foreigners of all nations who had been invited to enjoy it—a sweet blue sky, a fresh and delicate air, a broad glow of soft and mellow sunshine, of a quality to sufficiently account for the holiday-making propensities of the Australian people, and for the fascination that draws them home, in spite of all intentions to the contrary, when they have gone to look for happiness in other lands. The great racing-ground was in its finest order, the running track sanded and rolled, the lawns watered to a velvet greenness, the promenade level and speckless and elastic to the feet as a ball-room floor; and by noon more than a hundred thousand spectators, well-dressed and well-to-do—so orderly in their coming and going, and when congregated in solid masses together, that the policeman, though doubtless ubiquitous, was forgotten—were waiting to see the triumph of Grand Flâneur. At which time, and throughout the afternoon, Melbourne city was as a city of the dead; shops and warehouses deserted, and the empty streets echoing to a passing footfall with the hollow distinctness of midnight or the early hours of Sunday morning.

While a full half of the crowd was being conveyed to the course by innumerable trains, the sunny road was alive with vehicles of every description—spring-carts and lorries, cabs and buggies, broughams and landaus, and four-in-hand coaches—all filled to their utmost capacity, and displaying the sweetest things in bonnets and parasols. And amongst the best-appointed carriages Major Duff-Scott's was conspicuous, not only for its build and finish, and the excellence of the horses that drew it, and the fit of the livery of the coachman who drove it, but for the beauty and charming costumes of the ladies inside. The major himself, festive in light grey, with his member's card in his button-hole and his field-glass slung over his shoulder, occupied the place of the usual footman on the box seat in order that all the three sisters should accompany his wife; and Mrs. Duff-Scott, having set her heart on dressing her girls for the occasion, had been allowed to have her own way, with the happiest results. The good woman sat back in her corner, forgetting her own Parisian elegance and how it would compare with the Cup Day elegance of rival matrons in the van of rank and fashion, while she revelled in the contemplation of the young pair before her, on whom her best taste had been exercised. Elizabeth, by her side, was perfectly satisfactory in straw-coloured Indian silk, ruffled with some of her own fine old lace, and wearing a delicate French bonnet and parasol to match, with a bunch of Camille de Rohan roses at her throat for colour; but Elizabeth was not a striking beauty, nor of a style to be experimented on. Patty and Eleanor were; and they had been "treated" accordingly. Patty was a harmony in pink—the faintest shell-pink—and Eleanor a study in the softest, palest shade of china-blue; both their dresses being of muslin, lightly frilled, and tied round the waist with sashes; while they wore bewitching little cap-like bonnets, with swathes of tulle under their chins. The effect—designed for a sunny morning, and to be set off by the subdued richness of her own olive-tinted robes—was all that Mrs. Duff-Scott anticipated. The two girls were exquisitely sylph-like, and harmonious, and refined—looking prettier than they had ever done in their lives, because they knew themselves that they were looking so—and it was confidently expected by their chaperon that they would do considerable execution before the day was over. At the back of the carriage was strapped a hamper containing luncheon sufficient for all the potential husbands that the racecourse might produce, and Mrs. Duff-Scott was prepared to exercise discriminating but extensive hospitality.

It was not more than eleven o'clock when they entered the carriage enclosure and were landed at the foot of the terrace steps, and already more carriages than one would have imagined the combined colonies could produce were standing empty and in close order in the paddock on one hand, while on the other the grand stand was packed from end to end. Lawn and terrace were swarming with those brilliant toilets which are the feature of our great annual *fête* day, and the chief subject of interest in the newspapers of the day after.

"Dear me, what a crowd!" exclaimed Mrs. Duff-Scott, as her horses drew up on the smooth gravel, and she glanced eagerly up the steps. "We shall not be able to find anyone."

But they had no sooner alighted and shaken out their skirts than down from the terrace stepped Mr. Westmoreland, the first and most substantial instalment of expected cavaliers, to assist the major to convoy his party to the field. Mr. Westmoreland was unusually alert and animated, and he pounced upon Eleanor, after hurriedly saluting the other ladies, with such an open preference that Mrs. Duff-Scott readjusted her schemes upon the spot. If the young man insisted upon choosing the youngest instead of the middle one, he must be allowed to do so, was the matron's prompt conclusion. She would rather have begun at the top and worked downwards, leaving fair Eleanor to be disposed of after the elder sisters were settled; but she recognised the wisdom of taking the goods the gods provided as she could get them.

"I do declare," said Mr. Westmoreland, looking straight at the girl's face, framed in the soft little bonnet, and the pale blue disc of her parasol, "I do declare I never saw anybody look so—so—"

"Come, come," interrupted the chaperon, "I don't allow speeches of that sort." She spoke quite sharply, this astute diplomatist, so that the young man who was used to being allowed, and even encouraged, to make speeches of that sort, experienced the strange sensation of being snubbed, and was half inclined to be sulky over it; and at the same moment she quietly seconded his manoeuvres to get to Eleanor's side, and took care that he had his chances generally for the rest of the day.

They joined the two great streams of gorgeous promenaders slowly pacing up and down the long green lawn. Every seat in the stand was occupied and the gangways and gallery so tightly packed that when the Governor arrived presently, driving his own four-in-hand, with the Duke of Manchester beside him, there was some difficulty in squeezing out a path whereby he and his party might ascend to their box. But there were frequent benches on the grass, and it was of far more consequence to have freedom to move and display one's clothes, and opportunities of meeting one's friends, and observing the social aspect of the affair generally, than it was to see the racing to the best advantage—since one had to choose between the two. At least, that was understood to be the opinion of the ladies present; and Cup Day, notwithstanding its tremendous issues, is a ladies' day. The major, than whom no man better loved a first-class race, had had a good time at the Derby on the previous Saturday, and looked forward to enjoying himself as a man and a sportsman when Saturday should come again; but to-day, though sharing a warm interest in the great event with those who thronged the betting and saddling paddock, he meekly gave himself up to be his wife's attendant and to help her to entertain her *protégées*. He did not find this task a hard one, nor wanting in abundant consolations. He took off Elizabeth, in the first place, to show her the arrangements of the course, of which, by virtue of the badge in his button-hole, he was naturally proud; and it pleased him to meet his friends at every step, and to note the grave respect with which they saluted him out of compliment to the lady at his side—obviously wondering who was that fine creature with Duff-Scott. He showed her the scratching-house, with its four-faced clock in its tall tower, and made erasures on his own card and hers from the latest corrected lists that it displayed; and he taught her the rudiments of betting as practised by her sex. Then he initiated her into the mysteries of the electric bells and telegraphs, and all the other V.R.C. appliances for conducting business in an enlightened manner; showed her the bookmakers noisily pursuing their ill-fated enterprises; showed her the beautiful horses pacing up and down and round and round, fresh and full of enthusiasm for their day's work. And he had much satisfaction in her intelligent and cheerful appreciation of these new experiences.

Meanwhile Mrs. Duff-Scott, in the care of Mr. Westmoreland, awaited their return on the lawn, slowly sweeping to and fro, with her train rustling over the grass behind her, and feeling that she had never enjoyed a Cup Day half so much before. Her girls were admired to her heart's content, and she literally basked in the radiance of their success. She regarded them, indeed, with an enthusiasm of affection and interest that her husband felt to be the most substantial safeguard against promiscuous philanthropy that had yet been afforded her. How hungrily had she longed for children of her own! How she had envied other women their grown-up daughters!— always with the sense that hers would have been, like her cabinets of china, so much more choice and so much better "arranged" than theirs. And now that she had discovered these charming orphans, who had beauty, and breeding, and culture, and not a relative or connection in the world, she did not know how to restrain the extravagance of her satisfaction. As she rustled majestically up and down the lawn, with one fair girl on one side of her and one on the other, while men and women turned at every step to stare at them, her heart swelled and throbbed with the long-latent pride of motherhood, and a sense that she had at last stumbled upon the particular "specimen" that she had all her life been hunting for. The only drawback to her enjoyment in them was the consciousness that, though they were nobody else's, they were not altogether hers. She would have given half her fortune to be able to buy them, as she would buy three bits of precious crockery, for her absolute possession, body and soul—to dress, to manage, to marry as she liked.

The major kept Elizabeth walking about with him until the hour approached for the Maiden Plate race and luncheon. And when at last they joined their party they found that Mrs. Duff-Scott was already getting together her guests for the latter entertainment. She was seated on a bench, between Eleanor and Patty, and before her stood a group of men, in various attitudes of animation and repose, conspicuous amongst whom was the tall form of Mr. Kingscote Yelverton. Elizabeth had only had distant glimpses of him during the four weeks that had passed since he was introduced to her, her chaperon not having seemed inclined to cultivate his acquaintance— probably because she had not sought it for herself; but now the girl saw, with a quickened pulse, that the happiness of speaking to him again was in store for her. He seemed to be aware of her approach as soon as she was within sight, and lifted his head and turned to watch her—still sustaining his dialogue with Mrs. Duff-Scott, who had singled him out to talk to; and Elizabeth, feeling his eyes upon her, had a sudden sense of discomfort in her beautiful dress and her changed surroundings. She was sure that he would draw comparisons, and she did not feel herself elevated by the new dignities that had been conferred upon her.

Coming up to her party, she was introduced to several strangers— amongst others, to the husband Mrs. Duff-Scott had selected for her, a portly widower with a grey beard—and in the conversation that ensued she quite ignored the only person in the group of whose presence she was distinctly conscious. She neither looked at him nor spoke to him, though aware of every word and glance and movement of his; until presently they were all standing upon the slope of grass connecting the terrace with the lawn to see the first race as best they could, and then she found herself once more by his side. And not only by his side, but, as those who could not gain a footing upon the stand congregated upon the terrace elevation, gradually wedged against him almost as tightly as on the former memorable occasion. Below them stood Mrs. Duff-Scott, protected by Mr. Westmoreland, and Patty and Eleanor, guarded vigilantly by the little major. It was Mr. Yelverton himself who had quietly seen and seized upon his chance of renewing his original relations with Elizabeth.

"Miss King," he said, in a low tone of authority, "take my arm—it will steady you."

She took his arm, and felt at once that she was in shelter and safety. Strong as she was, her impulse to lean on him was almost irresistible.

"Now, give me your parasol," he said. The noonday sun was pouring down, but at this critical juncture the convenience of the greatest number had to be considered, and unselfish women were patiently exposing their best complexions to destruction. Of course Elizabeth declared she should do very well until the race was over. Whereupon her companion took her parasol gently from her hand, opened it, and held it—as from his great height he was able to do—so that it shaded her without incommoding other people. And so they stood, in silent enjoyment, both thinking of where and how something like this—and yet something so very different—had happened before, but neither of them saying a word to betray their thoughts, until the first race was run, and the excitement of it cooled down, and they were summoned by Mrs. Duff-Scott to follow her to the carriage-paddock for lunch.

Down on the lawn again they sauntered side by side, finding themselves *tête-à-tête* without listeners for the first time since they had been introduced to each other. Elizabeth made a tremendous effort to ignore the secret intimacy between them. "It is a lovely day, is it not?" she lightly remarked, from under the dome of her straw-coloured parasol. "I don't think there has been such a fine Cup Day for years."

"Lovely," he assented. "Have you often been here before?"

"I?—oh, no. I have never been here before."

He was silent a moment, while he looked intently at what he could see of her. She had no air of rustic inexperience of the world to-day. "You are beginning to understand crowds," he said.

"Yes—I am, a little." Then, glancing up at him, she said, "How does *this* crowd affect you? Do you find it all interesting?"

He met her eyes gravely, and then lifted his own towards the hill above the grand stand, which was now literally black with human beings, like a swarming ant-hill.

"I think it might be more interesting up yonder," he said; and then added, after a pause—"if we could be there."

Eleanor was walking just in front of them, chatting airily with her admirer, Mr. Westmoreland, who certainly was making no secret of his admiration; and she turned round when she heard this. "Ah, Mr. Yelverton," she said, lightly, "you are very disappointing. You don't care for our great Flemington show. You are not a connoisseur in ladies' dresses, I suppose."

"I know when a lady's dress is becoming, Miss Eleanor," he promptly responded, with a smile and bow. At which she blushed and laughed, and turned her back again. For the moment he was a man like other men who enjoy social success and favour—ready to be all things to all women; but it was only for the moment. Elizabeth noted, with a swelling sense of pride and pleasure, that he was not like that to her.

"I am out of my element in an affair of this kind," he said, in the undertone that was meant for her ear alone.

"What is your element?"

"Perhaps I oughtn't to call it my element—the groove I have got into—my 'walk of life,' so to speak."

"Yes?"

"I'll tell you about it some day—if I ever get the chance. I can't here."

"I should like to know. And I can guess a little. You don't spend life wholly in getting pleasure for yourself—you help others."

"What makes you think that?"

"I am sure of it."

"Thank you."

Elizabeth blushed, and could not think of a remark to make, though she tried hard.

"Just at present," he went on, "I am on pleasure bent entirely. I am taking several months' holiday—doing nothing but amusing myself."

"A holiday implies work."

"I suppose we all work, more or less."

"Oh, no, we don't. Not voluntarily—not disinterestedly—in that way."

"You mean in my way?"

"Yes."

"Ah, I see that Westmoreland has been romancing."

"I have not heard a word from Mr. Westmoreland—he has never spoken of you to me."

"Who, then?"

"Nobody."

"These are your own conjectures?"

She made no reply, and they crossed the gravelled drive and entered the labyrinth of carriages where the major's servants had prepared luncheon in and around his own spacious vehicle, which was in a position to lend itself to commissariat purposes. They all assembled there, the ladies in the carriage, the gentlemen outside, and napkins and plates were handed round and champagne uncorked; and they ate and drank together, and were a very cheerful party. Mr. Yelverton contributed witty nothings to the general entertainment—with so much happy tact that Mrs. Duff-Scott was charmed with him, and said afterwards that she had never met a man with finer manners. While the other men waited upon their hostess and the younger sisters, he stood for the most part quietly at Elizabeth's elbow, joining freely in the badinage round him without once addressing her—silently replenishing her plate and her glass when either required it with an air of making her his special charge that was too unobtrusive to attract outside attention, but which was more eloquent than any verbal intercourse could have been to themselves. Elizabeth attempted no analysis of her sweet and strange sensations. She took them from his hand, as she took her boned turkey and champagne, without question or protest. She only felt that she was happy and satisfied as she had never been before.

Later in the afternoon, when the great Cup race and all the excitement of the day was over, Mrs. Duff-Scott gathered her brood together and took leave of her casual male guests.

"*Good*-bye, Mr. Yelverton," she said cordially, when his turn came to bid her adieu; "you will come and see me at my own house, I hope?"

Elizabeth looked up at him when she heard the words. She could not help it—she did not know what she did. And in her eyes he read the invitation that he declared gravely he would do himself the honour to accept.

CHAPTER XXII
CROSS PURPOSES

While Elizabeth was thus happily absorbed in her "young man," and Eleanor making an evident conquest of Mr. Westmoreland, Patty, who was rather accustomed to the lion's share of whatever interesting thing was going on, had very little enjoyment. For the first hour or two she was delighted with the beauty of the scene and the weather and her own personal circumstances, and she entered into the festive spirit of the day with the ardour of her energetic temperament. But in a little while the glamour faded. A serpent revealed itself in Paradise, and all her innocent pleasure was at an end.

That serpent was Mrs. Aarons. Or, rather, it was a hydra-headed monster, consisting of Mrs. Aarons and Paul Brion combined. Poor Paul had come to spend a holiday afternoon at the races like everybody else, travelling to the course by train along with the undistinguished multitude, with the harmless intention of recruiting his mind, and, at the same time, storing it with new impressions. He had meant to enjoy himself in a quiet and independent fashion, strolling amongst the crowd and studying its various aspects from the point of view of a writer for the press to whom men and women are "material" and "subjects," and then to go home as soon as the Cup race was over, and, after an early dinner, to spend a peaceful solitary evening, embodying the results of his observations in a brilliant article for his newspaper. But, before he had well thought out the plan of his paper, he encountered Mrs. Aarons; and to her he was a helpless captive for the whole live-long afternoon. Mrs. Aarons had come to the course in all due state, attired in one of the few real amongst the many reputed Worth dresses of the day, and reclining in her own landau, with her long-nosed husband at her side. But after her arrival, having lost the shelter of her carriage, and being amongst the many who were shut out from the grand stand, she had felt just a little unprotected and uncared-for. The first time she stopped to speak to a friend, Mr. Aarons took the opportunity to slip off to the saddling paddock, where the astute speculator was speedily absorbed in a more congenial occupation than that of idling up and down the promenade; and the other gentlemen who were so assiduous in their attendance upon her in the ordinary way had their own female relatives to look after on this extraordinary occasion. She joined one set and then another of casual acquaintances whom she chanced to meet, but her hold upon them all was more or less precarious; so that when by-and-bye she saw Paul Brion, threading his way alone amongst the throng, she pounced upon him thankfully, and confided herself to his protection. Paul had no choice but to accept the post of escort assigned to him under such circumstances, nor was he at all unwilling to become her companion. He had been rather out in the cold lately. Patty, though nominally at home in Myrtle Street, had been practically living with Mrs. Duff-Scott for the last few weeks, and he had scarcely had a glimpse of her, and he had left off going to Mrs. Aarons's Fridays since the evening that she snubbed him for Patty's sake. The result was that he was in a mood to appreciate women's society and to be inclined to melt when the sunshine of his old friend's favour was poured upon him again.

They greeted each other amicably, therefore, and made up the intangible quarrel that was between them. Mrs. Aarons justified her reputation as a clever woman by speedily causing him to regard her as the injured party, and to wonder how he could have been such a brute as to wound her tender susceptibilities as he had done. She insinuated, with the utmost tact, that she had suffered exceedingly from the absence of his society, and was evidently in a mood to revive the slightly sentimental intercourse that he had not found disagreeable in earlier days. Paul, however, was never less inclined to be sentimental in her company than he was to-day, in spite of his cordial disposition. He was changed from what he was in those earlier days; he felt it as soon as she began to talk to him, and perfectly understood the meaning of it. After a little while she felt, too, that he was changed, and she adapted herself to him accordingly. They fell into easy chat as they strolled up and down, and were very friendly in a harmless way. They did not discuss their private feelings at all, but only the topics that were in every-day use—the weather, the races, the trial of Ned Kelly, the wreck of the Sorata, the decay of Berryism—anything that happened to come into their heads or to be suggested by the scene around them. Nevertheless, they had a look of being very intimate with each other to the superficial eye of Mrs. Grundy. People with nothing better to do stared at them as they meandered in and out amongst the crowd, he and she *tête-à-tête* by their solitary selves; and those who knew they were legally unrelated were quick to discover a want of conventional discretion in their behaviour. Mrs. Duff-Scott, for instance, who abhorred scandal, made use of them to point a delicate moral for the edification of her girls.

Paul, who was a good talker, was giving his companion an animated account of the French plays going on at one of the theatres just then— which she had not yet been to see—and describing with great warmth the graceful and finished acting of charming Madame Audrée, when he was suddenly aware of Patty King passing close beside him. Patty was walking at her chaperon's side, with her head erect, and her white parasol, with its pink lining, held well back over her shoulder, a vision of loveliness in her diaphanous dress. He caught his breath at sight of her, looking so different from her ordinary self, and was about to raise his hat, when—to his deep dismay and surprise—she swept haughtily past him, meeting his eyes fairly, with a cold disdain, but making no sign of recognition.

The blood rushed into his face, and he set his teeth, and walked on silently, not seeing where he went. For a moment he felt stunned with the shock. Then he was brought to himself by a harsh laugh from Mrs. Aarons. "Dear me," said she, in a high tone, "the Miss Kings have become so grand that we are beneath their notice. You and I are not good enough for them now, Mr. Brion. We must hide our diminished heads."

"I see," he assented, with savage quietness. "Very well. I am quite ready to hide mine."

Meanwhile Patty, at the farther end of the lawn, was overwhelmed with remorse for what she had done. At the first sight of him, in close intercourse with that woman who, Mrs. Duff-Scott again reminded her, was not "nice"—who, though a wife and mother, liked men to "dangle" round her—she had arraigned and judged and sentenced him with the swift severity of youth, that knows nothing of the complex trials and sufferings which teach older people to bear and forbear with one another. But when it was over, and she had seen his shocked and bewildered face, all her instinctive trust in him revived, and she would have given anything to be able to make reparation for her cruelty. The whole afternoon she was looking for him, hoping for a chance to show him somehow that she did not altogether "mean it," but, though she saw him several times—eating his lunch with Mrs. Aarons under the refreshment shed close by the Duff-Scott carriage, watching Grand Flâneur win the greatest of his half-dozen successive victories from the same point of view as that taken by the Duff-Scott party—he never turned his head again in her direction or seemed to have the faintest consciousness that she was there.

And next day, when no longer in her glorious apparel, but walking quietly home from the Library with Eleanor, she met him unexpectedly, face to face, in the Fitzroy Gardens. And then *he* cut *her*—dead.

CHAPTER XXIII
MR. YELVERTON'S MISSION

On a Thursday evening in the race week—two days after the "Cup," Mrs. Duff-Scott took her girls to the Town Hall to one of a series of concerts that were given at that time by Henri Ketten, the Hungarian pianist, and the Austrian band that had come out to Melbourne to give *éclat* to the Exhibition.

It was a fine clear night, and the great hall was full when they arrived, notwithstanding the fact that half-a-dozen theatres were open and displaying their most attractive novelties, for music-loving souls are pretty numerous in this part of the world, taking all things into consideration. Australians may not have such an enlightened appreciation of high-class music as, say, the educated Viennese, who live and breathe and have their being in it. There are, indeed, sad instances on record of a great artist, or a choice combination of artists, having appealed in vain for sympathy to the Melbourne public— that is to say, having found not numbers of paying and applauding listeners, but only a select and fervent few. But such instances are rare, and to be accounted for as the result, not of indifference, but of inexperience. The rule is—as I think most of our distinguished musical visitors will testify—that we are a people peculiarly ready to recognise whatever is good that comes to us, and to acknowledge and appreciate it with ungrudging generosity. And so the Austrian band, though it had many critics, never played to a thin audience or to inattentive ears; and no city in Europe (according to his own death-bed testimony) ever offered such incense of loving enthusiasm to Ketten's genius as burnt steadily in Melbourne from the moment that he laid his fingers on the keyboard, at the Opera House, until he took his reluctant departure. This, I hasten to explain (lest I should be accused of "blowing"), is not due to any exceptional virtue of discrimination on our part, but to our good fortune in having inherited an enterprising and active intelligence from the brave men who had the courage and energy to make a new country, and to that country being such a land of plenty that those who live in it have easy times and abundant leisure to enjoy themselves.

Mrs. Duff-Scott sailed into the hall, with her girls around her, and many eyes were turned to look at them and to watch their progress to their seats. By this time "the pretty Miss Kings" had become well-known and much talked about, and the public interest in what they wore, and what gentlemen were in attendance on them, was apt to be keen on these occasions. To-night the younger girls, with their lovely hair lifted from their white necks and coiled high at the back of their heads, wore picturesque flowered gowns of blue and white stuff, while the elder sister was characteristically dignified in black. And the gentlemen in attendance upon them were Mr. Westmoreland, still devoted to Eleanor, and the portly widower, whom Mrs. Duff-Scott had intended for Elizabeth, but who was perversely addicted to Patty. The little party took their places in the body of the hall, in preference to the gallery, and seated themselves in two rows of three—the widower behind Mrs. Duff-Scott, Patty next him behind Eleanor, and Elizabeth behind Mr. Westmoreland. And when the concert began there was an empty chair beside Elizabeth.

By-and-bye, when the overture was at an end—when the sonorous tinkling and trumpeting of the orchestra had ceased, and she was listening, in soft rapture, to Ketten's delicate improvisation, at once echo and prelude, reminiscent of the idea that the band had been elaborating, and prophetic of the beautiful Beethoven sonata that he was thus tenderly approaching, Elizabeth was aware that the empty chair was taken, and knew, without turning her head, by whom. She tried not to blush and feel fluttered—she was too old, she told herself, for that nonsense—but for half a minute or so it was an effort to control these sentimental tendencies. He laid his light overcoat over the back of his chair, and sat down quietly. Mrs. Duff-Scott looked over her shoulder, and gave him a pleasant nod. Mr. Westmoreland said, "Hullo! Got back again?" And then Elizabeth felt sufficiently composed to turn and hold out her hand, which he took in a strong clasp that was not far removed from a squeeze. They did not speak to each other; nor did they look at each other, though Mr. Yelverton was speedily informed of all the details of his neighbour's appearance, and she took no time to ascertain that he looked particularly handsome in his evening dress (but *she* always thought him handsome; big nose, leather cheeks, red moustache, and all), and that his well-cut coat and trousers were not in their first freshness. Then the concert went on as before—but not as before—and they sat side by side and listened. Elizabeth's programme lay on her knee, and he took it up to study it, and laid it lightly on her knee again. Presently she pointed to one and another of the selections on the list, about which she had her own strong musical feelings, and he looked down at them and nodded, understanding what she meant. And again they sat back in their chairs, and gazed serenely at the stage under the great organ, at Herr Wildner cutting the air with his baton, or at poor Ketten, with his long, white, solemn face, sitting at the piano in a bower of votive wreaths and bouquets, raining his magic finger-tips like a sparkling cascade upon the keyboard, and wrinkling the skin of his forehead up and down. But they had no audible conversation throughout the whole performance. When, between the two divisions of the programme, the usual interval occurred for the relaxation and refreshment of the performers and their audience, Mr. Westmoreland turned round, with his elbow over the back of his chair, and appropriated an opportunity to which they had secretly been looking forward. "So you've got back?" he remarked for the second time. "I thought you were going to make a round of the country?"

"I shall do it in instalments," replied Mr. Yelverton.

"You won't have time to do much that way, if you are going home again next month. Will you?"

"I can extend my time a little, if necessary."

"Can you? Oh, I thought there was some awfully urgent business that you had to get back for—a new costermonger's theatre to open, or a street Arab's public-house—eh?"

Mr. Westmoreland laughed, as at a good joke that he had got hold of, but Mr. Yelverton was imperturbably grave. "I have business in Australia just now," he said, "and I'm going to finish that first."

Here the portly widower, who had overheard the dialogue, leaned over Patty to join in the conversation. He was a wealthy person of the name of Smith, who, like Mr. Phillips's father in the *Undiscovered Country*, had been in business "on that obscure line which divides the wholesale merchant's social acceptability from the lost condition of the retail trader," but who, on his retirement with a fortune, had safely scaled the most exclusive heights of respectability. "I say," he called out, addressing Mr. Yelverton, "you're not going to write a book about us, I hope, like Trollope and those fellows? We're suspicious of people who come here utter strangers, and think they can learn all about us in two or three weeks."

Mr. Yelverton reassured him upon this point, and then Mrs. Duff-Scott broke in. "You have not been to call on me yet, Mr. Yelverton."

"No. I hope to have that pleasure to-morrow," he replied. "I am told that Friday is your reception day."

"Oh, you needn't have waited for that. Any day before four. Come to-morrow and dine with us, will you? We are going to have a few friends and a little music in the evening. I suppose you are fond of music—being here."

Mr. Yelverton said he was very fond of music, though he did not understand much about it, and that he would be very happy to dine with her next day. Then, after a little more desultory talk, the orchestra returned to the stage and began the second overture—from Mozart this time—and they all became silent listeners again.

When at last the concert was over, Elizabeth and her "young man" found themselves once more navigating a slow course together through a crowd. Mrs. Duff-Scott, with Mr. Westmoreland and Eleanor, moved off in advance; Mr. Smith offered his arm to Patty and followed; and so, by the favour of fate and circumstances, the remaining pair were left with no choice but to accompany each other. "Wait a moment," said Mr. Yelverton, as she stepped out from her seat, taking her shawl—a soft white Rampore chuddah, that was the fairy godmother's latest gift—from her arms. "You will feel it cold in the passages." She stood still obediently, and he put the shawl over her shoulders and folded one end of it lightly round her throat. Then he held his arm, and her hand was drawn closely to his side; and so they set forth towards the door, having put a dozen yards between themselves and the rest of their party.

"You are living with Mrs. Duff-Scott, are you not?" he asked abruptly.

"Not quite that," she replied. "Mrs. Duff-Scott would like us to be there always, but we think it better to be at home sometimes."

"Yes—I should think it is better," he replied.

"But we are with her very often—nearly every day," she added.

"Shall you be there to-morrow?" he asked, not looking at her. "Shall I see you there in the evening?"

"I think so," she replied rather unsteadily. And, after a little while, she felt emboldened to ask a few questions of him. "Are you really only making a flying visit to Australia, Mr. Yelverton?"

"I had intended that it should be very short," he said; "but I shall not go away quite yet."

"You have many interests at home—to call you back?" she ventured to say, with a little timidity about touching on his private affairs.

"Yes. You are thinking of what Westmoreland said? He is a scoffer—he doesn't understand. You mustn't mind what he says. But I should like," he added, as they drew near the door and saw Mrs. Duff-Scott looking back for them, "I should very much like to tell you something about it myself. I think—I feel sure—it would interest you. Perhaps I may have an opportunity to-morrow night."

Here Mrs. Duff-Scott's emissary, Mr. Smith, who had been sent back to his duty, claimed Elizabeth on her chaperon's behalf. She and her lover had no time to say anything more, except good-night. But that good-night—and their anticipations—satisfied them.

On reaching Mrs. Duff-Scott's house, where the girls were to sleep, they found the major awaiting their return, and were hospitably invited—along with Mr. Westmoreland, who had been allowed to "see them safely home," on the box-seat of the carriage—into the library, where they found a bright little fire in the grate, and refreshments on the table. The little man, apparently, was as paternal in his dispositions towards the orphans as his wife could desire, and was becoming quite weaned from his bad club habits under the influence of his new domestic ties.

"Dear me, *how* nice!—*how* comfortable!" exclaimed Mrs. Duff-Scott, sailing up to the hearth and seating herself in a deep leather chair. "Come in, Mr. Westmoreland. Come along to the fire, dears." And she called her brood around her. Eleanor, who had caressing ways, knelt down at her chaperon's feet on the soft oriental carpet, and she pulled out the frills of lace round the girl's white neck and elbows with a motherly gesture.

"Dear child!" she ejaculated fondly, "doesn't she"—appealing to her husband—"remind you exactly of a bit of fifteenth century Nankin?"

"I should like to see the bit of porcelain, Nankin or otherwise, that would remind me exactly of Miss Nelly," replied the gallant major, bowing to the kneeling girl. "I would buy that bit, whatever price it was."

"That's supposing you could get it," interrupted Mr. Westmoreland, with a laugh.

"It is the very shade of blue, with that grey tinge in it," murmured Mrs. Duff-Scott. But at the same time she was thinking of a new topic. "I have asked Mr. Yelverton to dine with us to-morrow, my dear," she remarked, suddenly, to her spouse. "We wanted another man to make up our number."

"Oh, have you? All right. I shall be very glad to see him. He's a gentlemanly fellow, is Yelverton. Very rich, too, they tell me. But we don't see much of him."

"No," said Mr. Westmoreland, withdrawing his eyes from the contemplation of Eleanor and her æsthetic gown, "he's not a society man. He don't go much into clubs, Yelverton. He's one of the richest commoners in Great Britain—give you my word, sir, he's got a princely fortune, all to his own cheek—and he lets his places and lives in chambers in Piccadilly, and spends nearly all his time when he's at home in the slums and gutters of Whitechapel. He's got a mania for philanthropy, unfortunately. It's an awful pity, for he really *would* be a good fellow."

At the word "philanthropy," the major made a clandestine grimace to Elizabeth, but composed his face immediately, seeing that she was not regarding him, but gazing with serious eyes at the narrator of Mr. Yelverton's peculiarities.

"He's been poking into every hole and corner," continued Mr. Westmoreland, "since he came here, overhauling the factory places, and finding out the prices of things, and the land regulations, and I don't know what. He's just been to Sandhurst, to look at the mines—doing a little amateur emigration business, I expect. Seems a strange thing," concluded the young man, thoughtfully, "for a rich swell of his class to be bothering himself about things of that sort."

Mrs. Duff-Scott had been listening attentively, and at this she roused herself and sat up in her chair. "It is the rich who *should* do it," said she, with energy. "And I admire him—I admire him, that he has given up his own selfish ease to help those whose lives are hard and miserable. I believe the squalid wretchedness of places like Whitechapel—though I have never been there—is something dreadful—dreadful! I admire him," she repeated defiantly. "I think it's a pity a few more of us are not like him. I shall talk to him about it. I—I shall see if I can't help him."

This time Elizabeth did look at the major, who was making a feint of putting his handkerchief to his eyes. She smiled at him sweetly, and then she walked over to Mrs. Duff-Scott, put her strong arms round the matron's shoulders, and kissed her fervently.

CHAPTER XXIV
AN OLD STORY

Mrs. Duff-Scott's drawing-room, at nine or ten o'clock on Friday evening, was a pleasant sight. Very spacious, very voluptuous, in a subdued, majestic, high-toned way; very dim—with splashes of richness—as to walls and ceilings; very glowing and splendid—with folds of velvety darkness—as to window curtains and portières. The colouring of it was such as required a strong light to show how beautiful it was, but with a proud reserve, and to mark its unostentatious superiority over the glittering salons of the uneducated *nouveaux riches*, it was always more or less in a warm and mellow twilight, veiling its sombre magnificence from the vulgar eye. Just now its main compartment was lit by wax candles in archaic candlesticks amongst the flowers and *bric-à-brac* of an *étagère* over the mantelpiece, and by seven shaded and coloured lamps, of various artistic devices, judiciously distributed over the abundant table-space so as to suffuse with a soft illumination the occupants of most of the wonderfully stuffed and rotund chairs and lounges grouped about the floor; and yet the side of the room was decidedly bad for reading in. "It does not light up well," was the consolation of women of Mrs. Duff-Scott's acquaintance, who still clung to pale walls and primary colours and cut-glass chandeliers, either from necessity or choice. "Pooh!" Mrs. Duff-Scott used to retort, hearing of this just criticism; "as if I *wanted* it to light up!" But she had compromised with her principles in the arrangement of the smaller division of the room, where, between and beyond a pair of vaguely tinted portières, stood the piano, and all other material appliances for heightening the spiritual enjoyment of musical people. Here she had grudgingly retained the gas-burner of utilitarian Philistinism. It hung down from the ceiling straight over the piano, a circlet of gaudy yellow flames, that made the face of every plaque upon the wall to glitter. But the brilliant corona was borne in no gas-fitter's vehicle; its shrine was of dull brass, mediæval and precious, said to have been manufactured, in the first instance, for either papal or imperial purposes—it didn't matter which.

In this bright music-room was gathered to-night a little company of the elect—Herr Wüllner and his violin, together with three other stringed instruments and their human complement. Patty at the piano, Eleanor, Mrs. Duff-Scott, and half-a-dozen more enthusiasts—with a mixed audience around them. In the dim, big room beyond, the major entertained the inartistic, outlawed few who did not care, nor pretend to care, for aught but the sensual comfort of downy chairs and after dinner chit-chat. And, at the farthest end, in a recess of curtained window that had no lamps about it, sat Elizabeth and Mr. Yelverton, side by side, on a low settee—not indifferent to the pathetic wail of the far-distant violins, but finding more entertainment in their own talk than the finest music could have afforded them.

"I had a friend who gave up everything to go and work amongst the London poor—in the usual clerical way, you know, with schools and guilds and all the right and proper things. He used to ask me for money, and insist on my helping him with a lecture or a reading now and then, and I got drawn in. I had always had an idea of doing something—taking a line of some sort—and somehow this got hold of me. I couldn't see all that misery—you've no idea of it, Miss King—"

"I have read of it," she said.

"You would have to see it to realise it in the least. After I saw it I couldn't turn my back and go home and enjoy myself as if nothing had happened. And I had no family to consider. I got drawn in."

"And *that* is your work?" said Elizabeth. "I *knew* it."

"No. My friend talks of 'his work'—a lot of them have 'their work'—it's splendid, too—but they don't allow me to use that word, and I don't want it. What I do is all wrong, they say—not only useless, but mischievous."

"I don't believe it," said Elizabeth.

"Nor I, of course—though they may be right. We can only judge according to our lights. To me, it seems that when things are as bad as possible, a well meaning person can't make them worse and *may* make them better. They say 'no,' and argue it all out as plainly as possible. Yet I stick to my view—I go on in my own line. It doesn't interfere with theirs, though they say it does."

"And what is it?" she asked, with her sympathetic eyes.

"Well, you'll hardly understand, for you don't know the class—the lowest deep of all—those who can't be dealt with by the Societies—the poor wretches whom nothing will raise, and who are abandoned as hopeless, outside the pale of everything. They are my line."

"Can there be any abandoned as hopeless?"

"Yes. They really are so, you know. Neither religion nor political economy can do anything for them, though efforts are made for the children. Poor, sodden, senseless, vicious lumps of misery, with the last spark of soul bred out of them—a sort of animated garbage that cumbers the ground and makes the air stink—given up as a bad job, and only wanted out of the way—from the first they were on my mind more than all the others. And when I saw them left to rot like that, I felt I might have a free hand."

"And can you succeed where so many have failed?"

"Oh, what I do doesn't involve success or failure. It's outside all that, just as they are. They're only brutes in human shape—hardly human shape either; but I have a feeling for brutes. I love horses and dogs—I can't bear to see things suffer. So that's all I do—just comfort them where I can, in their own way; not the parson's way—that's no use. I wouldn't mock them by speaking of religion—I suppose religion, as we know it, has had a large hand in making them what they are; and to go and tell them that God ordained their miserable pariah-dog lot would be rank blasphemy. I leave all that. I don't bother about their souls, because I know they haven't got any; I see their wretched bodies, and that's enough for me. It's something not to let them go out of the world without *ever* knowing what it is to be physically comfortable. It eases my conscience, as a man who has never been hungry, except for the pleasure of it."

"And do they blame you for that?"

"They say I pauperise them and demoralise them," he answered, with a sudden laugh; "that I disorganise the schemes of the legitimate workers— that I outrage every principle of political economy. Well, I do *that*, certainly. But that I make things worse—that I retard the legitimate workers—I won't believe. If I do," he concluded, "I can't help it."

"No," breathed Elizabeth, softly.

"There's only one thing in which I and the legitimate workers are alike—everybody is alike in that, I suppose—the want of money. Only in the matter of beer and tobacco, what interest I could get on a few hundred pounds! What I could do in the way of filling empty stomachs and easing aches and pains if I had control of large means! What a good word 'means' is, isn't it? We want 'means' for all the ends we seek—no matter what they are."

"I thought," said Elizabeth, "that you were rich. Mr. Westmoreland told us so."

"Well, in a way, I am," he rejoined. "I hold large estates in my own name, and can draw fifty or sixty thousand a year interest from them if I like. But there have been events—there are peculiar circumstances in connection with the inheritance of the property, which make me feel myself not quite entitled to use it freely—not yet. I *will* use it, after this year, if nothing happens. I think I *ought* to; but I have put it off hitherto so as to make as sure as possible that I was lawfully in possession. I will tell you how it is," he proceeded, leaning forward and clasping his knee with his big brown hands. "I am used to speaking of the main facts freely, because I am always in hopes of discovering something as I go about the world. A good many years ago my father's second brother disappeared, and was never heard of afterwards. He and the eldest brother, at that time the head of the family, and in possession of the property, quarrelled about—well, about a woman whom both were in love with; and the elder one was found dead—shot dead—in a plantation not far from the house on the evening of the day of the quarrel, an hour after the total disappearance of the other. My uncle Kingscote—I was named after him, and he was my godfather—was last seen going out towards the plantation with his gun; he was traced to London within the next few days; and it was almost—but just not quite certainly—proved that he had there gone on board a ship that sailed for South America and was lost. He was advertised for in every respectable newspaper in the world, at intervals, for twenty years afterwards—during which time the estate was in Chancery, before they would grant it to my father, from whom it descended to me—and I should think the agony columns of all countries never had one message cast into such various shapes. But he never gave a sign. All sorts of apparent clues were followed up, but they led to nothing. If alive he must have known that it was all right, and would have come home to take his property. He *must* have gone down in that ship."

"But—oh, surely he would never have come back to take the property of a murdered brother!" exclaimed Elizabeth, in a shocked voice.

"His brother was not murdered," Mr. Yelverton replied. "Many people thought so, of course—people have a way of thinking the worst in these cases, not from malice, but because it is more interesting—and a tradition to that effect survives still, I am afraid. But my uncle's family never suspected him of such a crime. The thing was not legally proved, one way or the other. There were strong indications in the position of the gun which lay by his side, and in the general appearance of the spot where he was found, that my uncle, Patrick Yelverton, accidentally shot himself; that was the opinion of the coroner's jury, and the conviction of the family. But poor Kingscote evidently assumed that he would be accused of murder. Perhaps—it is very possible—some rough-tempered action of his might have caused the catastrophe, and his remorse have had the same effect as fear in prompting him to efface himself. Anyway, no one who knew him well believed him capable of doing his brother a mischief wilfully. His innocence was, indeed, proved by the fact that he married the lady who had been at the bottom of the trouble—by no fault of hers, poor soul!—after he escaped to London; and, wherever he went to, he took her with him. She disappeared a few days after he did, and was lost as completely, from that time. The record and circumstances of their marriage were discovered; and that was all. He would not have married her—she would not have married him—had he been a murderer."

"Do you think not?" said Elizabeth. "That is always assumed as a matter of course, in books—that murder and—and other disgraces are irrevocable barriers between those who love each other, when they discover them. But I do not understand why. With such an awful misery to bear, they would want all that their love could give them so much *more*—not less."

"You see," said Mr. Yelverton, regarding her with great interest, "it is a sort of point of honour with the one in misfortune not to drag the other down. When we are married, as when we are dead, 'it is for a long time.'"

Elizabeth made no answer, but there was a quiet smile about her lips that plainly testified to her want of sympathy with this view. After a silence of a few seconds, her companion leaned forward and looked directly into her face. "Would *you* stick to the man you loved if he had forfeited his good name or were in risk of the gallows?—I mean if he were really a criminal, and not only a suspected one?" he asked with impressive slowness.

"If I had found him worthy to be loved before that," she replied, speaking collectedly, but dismayed to find herself growing crimson, "and if he cared for me—and leant on me—oh, yes! It might be wrong, but I should do it. Surely any woman would. I don't see how she could help herself."

He changed his position, and looked away from her face into the room with a light in his deep-set eyes. "You ought to have been Elizabeth Leigh's daughter," he said. "I did not think there were any more women like her in the world."

"I am like other women," said Elizabeth, humbly, "only more ignorant."

He made no comment—they both found it rather difficult to speak at this point—and, after an expressive pause, she went on, rather hurriedly, "Was Elizabeth Leigh the lady who married your uncle?"

"Yes," he replied, bringing himself back to his story with an effort, "she was. She was a lovely woman, bright and clever, fond of dress and fun and admiration, like other women; but with a solid foundation to her character that you will forgive my saying is rare to your sex—as far, at least, as I am able to judge. I saw her when I was a little schoolboy, but I can picture her now, as if it were but yesterday. What vigour she had! What a wholesome zest for life! And yet she gave up everything to go into exile and obscurity with the man she loved. Ah, *what* a woman! She *ought* not to have died. She should have lived and reigned at Yelverton, and had a houseful of children. It is still possible—barely, barely possible—that she did live, and that I shall some day stumble over a handsome young cousin who will tell me that he is the head of the family."

"O no," said Elizabeth, "not after all these years. Give up thinking of such a thing. Take your own money now, as soon as you go home, and"— looking up with a smile—"buy all the beer and tobacco that you want."

CHAPTER XXV
OUT IN THE COLD

Paul Brion, meanwhile, plodded on in his old groove, which no longer fitted him as it used to do, and vexed the soul of his benevolent landlady with the unprecedented shortness of his temper. She didn't know how to take him, she said, he was that cantankerous and "contrary:" but she triumphantly recognised the result that she had all along expected would follow a long course of turning night into day, and therefore was not surprised at the change in him. "Your brain is over-wrought," she said, soothingly, when one day a compunctious spirit moved him to apologise for his moroseness; "your nervous system is unstrung. You've been going on too long, and you want a spell. You just take a holiday straight off, and go right away, and don't look at an ink-bottle for a month. It will save you a brain fever, mark my words." But Paul was consistent in his perversity, and refused to take good advice. He did think, for a moment, that he might as well have a little run and see how his father was getting on; and for several days he entertained the more serious project of "cutting" the colony altogether and going to seek his fortune in London. All the same, he stayed on with Mrs. M'Intyre, producing his weekly tale of political articles and promiscuous essays, and sitting up all night, and sleeping all the morning, with his habitual irregular regularity. But the flavour had gone out of work and recreation alike, and not all Mrs. Aarons's blandishments, which were now exercised upon him for an hour or two every Friday evening, were of any avail to coax it back again. Those three Miss Kings, whom his father had sent to him, and whom Mrs. Duff-Scott had taken away from him, had spoiled the taste of life. That was the fact, though he would not own it. "What care I? They are nothing to me," he used to say to himself when fighting an occasional spasm of rage or jealousy. He really persuaded himself very often that they were nothing to him, and that his bitter feeling was caused solely by the spectacle of their deterioration. To see them exchanging all their great plans and high aspirations for these vulgar social triumphs—giving up their studies at the Library to attend dancing classes, and to dawdle about the Block, and gossip in the Exhibition—laying aside their high-bred independence to accept the patronage of a fine lady who might drop them as suddenly as she took them up—was it not enough to make a man's heart bleed?

As for Patty, he made up his mind that he could never forgive *her*. Now and then he would steal out upon his balcony to listen to a Schubert serenade or a Beethoven sonata in the tender stillness of a summer night, and then he would have that sensation of bleeding at the heart which melted, and unnerved, and unmanned him; but, for the most part, every sight and sound and reminiscence of her were so many fiery styptics applied to his wound, scorching up all tender emotions in one great angry pain. Outwardly he shunned her, cut her—withered her up, indeed—with his ostentatiously expressed indifference; but secretly he spent hours of the day and night dogging her from place to place, when he ought to have been at work or in his bed, merely that he might get a glimpse of her in a crowd, and some notion of what she was doing. He haunted the Exhibition with the same disregard for the legitimate attractions of that social head-centre as prevailed with the majority of its visitors, to whom it was a daily trysting-place; and there he had the doubtful satisfaction of seeing her every now and then. Once she was in the Indian Court, so fragrant with sandalwood, and she was looking with ardent eyes at gossamer muslins and embroidered cashmeres, while young Westmoreland leaned on the glass case beside her in an attitude of insufferable familiarity. It was an indication, to the jealous lover, that the woman who had elevated her sex from the rather low place that it had held in his estimation before he knew her, and made it sacred to him for her sake, was, after all, "no better than the rest of them." He had dreamed of her as a man's true helpmate and companion, able to walk hand in hand with him on the high roads of human progress, and finding her vocation and her happiness in that spiritual and intellectual fellowship; and here she was lost in the greedy contemplation of a bit of fine embroidery that had cost some poor creature his eyesight already, and was presently to cost again what would perhaps provision a starving family for a twelvemonth—just like any other ignorant and frivolous female who had sold her soul to the demon of fashion. He marched home to Myrtle Street with the zeal of the reformer (which draws its inspiration from such unsuspected sources) red-hot in his busy brain. He lit his pipe, spread out his paper, dipped his pen in the ink-bottle, and began to deal with the question of "Woman's Clothes in Relation to her Moral and Intellectual Development" in what he conceived to be a thoroughly impersonal and benevolent temper. His words should be brief, he said to himself, but they should be pregnant with suggestive truth. He would lay a light touch upon this great sore that had eaten so deeply into one member of the body politic, causing all the members to suffer with it; but he would diagnose it faithfully, without fear or favour, and show wherein it had hindered the natural advancement of the race, and to what fatal issues its unchecked development tended. It was a serious matter, that had too long been left unnoticed by the leaders of the thought of the day. "It is a *problem*," he wrote, with a splutter of his pen, charging his grievance full tilt with his most effective term; "it is, we conscientiously believe, one of the great problems of this problem-haunted and problem-fighting age—one of the wrongs that it is the mission of the reforming Modern Spirit to set right—though the subject is so inextricably entangled and wrapped up in its amusing associations that at present its naked gravity is only recognised by the philosophic few. It is all very well to make fun of it; and, indeed, it is a very good thing to make fun of it—for every reform must have a beginning, and there is no better weapon than just and judicious ridicule wherewith Reason can open her attack upon the solid and solemn front of time-honoured Prejudice. The heavy artillery of argument has no effect until the enemy has contracted an internal weakness by being made to imbibe the idea that he is absurd. A little wit, in the early stage of the campaign, is worth a deal of logic. But still there it stands—this great, relentless, crushing, cruel CUSTOM (which requires capital letters to emphasise it suitably)—and there are moments when we *can't* be witty about it—when our hearts burn within us at the spectacle of our human counterpart still, with a few bright exceptions, in the stage of intellectual childhood, while we fight the battle of the world's progress alone—"

Here the typical strong-minded female, against whom he had fulminated in frequent wrath, suddenly appeared before him, side by side with a vision of Patty in her shell-pink Cup dress; and his sword arm failed him. He paused, and laid down his pen, and leaned his head on his hand; and he was thereupon seized with a raging desire to be rich, in order that he might buy Indian embroideries for his beloved, and clothe her like a king's daughter in glorious apparel. Somehow that remarkable paper which was to inaugurate so vast a revolution in the social system never got written. At least, it did not for two or three years, and then it came forth in so mild a form that its original design was unrecognisable. (N.B.—In this latest contribution to the Dress Reform Question, women, to the peril of their immortal intellects, were invited to make themselves as pretty as they could, no hard condition being laid upon them, save that they should try to dress to please the eyes of men instead of to rival and outshine each other—that they should cultivate such sense of art and reason as might happily have survived in them—and, above all, from the high principles of religion and philanthropy, that they should abstain from bringing in new fashions violently—or, indeed, at all— leaving the spirit of beauty and the spirit of usefulness to produce their healthy offspring by the natural processes. In the composition of this paper he had the great advantage of being able to study both his own and the woman's point of view.)

The next day he went to the Exhibition again, and again he saw Patty, with no happier result than before. She was standing amongst the carriages with Mr. Smith—popularly believed to have been for years on the look-out for a pretty young second wife—who was pointing out to her the charms of a seductive little lady's phaeton, painted lake and lined with claret, with a little "dickey" for a groom behind; no doubt tempting her with the idea of driving such a one of her own some day. This was even more bitter to Paul than the former encounter. He could bear with Mr. Westmoreland, whose youth entitled him to place himself somewhat on an equality with her, and whom, moreover, his rival (as he thought himself) secretly regarded as beneath contempt; but this grey-bearded widower, whose defunct wife might almost have been her grandmother, Paul felt he could *not* bear, in any sort of conjunction with his maiden queen, who, though in such dire disgrace, was his queen always. He went hastily away that he might not see them together, and get bad thoughts into his head—such as, for instance, that Patty might be contemplating the incredible degradation of matrimony with the widower, in order to be able to drive the prettiest pony carriage in town.

He went away, but he came back again in a day or two. And then he saw her standing in the nave, with Mr. Smith again, looking at Kate Kelly, newly robed in black, and prancing up and down, in flowing hair and three-inch veil, and high heels and furbelows, putting on all sorts of airs and graces because, a few hours before, Ned had crowned his exploits and added a new distinction to the family by being hung in gaol; and she (Patty) could not only bear that shabby and shameless spectacle, but was even listening while Mr. Smith cut jokes about it—this pitiful demolishment of our imagined Kate Kelly, our Grizell Hume of the bush—and smiling at his misplaced humour. The fact being that poor Patty was aware of her lover's proximity, and was moved to unnatural and hysteric mirth in order that he might not carry away the mistaken notion that she was fretting for him. But Paul, who could see no further through a stone wall than other men, was profoundly shocked and disgusted.

And yet once more he saw his beloved, whom he tried so hard to hate. On the night of the 17th—a Wednesday night—he had yawned through an uninteresting, and to him unprofitable, session of the Assembly, dealing with such mere practical matters as the passing in committee of clauses of railway bills and rabbit bills, which neither enlivened the spirits and speeches of honourable members nor left a press critic anything in particular to criticise; and at a few minutes after midnight he was sauntering through the streets to his office, and chanced to pass the Town Hall, where the great ball of the Exhibition year was going on. It was not chance, perhaps, that led him that way—along by the chief entrance, round which carriages and cabs were standing in a dense black mass, and where even the pavements were too much crowded by loiterers to be comfortable to the pedestrian abroad on business. But it was chance that gave him a glimpse of Patty at the only moment of the night when he could have seen her. As he went by he looked up at the lighted vestibule with a sneer. He was not himself of the class which went to balls of that description—he honestly believed he had no desire to be, and that, as a worker for his bread, endowed with brains instead of money, he was at an infinite advantage over those who did; but he knew that the three Miss Kings would be numbered with the elect. He pictured Patty in gorgeous array, bare-necked and bare-armed, displaying her dancing-class acquirements for the edification of the gilded youth of the Melbourne Club, whirling round and round, with flushed cheeks and flying draperies, in the arms of young Westmoreland and his brother hosts, intoxicated with flattery and unwholesome excitement, and he made up his mind that she was only beginning the orgy of the night, and might be expected to trail home, dishevelled, when the stars grew pale in the summer dawn. However, as this surmise occurred to him it was dispelled by the vision of Mrs. Duff-Scott coming out of the light and descending the flight of steps in front of him. He recognised her majestic figure in spite of its wraps, and the sound of her voice directing the major to call the carriage up. She had a regal—or, I should rather say, vice-regal—habit of leaving a ball-room early (generally after having been amongst the first to be taken to supper), as he might have known had he known a little more about her. It was one of the trivial little customs that indicated her rank. Paul looked up at her for a moment, to make sure that she had all her party with her; and then he drew into the shadow of a group of bystanders to watch them drive off.

First came the chaperon herself, with Eleanor leaning lightly on her arm, and a couple of hosts in attendance. Eleanor was not bare-armed and necked, nor was she dishevelled; she had just refreshed herself with chicken and champagne, and was looking as composed and fair and refined as possible in her delicate white gown and unruffled yellow hair—like a tall lily, I feel I ought (and for a moment was tempted) to add, only that I know no girl ever did look like a lily since the world was made, nor ever will, no matter what the processes of evolution may come to. This pair, or quartette, were followed by Elizabeth, escorted on one side by the little major and on the other by big Mr. Yelverton. She, too, had neither tumbled draperies nor towsled head, but looked serene and dignified as usual, holding a bouquet to her breast with the one hand, and with the other thriftily guarding her skirts from contact with the pavement. But Mr. Brion took no notice of her. His attention was concentrated on his Patty, who appeared last of all, under the charge of that ubiquitous widower (whom he was beginning to hate with a deadly hatred), Mr. Smith. She was as beautiful as—whatever classical or horticultural object the reader likes to imagine—in the uncertain light and in her jealous lover's estimation, when she chanced, after stepping down to his level, to stand within a couple of yards of him to wait for the carriage. No bronze, or dead leaf, or half-ripe chestnut (to which I inadvertently likened it) was fit to be named in the same breath with that wavy hair that he could almost touch, and not all the jewellers' shops in Melbourne could have furnished a comparison worthy of her lovely eyes. She, too, was dressed in snowy, foamy, feathery white (I use these adjectives in deference to immemorial custom, and not because they accurately describe the finer qualities of Indian muslin and Mechlin lace), ruffled round her white throat and elbows in the most delicately modest fashion; and not a scrap of precious stone or metal was to be seen anywhere to vulgarise the maidenly simplicity of her attire. He had never seen her look so charming— he had never given himself so entirely to the influence of her beauty. And she stood there, so close that he could see the rise and fall of the laces on her breast with her gentle breathing, silent and patient, paying no attention to the blandishments of her cavalier, looking tired and pre-occupied, and as far as possible from the condition in which he had pictured her. Yet, when presently he emerged from his obscurity, and strode away, he felt that he had never been in such a rage of wrath against her. And why, may it be asked? What had poor Patty done this time? *She had not known that he was there beside her.* It was the greatest offence of all that she had committed, and the culmination of his wrongs.

CHAPTER XXVI
WHAT PAUL COULD NOT KNOW

It was a pity that Paul Brion, looking at Patty's charming figure in the gaslight, could not have looked into her heart. It is a pity, for us all, that there is no Palace of Truth amongst our sacred edifices, into which we could go—say, once a week—and show ourselves as we are to our neighbours and ourselves. If we could know our friends from our enemies, whom to trust and whom to shun—if we could vindicate ourselves from the false testimony of appearances in the eyes of those whom we love and by whom we desire to be loved—not to speak of larger privileges—what a different world it would be! But we can't, unfortunately. And so Paul carried away with him the impression that his Patty had become a fine lady—too fine to have any longer a thought for him—than which he had never conceived a baser calumny in his life.

Nor was he the only one who misread her superficial aspect that night. Mrs. Duff-Scott, the most discerning of women, had a fixed belief that her girls, all of them, thoroughly enjoyed their first ball. From the moment that they entered the room, a few minutes in advance of the Governor's party, received by a dozen or two of hosts drawn up in line on either side of the doorway, it was patent to her that they would do her every sort of credit; and this anticipation, at any rate, was abundantly realised. For the greater part of the evening she herself was enthroned under the gallery, which roofed a series of small drawing-rooms on this occasion, eminently adapted to matronly requirements; and from her arm-chair or sofa corner she looked out through curtains of æsthetic hues upon the pretty scene which had almost as fresh an interest for her to-night as it had for them. And no mother could have been more proud than she when one or other was taken from her side by the most eligible and satisfactory partners, or when for brief minutes they came back to her and gave her an opportunity to pull out a fold or a frill that had become disarranged, or when at intervals during their absence she caught sight of them amongst the throng, looking so distinguished in their expensively simple toilettes—those unpretending white muslins upon which she had not hesitated to spend the price of her own black velvet and Venetian point, whereof the costly richness was obvious to the least instructed observer—and evidently receiving as much homage and attention as they well knew what to do with. Now it was Eleanor going by on the arm of a naval foreigner, to whom she was chatting in that pure German (or equally pure French) that was one of her unaccountable accomplishments, or dancing as if she had danced from childhood with a more important somebody else. Now it was Patty, sitting bowered in azaleas on the steps under the great organ, while the Austrian band (bowered almost out of sight) discoursed Strauss waltzes over her head, and Mr. Smith sat in a significant attitude on the crimson carpet at her feet. And again it was Elizabeth, up in the gallery, which was a forest of fern trees to-night, sitting under the shade of the great green fronds with Mr. Yelverton, who had such an evident partiality for her society. Strange to say, Mrs. Duff-Scott, acute as she was in such matters, had never thought of Mr. Yelverton as a possible husband, and did not so think of him now—while noting his proceedings. She was taking so deep an interest in him as a philanthropist and social philosopher that she forgot he might have other and less exceptional characteristics; and she left off scheming for Elizabeth when Mr. Smith made choice of Patty, and was fully occupied in her manoeuvres and anxieties for the welfare of the younger sisters. That Patty should be the second Mrs. Smith she had quite made up her mind, and that Eleanor should be Mrs. Westmoreland was equally a settled thing. With these two affairs approaching a crisis together, she had quite enough to think of; and, with the prospect of losing two of her children so soon after becoming possessed of them, she was naturally in no hurry to deprive herself of the third. She was beginning to regard Elizabeth as destined to be her surviving comfort when the others were gone, and therefore abandoned all matrimonial projects on her behalf. Concerning Patty, the fairy godmother felt that her mind was at rest; half-a-dozen times in an hour and a half did she see the girl in some sort of association with Mr. Smith—who finally took her in to supper, and from supper to the cloak-room and carriage. For her she had reached the question of the trousseau and whom she would invite for bridesmaids. About Eleanor she was not so easy. It did not seem that Mr. Westmoreland lived up to his privileges; he did not dance with her at all, and was remarkably attentive to a plain heiress in a vulgar satin gown and diamonds. However, that was nothing. The bachelors of the club had all the roomful to entertain, and were obliged to lay aside their private preferences for the occasion. He had made his attentions to Eleanor so conspicuous that his proposal was only required as a matter of form; and Mrs. Duff-Scott felt that she would rather get the fuss of one engagement over before another came on. So, when the dissipations of the night were past, she retired from the field with a pleasant sense of almost unalloyed success, and fondly believed that her pretty *protégées* were as satisfied with the situation as she was.

But she was wrong. She was mistaken about them all—and most of all about Patty. When she first came into the room, and the fairy-land effect of the decorations burst upon her—when she passed up the lane of bachelor hosts, running the gauntlet of their respectful but admiring observation, like a young queen receiving homage—when the little major took her for a slow promenade round the hall and made her pause for a moment in front of one of the great mirrors that flanked the flowery orchestra, to show her herself in full length and in the most charming relief against her brilliant surroundings—the girl certainly did enjoy herself in a manner that bordered closely upon intoxication. She said very little, but her eyes were radiant and her whole face and figure rapturous, all her delicate soul spread out like a flower opened to the sunshine under the sensuous and artistic influences thus suddenly poured upon her. And then, after an interval of vague wonder as to what it was that was missing from the completeness of her pleasure—what it was that, being absent, spoiled the flavour of it all—there came an overpowering longing for her lover's presence and companionship, that lover without whom few balls are worth the trouble of dressing for, unless I am much mistaken. And after she found out that she wanted Paul Brion, who was not there, her gaiety became an excited restlessness, and her enjoyment of the pretty scene around her changed to passionate discontent. Why was he not there? She curled her lip in indignant scorn. Because he was poor, and a worker for his bread, and therefore was not accounted the equal of Mr. Westmoreland and Mr. Smith. She was too young and ardent to take into account the multitudes of other reasons which entirely removed it from the sphere of social grievances; like many another woman, she could see only one side of a subject at a time, and looked at that through a telescope. It seemed to her a despicably vulgar thing, and an indication of the utter rottenness of the whole fabric of society, that a high-born man of distinguished attainments should by common consent be neglected and despised simply because he was not rich. That was how she looked at it. And if Paul Brion had not been thought good enough for a select assembly, why had *she* been invited? Her answer to this question was a still more painful testimony to the generally improper state of things, and brought her to long for her own legitimate and humble environment, in which she could enjoy her independence and self-respect, and (which was the idea that tantalised her most just now) solace her lover with Beethoven sonatas when he was tired of writing, and wanted a rest. From the longing to see him in the ballroom, to have him with her as other girls had their natural counterparts, to share with her in the various delights of this great occasion, she fell to longing to go home to him—to belong to Myrtle Street and obscurity again, just as he did, and because he did. Why should she be listening to the Austrian band, eating ices and strawberries, rustling to and fro amongst the flowers and fine ladies, flaunting herself in this dazzling crowd of rich and idle people, while he plodded at his desk or smoked a lonely pipe on his balcony, out of it all, and with nothing to cheer him? Then the memory of their estrangement, and how it had come about, and how little chance there seemed now of any return to old relations and those blessed opportunities that she had so perversely thrown away, wrought upon her high-strung nerves, and inspired her with a kind of heroism of despair. Poor, thin-skinned Patty! She was sensitive to circumstances to a degree that almost merited the term "morbid," which is so convenient as a description of people of that sort. A ray of sunshine would light up the whole world, and show her her own pathway in it, shining into the farthest future with a divine effulgence of happiness and success; and the patter of rain upon the window on a dark day could beat down hope and discourage effort as effectually as if its natural mission were to bring misfortune. At one moment she would be inflated with a proud belief in herself and her own value and dignity, that gave her the strength of a giant to be and do and suffer; and then, at some little touch of failure, some discovery that she was mortal and a woman liable to blunder, as were other women, she would collapse into nothing and fling herself into the abysses of shame and self-condemnation as a worthless and useless thing. When this happened, her only chance of rescue and restoration in her own esteem was to do penance in some striking shape—to prove herself to herself as having some genuineness of moral substance in her, though it were only to own honestly how little it was. It was above all things necessary to her to have her own good opinion; what others thought of her was comparatively of no consequence.

She had been dancing for some time before the intercourse with Mr. Smith, that so gratified Mrs. Duff-Scott, set in. The portly widower found her fanning herself on a sofa in the neighbourhood of her chaperon, for the moment unattended by cavaliers; and, approaching her with one of the frequent little plates and spoons that were handed about, invited her favour through the medium of three colossal strawberries veiled in sugar and cream.

"I am so grieved that I am not a dancing man," he sighed as she refused his offering on the ground that she had already eaten strawberries twice; "I would ask leave to inscribe my humble name on your programme, Miss Patty."

"I don't see anything to grieve about," she replied, "in not being a dancing man. I am sure I don't want to dance. And you may inscribe your name on my programme and welcome"—holding it out to him. "It will keep other people from doing it."

The delighted old fellow felt that this was indeed meeting him half way, and he put his name down for all the available round dances that were to take place before morning, with her free permission. Then, as the band struck up for the first of them, and the people about them began to crystallise into pairs and groups, and the smart man-o'-wars men stretched their crimson rope across the hall to divide the crowd, Mr. Smith took his young lady on his arm and went off to enjoy himself. First to the buffet, crowned with noble icebergs to cool the air, and groaning with such miscellaneous refreshment that supper, in its due course, came to her as a surprise and a superfluity, where he insisted that she should support her much-tried strength (as he did his own) with a sandwich and champagne. Then up a narrow staircase to the groves above—where already sat Elizabeth in a distant and secluded bower with Mr. Yelverton, lost, apparently, to all that went on around her. Here Mr. Smith took a front seat, that the young men might see and envy him, and set himself to the improvement of his opportunity.

"And so you don't care about dancing," he remarked tenderly; "you, with these little fairy feet! I wonder why that is?"

"Because I am not used to it," said Patty, leaning her white arms on the ledge in front of her and looking down at the shining sea of heads below. "I have been brought up to other accomplishments."

"Music," he murmured; "and—and—"

"And scrubbing and sweeping, and washing and ironing, and churning and bread-making, and cleaning dirty pots and kettles," said Patty, with elaborate distinctness.

"Ha-ha!" chuckled Mr. Smith. "I should like to see you cleaning pots and kettles! Cinderella after twelve o'clock, eh?"

"Yes," said she; "you have expressed it exactly. After twelve o'clock— what time is it now?—after twelve o'clock, or it may be a little later, I shall be Cinderella again. I shall take off my glass slippers, and go back to my kitchen." And she had an impulse to rise and run round the gallery to beg Elizabeth to get permission for their return to their own lodgings after the ball; only Elizabeth seemed to be enjoying her *tête-à-tête* so much that she had not the heart to disturb her. Then she looked up at Mr. Smith, who stared at her in a puzzled and embarrassed way. "You don't seem to believe me," she said, with a defiant smile. "Did you think I was a fine lady, like all these other people?"

"I have always thought you the most lovely—the most charming—"

"Nonsense. I see you don't understand at all. So just listen, and I will tell you." Whereupon Patty proceeded to sketch herself and her domestic circumstances in what, had it been another person, would have been a simply brutal manner. She made herself out to be a Cinderella indeed, in her life and habits, a parasite, a sycophant, a jay in borrowed plumage—everything that was sordid and "low," and calculated to shock the sensibilities of a "new rich" man; making her statement with calm energy and in the most terse and expressive terms. It was her penance, and it did her good. It made her feel that she was genuine in her unworthiness, which was the great thing just now; and it made her feel, also, that she was set back in her proper place at Paul Brion's side—or, rather, at his feet. It also comforted her, for some reason, to be able, as a matter of duty, to disgust Mr. Smith.

But Mr. Smith, though he was a "new rich" man, and not given to tell people who did not know it what he had been before he got his money, was still a man, and a shrewd man too. And he was not at all disgusted. Very far, indeed, from it. This admirable honesty, so rare in a young person of her sex and charms—this touching confidence in him as a lover and a gentleman—put the crowning grace to Patty's attractions and made her irresistible. Which was not what she meant to do at all.

CHAPTER XXVII
SLIGHTED

Some hours earlier on the same evening, Eleanor, dressing for dinner and the ball in her spacious bedroom at Mrs. Duff-Scott's house, felt that *she*, at any rate, was arming herself for conquest. No misgivings of any sort troubled the serene and rather shallow waters of that young lady's mind. While her sisters were tossing to and fro in the perturbations of the tender passion, she had calmly taken her bearings, so to speak, and was sailing a straight course. She had summed up her possibilities and arranged her programme accordingly. In short, she had made up her mind to marry Mr. Westmoreland—who, if not all that could be desired in a man and a husband, was well enough—and thereby to take a short cut to Europe, and to all those other goals towards which her feet were set. As Mr. Westmoreland himself boasted, some years afterwards, Eleanor was not a fool; and I feel sure that this negative excellence, herein displayed, will not fail to commend itself to the gentle reader of her little history.

She had made up her mind to marry Mr. Westmoreland, and to-night she meant that he should ask her. Looking at her graceful person in the long glass, with a soft smile on her face, she had no doubt of her power to draw forth that necessary question at any convenient moment. It had not taken her long to learn her power; nor had she failed to see that it had its limitations, and that possibly other and greater men might be unaffected by it. She was a very sensible young woman, but I would not have any one run off with the idea that she was mercenary and calculating in the sordid sense. No, she was not in love, like Elizabeth and Patty; but that was not her fault. And in arranging her matrimonial plans she was actuated by all sorts of tender and human motives. In the first place, she liked her admirer, who was fond of her and a good comrade, and whom she naturally invested with many ideal excellences that he did not actually possess; and she liked (as will any single woman honestly tell me that she does not?) the thought of the dignities and privileges of a wife, and of that dearer and deeper happiness that lay behind. She was in haste to snatch at them while she had the chance, lest the dreadful fate of a childless old maid should some day overtake her—as undoubtedly it did overtake the very prettiest girls sometimes. And she was in love with the prospect of wealth at her own disposal, after her narrow experiences; not from any vulgar love of luxury and display, but for the sake of the enriched life, bright and full of beauty and knowledge, that it would make possible for her sisters as well as herself. If these motives seem poor and inadequate, in comparison with the great motive of all (as no doubt they are), we must remember that they are at the bottom of a considerable proportion of the marriages of real life, and not perhaps the least successful ones. It goes against me to admit so much, but one must take things as one finds them.

Elizabeth came in to lace up her bodice—Elizabeth, whose own soft eyes were shining, and who walked across the floor with an elastic step, trailing her long robes behind her; and Eleanor vented upon her some of the fancies which were seething in her small head. "Don't we look like brides?" she said, nodding at their reflections in the glass.

"Or bridesmaids," said Elizabeth. "Brides wear silks and satins mostly, I believe."

"If they only knew it," said Eleanor reflectively, "muslin and lace are much more becoming to the complexion. When I am married, Elizabeth, I think I shall have my dress made of that 'woven dew' that we were looking at in the Exhibition the other day."

"My dear girl, when you are married you will do nothing so preposterous. Do you suppose we are always going to let Mrs. Duff-Scott squander her money on us like this? I was telling her in her room just now that we must begin to draw the line. It is *too* much. The lace on these gowns cost a little fortune. But lace is always family property, and I shall pick it off and make her take it back again. So just be very careful not to tear it, dear."

"She won't take it back," said Eleanor, fingering it delicately; "she looks on us as her children, for whom nothing is too good. And perhaps—perhaps some day we may have it in our power to do things for *her*."

"I wish I could think so. But there is no chance of that."

"How can you tell? When we are married, we may be very well off—"

"That would be to desert her, Nelly, and to cut off all our opportunities for repaying her."

"No. It would please her more than anything. We might settle down close to her—one of us, at any rate—and she could advise us about furnishing and housekeeping. To have the choosing of the colours for our drawing-rooms, and all that sort of thing, would give her ecstasies of delight."

"Bless her!" was Elizabeth's pious and fervent rejoinder.

Then Eleanor laid out her fan and gloves for the evening, and the girls went down to dinner. Patty was in the music-room, working off her excitement in one of Liszt's rhapsodies, to which Mrs. Duff-Scott was listening with critical approval—the girl very seldom putting her brilliant powers of execution to such evident proof; and the major was smiling to himself as he paced gently up and down the Persian carpeted parquet of the long drawing-room beyond, waiting for the sound of the dinner bell, and the appearance of his dear Elizabeth. As soon as she came in, he went up to her, still subtly smiling, carrying a beautiful bouquet in his hand. It was composed almost entirely of that flower which is so sweet and lovely, but so rare in Australia, the lily of the valley (and lest the reader should say it was impossible, I can tell him or her that I saw it and smelt it that very night, and in that very Melbourne ballroom where Elizabeth disported herself, with my own eyes and nose), the great cluster of white bells delicately thinned and veiled in the finest and most ethereal feathers of maiden-hair. "For you," said the major, looking at her with his sagacious eyes.

"Oh!" she cried, taking it with tremulous eagerness, and inhaling its delicious perfume in a long breath. "Real lilies of the valley, and I have never seen them before. But not for me, surely," she added; "I have already the beautiful bouquet you told the gardener to cut for me."

"You may make that over to my wife," said the major, plaintively. "I thought she was above carrying flowers about with her to parties—she used to say it was bad art—you did, my dear, so don't deny it; you told me distinctly that that was not what flowers were meant for. But she says she will have your bouquet, Elizabeth, so that you may not be afraid of hurting my feelings by taking this that is so much better. Where the fellow got it from I can't imagine. I only know of one place where lilies of the valley grow, and they are not for sale *there*."

Elizabeth looked at him with slowly-crimsoning cheeks. "What fellow?" she asked.

He returned her look with one that only Major Duff-Scott's eyes could give. "I don't know," he said softly.

"He *does* know," his wife broke in; "I can see by his manner that he knows perfectly well."

"I assure you, on my word of honour, that I don't," protested the little major, still with a distant sparkle in his quaint eyes. "It was brought to the door just now by somebody, who said it was for Miss King—that's all."

"It might be for any of them," said Mrs. Duff-Scott, slightly put out by the liberty that somebody had taken without her leave. "They are all Miss Kings to outside people. It was a very stupid way of sending it."

"Will you take it for yourself?" said Elizabeth, holding it out to her chaperon. "Let me keep my own, and you take this."

"O no," said Mrs. Duff-Scott, flinging out her hands. "That would never do. It was meant for one of you, of course—not for me. *I* think Mr. Smith sent it. It must have been either he or Mr. Westmoreland, and I fancy Mr. Westmoreland would not choose lilies of the valley, even if he could get them. I think you had better draw lots for it, pending further information."

Patty, rising from the piano with a laugh, declared that *she* would not have it, on any account. Eleanor believed that it was meant for her, and that Mr. Westmoreland had better taste than people gave him credit for; and she had a mind to put in her claim for it. But the major set her aside gently. "No," he said, "it belongs to Elizabeth. I don't know who sent it—you may shake your head at me, my dear; I can't help it if you don't believe me—but I am convinced that it is Elizabeth's lawful property."

"As if that didn't *prove* that you know!" retorted Mrs. Duff-Scott.

He was still looking at Elizabeth, who was holding her lilies of the valley to her breast. His eyes asked her whether she did not endorse his views, and when she lifted her face at the sound of the dinner bell, she satisfied him, without at all intending to do so, that she did. *She* knew that the bouquet had been sent for her.

It was carefully set into the top of a cloisonné pot in a cool corner until dinner was over, and until the girls were wrapped up and the carriage waiting for them at the hall door. Then the elder sister fetched it from the drawing-room, and carried it out into the balmy summer night, still held against her breast as if she were afraid it might be taken from her; and the younger sister gazed at it smilingly, convinced that it was Mr. Westmoreland's tribute to herself, and magnanimously determined to beg him not to let Elizabeth know it. Thus the evening began happily for both of them. And by-and-bye their carriage slowly ploughed its way to the Town Hall entrance, and they went up the stone stairs to the vestibule and the cloak-room and the ball-room, and had their names shouted out so that every ear listening for them should hear and heed, and were received by the hospitable bachelors and passed into the great hall that was so dazzlingly splendid to their unsophisticated eyes; and the first face that Eleanor was aware of was Mr. Westmoreland's, standing out solidly from the double row of them that lined the doorway. She gave him a side-long glance as she bowed and passed, and then stood by her chaperon's side in the middle of the room, and waited for him to come to her. But he did not come. She waited, and watched, and listened, with her thanks and explanations all ready, chatting smilingly to her party the while in perfect ease of mind; but, to her great surprise, she waited in vain. Perhaps he had to stand by the door till the Governor came; perhaps he had other duties to perform that kept him from her and his private pursuits; perhaps he had forgotten that he had asked her for the first dance two days ago; perhaps he had noticed her bouquet, and had supposed that she had given it away, and was offended with her. She had a serene and patient temperament, and did not allow herself to be put out; it would all be explained presently. And in the meantime the major introduced his friends to her, and she began to fill her programme rapidly.

The evening passed on. Mrs. Duff-Scott settled herself in the particular one of the series of boudoirs under the gallery that struck her as having a commanding prospect. The Governor came, the band played, the guests danced, and promenaded, and danced again; and Mr. Westmoreland was nowhere to be seen. Eleanor was beset with other partners, and thought it well to punish him by letting them forestall him as they would; and, provisionally, she captivated a couple of naval officers by her proficiency in foreign languages, and made various men happy by her graceful and gay demeanour. By-and-bye, however, she came across her recreant admirer— as she was bound to do some time. He was leaning against a pillar, his dull eyes roving over the crowd before him, evidently looking for some one. She thought he was looking for her.

"Well?" she said, archly, pausing before him, on the arm of an Exhibition commissioner with whom she was about to plunge into the intricacies of the lancers. Mr. Westmoreland looked at her with a start and in momentary confusion.

"Oh—er," he stammered, hurriedly, "*here* you are! Where have you been hiding yourself all the evening?" Then, after a pause, "Got any dances saved for me?"

"*Saved*, indeed!" she retorted. "What next? When you don't take the trouble to come and ask for them!"

"I am so engaged to-night, Miss Eleanor——"

"I see you are. Never mind—I can get on without you." She walked on a step, and turned back. "Did you send me a pretty bouquet just now?" she whispered, touching his arm. "I think you did, and it was so good of you, but there was some mistake about it—" She checked herself, seeing a blank look in his face, and blushed violently. "Oh, it was *not* you!" she exclaimed, in a shocked voice, wishing the ball-room floor would open and swallow her up.

"Really," he said, "I—I was very remiss—I'm awfully sorry." And he gave her to understand, to her profound consternation, that he had fully intended to send her a bouquet, but had forgotten it in the rush of his many important engagements.

She passed on to her lancers with a wan smile, and presently saw him, under those seductive fern trees upstairs, with the person whom he had been looking for when she accosted him. "There's Westmoreland and his old flame," remarked her then partner, a club-frequenting youth who knew all about everybody. "*He* calls her the handsomest woman out—because she's got a lot of money, I suppose. All the Westmorelands are worshippers of the golden calf, father and son—a regular set of screws the old fellows were, and he's got the family eye to the main chance. Trust him! *I* can't see anything in her; can you? She's as round as a tub, and as swarthy as a gipsy. I like women"—looking at his partner—"to be tall, and slender, and fair. That's *my* style."

This was how poor Eleanor's pleasure in her first ball was spoiled. I am aware that it looks a very poor and shabby little episode, not worthy of a chapter to itself; but then things are not always what they seem, and, as a matter of fact, the life histories of a large majority of us are made up of just such unheroic passages.

CHAPTER XXVIII
"WRITE ME AS ONE WHO
LOVES HIS FELLOW MEN"

When Elizabeth went into the room, watchfully attended by the major, who was deeply interested in her proceedings, she was perhaps the happiest woman of all that gala company. She was in love, and she was going to meet her lover—which things meant to her something different from what they mean to girls brought up in conventional habits of thought. Eve in the Garden of Eden could not have been more pure and unsophisticated, more absolutely natural, more warmly human, more blindly confiding and incautious than she; therefore she had obeyed her strongest instinct without hesitation or reserve, and had given herself up to the delight of loving without thought of cost or consequences. Where her affections were concerned she was incapable of compromise or calculation; it was only the noble and simple rectitude that was the foundation of her character and education which could "save her from herself," as we call it, and that only in the last extremity. Just now she was in the full flood-tide, and she let herself go with it without an effort. Adam's "graceful consort" could not have had a more primitive notion of what was appropriate and expected of her under the circumstances. She stood in the brilliant ball-room, without a particle of self-consciousness, in an attitude of unaffected dignity, and with a radiance of gentle happiness all over her, that made her beautiful to look at, though she was not technically beautiful. The major watched her with profound interest, reading her like an open book; he knew what was happening, and what was going to happen (he mostly did), though he had a habit of keeping his own counsel about his own discoveries. He noted her pose, which, besides being so admirably graceful, so evidently implied expectancy; the way she held her flowers to her breast, her chin just touched by the fringes of maiden-hair, while she gently turned her head from side to side. And he saw her lift her eyes to the gallery, saw at the same moment a light spread over her face that had a superficial resemblance to a smile, though her sensitive mouth never changed its expression of firm repose; and, chuckling silently to himself, he walked away to find a sofa for his wife.

Presently Mrs. Duff-Scott, suitably enthroned, and with her younger girls already carried off by her husband from her side, saw Mr. Yelverton approaching her, and rejoiced at the prospect of securing his society for herself and having the tedium of the chaperon's inactivity relieved by sensible conversation. "Ah, so you are here!" she exclaimed cordially; "I thought balls were things quite out of your line."

"So they are," he said, shaking hands with her and Elizabeth impartially, without a glance at the latter. "But I consider it a duty to investigate the customs of the country. I like to look all round when I am about it."

"Quite right. This is distinctly one of our institutions, and I am very glad you are not above taking notice of it."

"I am not above taking notice of anything, I hope."

"No, of course not. You are a true philosopher. There is no dilettantism about you. That is what I like in you," she added frankly. "Come and sit down here between Miss King and me, and talk to us. I want to know how the emigration business is getting on."

He sat down between the two ladies, Elizabeth drawing back her white skirts.

"I have been doing no business, emigration or other," he said; "I have been spending my time in pleasure."

"Is it possible? Well, I am glad to hear it. I should very much like to know what stands for pleasure with you, only it would be too rude a question."

"I have been in the country," he said, smiling.

"H—m—that's not saying much. You don't mean to tell me, I see. Talking of the country—look at Elizabeth's bouquet. Did you think we could raise lilies of the valley like those?"

He bent his head slightly to smell them. "I heard that they did grow hereabouts," he said; and his eyes and Elizabeth's met for a moment over the fragrant flowers that she held between them, while Mrs. Duff-Scott detailed the negligent circumstances of their presentation, which left it a matter of doubt where they came from and for whom they were intended.

"I want to find Mr. Smith," said she; "I fancy he can give us information."

"I don't think so," said Mr. Yelverton; "he was showing me a lily of the valley in his button-hole just now as a great rarity in these parts."

Then it flashed across Mrs. Duff-Scott that Paul Brion might have been the donor, and she said no more.

For some time the trio sat upon the sofa, and the matron and the philanthropist discussed political economy in its modern developments. They talked about emigration; they talked about protection—and wherein a promising, but inexperienced, young country was doing its best to retard the wheels of progress—as if they were at a committee meeting rather than disporting themselves at a ball. The major found partners for the younger girls, but he left Elizabeth to her devices; at least he did so for a long time—until it seemed to him that she was being neglected by her companions. Then he started across the room to rescue her from her obscurity. At the moment that he came in sight, Mr. Yelverton turned to her. "What about dancing, Miss King?" he said, quickly. "May I be allowed to do my best?"

"I cannot dance," said Elizabeth. "I began too late—I can't take to it, somehow."

"My dear," said Mrs. Duff-Scott, "that is nonsense. All you want is practice. And I am not going to allow you to become a wall-flower." She turned her head to greet some newly-arrived friends, and Mr. Yelverton rose and offered his arm to Elizabeth.

"Let us go and practise," he said, and straightway they passed down the room, threading a crowd once more, and went upstairs to the gallery, which was a primeval forest in its solitude at this comparatively early hour. "There is no reason why you should dance if you don't like it," he remarked; "we can sit here and look on." Then, when she was comfortably settled in her cushions under the fern trees, he leaned forward and touched her bouquet with a gesture that was significant of the unacknowledged but well-understood intimacy between them. "I am so glad I was able to get them for you," he said; "I wanted you to know what they were really like—when you told me how much your mother had loved them."

"I can't thank you," she replied.

"Do not," he said. "It is for me to thank you for accepting them. I wish you could see them in my garden at Yelverton. There is a dark corner between two gables of the house where they make a perfect carpet in April."

She lifted those she held to her face, and sniffed luxuriously.

"There is a room in that recess," he went on, "a lady's sitting-room. Not a very healthy spot, by the way, it is too dank and dark. It was fitted up for poor Elizabeth Leigh when my two uncles, Patrick and Kingscote, expected her to come and live there, each wanting her for his wife—so my grandmother used to say. It has never been altered, though nearly all the rest of the house has been turned inside out. I think the lilies of the valley were planted there for her. I wish you could see that room. You would like sitting by the open window—it is one of those old diamond-paned casements, and has got some interesting stained glass in it—and seeing the sun shine on the grey walls outside, and smelling the lilies in that green well that the sun cannot reach down below. It is just one of those things that would suit you."

She listened silently, gazing at the great organ opposite, towering out of the groves of flowers at its base, without seeing what it was she looked at. After a pause he went on, still leaning forward, with his arms resting on his knees. "I can think of nothing now but how much I want you to see and know everything that makes my life at home," he said.

"Tell me about it," she said, with the woman's instinctive desire for delay at this juncture, not because she didn't want to hear the rest, but to prolong the sweetness of anticipation; "tell me what your life at Yelverton is like."

"I have not had much of it at present," he replied, after a brief pause. "The place was let for a long while. Then, when I took it over again, I made it into a sort of convalescent home, and training-place, and general starting-point for girls and children—*protégées* of my friend who does slumming in the orthodox way. Though he disapproves of me he makes use of me, and, of course, I don't disapprove of him, and am very glad to help him. The house is too big for me alone, and it seems the best use I can put it to. Of course I keep control of it; I take the poor things in on the condition that they are to be disciplined after my system and not his—his may be the best, but they don't enjoy it as they do mine—and when I am at home I run down once a week or so to see how they are getting on."

"And how is it now?"

"Now the house is just packed, I believe, from top to bottom. I got a letter a few days ago from my faithful lieutenant, who looks after things for me, to say that it couldn't hold many more, and that the funds of the institution are stretched to their utmost capacity to provide supplies."

"The funds? Oh, you must certainly use that other money now!"

"Yes, I shall use it now. I have, indeed, already appropriated a small instalment. I told Le Breton to draw on it, rather than let one child go that we could take—rather than let one opportunity be lost."

"You have other people working with you, then?"

"A good many—yes, and a very miscellaneous lot you would think them. Le Breton is the one I trust as I do myself. I could not have been here now if it had not been for him. He is my right hand."

"Who is he?" she asked, fascinated, in spite of her preoccupations, by this sketch of a life that had really found its mission in the world, and one so beneficent and so satisfying.

"He is a very interesting man," said Mr. Yelverton, who still leaned towards her, touching her flowers occasionally with a tender audacity; "a man to respect and admire—a brave man who would have been burnt at the stake had he lived a few centuries ago. He was once a clergyman, but he gave that up."

"He gave it up!" repeated Elizabeth, who had read "Thomas à Kempis" and the *Christian Year* daily since she was a child, as her mother had done before her.

"He couldn't stand it," said Mr. Yelverton, simply. "You see he was a man with a very literal, and straight-going, and independent mind—a mind that could nohow bend itself to the necessities of the case. I don't suppose he ever really gave himself up out of his own control, but, at any rate, when he got to know the world and the kind of time that we had come to, he couldn't pretend to shut his eyes. He couldn't make-believe that he was all the same as he had been when a mere lad of three-and-twenty, and that nothing had happened to change things while he had been learning and growing. And once he fell out with his conscience there was no patching up the breach with compromises for *him*. He tried it, poor fellow—he had a tough tussle before he gave in. It was a great step to take, you know—a martyrdom with all the pain and none of the glory—that nobody could sympathise with or understand."

Elizabeth was sitting very still, watching with unseeing eyes the glitter of a conspicuous diamond tiara in the moving crowd below. She, at any rate, could neither sympathise nor understand.

"He was in the thick of his troubles when I first met him," Mr. Yelverton went on. "He was working hard in one of the East End parishes, doing his level best, as the Yankees say, and tormented all the time, not only by his own scruples and self-accusations, but by a perfect hornet's nest of ecclesiastical persecutors. I said to him. 'Be an honest man, and give up being a parson—'"

"Isn't it possible to be *both?*" Elizabeth broke in.

"No doubt it is. But it was not possible for him. Seeing that, I advised him to let go, and leave those that could to hold on—as I am glad they do hold on, for we want the brake down at the rate we are going. He was in agonies of dread about the future, because he had a wife and children, so I offered him a salary equal to the emoluments of his living to come and work with me. 'You and I will do what good we can together,' I said, 'without pretending to be anything more than what we *know* we are.' And so he cast in his lot with me, and we have worked together ever since. They call him all sorts of bad names, but he doesn't care—at least not much. It is such a relief to him to be able to hold his head up as a free man—and he does work with such a zest compared to what he did!"

"And you," said Elizabeth, drawing short breaths, "what are you?—are you a Dissenter, too?"

"Very much so, I think," he said, smiling at a term that to him, an Englishman, was obsolete, while to her, an Australian born, it had still its ancient British significance (for she had been born and reared in her hermit home, the devoutest of English-churchwomen).

"And yet, in one sense, no one could be less so."

"But *what* are you?" she urged, suddenly revealing to him that she was frightened by this ambiguity.

"Really, I don't know," he replied, looking at her gravely. "I think if I had to label my religious faith in the usual way, with a motto, I should say I was a Humanitarian. The word has been a good deal battered about and spoiled, but it expresses my creed better than any other."

"A Humanitarian!" she ejaculated with a cold and sinking heart. "Is that all?" To her, in such a connection, it was but another word for an infidel.

CHAPTER XXIX
PATTY CONFESSES

A little group of their male attendants stood in the lobby, while Mrs. Duff-Scott and the girls put on their wraps in the cloak-room. When the ladies reappeared, they fell into the order in which Paul, unseen in the shadows of the street, saw them descend the steps to the pavement.

"May I come and see you to-morrow morning?" asked Mr. Yelverton of Elizabeth, whom he especially escorted.

"Not—not to-morrow," she replied. "We shall be at Myrtle Street, and we never receive any visitors there."

"At Myrtle Street!" exclaimed the major, who also walked beside her. "Surely you are not going to run off to Myrtle Street to-morrow?"

"We are going there now," said she, "if we can get in. Mrs. Duff-Scott knows."

"Let them alone," said the chaperon, looking back over her shoulder. "If they have a fancy to go home they shall go. I won't have them persuaded." She was as reluctant to leave them at Myrtle Street as the major could be, but she carefully abstained, as she always did, from interfering with their wishes when nothing of importance was involved. She was wise enough to know that she would have the stronger hold on them by seeming to leave them their liberty.

They were put into the carriage by their attentive cavaliers, the major taking his now frequent box seat in order to accompany them; and Mr. Smith and Mr. Yelverton were left standing on the pavement. Arrived at Myrtle Street, it was found that the house was still open, and the girls bade the elder couple an effusively affectionate and compunctious good-night.

"And when shall I see you again?" Mrs. Duff-Scott inquired, with a carefully composed smile and cheerful air.

"To-morrow," said Elizabeth, eagerly; "to-morrow, of course, some of us will come." All three girls had a painful feeling that they were ungrateful, while under obligations to be grateful, in spite of their friend's effort to prevent it, as they stood a moment in the warm night at their street door, and watched the carriage roll away. And yet they were so glad to be on their own "tauri" to-night—even Eleanor, who had grown more out of tune with the old frugal life than any of them.

They were let in by the ground-floor landlady, with whom they chatted for a few minutes, arranging about the materials for their breakfast; then they went upstairs to their lonely little bedrooms, where they lit their candles and began at once to prepare for bed. They were dead tired, they said, and wanted to sleep and not to talk.

But a full hour after their separation for the night, each one was as wide awake as she had been all day. Elizabeth was kneeling on the floor by her bedside, still half-dressed—she had not changed her attitude for a long time, though the undulations of her body showed how far from passive rest she was—when Patty, clothed only in her night-gown, crept in, making no noise with her bare feet.

"Elizabeth," she whispered, laying her hand on her sister's shoulder, "are you asleep?—or are you saying your prayers?"

Elizabeth, startled, lifted up her head, and disclosed to Patty's gaze in the candle-light a pale, and strained, and careworn face, "I was saying my prayers," she replied, with a dazed look. "Why are you out of bed, my darling? What is the matter?"

"That is what I want to know," said Patty, sitting down on the bed. "What is the matter with us all? What has come to us? Nelly has been crying ever since I put the light out—she thought I couldn't hear her, but she was mistaken—sobbing and sniffing under the bedclothes, and blowing her nose in that elaborately cautious way—"

"Oh, poor, dear child!" interrupted the maternal elder sister, making a start towards the door.

"No, don't go to her," said Patty, putting out her hand; "leave her alone—she is quiet now. Besides, you couldn't do her any good. Do you know what she is fretting about? Because Mr. Westmoreland has been neglecting her. Would you believe it? She is caring about it, after all—and we thought it was only fun. She doesn't care about *him*, she couldn't do that—"

"We can't tell," interrupted Elizabeth. "It is not for us to say. Perhaps she does, poor child!"

"Oh, she *couldn't*," Patty scornfully insisted. "That is quite impossible. No, she has got fond of this life that we are living now with Mrs. Duff-

Scott—I have seen it, how it has laid hold of her—and she would like to marry him so that she could have it always. That is what *she* has come to. Oh, Elizabeth, don't you wish we had gone to Europe at the very first, and never come to Melbourne at all!" Here Patty herself broke down, and uttered a little shaking, hysterical sob. "Everything seems to be going wrong with us here! It does not look so, I know, but at the bottom of my heart I feel it. Why did we turn aside to waste and spoil ourselves like this, instead of going on to the life that we had laid out—a real life, that we should never have had to be ashamed of?"

Elizabeth was silent for a few minutes, soothing her sister's excitement with maternal caresses, and at the same time thinking with all her might. "We must try not to get confused," she said presently. "Life is life, you know, Patty, wherever you are—all the other things are incidental. And we need not try to struggle with everything at once. I think we have done our best, when we have had anything to do—any serious step to take—since we came to Melbourne; and in Europe we could have done no more. It seemed right to please Mrs. Duff-Scott, and to accept such a treasure as her friendship when it came to us in what seemed such a providential way—did it not? It seemed so to me. It would have been ungenerous to have held out against her—and we were always a little given to be too proud of standing alone. It makes her happy to have us. I don't know what work we could have done that would have been more profitable than that. Patty"—after another thoughtful pause—"I don't think it is that *things* are going wrong, dear. It is only that we have to manage them, and to steer our way, and to take care of ourselves, and that is so trying and perplexing. God knows *I* find it difficult! So, I suppose, does everyone."

"You, Elizabeth? *You* always seem to know what is right. And you are so good that you never ought to have troubles."

"If Nelly is susceptible to such a temptation as Mr. Westmoreland—Mr. Westmoreland, because he is rich—she would not have gone far with us, in any case," Elizabeth went on, putting aside the allusion to herself. "Europe would not have strengthened her. It would have been all the same. While, as for you, my darling—"

"I—I!" broke in Patty excitedly. "I should have been happy now, and not as I am! I should have been saved from making a fool of myself if I had gone to Europe! I should have been worth something, and able to do something, there!"

"How can you tell, dear child? And why do you suppose you have been foolish? *I* don't think so. On the contrary, it has often seemed to me that you have been the sensible one of us all."

"O, Elizabeth, don't laugh at me!" wailed Patty, reproachfully.

"I laugh at you, my darling! What an idea! I mean it, every word. You see everything in a distorted and exaggerated way just now, because you are tired and your nerves are over-wrought. You are not yourself to-night, Patty. You will cheer up—we shall all cheer up—when we have had a good sleep and a little quiet time to think things over."

"No, I am not myself, indeed," assented Patty, with moody passion. "I am not myself at all—to be made to feel so weak and miserable!" She put her face down in her hands and began to cry with more abandonment at the thought of how weak she had become.

"But Patty, dearest, there must be something the matter with you," her motherly elder sister cried, much distressed by this abnormal symptom. "Are you feeling ill? Don't frighten me like this."

The girl laid her head upon her sister's shoulder, and there let herself loose from all restraint. "You *know* what is the matter," she sobbed; "you know as well as I do what is the matter—that it is Paul Brion who worries me so and makes me so utterly wretched."

"Paul Brion! *He* worry you, Patty—*he* make you wretched?"

"You have always been delicate and considerate, Elizabeth—you have never said anything—but I know you know all about it, and how spoiled I am, and how spoiled everything is because of him. I hate to talk of it—I can't bear even you to see that I am fretting about him—but I can't help it! and I know you understand. When I have had just one good cry," she concluded, with a fresh and violent burst of tears, "perhaps I shall get on better."

Elizabeth stared at the wall over her sister's head in dumb amazement, evidently not deserving the credit for perspicacity accorded to her. "Do you mean," she said slowly, "do you really mean—"

"Yes," sobbed Patty, desperate, for the moment dead to shame.

"Oh, how blind—how wickedly blind—how stupid—how selfish I have been!" Elizabeth exclaimed, after another pause in which to collect her shocked and bewildered faculties. "I never dreamt about it, my darling— never, for a single moment. I thought—I always had the settled impression that you did not like him."

"I don't like him," said Patty, fiercely, lifting herself up. "I love him—I *love* him! I must say it right out once, if I never speak another word," and she bent her head back a little, and stretched out her arms with an indescribable gesture as if she saw him standing before her. "He is a man—a real, true, strong man—who works, and thinks, and lives—lives! It is all serious with him, as I wanted it to be with me—and I *might* have been worthy of him! A little while ago we were so near to each other—so near that we almost *touched*—and now no two people could be farther apart. I have done him wrong—I have been a wicked fool, but I am punished for it out of all proportion. *He* flirt with a married woman! What could I have been dreaming of? Oh, how *disgusting* I must be to have allowed such an idea to come into my head! And yet it was only a little thing, Elizabeth, when you come to think of it relatively—the only time I ever really did him injustice, and it was only for a moment. No one can always do what is right and fair without making a mistake sometimes—it was just a mistake for want of thinking. But it has taken him from me as completely as if I had committed suicide, and was dead and buried and done with. It has made him *hate* me. No wonder! If he cared about me, I wouldn't be too proud to beg his pardon, but he doesn't—he doesn't! And so I must face it out, or else he will think I am running after him, and he will despise me more than he does already."

"But if he was doing no harm," said Elizabeth, soothingly, "he could not suppose that you thought he was."

"No," said Patty, "he will never think I was so disgusting as to think *that* of him. But it is as bad as if he did. That at least was a great, outrageous, downright wrong, worth fighting about, and not the pitiful shabby thing that it appears to him. For, of course, he thinks I did it because I was too grand to notice him while I was wearing a fine dress and swelling about with great people. It never occurred to me that it would be possible for him or anybody to suspect me of *that*," said Patty, proudly, drawing herself up; "but afterwards I saw that he could not help doing it. And ever since then it has been getting worse and worse—everything has seemed to point to its being so. Haven't you noticed? I never see him except I am with people who *are* above noticing him; and Mr. Smith—oh, what I have suffered from Mr. Smith to-night, Elizabeth!—has all this time been thinking I was going to marry him, and I can see now how it must have looked to other people as if I was. Just think of it!"—with a gesture of intense disgust. "As if any girl could stoop to that, after having had such a contrast before her eyes! No wonder he hates me and despises me—no wonder he looks at me as if I were the dirt beneath his feet. I wish I were," she added, with reckless passion; "oh, my dear love, I only wish I were!"

When she was about it, Patty cleansed her stuffed bosom thoroughly. It was not her way to do things by halves. She rhapsodised about her love and her lover with a wild extravagance that was proportionate to the strained reserve and restraint that she had so long put upon her emotions. After which came the inevitable reaction. The fit being over, she braced herself up again, and was twice as strong-minded and self-sufficient as before. When the morning came, and she and Elizabeth busied themselves with housework—Eleanor being relegated to the sofa with a sick headache—the girl who had dissolved herself in tears and given way to temporary insanity, as she chose herself to call it, so recently, was bright, and brusque, and cheerful, in spite of sultry weather; and not only did she pretend, even to her confidante, that the young man on the other side of the wall had no place in her thoughts, but she hardened her heart to adamant against *him*, for having been the cause of her humiliating lapse from dignity. It was quite a lucky chance, indeed, that she did not straightway go and accept the hand and fortune of Mr. Smith, by way of making reparation for the outrage committed vicariously by Paul Brion on her self-respect.

CHAPTER XXX
THE OLD AND THE NEW

The weather was scorchingly hot and a thunderstorm brewing when the girls sat down to their frugal lunch at mid-day. It was composed of bread and butter and pickled fish, for which, under the circumstances, they had not appetite enough. They trifled with the homely viands for awhile, in a manner quite unusual with them, in whatever state of the atmosphere; and then they said they would "make up" at tea time, if weather permitted, and cleared the table. Eleanor was sent to lie down in her room, Patty volunteered to read a pleasant novel to the invalid, and Elizabeth put on her bonnet to pay her promised visit to Mrs. Duff-Scott.

She found her friend in the cool music-room, standing by the piano, on which some loose white sheets were scattered. The major sat on a sofa, surveying the energetic woman with a sad and pensive smile.

"Are you looking over new music?" asked Elizabeth, as she walked in.

"O my dear, is that you? How good of you to venture out in this heat!— but I knew you would," exclaimed the lady of the house, coming forward with outstretched arms of welcome. "Music, did you say?—O *dear* no!" as if music were the last thing likely to interest her. "It is something of far more importance."

"Yelverton has been here," said the major, sadly; "and he has been sketching some plans for Whitechapel cottages. My wife thinks they are most artistic."

"So they are," she insisted, hardly, "though I don't believe I used the word; for things are artistic when they are suitable for the purpose they are meant for, and only pretend to be what they are. Look at this, Elizabeth. You see it is of no use to build Peabody houses in these frightfully low neighbourhoods, where half-starved creatures are packed together like herrings in a barrel—Mr. Yelverton has explained that quite clearly. The better class of poor come to live in them, and the poorest of all are worse off instead of better, because they have less room than they had before. You *must* take into consideration that there is only a certain amount of space, and if you build model lodgings here, and a school there, and a new street somewhere else, you do good, of course, but you herd the poor street-hawkers and people of that class more and more thickly into their wretched dens, where they haven't enough room to breathe as it is—"

"I think I'll go, my dear, if you'll excuse me," interrupted the major, humbly, in tones of deep dejection.

"And therefore," proceeded Mrs. Duff-Scott, taking no notice of her husband, "the proper and reasonable thing to do—if you want to help those who are most in need of help—is to let fine schemes alone. Mr. Yelverton expects to come into a large property soon, and he means to buy into those wretched neighbourhoods, where he can, and to build for one-room tenants—for cheapness and low rents. He will get about four per cent. on his money, but that he will use to improve with—I mean for putting them in the way of sanitary habits, poor creatures. He makes a great point of teaching them sanitation. He seems to think more of that than about teaching them the Bible, and really one can hardly wonder at it when one sees the frightful depravity and general demoralisation that come of ignorance and stupidity in those matters—and he sees so much of it. He seems to be always rooting about in those sewers and dunghills, as he calls them—he is rather addicted to strong expressions, if you notice—and turning things out from the very bottom. He is queer in some of his notions, but he is a good man, Elizabeth. One can forgive him his little crotchets, for the sake of all the good he does—it must be incalculable! He shrinks from nothing, and spends himself trying to better the things that are so bad that most people feel there is nothing for it but to shut their eyes to them—without making any fuss about it either, or setting himself up for a saint. Oh!" exclaimed Mrs. Duff-Scott, throwing a contemptuous glance around her museum of precious curiosities, "how inconceivably petty and selfish it seems to care for rubbish like this, when there are such miseries in the world that we might lighten, as he does, if we would only set ourselves to it in the same spirit."

Rubbish!—those priceless pots and plates, those brasses and ivories and enamels, those oriental carpets and tapestries, those unique miscellaneous relics of the mediæval prime! Truly the Cause of Humanity had taken hold of Mrs. Duff-Scott at last.

She sat down in an arm-chair, having invited Elizabeth to take off her hat and make herself as comfortable as the state of the weather permitted, and began to wave a large fan to and fro while she looked into vacant space with shining eyes.

"He is a strange man," she said musingly. "A most interesting, admirable man, but full of queer ideas—not at all like any man I ever met before. He has been lunching with us, Elizabeth—he came quite early—and we have had an immense deal of talk. I wish you had been here to listen to him—though I don't know that it would have been very good for you, either. He is extremely free, and what you might call revolutionary, in his opinions; he treats the most sacred subjects as if they were to be judged and criticised like common subjects. He talks of the religions of the world, for instance, as if they were all on the same foundation, and calls the Bible our Veda or Koran—says they are all alike inspired writings because they respectively express the religious spirit, craving for knowledge of the mystery of life and the unseen, that is an integral part of man's nature, and universal in all races, though developed according to circumstances. He says all mankind are children of God, and brothers, and that he declines to make invidious distinctions. And personal religion to him seems nothing more than the most rudimentary morality—simply to speak the truth and to be unselfish—just as to be selfish or untrue are the only sins he will acknowledge that we are responsible for out of the long catalogue of sins that stain this unhappy world. He won't call it an unhappy world, by the way, in spite of the cruel things he sees; he is the most optimistic of unbelievers. It will all come right some day—and our time will be called the dark ages by our remote descendants. Ever since men and women came first, they have been getting better and higher—the world increases in human goodness steadily, and will go on doing so as long as it is a world—and that because of the natural instincts and aspirations of human nature, and not from what we have always supposed all our improvement came from—rather in spite of that, indeed."

Mrs. Duff-Scott poured out this information, which had been seething in her active mind, volubly and with a desire to relieve herself to some one; but here she checked herself, feeling that she had better have left it all unsaid, not less for Elizabeth's sake than for her own. She got up out of her seat and began to pace about the room with a restless air. She was genuinely troubled. It was as if a window in a closed chamber had been opened, letting in a too strong wind that was blowing the delicate furniture all about; now, with the woman's instinctive timidity and fear (that may be less a weakness than a safeguard), she was eager to shut it to again, though suspecting that it might be too late to repair the damage done. Now that she took time to think about it, she felt particularly guilty on Elizabeth's account, who had not had her experience, and was not furnished with her ripe judgment and powers of discrimination as a preservative against the danger of contact with heterodox ideas.

"I ought not to repeat such things," she exclaimed, vexedly, beginning to gather up the plans of the Whitechapel cottages, but observing only her companion's strained and wistful face. "The mere independent hypotheses and speculations of one man, when no two seem ever to think alike! I suppose those who study ancient history and literatures, and the sciences generally, get into the habit of pulling things to pieces—"

"Those who learn most *ought* to know most," suggested Elizabeth.

"They ought, my dear; but it doesn't follow."

"Not when they are so earnest in trying to find out?"

"No; that very earnestness is against them—they over-reach themselves. They get confused, too, with learning so much, and mixing so many things up together." Mrs. Duff-Scott was a little reckless as to means so long as she could compass the desired end—which was the shutting of that metaphorical window which she had incautiously set (or left) open.

"Well, he believes in God—that all men are God's children," the girl continued, clinging where she could. "That seems like religion to me—it is a good and loving way to think of God, that He gave His spirit to all alike from the beginning—that He is so just and kind to all, and not only to a few."

"Yes, he believes in God. He believes in the Bible, too, in a sort of a way. He says he would have the lessons of the New Testament and the life of Christ disseminated far and wide, but not as they are now, with the moral left out, and not as if those who wrote them were wise enough for all time. But, whatever his beliefs may be," said Mrs. Duff-Scott, "they are not what will satisfy us, Elizabeth. You and I must hold fast to our faith in Christ, dear child, or I don't know what would become of us. We will let 'whys' alone—we will not trouble ourselves to try and find out mysteries that no doubt are wisely withheld from us, and that anyhow we should never be able to understand."

Here the servant entered with a gliding step, opened a little Sutherland table before his mistress's chair, spread the æsthetic cloth, and set out the dainty tea service. Outside the storm had burst, and was now spending itself and cooling the hot air in a steady shower that made a rushing sound on the gravel. Mrs. Duff-Scott, who had reseated herself, leant back silently with an air of reaction after her strong emotion in the expression of her handsome face and form, and Elizabeth mechanically got up to pour out the tea. Presently, as still in silence they began to sip and munch their afternoon repast, the girl saw on the piano near which she stood a photograph that arrested her attention. "What is this?" she asked. "Did he bring this too?" It was a copy of Luke Fildes' picture of "The Casuals." Mrs. Duff-Scott took it from her hand.

"No, it is mine," she said. "I have had it here for some time, in a portfolio amongst others, and never took any particular notice of it. I just had an idea that it was an unpleasant and disagreeable subject. I never gave it a thought—what it really meant—until this morning, when he was talking to me, and happened to mention it. I remembered that I had it, and I got it out to look at it. Oh!" setting down her teacup and holding it fairly in both hands before her—"isn't it a terrible sermon? Isn't it heartbreaking to think that it is *true?* And he says the truth is understated."

Like the great Buddha, when he returned from his first excursion beyond his palace gates, Elizabeth's mind was temporarily darkened by the new knowledge of the world that she was acquiring, and she looked at the picture with a fast-beating heart. "Sphinxes set up against that dead wall," she quoted from a little printed foot-note, "and none likely to be at the pains of solving them until the general overthrow." She was leaning over her friend's shoulder, and the tears were dropping from her eyes.

"They are Dickens's words," said Mrs. Duff-Scott.

"Why is it like this, I wonder?" the girl murmured, after a long, impressive pause. "We must not think it is God's fault—that can't be. It must be somebody else's fault. It cannot have been *intended* that a great part of the human race should be forced, from no fault of their own, to accept such a cruel lot—to be made to starve, when so many roll in riches—to be driven to crime because they cannot help it—to be driven to *hell* when they *need not* have gone there—if there is such a place—if there is any truth in what we have been taught. But"—with a kind of sad indignation—"if religion has been doing its best for ever so many centuries, and this is all that there is to show for it—doesn't that seem to say that *he* may be right, and that religion has been altogether misinterpreted—that we have all along been making mistakes—" She checked herself, with a feeling of dismay at her own words; and Mrs. Duff-Scott made haste to put away the picture, evidently much disturbed. Both women had taken the "short views" of life so often advocated, not from philosophical choice, but from disinclination, and perhaps inability, to take long ones; and they had the ordinary woman's conception of religion as exclusively an ecclesiastical matter. This rough disturbance of old habits of thought and sentiments of reverence and duty was very alarming; but while Elizabeth was rashly confident, because she was inexperienced, and because she longed to put faith in her beloved, Mrs. Duff-Scott was seized with a sort of panic of remorseful misgiving. To shut that window had become an absolute necessity, no matter by what means.

"My dear," she said, in desperation, "whatever you do, you must not begin to ask questions of that sort. We can never find out the answers, and it leads to endless trouble. God's ways are not as our ways—we are not in the secrets of His providence. It is for us to trust Him to know what is best. If you admit one doubt, Elizabeth, you will see that everything will go. Thousands are finding that out now-a-days, to their bitter cost. Indeed, I don't know what we are coming to—the 'general overthrow,' I suppose. I hope I, at any rate, shall not live to see it. What would life be worth to us—*any* of us, even the best off—if we lost our faith in God and our hope of immortality? Just try to imagine it for a moment."

Elizabeth looked at her mentor, who had again risen and was walking about the room. The girl's eyes were full of solemn thought. "Not much," she replied, gravely. "But I was never afraid of losing faith in God."

"It is best to be afraid," replied Mrs. Duff-Scott, with decision. "It is best not to run into temptation. Don't think about these difficulties, Elizabeth—leave them, leave them. You would only unsettle yourself and become wretched and discontented, and you would never be any the wiser."

Elizabeth thought over this for a few minutes, while Mrs. Duff-Scott mechanically took up a brass lota and dusted it with her handkerchief.

"Then you think one ought not to read books, or to talk to people—to try to find out the ground one stands on——"

"No, no, no—let it alone altogether. You know the ground you ought to stand on quite well. You don't want to see where you are if you can feel that God is with you. Blessed are they that have not seen and yet have believed!" she ended in a voice broken with strong feeling, clasping her hands with a little fervent, prayerful gesture.

Elizabeth drew a long breath, and in her turn began to walk restlessly up and down the room. She had one more question to ask, but the asking of it almost choked her. "Then you would say—I suppose you think it would be wrong—for one who was a believer to marry one who was not?—however good, and noble, and useful he or she might be—however religious *practically*—however blameless in character?"

Mrs. Duff-Scott, forgetting for the moment that there was such a person as Mr. Yelverton in the world, sat down once more in an arm-chair, and addressed herself to the proposition on its abstract merits. She had worked herself up, by this time, into a state of highly fervid orthodoxy. Her hour of weakness was past, and she was fain to put forth and test her reserves of strength. Wherefore she had very clear views as to the iniquity of an unequal yoking together with unbelievers, and the peril of touching the unclean thing; and she stated them plainly and with all her wonted incisive vigour.

When it was all over, Elizabeth put on her hat and walked back through the pattering rain to Myrtle Street, heavy-hearted and heavy-footed, as if a weight of twenty years had been laid on her since the morning.

"Patty," she said, when her sister, warmly welcoming her return, exclaimed at her pale face and weary air, and made her take the sofa that Eleanor had vacated, "Patty, let us go away for a few weeks, shall we? I want a breath of fresh air, and to be in peace and quiet for a little, to think things over."

"So do I," said Patty. "So does Nelly. Let us write to Sam Dunn to find us lodgings."

CHAPTER XXXI
IN RETREAT

"Is it possible that we have only been away for nine months?" murmured Elizabeth, as the little steamer worked its way up to the well-remembered jetty, and she looked once more on surf and headland, island rock and scattered township, lying under the desolate moorlands along the shore. "Doesn't it seem *at least* nine years?"

"Or ninety," replied Patty. "I feel like a new generation. How exactly the same everything is! Here they have all been going on as they always did. There is Mrs. Dunn, dear old woman!—in the identical gown that she had on the day we went away."

Everything was the same, but they were incredibly changed. There was no sleeping on the nose of the vessel now; no shrinking from association with their fellow-passengers. The skipper touched his cap to them, which he never used to do in the old times; and the idlers on the pier, when the vessel came in, stared at them as if they had indeed been away for ninety years. Mrs. Dunn took in at a glance the details of their travelling costumes, which were of a cut and quality not often seen in those parts; and, woman-like, straightway readjusted her smiles and manners, unconsciously becoming at once more effusive and more respectful than (with the ancient waterproofs in her mind's eye) she had prepared herself to be. But Sam saw only the three fair faces, that were to him as unchanged as his own heart; and he launched himself fearlessly into the boat as soon as it came alongside, with horny hand outstretched, and boisterous welcomes.

"So y'are come back again?" he cried, "and darn glad I am to see yer, and no mistake." He added a great deal more in the way of greeting and congratulation before he got them up the landing stage and into the capacious arms of Mrs. Dunn—who was quite agreeably surprised to be hugged and kissed by three such fashionable young ladies. Then he proceeded to business with a triumphant air. "Now, Miss 'Lisbeth, yer see here's the cart—that's for the luggage. Me and the old hoss is going to take it straight up. And there is a buggy awaiting for you. And Mr. Brion told me to say as he was sorry he couldn't come down to the boat, but it's court day, yer see, and he's got a case on, and he's obliged to stop till he's done wi' that."

"Oh," exclaimed Elizabeth, hastily, "did you tell Mr. Brion that we were coming?"

"Why, of course, miss. I went and told him the very first thing—'twas only right, him being such a friend—your only friend here, as one may say."

"Oh, no, Sam, we have you."

"Me!"—with scornful humility—"I'm nothing. Yes, of course I went and told him. And he wouldn't let us get no lodgings; he said you was just to go and stay wi' Mrs. Harris and him. He would ha' wrote to tell yer, but there worn't time."

"And much more comfortable you'll be than at them lodging places," put in Mrs. Dunn. "There's nothing empty now that's at all fit for you. The season is just a-coming on, you see, and we're like to be pretty full this year."

"But we wanted to be away from the town, Mrs. Dunn."

"And so you will be away from the town. Why, bless me, you can't be much farther away—to be anywhere at all—than up there," pointing to the headland where their old home was dimly visible in the November sunshine. "There's only Mrs. Harris and the gal, and *they* won't interfere with you."

"Up *there!*" exclaimed the sisters in a breath. And Mr. and Mrs. Dunn looked with broad grins at one another.

"Well, I'm blowed!" exclaimed the fisherman. "You don't mean as Master Paul never let on about his pa and him buying the old place, do you? Why, they've had it, and the old man has been living there—he comes down every morning and goes up every night—walks both ways, he do, like a young chap—this two or three months past. Mrs. Hawkins she couldn't bear the lonesomeness of it when the winter come on, and was right down glad to get out of it. They gave Hawkins nearly double what *you* got for it. I told yer at the time that yer was a-throwing of it away."

The girls tried to look as if they had known all about it, while they digested their surprise. It was a very great surprise, almost amounting to a shock.

"And how *is* Mr. Paul?" asked Mrs. Dunn of Patty. "Dear young man, it's a long time since we've seen anything of him! I hope he's keeping his health well!"

"I think so—I hope so," said Patty gently. "He works very hard, you know, writing things for the papers. He is wanted too much to be able to take holidays like ordinary people. They couldn't get on without him."

Elizabeth turned round in astonishment: she had expected to see her sister in a blaze of wrath over Sam's unexpected communications. "I'm afraid you won't like this arrangement, dearie," she whispered. "What had we better do?"

"Oh, go—go," replied Patty, with a tremulous eagerness that she vainly tried to hide. "I don't mind it. I—I am glad to see Mr. Brion. It will be very nice to stay with him—and in our own dear old house too. Oh, I wouldn't refuse to go for anything! Besides we *can't*."

"No, I don't see how we can," acquiesced Elizabeth, cheerfully. Patty having no objection, she was delighted with the prospect.

They walked up the little pier in a group, the "hoss" following them with the reins upon his neck; and, while Elizabeth and Patty mounted the buggy provided by Mr. Brion, Eleanor gratified the old fisherman and his wife by choosing to stay with them and ride up in the cart. It was a lovely morning, just approaching noon, the sky as blue as—no, *not* as a turquoise or a sapphire—but as nothing save itself can be in a climate like ours, saturated with light and lucent colour, and giving to the sea its own but an intenser hue. I can see it all in my mind's eye—as my bodily eyes have seen it often—that dome above, that plain below, the white clouds throwing violet shadows on the water, the white gulls dipping their red legs in the shining surf and reflecting the sunlight on their white wings; but I cannot describe it. It is beyond the range of pen and ink, as of brush and pigments. As the buggy lightly climbed the steep cliff, opening the view wider at every step, the sisters sat hand in hand, leaning forward to take it all in; but they, too, said nothing—only inhaled long draughts of the delicious salt air, and felt in every invigorated fibre of them that they had done well to come. Reaching the crest of the bluff, and descending into the broken basin—or saucer, rather—in which Seaview Villa nestled, they uttered simultaneously an indignant moan at the spectacle of Mrs. Hawkins's devastations. There was the bright paint, and the whitewash, and the iron roof, and the fantastic trellis; and there was *not* the ivy that had mantled the eaves and the chimney stacks, nor the creepers that had fought so hard for existence, nor the squat verandah posts which they had bountifully embraced—nor any of the features that had made the old house distinct and characteristic.

"Never mind," said Patty, who was the first to recover herself. "It looks very smart and tidy. I daresay it wanted doing up badly. After all, I'd sooner see it look as unlike home as possible, now that it isn't home."

Mrs. Harris came out and warmly welcomed them in Mr. Brion's name. She took them into the old sitting-room, now utterly transformed, but cosy and inviting, notwithstanding, with the lawyer's substantial old leather chairs and sofas about it, and a round table in the middle set out for lunch, and the sea and sky shining in through the open verandah doors. She pressed them to have wine and cake to "stay" them till Eleanor and lunch time arrived; and she bustled about with them in their rooms—their own old bedrooms, in one of which was a collection of Paul's schoolboy books and treasures, while they took off their hats and washed their hands and faces; and was very motherly and hospitable, and made them feel still more pleased that they had come. They feasted, with fine appetites, on fish and gooseberry-fool at one o'clock, while Sam and Mrs. Dunn were entertained by the housekeeper in the kitchen; and in the afternoon, the cart and "hoss" having departed, they sat on the verandah in basket chairs, and drank tea, and idled, and enjoyed the situation thoroughly. Patty got a dog's-eared novel of Mayne Reid's from the book-case in her bedroom, and turned over the pages without reading them to look at the pencil marks and thumb stains; and Eleanor dozed and fanned herself; and Elizabeth sewed and thought. And then their host came home, riding up from the township on a fast and panting steed, quite thrown off his balance by emotion. He was abject in his apologies for having been deterred by cruel fate and business from meeting them at the steamer and conducting them in person to his house, and superfluous in expressions of delight at the honour they had conferred on him.

"And how did you leave my boy?" he asked presently, when due inquiries after their own health and welfare had been satisfied. He spoke as if they and Paul had all been living under one roof. "And when is he coming to see his old father again?"

Patty, who was sitting beside her host—"in his pocket," Nelly declared—and was simply servile in her affectionate demonstrations, undertook to describe Paul's condition and circumstances, and she implied a familiar knowledge of them which considerably astonished her sisters. She also gave the father a full history of all the son's good deeds in relation to themselves—described how he had befriended them in this and that emergency, and asserted warmly, and with a grave face, that she didn't know what they *should* have done without him.

"That's right—that's right!" said the old man, laying her hand on his knee and patting it fondly. "I was sure he would—I knew you'd find out his worth when you came to know him. We must write to him to-morrow, and tell him you have arrived safely. He doesn't know I have got you, eh? We must tell him. Perhaps we can induce him to take a little holiday himself—I am sure it is high time he had one—and join us for a few days. What do you think?"

"Oh, I am *sure* he can't come away just now," protested Patty, pale with eagerness and horror. "In the middle of the Exhibition—and a parliamentary crisis coming on—it would be quite impossible!"

"I don't know—I don't know. I fancy 'impossible' is not a word you will find in his dictionary," said the old gentleman encouragingly. "When he hears of our little arrangement, he'll want to take a hand, as the Yankees say. He won't like to be left out—no, no."

"But, dear Mr. Brion," Patty strenuously implored—for this was really a matter of life and death, "do think what a critical time it is! They never *can* spare him now."

"Then they ought to spare him. Because he is the best man they have, that is no reason why they should work him to death. They don't consider him sufficiently. He gives in to them too much. He is not a machine."

"Perhaps he would come," said Patty, "but it would be against his judgment—it would be at a heavy cost to his country—it would be just to please us—oh, don't let us tempt him to desert his post, which *no* one could fill in his absence! Don't let us unsettle and disturb him at such a time, when he is doing so much good, and when he wants his mind kept calm. Wait for a little while; he might get away for Christmas perhaps."

"But by Christmas, I am afraid, you would be gone."

"Never mind. We see him in Melbourne. And we came here to get away from all Melbourne associations."

"Well, well, we'll see. But I am afraid you will be very dull with only an old fellow like me to entertain you."

"Dull!" they all exclaimed in a breath. It was just what they wanted, to be so peaceful and quiet—and, above all things, to have him (Mr. Brion, senior) entirely to themselves.

The polite old man looked as if he were scarcely equal to the weight of the honour and pleasure they conferred upon him. He was excessively happy. As the hours and days went on, his happiness increased. His punctilious courtesy merged more and more into a familiar and paternal devotion that took all kinds of touching shapes; and he felt more and more at a loss to express adequately the tender solicitude and profound satisfaction inspired in his good old heart by the sojourn of such charming guests within his gates. To Patty he became especially attached; which was not to be wondered at, seeing how susceptible he was and how lavishly she exercised her fascinations upon him. She walked to his office with him in the morning; she walked to meet him when he came hastening back in the afternoon; she read the newspaper (containing Paul's peerless articles) to him in the evening, and mixed his modest glass of grog for him before he went to bed. In short, she made him understand what it was to have a charming and devoted daughter, though she had no design in doing so—no motive but to gratify her affection for Paul in the only way open to her. So the old gentleman was very happy—and so were they. But still it seemed to him that he must be happier than they were, and that, being a total reversal of the proper order of things, troubled him. He had a pang every morning when he wrenched himself away from them—leaving them, as he called it, alone—though loneliness was the very last sensation likely to afflict them. It seemed so inhospitable, so improper, that they should be thrown upon their own resources, and the company of a housekeeper of humble status, for the greater part of the day—that they should be without a male attendant and devotee, while a man existed who was privileged to wait on them. If only Paul had been at home! Paul would have taken them for walks, for drives, for boating excursions, for pic-nics; he would have done the honours of Seaview Villa as the best of hosts and gentlemen. However, Paul, alas! was tied to his newspaper in Melbourne, and the old man had a business that he was cruelly bound to attend to—at any rate, sometimes. But at other times he contrived to shirk his business and then he racked his brains for projects whereby he might give them pleasure.

"Let's see," he said one evening, a few days after their arrival; "I suppose you have been to the caves too often to care to go again?"

"No," said Elizabeth; "we have never been to the caves at all."

"What—living within half-a-dozen miles of them all your lives! Well, I believe there are many more like you. If they had been fifty miles away, you would have gone about once a twelvemonth."

"No, Mr. Brion; we were never in the habit of going sight-seeing. My father seldom left the house, and my mother only when necessary; and we had no one else to take us."

"Then I'll take you, and we will go to-morrow. Mrs. Harris shall pack us a basket for lunch, and we'll make a day of it. Dear, dear, what a pity Paul couldn't be here, to go with us!"

The next morning, which was brilliantly fine, brought the girls an anxiously-expected letter from Mrs. Duff-Scott. Sam Dunn, who was an occasional postman for the solitary house, delivered it, along with a present of fresh fish, while Mr. Brion was absent in the township, negotiating for a buggy and horses for his expedition. The fairy godmother had given but a grudging permission for this *villeggiatura* of theirs, and they were all relieved to have her assurance that she was not seriously vexed with them. Her envelope was inscribed to "Miss King," but the long letter enclosed was addressed to her "dearest children" collectively, tenderly inquiring how they were getting on and when they were coming back, pathetically describing her own solitude—so unlike what it was before she knew the comfort of their companionship—and detailing various items of society news. Folded in this, however, was the traditional lady's postscript, scribbled on a small half-sheet and marked "private," which Elizabeth took away to read by herself. She wondered, with a little alarm, what serious matter it was that required a confidential postscript, and this was what she read:—

"I have been thinking over our talk the other day, dear. Perhaps I spoke too strongly. One is apt to make arbitrary generalisations on the spur of the moment, and to forget how circumstances may alter cases. There is another side to the question that should not be overlooked. The believing wife or husband may be the salvation of *the other*, and when the other is *honest* and *earnest*, though *mistaken*, there is the strongest hope of this. It requires thinking of on *all* sides, my darling, and I fear I spoke without thinking enough. Consult your own heart—I am sure it will advise you well."

Elizabeth folded up the note, and put it into her pocket. Then—for she was alone in her own little bedroom—she sat down to think of it; to wonder what had reminded Mrs. Duff-Scott of their conversation the "other day"—what had induced her to temporise with the convictions which then appeared so sincere and absolute. But she could make nothing of it. It was a riddle without the key.

Then she heard the sound of buggy wheels, hurried steps on the verandah, and the voice of Mr. Brion calling her.

"My dear," said the old man when she went out to him, speaking in some haste and agitation, "I have just met at the hotel a friend of yours from Melbourne—Mr. Yelverton. He came by the coach last night. He says Mrs. Duff-Scott sent him up to see how you are getting on, and to report to her. He is going away again to-morrow, and I did not like to put off our trip, so I have asked him to join us. I hope I have not done wrong"—looking anxiously into her rapidly changing face—"I hope you won't think that I have taken a liberty, my dear."

CHAPTER XXXII
HISTORY REPEATS ITSELF

He was talking to Patty and Eleanor in the garden when Elizabeth went out to him, looking cool and colonial in a silk coat and a solar topee. The girls were chatting gaily; the old lawyer was sketching a programme of the day's proceedings, and generally doing the honours of his neighbourhood with polite vivacity. Two buggies, one single and one double, in charge of a groom from the hotel, were drawn up by the gate, and Mrs. Harris and "the gal" were busily packing them with luncheon baskets and rugs. There was a cloudless summer sky overhead—a miracle of loveliness spread out before them in the shining plain of the sea; and the delicate, fresh, salt air, tremulous with the boom of subterranean breakers, was more potent than any wine to make glad the heart of man and to give him a cheerful countenance.

Very cheerfully did Mr. Yelverton come forward to greet his beloved, albeit a little moved with the sentiment of the occasion. He had parted from her in a ball-room, with a half-spoken confession of—something that she knew all about quite as well as he did—on his lips; and he had followed her now to say the rest, and to hear what she had to reply to it. This was perfectly understood by both of them, as they shook hands, with a little conventional air of unexpectedness, and he told her that he had come at Mrs. Duff-Scott's orders.

"She could not rest," he said, gravely, "until she was sure that you had found pleasant quarters, and were comfortable. She worried about you—and so she sent me up."

"It was troubling you too much," Elizabeth murmured, evading his direct eyes, but quite unable to hide her agitation from him.

"You say that from politeness, I suppose? No, it was not troubling me at all—quite the contrary. I am delighted with my trip. And I am glad," he concluded, dropping his voice, "to see the place where you were brought up. This was your home, was it not?" He looked all round him.

"It was not like this when we were here," she replied. "The house was old then—now it is new. They have done it up."

"I see. Have you a sketch of it as it used to be? You draw, I know. Mrs. Duff-Scott has been showing me your drawings."

"Yes, I have one. It hangs in the Melbourne sitting-room."

Mr. Brion broke in upon this dialogue. "Now, my dears, I think we are all ready," he said. "Elizabeth, you and I will go in the little buggy and lead the way. Perhaps Mr. Yelverton will be good enough to take charge of the two young ladies. Will you prefer to drive yourself, Mr. Yelverton?"

Mr. Yelverton said he preferred to be driven, as he was not acquainted with the road; and Elizabeth, throned in the seat of honour in the little buggy, looked back with envious eyes to watch his arrangements for her sisters' comfort. He put Patty beside the groom on the front seat, and carefully tucked her up from the dust; and then he placed Eleanor at the back, climbed to her side, and opened a large umbrella which he held so that it protected both of them. In this order the two vehicles set forth, and for the greater part of the way, owing to the superior lightness of the smaller one, they were not within sight of each other; during which time Elizabeth was a silent listener to her host's amiable prattle, and reproaching herself for not feeling interested in it. She kept looking through the pane of glass behind her, and round the side of the hood, and wondering where the others were, and whether they were keeping the road.

"Oh, they can't miss it," was Mr. Brion's invariable comment. "They will follow our tracks. If not, the man knows our destination."

For the old lawyer was making those short cuts which are so dear to all Jehus of the bush; preferring a straight mile of heavy sand to a devious mile and a quarter of metal, and ploughing through the stiff scrub that covered the waste moors of the district rather by the sun's than by the surveyor's direction. It made the drive more interesting, of course. The bushes that rustled through the wheels and scratched the horses' legs were wonderful with wild flowers of every hue, and the orchids that were trampled into the sand, and gathered by handfuls to die in the buggy, were remarkable for their fantastic variety. And then there were lizards and butterflies, and other common objects of the country, not so easily discerned on a beaten track. But Elizabeth could not bring herself to care much for these things to-day.

They reached high land after a while, whence, looking back, they saw the other buggy crawling towards them a mile or two away, and, looking forward, saw, beyond a green and wild foreground, the brilliant sea again, with a rocky cape jutting out into it, sprinkled with a few white houses on its landward shoulder—a scene that was too beautiful, on such a morning, to be disregarded. Here the girl sat at ease, while the horses took breath, thoroughly appreciating her opportunities; wondering, not what Mr. Yelverton was doing or was going to do, but how it was that she had never been this way before. Then Mr. Brion turned and drove down the other side of the hill, and exclaimed "Here we are!" in triumph.

It was a shallow basin of a dell, in the midst of romantic glens, sandy, and full of bushes and wild flowers, and bracken and tussocky grass, and shady with tall-stemmed gum trees. As the buggy bumped and bounced into the hollow, shaving the dead logs that lay about in a manner which reflected great credit upon the lawyer's navigation, Elizabeth, feeling the cool shadows close over her head, and aware that they had reached their destination, looked all round her for the yawning cavern that she had specially come to see.

"Where are the caves?" she inquired—to Mr. Brion's intense gratification.

"Ah, where are they?" he retorted, enjoying his little joke. "Well, we have just been driving over them."

"But the mouth, I mean?"

"Oh, the mouth—the mouth is here. We were very nearly driving over that too. But we'll have lunch first, my dear, before we investigate the caves—if it's agreeable to you. I will take the horses out, and we'll find a nice place to camp before they come."

Presently the other buggy climbed over the ridge and down into the hollow; and Mr. Yelverton beheld Elizabeth kneeling amongst the bracken fronds, with the dappled sun and shade on her bare head and her blue cotton gown, busily trying to spread a table-cloth on the least uneven piece of ground that she could find, where it lay like a miniature snow-clad landscape, all hills except where the dishes weighed it to the earth. He hastened to help her as soon as he had lifted Patty and Eleanor from their seats.

"You are making yourself hot," he said, with his quiet air of authority and proprietorship. "You sit down, and let me do it. I am quite used to commissariat business, and can set a table beautifully." He took some tumblers from her hand, and, looking into her agitated face, said suddenly, "I could not help coming, Elizabeth—I could not leave it broken off like that—I wanted to know why you ran away from me—and Mrs. Duff-Scott gave me leave. You will let me talk to you presently?"

"Oh, not now—not now!" she replied, in a hurried, low tone, turning her head from side to side. "I must have time to think—"

"Time to think!" he repeated, with just a touch of reproach in his grave surprise. And he put down the tumblers carefully, got up, and walked away. Upon which, Elizabeth, reacting violently from the mood in which she had received him, had an agonising fear that he would impute her indecision to want of love for him, or insensibility to his love for her—though, till now, that had seemed an impossibility. In a few minutes he returned with her sisters and Mr. Brion, all bearing dishes and bottles, and buggy cushions and rugs; and, when the luncheon was ready, and the groom had retired to feed and water his horses, she lifted her eyes to her tall lover's face with a look that he understood far better than she did. He quietly came round from the log on which he had been about to seat himself, and laid his long limbs on the sand and bracken at her side.

"What will you have?" he asked carelessly; "roast beef and salad, or chicken pie? I can recommend the salad, which has travelled remarkably well." And all the time he was looking at her with happy contentment, a little smile under his red moustache; and her heart was beating so that she could not answer him.

The luncheon was discussed at leisure, and, as far as Mr. Brion could judge, was a highly successful entertainment. The younger girls, whatever might be going to happen to-morrow, could not help enjoying themselves to-day—could not help getting a little intoxicated with the sweetness of the summer air and the influences of the scene generally, and breaking out in fun and laughter; even Elizabeth, with her desperate anxieties, was not proof against the contagion of their good spirits now and then. The travelled stranger, who talked a great deal, was the most entertaining of guests, and the host congratulated himself continually on having added him to the party. "We only want Paul now to make it all complete," said the happy old man, as he gave Patty, who had a dreadful appetite after her long drive, a second helping of chicken pie.

When the sylvan meal was ended, and the unsightly remnants cleared away, the two men smoked a soothing cigarette under the trees, while the girls tucked up their clean gowns a little and tied handkerchiefs over their heads, and then Mr. Brion, armed with matches and a pound of candles, marched them off to see the caves. He took them but a little way from where they had camped, and disclosed in the hillside what looked like a good-sized wombat or rabbit hole. "Now, you stay here while I go and light up a bit," he said, impressively, and he straightway slid down and disappeared into the hole. They stooped and peered after him, and saw a rather muddy narrow shaft slanting down into the earth, through which the human adult could only pass "end on." The girls were rather dismayed at the prospect.

"It is a case of faith," said Mr. Yelverton. "We must trust ourselves to Mr. Brion entirely or give it up."

"We will trust Mr. Brion," said Elizabeth.

A few minutes later the old man's voice was heard from below. "Now, come along! Just creep down for a step or two, and I will reach your hand. Who is coming first?"

They looked at each other for a moment, and Patty's quick eye caught something from Mr. Yelverton's. "I will go first," she said; "and you can follow me, Nelly." And down she went, half sliding, half sitting, and when nearly out of sight stretched up her arm to steady her sister. "It's all right," she cried; "there's plenty of room. Come along!"

When they had both disappeared, Mr. Yelverton took Elizabeth's unlighted candle from her hand and put it into his pocket. "There is no need for you to be bothered with that," he said: "one will do for us." And he let himself a little way down the shaft, and put up his hand to draw her after him.

In a few seconds they stood upright, and were able, by the light of the three candles just dispersing into the interior, to see what kind of place they had come to. They were limestone caves, ramifying underground for a quarter of a mile or so in direct length, and spreading wide on either side in a labyrinth of chambers and passages. The roof was hung with a few stalactites, but mostly crusted with soft bosses, like enormous cauliflowers, that yielded to the touch; lofty in places, so that the candle-light scarcely reached it, and in places so low that one could not pass under it. The floor, if floor it could be called, was a confusion of hills and vales and black abysses, stony here, and dusty there, and wet and slippery elsewhere—altogether an uncanny place, full of weird suggestions. The enterprising and fearless Patty was far ahead, exploring on her own account, and Mr. Brion, escorting Eleanor, dwindling away visibly into a mere pin's point, before Mr. Yelverton and Elizabeth had got their candle lighted and begun their investigations. A voice came floating back to them through the immense darkness, duplicated in ever so many echoes: "Are you all right, Elizabeth?"

"Yes," shouted Mr. Yelverton instantly, like a soldier answering to the roll-call. Then he took her hand, and, holding the candle high, led her carefully in the direction of the voice. She was terribly nervous and excited by the situation, which had come upon her unawares, and she had an impulse to move on hastily, as if to join her sisters. Bat her lover held her back with a turn of his strong wrist.

"Don't hurry," he said, in a tone that revealed to her how he appreciated his opportunity, and how he would certainly turn it to account; "it is not safe in such a place as this. And you can trust *me* to take care of you as well as Mr. Brion, can't you?"

She did not answer, and he did not press the question. They crept up, and slid down, and leapt over, the dark obstructions in their devious course for a little while in silence—two lonely atoms in the vast and lifeless gloom. Fainter and fainter grew the voices in the distance—fainter and fainter the three tiny specks of light, which seemed as far away as the stars in heaven. There was something dreadful in their isolation in the black bowels of the earth, but an unspeakably poignant bliss in being thus cast away together. There was no room for thought of anything outside that.

Groping along hand in hand, they came to a chasm that yawned, bridgeless, across their path. It was about three feet wide, and perhaps it was not much deeper, but it looked like the bottomless pit, and was very terrifying. Bidding Elizabeth to wait where she was, Mr. Yelverton leaped over by himself, and, dropping some tallow on a boulder near him, fixed his candle to the rock. Then he held out his arms and called her to come to him.

For a moment she hesitated, knowing what awaited her, and then she leaped blindly, fell a little short, and knocked the candle from its insecure socket into the gulf beneath her. She uttered a sharp cry as she felt herself falling, and the next instant found herself dragged up in her lover's strong arms, and folded with a savage tenderness to his breast. *This* time he held her as if he did not mean to let her go.

"Hush!—you are quite safe," he whispered to her in the pitch darkness.

CHAPTER XXXIII
THE DRIVE HOME

The girls were boiling a kettle and making afternoon tea, while the men were getting their horses and buggy furniture together, at about four o'clock. Elizabeth was on her knees, feeding the gipsy fire with dry sticks, when Mr. Yelverton came to her with an alert step.

"I am going to drive the little buggy back," he said, "and you are coming with me. The others will start first, and we will follow."

She looked up with a startled expression that puzzled and disappointed him.

"*What!*" he exclaimed, "do you mean to say that you would rather not?"

"Oh, no, I did not mean that," she faltered hurriedly; and into her averted face, which had been deadly pale since she came out of the cave, the hot blood flushed, remembering how long he and she had stood there together in a profound and breathless solitude, and the very blackest night that ever Egypt knew, after he took her into his arms, and before they remembered that they had a second candle and matches to light it with. In that interval, when she laid her head upon his shoulder, and he his red moustache upon her responsive lips, she had virtually accepted him, though she had not meant to do so. "No," she repeated, as he silently watched her, "you know it is not that."

"What then? Do you think it is improper?"

"Of course not."

"You would really like it, Elizabeth?"

"Yes—yes. I will come with you. We can talk as we go home."

"We can. That was precisely my object in making the arrangement."

Eleanor, presiding over her crockery at a little distance, called to them to ask whether the water boiled—and they perceived that it did. Mr. Yelverton carried the kettle to the teapot, and presently busied himself in handing the cups—so refreshing at the close of a summer picnic, when exercise and sun and lunch together have resulted in inevitable lassitude and incipient headaches—and doling out slices of thin bread and butter as Patty deftly shaved them from the loaf. They squatted round amongst the fern fronds and tussocks, and poured their tea vulgarly into their saucers—being warned by Mr. Brion that they had no time to waste—and then packed up, and washed their hands, and tied on their hats, and shook out their skirts, and set forth home again, declaring they had had the most beautiful time. The large buggy started first, the host driving; and Mr. Yelverton was informed that another track would be taken for the return journey, and that he was to be very careful not to lose himself.

"If we do lose ourselves," said Mr. Yelverton, as his escort disappeared over the crest of the hill, and he still stood in the valley—apparently in no haste to follow—tucking a light rug over his companion's knees, "it won't matter very much, will it?"

"Oh, yes, it will," she replied anxiously. "I don't know the way at all."

"Very well; then we will keep them in sight. But only just in sight—no more. Will you have the hood up or down?"

"Down," she said. "The day is too lovely to be shut out."

"It is, it is. I think it is just about the most lovely day I ever knew—not even excepting the first of October."

"The first of October was not a lovely day at all. It was cold and dismal."

"That was its superficial appearance." He let down the hood and climbed to his seat beside her, taking the reins from her hand. He had completely laid aside his sedate demeanour, and, though self-contained still, had a light in his eyes that made her tremble. "On your conscience," he said, looking at her, "can you say that the first of October was a dismal day? We may as well begin as we mean to go on," he added, as she did not answer; "and we will make a bargain, in the first place, never to say a word that we don't mean, nor to keep back one that we do mean from each other. You will agree to that, won't you, Elizabeth?"—his disengaged arm was round her shoulder and he had drawn her face up to his. "Elizabeth, Elizabeth,"—repeating the syllables fondly—"what a sweet and honest name it is! Kiss me, Elizabeth."

Instead of kissing him she began to sob. "Oh, don't, don't!" she cried, making a movement to free herself—at which he instantly released her. "Let us go on—they will be wondering where we are. I am very foolish—I can't help it—I will tell you presently!"

She took out her handkerchief, and tried to calm herself as she sat back in the buggy; and he, without speaking, touched his horses with his whip and drove slowly out of the shady dell into the clear sunshine. For a mile or more of up-and-down tracking, where the wheels of the leading vehicle had left devious ruts in sand and grass to guide them, they sat side by side in silence—she fighting with and gradually overcoming her excitement, and he gravely waiting, with a not less strong emotion, until she had recovered herself. And then he turned to her, and laid his powerful hand on hers that had dropped dejectedly into her lap, and said gently, though with decision—"Now tell me, dear. What is the matter? I *must* know. It is not—it is *not*"—contracting his fingers sharply—"that you don't mean what you have been telling me, after all? For though not in words, you *have* been telling me, have you not?"

"No," she sighed; "it is not that."

"I knew it. I was sure it could not be. Then what else can matter?—what else should trouble you? Is it about your sisters? You *know* they will be all right. They will not lose you—they will gain me. I flatter myself they will be all the better for gaining me, Elizabeth. I hoped you would think so?"

"I do think so."

"What then? Tell me."

"Mr. Yelverton, it is so hard to tell you—I don't know how to do it. But I am afraid—I am afraid—"

"Of what? Of *me?*"

"Oh, no! But I want to do what is right. And it seems to me that to let myself be happy like this would be wrong—"

"Wrong to let yourself be happy? Good heavens! Who has been teaching you such blasphemy as that?"

"No one has taught me anything, except my mother. But she was so good, and she had so many troubles, and she said that she would never have been able to bear them—to have borne life—had she not been stayed up by her religious faith. She told us, when it seemed to her that we might some day be cast upon the world to shift for ourselves, never to let go of that—to suffer and renounce everything rather than be tempted to give up that."

"Who has asked you to give it up?" he responded, with grave and gentle earnestness. "Not I. I would be the last man to dream of such a thing."

"But you—*you* have given up religion!" she broke forth, despairingly.

"Have I? I don't think so. Tell me what you mean by religion?"

"I mean what we have been brought up to believe."

"By the churches?"

"By the Church—the English Church—which I have always held to be the true Church."

"My dear child, every Church holds itself to be the true Church, and all the others to be false ones. Why should yours be right any more than other people's?"

"My mother taught us so," said Elizabeth.

"Yes. Your mother made it true, as she would have made any other true, by the religious spirit that she brought into it. They are *all* true—not only those we know of, but Buddhism and Mohammedanism, and even the queer faiths and superstitions of barbarian races, for they all have the same origin and object; and at the same time they are all so adulterated with human errors and vices, according to the sort of people who have had the charge of them, that you can't say any one of them is pure. No more pure than we are, and no less. For you to say that the rest are mistaken is just the pot calling the kettle black, Elizabeth. You may be a few degrees nearer the truth than those are who are less educated and civilised, but even that at present does not look so certain that you are justified in boasting about it—I mean your Church, you know, not you."

"But we go by our Bible—we trust, not in ourselves, but in *that*."

"So do the 'Dissenters,' as you call them."

"Yes, I am speaking of all of us—all who are Christian people. What guide should we have if we let our Bible go?"

"Why should you let it go? I have not let it go. If you read it intelligently it is truly a Holy Scripture—far more so than when you make a sort of charm and fetish of it. You should study its origin and history, and try to get at its meaning as you would at that of any other book. It has a very wonderful history, which in its turn is derived from other wonderful histories, which people will perversely shut their eyes to; and because of this undiscriminating ignorance, which is the blindness of those who won't see or who are afraid to see, it remains to this day the least understood of all ancient records. Some parts of it, you know, are a collection of myths and legends, which you will find in the same shape in older writings—the first dim forms of human thought about God and man and the mysteries of creation; and a great many good people read *these* as gospel truth, in spite of the evidence of all their senses to the contrary, and take them as being of the same value and importance as the beautiful books of the later time. And there are other Bibles in the world besides ours, whether we choose to acknowledge them or not."

Elizabeth listened with terror. "And do you say it is *not* the light of the world after all?" she cried in a shaken voice.

"There should be no preaching to the heathen, and spreading the good tidings over all lands?"

"Yes, there should," he replied; "oh, yes, certainly there should. But it should be done as it was by Christ, to whom all were with Him who were not against Him, and with a feeling that we should share all we know, and help each other to find out the best way. Not by rudely wrenching from the heathen, as we call him, all his immemorial moral standards, which, if you study them closely, are often found, rough as they are, to be thoroughly effective and serviceable, and giving him nothing in their places except outworn myths, and senseless hymns, and a patter of Scripture phrases that he can't possibly make head or tail of. That, I often think, is beginning the work of salvation by turning him from a religious man into an irreligious one. Your Church creed," he went on, "is just the garment of religion, and you wear finely-woven stuffs while the blacks wear blankets and 'possum-skins; they are all little systems that have their day and cease to be—that change and change as the fashion of the world changes. But the spirit of man—the indestructible intelligence that makes him apprehend the mystery of his existence and of the great Power that surrounds it—which in the early stages makes him cringe and fear, and later on to love and trust—that is the *body*. That is religion, as I take it. It is in the nature of man, and not to be given or taken away. Only the more freely we let that inner voice speak and guide us, the better we are, and the better we make the world and help things on. That's my creed, Elizabeth. You confuse things," he went on, after a pause, during which she kept an attentive silence, "when you confound religion and churchism together, as if they were identical. I have given up churchism, in your sense, because, though I have hunted the churches through and through, one after another, I have found in them no adequate equipment for the work of my life. The world has gone on, and they have not gone on. The world has discovered breechloaders, so to speak, and they go to the field with the old blunderbusses of centuries ago. Centuries!—of the prehistoric ages, it seems, now. My dear, I have lived over forty years— did you know I was so old as that?—seeking and striving to get hold of what I could in the way of a light and a guide to help me to make the best of my life and to do what little I might to better the world and brighten the hard lot of the poor and miserable. Is that giving up religion? I am not a churchman—I would be if I could, it is not my fault—but if I can't accept those tests, which revolt the reason and consciousness of a thinking man, am I therefore irreligious? *Am* I, Elizabeth?"

"You bewilder me," she said; "I have never made these distinctions. I have been taught in the Church—I have found comfort there and help. I am afraid to begin to question the things that I have been taught—I should get lost altogether, trying to find a new way."

"Then don't begin," he said. "*I* will not meddle with your faith—God forbid! Keep it while you can, and get all possible help and comfort out of it."

"But you have meddled with it already," she said, sighing. "The little that you have said has shaken it like an earthquake."

"If it is worth anything," he responded, "it is not shaken so easily."

"And *you* may be able to do good in your own strength," she went on, "but how could I?—a woman, so weak, so ignorant as I?"

"Do you want a policeman to keep you straight? I have a better opinion of you. Oh, you will be all right, my darling; don't fear. If you only honestly believe what you *do* believe, and follow the truth as it reveals itself to you, no matter in what shape, and no matter where it leads you, you will be all right. Be only sincere with yourself, and don't pretend—don't, whatever you do, pretend to *anything*. Surely that is the best religion, whether it enables you to keep within church walls or drives you out into the wilderness. Doesn't it stand to reason? We can only do our best, Elizabeth, and leave it." He put his arm round her again, and drew her head down to his shoulder. They were driving through a lone, unpeopled land, and the leading buggy was but a speck on the horizon.

"Oh!" she sighed, closing her eyes wearily, "if I only knew *what* was best!"

"Well," he said, "I will not ask you to trust me since you don't seem equal to it. You must decide for yourself. But, Elizabeth, if you *knew* what a life it was that I had planned! We were to be married at once—within a few weeks—and I was to take you home to *my* home. Patty and Nelly were to follow us later on, with Mrs. Duff-Scott, who wants to come over to see my London work, which she thinks will help her to do something here when she returns. You and I were to go away alone—wouldn't you have liked that, my love?—to be always with me, and taken care of and kept from harm and trouble, as I kept you to-day and on that Exhibition morning. Yes, and we were to take up that fortune that has been accumulating so long, and take Yelverton, and make our home and head-quarters there; and we were to live a great deal in London, and go backwards and forwards and all about amongst those unhappy ones, brightening up their lives because our own were so bright and sweet. You were to help me, as only a woman like you—

the woman I have been looking for all my life—could help; but I was not going to let you work too hard—you were to be cared for and made happy, first of all—before all the world. And I *could* make you happy—I could, I could—if you would let me try." He was carried away for the moment with the rush of his passionate desire for that life that he was contemplating, and held her and kissed her as if he would compel her to come to him. Then with a strong effort he controlled himself, and went on quietly, though in a rather unsteady voice: "Don't you think we can be together without harming each other? We shall both have the same aims—to live the best life and do the most good that we can—what will the details matter? We could not thwart each other really—it would be impossible. The same spirit would be in us; it is only the letter we should differ about."

"If we were together," she said, "we should not differ about anything. Spirit or letter, I should grow to think as you did."

"I believe you would, Elizabeth—I believe you would. And I should grow to think as you did. No doubt we should influence each other—it would not be all on one side. Can't you trust me, my dear? Can't we trust each other? You will have temptations, wherever you go, and with me, at least, you will always know where you are. If your faith is a true faith it will stand all that I shall do to it, and if your love for me is a true love—"

He paused, and she looked up at him with a look in her swimming eyes that settled that doubt promptly.

"Then you will do it, Elizabeth?"

"Oh," she said, "you know you can *make* me do it, whether it is right or wrong!"

It was a confession of her love, and of its power over her that appealed to every sentiment of duty and chivalry in him. "No," he said, very gravely and with a great effort, "I will not make you do anything wrong. You shall feel that it is not wrong before you do it."

An hour later they had reached the shore again, and were in sight of the headland and the smoke from the kitchen chimney of Seaview Villa, and in sight of their companions dismounting at Mr. Brion's garden gate. They had not lost themselves, though they had taken so little heed of the way. The sun was setting as they climbed the cliff, and flamed gloriously in their faces and across the bay. Sea and sky were bathed in indescribable colour and beauty. Checking their tired horses to gaze upon the scene, on the eve of an indefinite separation, the lovers realised to the full the sweetness of being together and what it would be to part.

CHAPTER XXXIV
SUSPENSE

Mr. Brion stood at his gate when the little buggy drove up, beaming with contentment and hospitality. He respectfully begged that Mr. Yelverton would grant them the favour of his company a little longer—would take pot-luck and smoke an evening pipe before he returned to his hotel in the town, whither he, Mr. Brion, would be only too happy to drive him. Mr. Yelverton declared, and with perfect truth, that nothing would give him greater pleasure. Whereupon the hotel servant was dismissed in charge of the larger vehicle, and the horses of the other were put into the stable. The girls went in to wash and dress, and the housekeeper put forth her best efforts to raise the character of the dinner from the respectable to the genteel in honour of a guest who was presumably accustomed to genteel dining.

The meal was served in the one sitting-room of the house, by the light of a single lamp on the round table and a flood of moonlight that poured in from the sea through the wide-open doors. After the feasts and fatigues of the day, no one had any appetite to speak of for the company dishes that Mrs. Harris hastily compounded, course by course, in the kitchen; but everyone felt that the meal was a pleasant one, notwithstanding. Mr. Yelverton, his host, and Patty, who was unusually sprightly, had the conversation to themselves. Patty talked incessantly. Nelly was amiable and charming, but decidedly sleepy; and Elizabeth, at her lover's side, was not, perhaps, unhappy, but visibly pale and noticeably silent. After dinner they went out upon the verandah, and sat there in a group on the comfortable old chairs and about the floor, and drank coffee, and chatted in subdued tones, and looked at the lovely water shining in the moonlight, and listened to it booming and splashing on the beach below. The two men, by virtue of their respective and yet common qualities, "took to" each other, and, by the time the girls had persuaded them to light the soothing cigarette, Mr. Brion was talking freely of his clever lad in Melbourne, and Mr. Yelverton of the mysterious disappearance of his uncle, as if it were quite a usual thing with them to confide their family affairs to strangers. Eleanor meanwhile swayed herself softly to and fro in a ragged rocking chair, half awake and half asleep; Elizabeth, still irresistibly attracted to the neighbourhood of her beloved, sat in the shadow of his large form, listening and pondering, with her eyes fixed on the veiled horizon, and all her senses on the alert; Patty squatted on the edge of the verandah, leaning against a post and looking up into the sky. She was the leading spirit of the group to-night. It was a long time since she had been so lively and entertaining.

"I wonder," she conjectured, in a pause of the conversation, "whether the inhabitants of any of those other worlds are sitting out on their verandahs to-night, and looking at *us*. I suppose we are not so absolutely insignificant but that *some* of them, our own brother and sister planets, at any rate, can see us if they use their best telescopes—are we, Mr. Yelverton?"

"We will hope not," said Mr. Yelverton.

"To think that the moon—miserable impostor that she is!—should be able to put them out," continued Patty, still gazing at the palely-shining stars. "The other Sunday we heard a clergyman liken her to something or other which on its appearance quenched the ineffectual fires of the *lesser* luminaries—"

"He said the sun," corrected Elizabeth.

"Well, it's all the same. What's the sun? The stars he hides are better suns than he is—not to speak of their being no end to them. It shows how easily we allow ourselves to be taken in by mere superficial appearances."

"The sun and moon quench the stars for *us*, Patty."

"Pooh! That's a very petty parish-vestry sort of way to look at things. Just what you might expect in a little bit of a world like this. In Jupiter now"—she paused, and turned her bright eyes upon a deep-set pair that were watching her amusedly. "Mr. Yelverton, I hope you are not going to insist upon it that Jupiter is too hot to do anything but blaze and shine and keep life going on his little satellites—are you?"

"O dear no!" he replied. "I wouldn't dream of such a thing."

"Very well. We will assume, then, that Jupiter is a habitable world, as there is no reason why he shouldn't be that *I* can see—-just for the sake of enlarging Elizabeth's mind. And, having assumed that, the least we can suppose—seeing that a few billions of years are of no account in the chronology of the heavenly bodies—is that a world on such a superior scale was fully up to *our* little standard before we began. I mean our present standard. Don't you think we may reasonably suppose that, Mr. Yelverton?"

"In the absence of information to the contrary, I think we may," he said. "Though I would ask to be allowed to reserve my own opinion."

"Certainly. I don't ask for anybody's opinion. I am merely throwing out suggestions. I want to extend Elizabeth's vision in these matters beyond the range of the sun and moon. So I say that Jupiter—and if not Jupiter, one of the countless millions of cooler planets, perhaps ever so much bigger than he is, which lie out in the other sun-systems—was well on with his railways and telegraphs when we began to get a crust, and to condense vapours. You will allow me to say as much as that, for the sake of argument?"

"I think you argue beautifully," said Mr. Yelverton.

"Very well then. Millions of years ago, if you had lived in Jupiter, you could have travelled in luxury as long as your life lasted, and seen countries whose numbers and resources never came to an end. Think of the railway system, and the shipping interest, of a world of that size!"

"*Don't*, Patty," interposed Elizabeth. "Think what a little, little life it would have been, by comparison! If we can't make it do us now, what would its insufficiency be under such conditions?"

Patty waved her hand to indicate the irrelevancy of the suggestion. "In a planet where, we are told, there are no vicissitudes of climate, people can't catch colds, Elizabeth; and colds, all the doctors say, are the primary cause of illness, and it is because they get ill that people die. That is a detail. Don't interrupt me. So you see, Mr. Yelverton, assuming that they knew all that we know, and did all that we do, before the fire and the water made our rocks and seas, and the chalk beds grew, and the slimy things crawled, and primitive man began to chip stones into wedges to kill the saurians with— just imagine for a moment the state of civilisation that must exist in Jupiter, *now*. Not necessarily our own Jupiter—any of the older and more improved Jupiters that must be spinning about in space."

"I can't," said Mr. Yelverton. "My imagination is not equal to such a task."

"I want Elizabeth to think of it," said Patty. "She is a little inclined to be provincial, as you see, and I want to elevate her ideas."

"Thank you, dear," said Elizabeth.

"It is a pity," Patty went on, "that we can't have a Federal Convention. That's what we want. If only the inhabited planets could send representatives to meet and confer together somewhere occasionally, then we should all have broad views—then we might find out at once how to set everything right, without any more trouble."

"Space would have to be annihilated indeed, Miss Patty."

"Yes, I know—I know. Of course I know it can't be done—at any rate, not *yet*—not in the present embryonic stage of things. If a meteor takes a million years to travel from star to star, going at the rate of thousands of miles per second—and keeps on paying visits indefinitely—Ah, what was that?"

She sprang from her low seat suddenly, all her celestial fancies scattered to the mundane winds, at the sound of a wakeful magpie beginning to pipe plaintively on the house roof. She thought she recognised one of the dear voices of the past. "*Can* it be Peter?" she cried, breathlessly. "Oh, Elizabeth, I do believe it is Peter! Do come out and let us call him down!"

They hurried, hand in hand, down to the shelving terrace that divided the verandah from the edge of the cliff, and there called and cooed and coaxed in their most seductive tones. The magpie looked at them for a moment, with his head cocked on one side, and then flew away.

"No," said Patty, with a groan, "it is *not* Peter! They are all gone, every one of them. I have no doubt the Hawkins boys shot them—little bloodthirsty wretches! Come down to the beach, Elizabeth."

They descended the steep and perilous footpath zig-zagging down the face of the cliff, with the confidence of young goats, and reaching the little bathing-house, sat down on the threshold. The tide was high, and the surf seething within a few inches of the bottom step of the short ladder up and down which they had glided bare-footed daily for so many years. The fine spray damped their faces; the salt sea-breezes fanned them deliciously. Patty put her arms impulsively round her sister's neck.

"Oh, Elizabeth," she said, "I am so glad for you—I *am* so glad! It has crossed my mind several times, but I was never sure of it till to-day, and I wouldn't say anything until I was sure, or until you told me yourself."

"My darling," said Elizabeth, responding to the caress, "don't be sure yet. *I* am not sure."

"*You* are not!" exclaimed Patty, with derisive energy. "Don't try to make me believe you are a born idiot, now, because I know you too well. Why, a baby in arms could see it!"

"I see it, dear, of course; both of us see it. We understand each other. But—but I don't know yet whether I shall accept him, Patty."

"Don't you?" responded Patty. She had taken her arms from her sister's neck, and was clasping her knees with them in a most unsympathetic attitude. "Do you happen to know whether you love him, Elizabeth?"

"Yes," whispered Elizabeth, blushing in the darkness; "I know that."

"And whether he loves you?"

"Yes."

"Of course you do. You can't help knowing it. Nobody could. And if," proceeded Patty sternly, fixing the fatuous countenance of the man in the moon with a baleful eye, "if, under those circumstances, you don't accept him, you deserve to be a miserable, lonely woman for all the rest of your wretched life. That's my opinion if you ask me for it."

Elizabeth looked at the sea in tranquil contemplation for a few seconds. Then she told Patty the story of her perplexity from the beginning to the end.

"Now *what* would you do?" she finally asked of her sister, who had listened with the utmost interest and intelligent sympathy. "If it were your own case, my darling, and you wanted to do what was right, *how* would you decide?"

"Well, Elizabeth," said Patty; "I'll tell you the truth. I should not stop to think whether it was right or wrong."

"Patty!"

"No. A year ago I would not have said so—a year ago I might have been able to give you the very best advice. But now—but now"—the girl stretched out her hands with the pathetic gesture that Elizabeth had seen and been struck with once before—"now, if it were my own case, I should take the man I loved, no matter *what* he was, if he would take me."

Elizabeth heaved a long sigh from the bottom of her troubled heart. She felt that Patty, to whom she had looked for help, had made her burden of responsibility heavier instead of lighter. "Let us go up to the house again," she said wearily. "There is no need to decide to-night."

When they reached the house, they found Eleanor gone to bed, and the gentlemen sitting on the verandah together, still talking of Mr. Yelverton's family history, in which the lawyer was professionally interested. The horses were in the little buggy, which stood at the gate.

"Ah, here they are!" said Mr. Brion. "Mr. Yelverton is waiting to say good-night, my dears. He has to settle at the hotel, and go on board to-night."

Patty bade her potential brother-in-law an affectionate farewell, and then vanished into her bedroom. The old man bustled off at her heels, under pretence of speaking to the lad-of-all-work who held the horses; and Elizabeth and her lover were left for a brief interval alone.

"You will not keep me in suspense longer than you can help, will you?" Mr. Yelverton said, holding her hands. "Won't a week be long enough?"

"Yes," she said; "I will decide it in a week."

"And may I come back to you here, to learn my fate? Or will you come to Melbourne to me?"

"Had I not better write?"

"No. Certainly not."

"Then I will come to you," she said.

He drew her to him and kissed her forehead gravely. "Good-night, my love," he said. "You will be my love, whatever happens."

And so he departed to the township, accompanied by his hospitable host, and she went miserable to bed. And at the first pale streak of dawn the little steamer sounded her whistle and puffed away from the little jetty, carrying him back to the world, and she stood on the cliff, a mile away from Seaview Villa, to watch the last whiff of smoke from its funnels fade like a breath upon the horizon.

CHAPTER XXXV
HOW ELIZABETH MADE UP HER MIND

If we could trace back the wonderful things that happen to us "by accident," or, as some pious souls believe, by the operation of a special Providence or in answer to prayer, to their remote origin, how far should we not have to go? Into the mists of antiquity, and beyond—even to the primal source whence the world was derived, and the consideration of the accident of its separation from its parent globe; nay, of the accident which separated our sun itself from the countless dust of other suns that strew the illimitable ether—still leaving the root of the matter in undiscoverable mystery. The chain of causes has no beginning for us, as the sequence of effects has no end. These considerations occurred to me just now, when I sat down, cheerful and confident, to relate how it came to pass (and what multitudinous trifles could have prevented it from coming to pass) that an extraordinary accident happened to the three Miss Kings in the course of the week following Mr. Yelverton's departure. Thinking it over, I find that I cannot relate it. It would make this chapter like the first half-dozen in the book of Chronicles, only much worse. If Mr. King had not inherited a bad temper from his great-great-grandfathers—I could get as far as that. But the task is beyond me. I give it up, and content myself with a narration of the little event (in the immeasurable chain of events) which, at this date of which I am writing—in the ephemeral summer time of these three brief little lives—loomed so large, and had such striking consequences.

It happened—or, as far as my story is concerned, it began to happen—while the steamer that carried away Mr. Yelverton was still ploughing the ocean waves, with that interesting passenger on board. Seaview Villa lay upon the headland, serene and peaceful in the sunshine of as perfect a morning as visitors to the seaside could wish to see, all its door-windows open to the south wind, and the sibilant music of the little wavelets at its feet. The occupants of the house had risen from their beds, and were pursuing the trivial round and common task of another day, with placid enjoyment of its atmospheric charms, and with no presentiment of what was to befall them. The girls went down to their bath-house before breakfast, and spent half an hour in the sunny water, diving, and floating, and playing all the pranks of childhood over again; and then they attacked a dish of fried flathead with appetites that a schoolboy might have envied. After breakfast the lawyer had to go to his office, and his guests accompanied him part of the way. On their return, Sam Dunn came to see them, with the information that his best boat, which bore the inappropriate title of "The Rose in June," was moored on the beach below, and an invitation to his young ladies to come out for a sail in her while the sea was so calm and the wind so fair. This invitation Elizabeth declined for herself; she was still wondering in which direction the right path lay—whether towards the fruition of her desires or the renunciation of all that now made life beautiful and valuable to her— and finding no solution to the problem either in meditation or prayer; and she had little inclination to waste any of the short time that remained to her for making up her mind. But to Patty and Eleanor it was irresistible. They scampered off to their bedrooms to put on their oldest frocks, hats, and boots, rushed into the kitchen to Mrs. Harris to beg for a bundle of sandwiches, and set forth on their expedition in the highest spirits—as if they had never been away from Sam Dunn and the sea, to learn life, and love, and trouble, and etiquette amongst city folks.

When they were gone, the house was very still for several hours. Elizabeth sat on the verandah, sewing and thinking, and watching the white sail of "The Rose in June" through a telescope; then she had her lunch brought to her on a white-napkined tray; after eating which in solitude she went back to her sewing, and thinking, and watching again. So four o'clock—the fateful hour—drew on. At a little before four, Mr. Brion came home, hot and dusty from his long walk, had a bath and changed his clothes, and sat down to enjoy himself in his arm-chair. Mrs. Harris brought in the afternoon tea things, with some newly-baked cakes; Elizabeth put down her work and seated herself at the table to brew the refreshing cup. Then home came Patty and Eleanor, happy and hungry, tanned and draggled, and in the gayest temper, having been sailing Sam's boat for him all the day and generally roughing it with great ardour. They were just in time for the tea and cakes, and sat down as they were, with hats tilted back on their wind-roughened heads, to regale themselves therewith.

When Patty was in the middle of her third cake, she suddenly remembered something. She plunged her hand into her pocket, and drew forth a small object. It was as if one touched the button of that wonderful electric apparatus whereby the great ships that are launched by princesses are sent gliding out of dock into the sea. "Look," she said, opening her hand carefully, "what he has given me. It is a Queensland opal. A mate of his, he says, gave it to him, but I have a terrible suspicion that the dear fellow bought it. Mates don't give such things for nothing. Is it not a beauty?"—

and she held between her thumb and finger a silky-looking flattened stone, on which, when it caught the light, a strong blue sheen was visible. "I shall have it cut and made into something when we go back to town, and I shall keep it *for ever*, in memory of Sam Dunn," said Patty with enthusiasm.

And then, when they had all examined and appraised it thoroughly, she carried it to the mantelpiece, intending to place it there in safety until she went to her own room. But she had no sooner laid it down, pushing it gently up to the wall, than there was a little click and a faint rattle, and it was gone.

"Oh," she exclaimed, "what *shall* I do? It has fallen behind the mantelpiece! I *quite* forgot that old hole—and it is there still. Surely," she continued angrily, stamping her foot, "when Mr. Hawkins took the trouble to do all this"—and she indicated the surface of the woodwork, which had been painted in a wild and ghastly imitation of marble—"he might have taken a little more, and fixed the thing close up to the wall?"

Mr. Brion examined the mantelpiece, pushed it, shook it, peered behind it with one eye, and said that he had himself lost a valuable paper-knife in the same distressing manner, and had long intended to have the aperture closed up. "And I will get a carpenter to-morrow morning, my dear," he boldly declared, "and he shall take the whole thing to pieces and fix it again properly. Yes, I will—as well now as any other time—and we will find your opal."

Having pledged himself to which tremendous purpose, he and they finished their tea, and afterwards had their dinner, and afterwards sat on the verandah and gossiped, and afterwards went to bed—and in due time got up again—as if nothing out of the common way had happened!

In the morning Fate sent another of her humble emissaries from the township to Seaview Villa, with a bag of tools over his shoulder—tools that were keys to unlock one of her long-kept secrets. And half an hour after his arrival they found the opal, and several things besides. When, after Mrs. Harris had carefully removed the furniture and hearthrug, and spread cornsacks over the carpet, the carpenter wrenched the mantelpiece from its fastenings, such a treasure-trove was discovered in the rough hollows of the wall and floor as none of them had dreamed of. It did not look much at the first glance. There were the opal and the paper-knife, half a dozen letters (circulars and household bills of Mrs. King's), several pens and pencils, a pair of scissors, a silver fruit-knife, a teaspoon, a variety of miscellaneous trifles, such as bodkins and corks, and a vast quantity of dust. That seemed all. But, kneeling reverently to grope amongst these humble relics of the past, Elizabeth found, quite at the bottom of everything, a little card. It was an old, old card, dingy and fretted with age, and dried and curled up like a dead leaf, and it had a little picture on it that had almost faded away. She carefully wiped the dust from it with her handkerchief, and looked at it as she knelt; it was a crude and youthful water-colour drawing of an extensive Elizabethan house, with a great many gables and fluted chimney-stacks, and much exuberance of architectural fancy generally. It had been minutely outlined by a hand trained to good draughtsmanship, and then coloured much as a child would colour a newspaper print from a sixpenny paint-box, and less effectively, because there was no light and shade to go upon. It was flat and pale, like a builder's plan, only that it had some washy grass and trees about it, and a couple of dogs running a race in the foreground, which showed its more ambitious pretensions; and the whole thing had evidently been composed with the greatest care. Elizabeth, studying it attentively, and thinking that she recognised her father's hand in certain details, turned the little picture over in search of the artist's signature. And there, in a corner, written very fine and small, but with elaborate distinctness, she read these words:—"*Elizabeth Leigh, from Kingscote Yelverton, Yelverton, June, 1847.*"

She stared at the legend—in which she recognised a peculiar capital K of his own invention that her father always used—with the utmost surprise, and with no idea of its tremendous significance. "Why—why!" she gasped, holding it up, "it belongs to *him*—it has Mr. Yelverton's name upon it! How in the world did it come here? What does it mean? Did he drop it here the other day? But, no, that is impossible—it was quite at the bottom—it must have been lying here for ages. Mr. Brion, *what* does it mean?"

The old man was already stooping over her, trying to take it from her hand. "Give it to me, my dear, give it to me," he cried eagerly. "Don't tear it—oh, for God's sake, be careful!—let me see what it is first." He took it from her, read the inscription over and over and over again, and then drew a chair to the table and sat down with the card before him, his face pale, and his hands shaking. The sisters gathered round him, bewildered; Elizabeth still possessed with her first impression that the little picture was her lover's property, Eleanor scarcely aware of what was going on, and Patty—always the quickest to reach the truth—already beginning dimly to discern the secret of their discovery. The carpenter and the housekeeper stood by, open-mouthed and open-eyed; and to them the lawyer tremulously addressed himself.

"You had better go for a little while," he said; "we will put the mantelpiece up presently. Yet, stay—we have found a very important document, as I believe, and you are witnesses that we have done so. You had better examine it carefully before you go, that you may know it when you see it again." Whereupon he solemnly proceeded to print the said document upon their memories, and insisted that they should each take a copy of the words that made its chief importance, embodying it in a sort of affidavit, to which they signed their names. Then he sent them out of the room, and confronted the three sisters, in a state of great excitement. "I must see Paul," he said hurriedly. "I must have my son to help me. We must ransack that old bureau of yours—there must be more in it than we found that time when we looked for the will. Tell me, my dears, did your father let you have the run of the bureau, when he was alive?"

No, they told him; Mr. King had been extremely particular in allowing no one to go to it but himself.

"Ah," said the old man, "we must hunt it from top to bottom—we must break it into pieces, if necessary. I will telegraph to Paul. We must go to town at once, my dears, and investigate this matter—before Mr. Yelverton leaves the country."

"He will not leave the country yet," said Elizabeth. "What is it, Mr. Brion?"

"I think I see what it is," broke in Patty. "Mr. Brion thinks that father was Mr. Yelverton's uncle, who was lost so long ago. King—King—Mr. Yelverton told us the other day that they called *him* 'King,' for short—and he was named Kingscote Yelverton, like his uncle. Mother's name was Elizabeth. I believe Mr. Brion is right And, if so—"

"And, if so," Patty repeated, when that wonderful, bewildering day was over, and she and her elder sister were packing for their return to Melbourne in the small hours of the next morning—"if so, we are the heiresses of all those hundreds of thousands that are supposed to belong to our cousin Kingscote. Now, Elizabeth, do you feel like depriving him of everything, and stopping his work, and leaving his poor starved costermongers to revert to their original condition—or do you not?"

"I would not take it," said Elizabeth, passionately.

"Pooh!—as if we should be allowed to choose! People can't do as they like where fortunes and lawyers are concerned. For Nelly's sake—not to speak of mine—they will insist on our claim, if we have one; and then do you suppose *he* would keep your money? Of course not—it's a most insulting idea. Therefore the case lies in a nutshell. You will have to make up your mind quickly, Elizabeth."

"I have made up my mind," said Elizabeth, "if it is a question of which of us is most worthy to have wealth, and knows best how to use it."

CHAPTER XXXVI
INVESTIGATION

They did not wait for the next steamer, but hurried back to Melbourne by train and coach, and reached Myrtle Street once more at a little before midnight, the girls dazed with sleep and weariness and the strain of so much excitement as they had passed through. They had sent no message to Mrs. Duff-Scott at present, preferring to make their investigations, in the first place, as privately as possible; and Mr. Brion had merely telegraphed to his son that they were returning with him on important business. Paul was at the house when they arrived, but Mrs. M'Intyre had made hospitable preparations at No. 6 as well as at No. 7; and the tired sisters found their rooms aired and their beds arranged, a little fire lit, gas burning, kettle boiling, and a tempting supper laid out for them when they dragged their weary limbs upstairs. Mrs. M'Intyre herself was there to give them welcome, and Dan, who had been reluctantly left behind when they went into the country, was wild with rapture, almost tearing them to pieces in the vehemence of his delight at seeing them again, long past the age of gambols as he was. Mr. Brion was consoled for the upsetting of his own arrangements, which had been to take his charges to an hotel for the night, and there luxuriously entertain them; and he bade them an affectionate good-night, and went off contentedly to No. 7 under the wing of Paul's landlady, to doze in Paul's arm-chair until that brilliant ornament of the press should be released from duty.

Cheered by their little fire—for, summer though it was, their fatigues had made them chilly—and by Mrs. M'Intyre's ham and chicken and hot coffee, the girls sat, talking and resting, for a full hour before they went to bed; still dwelling on the strange discovery of the little picture behind the mantelpiece, which Mr. Brion had taken possession of, and wondering if it would really prove them to be the three Miss Yelvertons instead of the three Miss Kings, and co-heiresses of one of the largest properties in England.

As they passed the old bureau on their way to their rooms, Elizabeth paused and laid her hand on it thoughtfully. "It hardly seems to me possible," she said, "that father should have kept such a secret all these years, and died without telling us of it. He must have seen the advertisements—he must have known what difficulties he was making for everybody. Perhaps he did not write those names on the picture—handwriting is not much to go by, especially when it is so old as that; you may see whole schools of boys or girls writing in one style. Perhaps father was at school with Mr. Yelverton's uncle. Perhaps mother knew Elizabeth Leigh. Perhaps she gave her the sketch—or she might have come by it accidentally. One day she must have found it—slipped in one of her old music-books, maybe—and taken it out to show father; and she put it up on the mantelpiece, and it slipped down behind, like Patty's opal. If it had been of so much consequence as it seems to us—if they had desired to leave no trace of their connection with the Yelverton family—surely they would have pulled the house down but what they would have recovered it. And then we have hunted the bureau over— we have turned it out again and again—and never found anything."

"Mr. Brion thinks there are secret drawers," said Eleanor, who, of all the three, was most anxious that their golden expectations should be realised. "It is just the kind of cabinet work, he says, that is always full of hidden nooks and corners, and he is blaming himself that he did not search it more thoroughly in the first instance."

"And he thinks," continued Patty, "that father seemed like a man with things on his mind, and believes he *would* have told us had he had more warning of his death. But you know he was seized so suddenly, and could not speak afterwards."

"Poor father—poor father!" sighed Elizabeth, pitifully. They thought of his sad life, in the light of this possible theory, with more tender compassion than they had ever felt for him before; but the idea that he might have murdered his brother, accidentally or otherwise—and for that reason had effaced himself and done bitter penance for the rest of his days—never for a moment occurred to them. "Well, we shall know by to-morrow night," said the elder sister, gently. "If the bureau does not yield fresh evidence, there is none that we can allow Mr. Brion, or anyone else, to act upon. The more I think it over, the more I see how easily the whole thing could be explained— to mean nothing so important as Mr. Brion thinks. And, for myself, I should not be disappointed if we found ourselves only Miss Kings, without fortune or pedigree, as we have always been. We are very happy as we are."

"That is how I felt at first," said Patty. "But I must say I am growing more and more in love with the idea of being rich. The delightful things that you can do with plenty of money keep flashing into my mind, one after the other, till I feel that I never understood what being poor meant till now, and that I could not content myself with a hundred a year and Mrs. Duff-Scott's benefactions any more. No; the wish may be father to the thought, Elizabeth, but I *do* think it, honestly, that we shall turn out to be Mr. Yelverton's cousins—destined to supersede him, to a certain extent."

"I think so, too," said Eleanor, anxiously. "I can't—I *won't*—believe that Mr. Brion is mistaken."

So they went, severally affected by their strange circumstances, to bed. And in the morning they were up early, and made great haste to get their breakfast over, and their sitting-room in order, in readiness for the lawyer's visit. They were very much agitated by their suspense and anxiety, especially Patty, to whom the impending interview with Paul had become of more pressing consequence, temporarily, than even the investigations that he was to assist. She had had no communication with him whatever since she cut him on the racecourse when he was innocently disporting himself with Mrs. Aarons; and her nerves were shaken by the prospect of seeing and speaking to him again, and by the vehemence of her conflicting hopes and fears. She grew cold and hot at the recollection of one or two accidental encounters that had taken place *since* Cup Day, and at the picture of his contemptuous, unrecognising face that rose up vividly before her. Elizabeth noticed her unusual pallor and restless movements, and how she hovered about the window, straining her ears to catch a chance sound of the men's voices next door, and made an effort to divert her thoughts. "Come and help me, Patty," she said, putting her hand on her sister's shoulder. "We have nothing more to do now, so we may as well turn out some of the drawers before they come. We can look over dear mother's clothes, and see if they have any marks on them that we have overlooked. Mr. Brion will want to have everything examined."

So they began to work at the bureau with solemn diligence, and a fresh set of emotions were evolved by that occupation, which counteracted, without effacing, those others that were in Patty's mind. She became absorbed and attentive. They took out all Mrs. King's gowns, and her linen, and her little everyday personal belongings, searched them carefully for indications of ownership, and, finding none, laid them aside in the adjoining bedroom. Then they exhumed all those relics of an olden time which had a new significance at the present juncture—the fine laces, the faded brocades, the Indian shawl and Indian muslins, the quaint fans and little bits of jewellery—and arranged them carefully on the table for the lawyer's inspection.

"We know *now*," said Patty, "though we didn't know a few mouths ago, that these are things that could only belong to a lady who had been rich once."

"Yes," said Elizabeth. "But there is another point to be considered. Elizabeth Leigh ran away with her husband secretly and in haste, and under circumstances that make it seem *most* unlikely that she should have hampered herself and him with luggage, or bestowed a thought on such trifles as fans and finery."

The younger sisters were a little daunted for a moment by this view of the case. Then Eleanor spoke up. "How you do love to throw cold water on everything!" she complained, pettishly. "Why shouldn't she think of her pretty things? I'm sure if I were going to run away—no matter under what circumstances—I should take all *mine*, if I had half an hour to pack them up. So would you. At least, I don't know about you—but Patty would. Wouldn't you, Patty?"

"Well," said Patty, thoughtfully, sitting back on her heels and folding her hands in her lap, "I really think I should, Elizabeth. If you come to think of it, it is the heroines of novels who do those things. They throw away lovers, and husbands, and fortunes, and everything else, on the slightest provocation; it is a matter of course—it is the correct thing in novels. But in real life girls are fond of all nice things—at least, that is my experience—and they don't feel like throwing them away. Girls in novels would never let Mrs. Duff-Scott give them gowns and bonnets, for instance—they would be too proud; and they would burn a bureau any day rather than rummage in it for a title to money that a nice man, whom they cared for, was in possession of. Don't tell me. You are thinking of the heroines of fiction, Elizabeth, and not of Elizabeth Leigh. *She*, I agree with Nelly—however much she might have been troubled and bothered—did not leave her little treasures for the servants to pawn. Either she took them with her, or someone able to keep her destination a secret sent them after her."

"Well, well," said Elizabeth, who had got out her mother's jewellery and was gazing fondly at the miniature in the pearl-edged locket, "we shall soon know. Get out the books and music, dear."

They were turning over a vast pile of music, which required at least half a day to examine properly, when the servant of the house tapped at the door to ask, with Mr. Brion's compliments, when it would be convenient to Miss King to receive that gentleman. In a few minutes father and son were in the room, the former distributing hasty and paternal greetings all around, and the latter quietly shaking hands with an air of almost aggressive deliberation. Paul was quite polite, and to a certain extent friendly, but he was terribly, uncompromisingly business-like. Not a moment did he waste in mere social amenities, after shaking hands with Patty—which he did as if he were a wooden automaton, and without looking at her—but plunged at once into the matter of the discovered picture, as if time were money and nothing else of any consequence. Patty's heart sank, but her spirit rose; she determined not to "let herself down" or in any way to "make an exhibition of herself," if she could help it. She drew a little aside from the bureau, and went on turning over the music—which presently she was able to report valueless as evidence, except negative evidence, the name, wherever it had been written at the head of a sheet, having been cut out or erased; while Elizabeth took the remaining articles from their drawers and pigeon-holes, and piled them on the table and in Nelly's arms.

For some time they were all intent upon their search, and very silent; and it still seemed that they were to find nothing in the shape of that positive proof which Elizabeth, as the head of the family, demanded before she would give permission for any action to be taken. There were no names in the old volumes of music, and the fly-leaves had been torn from the older books. Some pieces of ancient silver plate—a pair of candlesticks, a pair of salt-cellars, a teapot and sugar basin (now in daily use), a child's mug, some Queen Anne spoons and ladles—were all unmarked by crest or monogram; and two ivory-painted miniatures and three daguerreotypes, representing respectively one old lady in high-crowned cap and modest kerchief, one young one with puffs all over her head, and a classic absence of bodice to her gown, one little fair-haired child, similarly scanty in attire, and one middle-aged gentleman with a large shirt frill and a prodigious quantity of neck-cloth—likewise failed to verify themselves by date or inscription when carefully prised out of their frames and leather cases with Paul Brion's pen-knife. These family portraits, understood by the girls to belong to the maternal side of the house, were laid aside, however, along with the pearl-rimmed locket and other jewels, and the picture that was found behind the mantelpiece; and then, nothing else being left, apparently, the two men began an inspection of the papers.

While this was going on, Patty, at a sign from Elizabeth, set up the leaves of a little tea-table by the window, spread it with a white cloth, and fetched in such a luncheon as the slender larder afforded—the remains of Mrs. M'Intyre's chicken and ham, some bread and butter, a plate of biscuits, and a decanter of sherry—for it was past one o'clock, and Mr. Brion and Paul had evidently no intention of going away until their investigations were complete. The room was quite silent. Her soft steps and the brush of her gown as she passed to and fro were distinctly audible to her lover, who would not so much as glance at her, but remained sternly intent upon the manuscripts before him. These were found to be very interesting, but to have no more bearing upon the matter in hand than the rest of the relics that had been overhauled; for the most part, they were studies in various arts and sciences prepared by Mr. and Mrs. King for their daughters during the process of their education, and such odds and ends of literature as would be found in a clever woman's common-place books. They had all been gone over at the time of Mr. King's death, in a vain hunt for testamentary documents; and Elizabeth, looking into the now bare shelves and apertures of the bureau, began to think how she could console her sisters for the disappointment of their hopes.

"Come and have some lunch," she said to Paul (Mr. Brion was already at the table, deprecating the trouble that his dear Patty was taking). "I don't think you will find anything more."

The young man stood up with his brows knitted over his keen eyes, and glanced askance at the group by the window. "We have not done yet," he said decisively; "and we have learned quite enough, in what we *haven't* found, to justify us in consulting Mr. Yelverton's solicitors."

"No," she said, "I'll have nothing said to Mr. Yelverton, unless the whole thing is proved first."

Never thinking that the thing would be proved, first or last, she advanced to the extemporised lunch table, and dispensed the modest hospitalities of the establishment with her wonted simple grace. Mr. Brion was accommodated with an arm-chair and a music-book to lay across his knees, whereon Patty placed the tit-bits of the chicken and the knobby top-crust of the loaf, waiting upon him with that tender solicitude to which he had grown accustomed, but which was so astonishing, and so interesting also, to his son.

"She has spoiled me altogether," said the old man fondly, laying his hand on her bright head as she knelt before him to help him to mustard and salt. "I don't know how I shall ever manage to get along without her now."

"Has this sad fate overtaken you in one short week?" inquired Paul, rather grimly. "Your sister should be labelled like an explosive compound, Miss King—'dangerous,' in capital letters." Paul was sitting in a low chair by Elizabeth, with his plate on his knee, and he thawed a good deal, in spite of fierce intentions to the contrary, under the influence of food and wine and the general conversation. He looked at Patty now and then, and by-and-bye went so far as to address a remark to her. "What did she think of the caves?" he asked, indifferently, offering her at the same moment a glass of sherry, which, though unaccustomed to fermented liquors, she had not the presence of mind to refuse—and which she took with such a shaking hand that she spilled some of it over her apron. And she plunged at once into rapid and enthusiastic descriptions of the caves and the delights of their expedition thereto, absurdly uplifted by this slight token of interest in her proceedings.

When luncheon was over, Elizabeth culled Eleanor—who, too restless to eat much herself, was hovering about the bureau, tapping it here and there with a chisel—to take her turn to be useful by clearing the table; and then, as if business were of no consequence, bade her guests rest themselves for a little and smoke a cigarette if they felt inclined.

"Smoke!" exclaimed Paul, with a little sarcastic laugh. "Oh, no, Miss King, that would never do. What would Mrs. Duff-Scott say if she were to smell tobacco in your sitting-room?"

"Well, what would she say?" returned Elizabeth, gently—she was very gentle with Paul to-day. "Mrs. Duff-Scott, I believe, is rather fond of the smell of tobacco, when it is good."

Mr. Brion having satisfied the demands of politeness with profuse protestations, suffered himself to indulge in a mild cigarette; but Paul would not be persuaded. He resumed his study of the manuscripts with an air of determination, as of a man who had idled away precious time. He conscientiously endeavoured to fix his attention on the important business that he had undertaken, and to forget everything else until he had finished it. For a little while Patty wandered up and down in an aimless manner, making neat heaps of the various articles scattered about the room and watching him furtively; then she softly opened the piano, and began to play, just above a whisper, the "Sonata Pathetique."

CHAPTER XXXVII
DISCOVERY

It was between two and three o'clock; Mr. Brion reposed in his arm-chair, smoking a little, talking a little to Elizabeth who sat beside him, listening dreamily to the piano, and feeling himself more and more inclined to doze and nod his head in the sleepy warmth of the afternoon, after his glass of sherry and his recent severe fatigues. Elizabeth, by way of entertaining him, sat at his elbow, thinking, thinking, with her fingers interlaced in her lap and her gaze fixed upon the floor. Patty, intensely alert and wakeful, but almost motionless in her straight back and delicately poised head, drooped over the keyboard, playing all the "soft things" that she could remember without notes; and Paul, who had resisted her enchantments as long as he could, leaned back in his chair, with his hand over his eyes, having evidently ceased to pay any attention to his papers. And, suddenly, Eleanor, who was supposed to be washing plates and dishes in the kitchen, flashed into the room, startling them all out of their dreams.

"Elizabeth, dear," she exclaimed tremulously, "forgive me for meddling with your things. But I was thinking and thinking what else there was that we had not examined, and mother's old Bible came into my head—the little old Bible that she always used, and that you kept in your top drawer. I could not help looking at it, and here"—holding out a small leather-bound volume, frayed at the corners and fastened with silver clasps—"here is what I have found. The two first leaves are stuck together—I remembered that—but they are only stuck round the edges; there is a little piece in the middle that is loose and rattles, and, see, there is writing on it." The girl was excited and eager, and almost pushed the Bible into Paul Brion's hands. "Look at it, look at it," she cried. "Undo the leaves with your knife and see what the writing is."

Paul examined the joined leaves attentively, saw that Eleanor was correct in her surmise, and looked at Elizabeth. "May I, Miss King?" he asked, his tone showing that he understood how sacred this relic must be, and how much it would go against its present possessor to see it tampered with.

"I suppose you had better," said Elizabeth.

He therefore sat down, laid the book before him, and opened his sharp knife. A sense that something was really going to happen now—that the secret of all this careful effacement of the little chronicles common and natural to every civilised family would reveal itself in the long-hidden page which, alone of all the records of the past, their mother had lacked the heart to destroy—fell upon the three girls; and they gathered round to watch the operation with pale faces and beating hearts. Paul was a long time about it, for he tried to part the leaves without cutting them, and they were too tightly stuck together. He had at last to make a little hole in which to insert his knife, and then it was a most difficult matter to cut away the plain sheet without injuring the written one. Presently, however, he opened a little door in the middle of the page, held the flap up, glanced at what was behind it for a moment, looked significantly at his father, and silently handed the open book to Elizabeth. And Elizabeth, trembling with excitement and apprehension, lifting up the little flap in her turn, read this clear inscription—

> "To my darling child, ELIZABETH,
> From her loving mother,
> ELEANOR D'ARCY LEIGH.
> Bradenham Abbey. Christmas, 1839.
> Psalm xv., 1, 2."

There was a dead silence while they all looked at the fine brown writing—that delicate caligraphy which, like fine needlework, went out of fashion when our grandmothers passed away—of which every letter, though pale, was perfectly legible. A flood of recollection poured into the minds of the three girls, especially the elder ones, at the sight of those two words, "Bradenham Abbey," in the corner of the uncovered portion of the page. "Leigh" and "D'Arcy" were both unfamiliar names—or had been until lately—but Bradenham had a place in the archives of memory, and came forth at this summons from its dusty and forgotten nook. When they were children their mother used to tell them stories by the firelight in winter evenings, and amongst those stories were several whose scenes were laid in the tapestried chambers and ghostly corridors, and about the parks and deer-drives and lake-shores of a great "place" in an English county—a place that had once been a famous monastery, every feature and aspect of which

Mrs. King had at various times described so minutely that they were almost as familiar with it as if they had seen it for themselves. These stories generally came to an untimely end by the narrator falling into an impenetrable brown study or being overtaken by an unaccountable disposition to cry—which gave them, of course, a special and mysterious fascination for the children. While still little things in pinafores, they were quick enough to perceive that mother had a personal interest in that wonderful place of which they never tired of hearing, and which evidently did not belong to the realms of Make-believe, like the palace of the Sleeping Beauty and Blue-beard's castle; and therefore they were always, if unconsciously, trying to understand what that interest was. And when, one day when she was painting a wreath of forget-me-nots on some little trifle intended for a bazaar, and, her husband coming to look over her, she said to him impulsively, "Oh, do you remember how they grew in the sedges round the Swan's Pool at Bradenham?"—and when he sternly bade her hush, and not speak of Bradenham unless she wished to drive him mad—then Patty and Elizabeth, who heard them both, knew that Bradenham was the name of the great house where monks had lived, in the grounds of which, as they had had innumerable proofs, pools and swans abounded. It was the first time they had heard it, but it was too important a piece of information to be forgotten. On this memorable day, so many years after, when they read "Bradenham Abbey" in the well-worn Bible, they looked at each other, immediately recalling that long-ago incident; but their hearts were too full to speak. It was Mr. Brion who broke the silence that had fallen upon them all.

"This, added to our other discoveries, is conclusive, I think," said the old lawyer, standing up in order to deliver his opinion impressively, and resting his hands on the table. "At any rate, I must insist on placing the results of our investigation before Mr. Yelverton—yes, Elizabeth, you must forgive me, my dear, if I take the matter into my own hands. Paul will agree with me that we have passed the time for sentiment. We will have another look into the bureau—because it seems incredible that any man should deliberately rob his children of their rights, even if he repudiated his own, and therefore I think there *must* be legal instruments *somewhere*; but, supposing none are with us, it will not be difficult, I imagine, to supply what is wanting to complete our case from other sources—from other records of the family, in fact. Mr. Yelverton himself, in five minutes, would be able to throw a great deal of light upon our discoveries. It is absolutely necessary to consult him."

"I would not mind so much," said Elizabeth, who was deadly pale, "if it were to be fought out with strangers. But *he* would give it all up at once, without waiting to see—without asking us to prove—that we had a strictly legal title."

"Don't you believe it," interposed Paul sententiously.

She rose from her chair in majestic silence, and moved towards the bureau. She would not bandy her lover's name nor discuss his character with those who did not know him as she did. Paul followed her, with his chisel in his hand.

"Let us look for that secret drawer, at any rate," he said. "I feel pretty certain there must be one, now. Mr. King took great pains to prevent identification during his lifetime, but, as my father says, that is a very different thing from disinheriting *you*. If you will allow me, I'll take every moveable part out first."

He did so, while she watched and assisted him. All the brass-handled drawers, and sliding shelves, and partitions were withdrawn from their closely-fitting sockets, leaving a number of holes and spaces each differing in size and shape from the rest. Then he drew up a chair in front of the exposed skeleton, and gazed at it thoughtfully; after which he began to make careful measurements inside and out, to tap the woodwork in every direction, and to prise some of its strong joints asunder. This work continued until four o'clock, when, notwithstanding the highly stimulating excitement of the day's proceedings, the girls began to feel that craving for a cup of tea which is as strong upon the average woman at this time as the craving for a nobbler of whisky is upon the—shall I say average man?—when the sight of a public-house appeals to his nobler appetite. Not that they wanted to eat and drink—far from it; the cup of tea was the symbol of rest and relief for a little while from the stress and strain of labour and worry, and that was what they were in need of. Elizabeth looked at her watch and then at Patty, and the two girls slipped out of the room together, leaving Eleanor to watch operations at the bureau. Reaching their little kitchen, they mechanically lit the gas in the stove, and set the kettle on to boil; and then they went to the open window, which commanded an unattractive view of the back yard, and stood there side by side, leaning on each other.

"In 1839," said Patty, "she must have been a girl, a child, and living at Bradenham *at home*. Think of it, Elizabeth—with a mother loving her and petting her as she did us. She was twenty-five when she married; she must have been about sixteen when that Bible was given to her—ever so much younger than any of us are now. *She* lived in those beautiful rooms with the gold Spanish leather on the walls—*she* danced in that long gallery with the painted windows and the slippery oak floor and the thirty-seven family portraits all in a row—no doubt she rode about herself with those hunting parties in the winter, and rowed and skated on the lake—I can imagine it, what a life it must have been. Can't you see her, before she grew stout and careworn, and her bright hair got dull, and her pretty hands rough with hard work—young, and lovely, and happy, and petted by everybody— wearing beautiful clothes, and never knowing what it was to have to do anything for herself? I can. And it seems dreadful to think that she had to remember all that, living as she did afterwards. If only he had made it up to her!—but I don't think he did, Elizabeth—I don't think he did. He used to be so cross to her sometimes. Oh, bless her, bless her! Why didn't she tell *us*, so that *we* could have done more to comfort her?"

"I don't think she ever repented," said Elizabeth, who remembered more about her mother than Patty could do. "She did it because she loved him better than Bradenham and wealth and her own personal comfort; and she loved him like that always, even when he was cross. Poor father! No wonder he was cross!"

"Why didn't he go back—for her sake, if not for ours—when he saw the advertisements? Elizabeth, my idea is that the death of his brother gave a permanent shock to his brain. I think he could never have been quite himself afterwards. It was a sort of mania with him to disconnect himself from everything that could suggest the tragedy—to get as far away as possible from any association with it."

"I think so, too," said Elizabeth.

Thus they talked by the kitchen window until the kettle bubbled on the stove; and then, recalled to the passing hour and their own personal affairs, they collected cups and saucers, sugar-basin and milk-jug, and cut bread and butter for the afternoon repast. Just as their preparations were completed, Eleanor came flying along the passage from the sitting-room. "They have found a secret drawer," she cried in an excited whisper. "At least not a drawer, but a double partition that seems to have been glued up; and Mr. Brion is sure, by the dull sound of the wood, that there are things in it. Come and see!"

She flew back again, not even waiting to help her sisters with the tea. Silently Elizabeth took up the tray of cups and saucers, and Patty the teapot and the plate of bread and butter; and they followed her with beating hearts. This was the crisis of their long day's trial. Paul was tearing at the intestines of the bureau like a cat at the wainscot that has just given sanctuary to a mouse, and his father was too much absorbed in helping him to notice their return.

"Now, pull, pull!" cried the old man, at the moment when the sisters closed the door behind them. "Break it, if it won't come. A—a—ah!" as a sudden crash of splintered wood resounded through the room, "there they are at last! I *thought* they must be here somewhere!"

"What is it?" inquired Elizabeth, setting down her tea-tray, and hastily running to his side. He was stripping a pink tape from a thin bundle of blue papers in a most unprofessional state of excitement and agitation.

"What is it?" he echoed triumphantly. "This is what it is, my dear"— and he began in a loud voice to read from the outside of the blue packet, to which he pointed with a shaking finger—"The will of Kingscote Yelverton, formerly of Yelverton, in the county of Kent—Elizabeth Yelverton, sole executrix."

CHAPTER XXXVIII
THE TIME FOR ACTION

Yes, it was their father's will—the will they had vainly hunted for a year ago, little thinking what manner of will it was; executed when Eleanor was a baby in long clothes, and providing for their inheritance of that enormous English fortune. When they were a little recovered from the shock of this last overwhelming surprise, Mr. Brion broke the seal of the document, and formally and solemnly read it to them. It was very short, but perfectly correct in form, and the testator (after giving to his wife, in the event of her surviving him, the sole control of the entire property, which was unentailed, for her lifetime) bequeathed to his younger daughters, and to any other children who might have followed them, a portion of thirty thousand pounds apiece, and left the eldest, Elizabeth, heiress of Yelverton and residuary legatee. Patty and Eleanor were thus to be made rich beyond *their* dreams of avarice, but Elizabeth, who had been her father's favourite, was to inherit a colossal fortune. That was, of course, supposing such wealth existed in fact as well as in the imagination of this incredible madman. Paul and his father found themselves unable to conceive of such a thing as that any one in his senses should possess these rare and precious privileges, so passionately desired and so recklessly sought and sinned for by those who had them not, and should yet abjure, them voluntarily, and against every natural temptation and moral obligation to do otherwise. It was something wholly outside the common course of human affairs, and unintelligible to men of business. Both of them felt that they must get out of the region of romance and into the practical domain of other lawyers' offices before they could cope effectively with the anomalies of the case. As it stood, it was beyond their grasp. While the girls, sitting together by the table, strove to digest the meaning of the legal phrases that had fallen so strangely on their ears, Mr. Brion and Paul exchanged *sotto voce* suggestions and opinions over the parchment spread out before them. Then presently the old man opened a second document, glanced silently down the first page, cleared his throat, and looking over his spectacles, said solemnly, "My dears, give me your attention for a few minutes."

Each changed her position a little, and looked at him steadily. Paul leaned back in his chair, and put his hand over his eyes.

"What I have just been reading to you," said Mr. Brion, "is your father's last will and testament, as I believe. It appears that his surname was Yelverton, and that King was only an abbreviation of his Christian name — assumed as the surname for the purpose of eluding the search made for him by his family. Now, certain circumstances have come to our knowledge lately, referring, apparently, to this inexplicable conduct on your father's part." He paused, coughed, and nervously smoothed out the sheets before him, glancing hither and thither over their contents. "Elizabeth, my dear," he went on, "I think you heard Mr. Yelverton's account of his uncle's strange disappearance after — ahem — after a certain unfortunate catastrophe?"

"Yes," said Elizabeth. "We all know about that."

"Well, it seems — of course we must not jump at conclusions too hastily, but still it appears to me a reasonable conjecture — that your father and Mr. Yelverton's lost uncle *were* one and the same person. The affair altogether is so extraordinary, so altogether unaccountable, on the face of it, that we shall require a great deal of proof — and of course Mr. Yelverton himself will require the very fullest and most absolute legal proof — before we can accept the theory as an established fact — "

"Did I not say so?" Elizabeth interrupted eagerly, surprised by the old man's sudden assumption of scepticism now that all doubt and uncertainty seemed to be over. "I wish that nothing should be done — that no steps of any sort should be taken — until it is all proved to the last letter."

"Well," said Mr. Brion, at once abandoning his cautious attitude, "we must take steps to obtain proof before we *can* obtain it. And, as it providentially happens, we have received the most opportune and, as I believe, the most unimpeachable testimony from Mr. Yelverton himself, who is the loser by our gain, and who gave us the information which is so singularly corroborated in these documents before the existence of such documents was known to anybody. But if more were wanted — "

"More *is* wanted," urged Elizabeth. "We cannot take advantage of his own admissions to ruin him."

"If more were wanted," Mr. Brion repeated, with growing solemnity of manner, "we have here a paper under your father's hand, and duly witnessed by the same persons who witnessed the will — where are you going, Paul?" For at this point Paul rose and walked quietly towards the door.

"Go on," said the young man. "I will come back presently."

"But where are you going?" his father repeated with irritation. "Can't you wait until this business is finished?"

"I think," said Paul, "that the Miss Kings—the Miss Yelvertons, I suppose I ought to say—would rather be by themselves while you read that paper. It is not just like the will, you know; it is a private matter—not for outsiders to listen to."

Elizabeth rose promptly and went towards him, laying her hand on his arm. "Do you think we consider *you* an outsider?" she said, reproachfully. "You are one of us—you are in the place of our brother—we want you to help us now more than we have ever done. Come and sit down—that is, of course, if you can spare time for our affairs when you have so many important ones of your own."

He went and sat down, taking the seat by Patty to which Elizabeth pointed him. Patty looked up at him wistfully, and then leaned her elbows on the table and put her face in her hands. Her lover laid his arm gently on the back of her chair.

"Shall I begin, my dear?" asked the lawyer hesitatingly. "I am afraid it will be painful to you, Elizabeth. Perhaps, as Paul says, it would be better for you to read it by yourselves. I will leave it with you for a little while, if you promise faithfully to be very careful with it."

But Elizabeth wished it to be read as the will was read, and the old man, vaguely suspecting that she might be illegally generous to the superseded representative of the Yelverton name and property, was glad to keep the paper in his own hands, and proceeded to recite its contents. "I, Kingscote Yelverton, calling myself John King, do hereby declare," &c.

It was the story of Kingscote Yelverton's unfortunate life, put on record in the form of an affidavit for the benefit of his children, apparently with the intention that they should claim their inheritance when he was gone. The witnesses were an old midwife, long since dead, and a young Scripture reader, now a middle-aged and prosperous ecclesiastic in a distant colony; both of whom the lawyer remembered as features of the "old days" when he himself was a new-comer to the out-of-the-world place that counted Mr. King as its oldest inhabitant. It was a touching little document, in the sad story that it told and the severe formality of the style of telling it. Kingscote Yelverton, it was stated, was the second of three brothers, sons of a long line of Yelvertons of Yelverton, of which three, however, according to hereditary custom, only one was privileged to inherit the ancestral wealth. This one, Patrick, a bachelor, had already come into his kingdom; the youngest, a briefless barrister in comfortable circumstances, had married a farmer's daughter in very early youth (while reading for university honours during a long vacation spent in the farmer's house), and was the father of a sturdy schoolboy while himself not long emancipated from the rule of pastors and masters; and Kingscote was a flourishing young captain in the Guards— when the tragedy which shattered the family to pieces, and threw its vast property into Chancery, took place. Bradenham Abbey was neighbour to Yelverton, and Cuthbert Leigh of Bradenham was kin to the Yelvertons of Yelverton. Cuthbert Leigh had a beautiful daughter by his first wife, Eleanor D'Arcy; when this daughter was sixteen her mother died, and a stepmother soon after took Eleanor D'Arcy's place; and not long after the stepmother came to Bradenham Cuthbert Leigh himself died, leaving an infant son and heir; and not long after *that* Mrs. Cuthbert Leigh married again, and her new husband administered Bradenham—in the interest of the heir eventually, but of himself and his own children in the meantime. So it happened that Elizabeth Leigh was rather elbowed out of her rights and privileges as her father's daughter; which being the case, her distant cousin and near friend, Mrs. Patrick Yelverton, mother of the ill-fated brothers (who lived, poor soul, to see her house left desolate), fetched the girl away from the home which was hers no more, and took her to live under her own wing at Yelverton. Then the troubles began. Elizabeth was young and fair; indeed, all accounts of her agreed in presenting the portrait of a woman who must have been irresistible to the normal and unappropriated man brought into close contact with her. At Yelverton she was the daily companion of the unwedded master of the house, and he succumbed accordingly. As an impartial chronicler, I may hazard the suggestion that she enjoyed a flirtation within lady-like limits, and was not without some responsibility in the matter. It was clear also that the dowager Mrs. Patrick, anxious to see her first-born suitably married and settled, and placed safely beyond the reach of designing farmers' daughters, contrived her best to effect a union between the two. But while Patrick was over head and ears in love, and Elizabeth was dallying with him, and the old mother planning new furniture for the stately rooms where the queen was to reign who should succeed her, Kingscote the guardsman—Kingscote, the handsome, strong-willed, fiery-tempered second son—came home. To him the girl's heart, with the immemorial and incurable perversity of hearts, turned forthwith, like a flower to the sun; and a very short furlough had but half run out when she was as deeply over head and ears in love with Kingscote as Patrick was with her. Kingscote also loved her passionately—on his own testimony, he loved her as never man loved before, though he made a proud confession that he had still been utterly unworthy of her; and so the materials for the tragedy were laid, like a housemaid's fire, ready for the match that kindled them. Elizabeth found her position untenable amid the strenuous and conflicting attentions bestowed on her by the mother and sons, and went away for a time to visit some of her other relatives; and when her presence and influence were withdrawn from Yelverton, the smothered enmity of the brothers broke out, and they had their first and last and fatal quarrel about her. She had left a miniature of herself hanging in their mother's boudoir; this miniature Patrick laid hands on, and carried off to his private rooms; wherefrom Kingscote, in a violent passion (as Elizabeth's accepted lover), abstracted it by force. Then the master of the house, always too much inclined to assert himself as such, being highly incensed in his turn at the liberty that had been taken with him, marched into his brother's bedroom, where the disputed treasure was hidden, found it, and put it in his breast until he could discover a safer place for it. They behaved like a pair of ill-regulated schoolboys, in short, as men do when love and jealousy combine to derange their nervous systems, and wrought their own irreparable ruin over this miserable trifle. Patrick, flushed with a lurid triumph at his temporary success, strolled away from the house for an aimless walk, but afterwards went to a gamekeeper's cottage to give some instructions that occurred to him. The gamekeeper was not at home, and the squire returned by way of a lonely track through a thick plantation, where some of the keeper's work had to be inspected. Here he met Kingscote, striding along with his gun over his shoulder. The guardsman had discovered his loss, and was in search of his brother, intending to make a calm statement of his right to the possession of the picture by virtue of his rights in the person of the fair original, but at the same time passionately determined that this sort of thing should be put a stop to. There was a short parley, a brief but fierce altercation, a momentary struggle—on one side to keep, on the other to take, the worthless little bone of contention—and it was all over. Patrick, sent backward by a sweep of his strong brother's arm, fell over the gun that had been carelessly propped against a sapling; the stock of the gun, flying up, was caught by a tough twig which dragged across the hammers, and as the man and the weapon tumbled to the ground together one hammer fell, and the exploded charge entered the squire's neck, just under the chin, and, passing upward to the brain, killed him. It was an accident, as all the family believed; but to the author of the mischance it was nothing less than murder. He was guilty of his brother's blood, and he accepted the portion of Cain—to be a fugitive and a vagabond on the face of the earth—in expiation of it. Partly with the idea of sparing pain and disgrace to his family (believing that the only evidence available would convict him of murder in a court of law), and partly because he felt that, if acquitted, it would be too horrible and impossible to take an inheritance that had come to him by such means, in the overwhelming desperation of his remorse and despair he took that determination to blot himself out which was never afterwards revoked.

Returning to the house, he collected some money and a few valuables, and, unsuspected and unnoticed, took leave of his home, and his name, and his place in the world, and was half way to London, and beyond recall, before the dead body in the plantation was discovered. In London Elizabeth Leigh was staying with an old Miss D'Arcy, quietly studying her music and taking a rest while the society which was so fond of her was out of town; and the stricken man could not carry out his resolve without bidding farewell to his beloved. He had a clandestine interview with Elizabeth, to whom alone he confided the circumstances of his wretched plight. The girl, of course, advised him to return to Yelverton, and bravely meet and bear whatever might befall; and it would have been well for him and for her if he had taken that advice. But he would not listen to it, nor be turned from his fixed purpose to banish and efface himself, if possible, for the rest of his life; seeing which, the devoted woman chose to share his fate. Whether he could and should have spared her that enormous sacrifice, or whether she was happier in making it than she would otherwise have been, only themselves ever knew. She did her woman's part in helping and sustaining and consoling him through all the blighted years that he was suffered to live and fret her with his brooding melancholy and his broken-spirited moroseness, and doubtless she found her true vocation in that thorny path of love.

The story, as told by himself for the information of his children (who, as children ever do, came in time to have interests of their own that transcended in importance those that were merely personal to their parents), was much more brief and bald than this, and the reading of it did not take many minutes. When he had finished it, in dead silence, the lawyer took from the packet of papers a third and smaller document, which he also proceeded to read aloud to those whom it concerned. This proved to be a certificate of the marriage of Kingscote Yelverton and Elizabeth Leigh, celebrated in an obscure London parish by a curate who had been the bridegroom's Eton and Oxford chum, and witnessed by a pair of humble folk who had had great difficulty in composing their respective signatures, on the 25th of November in the year 1849. And, finally, half-folded round the packet, there was a slip of paper, on which was written—"Not to be opened until my death."

"And it might never have been opened until you were *all* dead!" exclaimed the lawyer, holding up his hands. "He must have meant to give it to you at the last, and did not reckon on being struck helpless in a moment when his time came."

"Oh, poor father!" sobbed Elizabeth, whose head lay on the table, crushed down in her handkerchief. And the other sisters put their arms about her, Patty with a set white face and Eleanor whimpering a little. But

Mr. Brion and Paul were incensed with the dead man, and could not pity him at present.

It was late before the two friendly advisers, summoned to dinner by their landlady, went back to No. 7, and they did not like going. It did not seem to them at all right that the three girls should be left alone under present circumstances. Mr. Brion wanted to summon Mrs. Duff-Scott, or even Mrs. M'Intyre, to bear them company and see that they did not faint, or have hysterics, or otherwise "give way," under the exceptional strain put upon their nervous systems. Then he wanted them to come next door for that dinner which he felt they must certainly stand much in need of, and for which they did not seem to have adequate materials; or to let him take them to the nearest hotel, or to Mrs. Duff-Scott's; or, at least, to permit him to give them some brandy and water; and he was genuinely distressed because they refused to be nourished and comforted and appropriately cared for in any of these ways.

"We want to be quiet for a little, dear Mr. Brion, that we may talk things over by ourselves—if you don't mind," Elizabeth said; and the tone of her voice silenced all his protests. The old man kissed them, for the first time in his life, uttering a few broken words of congratulation on the wonderful change in their fortunes; and Paul shook hands with great gravity and without saying anything at all, even though Patty, looking up into his inscrutable face, mutely asked for his sympathy with her wistful, wet eyes. And they went away.

As they were letting themselves out of the house, assisted by the ground-floor domestic, who, scenting mystery in the air, politely volunteered to open the hall door in order that she might investigate the countenances of the Miss Kings' visitors and perchance gather some enlightenment therefrom, Patty, dry-eyed and excited, came flying downstairs, and pounced upon the old man.

"Mr. Brion, Mr. Brion, Elizabeth says she hopes you will be *sure* not to divulge what we have discovered to *anybody*," she panted breathlessly (at the same time glancing at her lover's back as he stood on the door-step). "It is of the utmost consequence to her to keep it quiet for a little longer."

"But, my dear, what object can Elizabeth have in waiting *now*? Surely it is better to have it over at once, and settled. I thought of walking up to the club by-and-bye, with the papers, and having a word with Mr. Yelverton."

"Of course it is better to have it over," assented Patty.

"I know your time is precious, and I myself am simply frantic till I can tell Mrs. Duff-Scott. So is Elizabeth. But there is something she must do first—I can't tell you the particulars—but she *must* have a few hours' start—say till to-morrow evening—before you speak to Mr. Yelverton or take any steps. I am sure she will do *whatever* you wish, after that."

The lawyer hesitated, suspicious of the wisdom of the delay, but not seeing how much harm could happen, seeing that he had all the precious documents in his own breast pocket; then he reluctantly granted Patty's request, and the girl went upstairs again with feet not quite so light as those that had carried her down. Upstairs, however, she subordinated her own interests to the consideration of her sister's more pressing affairs.

"Elizabeth," she said, with fervid and portentous solemnity, "this is a crisis for you, and you must be bold and brave. It is no time for shilly-shallying—you have twenty-four hours before you, and you must *act*. If you don't, you will see that he will just throw up everything, and be too proud to take it back. He will lose all his money and the influence for good that it gives him, and *you* will lose *him*."

"How shall I act?" asked Elizabeth, leaning instinctively upon this more courageous spirit.

"How?" echoed Patty, looking at her sister with brilliant eyes. "Oh!" drawing a long breath, and speaking with a yearning passion that it was beyond the power of good grammar to express—"oh, if it was only *me!*"

CHAPTER XXXIX
AN ASSIGNATION

That evening Mr. Yelverton was leisurely finishing his dinner at the club when a note was brought to him. He thought he knew the writing, though he had never seen it before, and put it into his pocket until he could politely detach himself from three semi-hosts, semi-guests, with whom he was dining. Then he went upstairs rather quickly, tearing open his letter as he went, and, arrived at the reading-room, sat down at a table, took pen in hand, and dashed off an immediate reply. "I will certainly be there," he wrote, in a hand more vigorous than elegant. "I will wait for you in the German picture gallery. Come as early as possible, while the place is quiet." And, having closed his missive and consigned it to the bag, he remained in a comfortable arm-chair in the quiet room, all by himself, meditating. He felt he had a great deal to think about, and it indisposed him for convivialities. The week since his parting with Elizabeth, long as it had seemed to him, had not quite run out, and she had made an assignation which, though it might have appeared unequivocal to the casual eye, was to him extremely perplexing. She had come back, and she wanted to see him, and she wanted to see him alone, and she asked him if he would meet her at the Exhibition in the morning. And she addressed him as her dearest friend, and signed herself affectionately his. He tried very hard, but he could not extract his expected comfort from such a communication, made under such circumstances.

In the morning he was amongst the first batch of breakfasters in the club coffee-room, and amongst the first to represent the public at the ticket-windows of the Carlton Palace. When he entered the great building, it was in the possession of officials and workmen, and echoed in a hollow manner to his solid footfall. Without a glance to right or left, he walked upstairs to the gallery and into that cosiest nook of the whole Exhibition, the German room, and there waited for his mistress. This restful room, with its carpeted floor and velvety settees (so grateful to the weary), its great Meissen vases in the middle, and casts of antique statues all round, was quite empty of visitors, and looked as pleasant and convenient a place of rendezvous as lovers could desire. If only Elizabeth would come quickly, he thought, they might have the most delicious quiet talk, sitting side by side on a semi-circular ottoman opposite to Lindenschmidt's "Death of Adonis"—not regarding that unhappy subject, of course, nor any other object but themselves. He would not sit down until she came, but strolled round and round, pausing now and then to investigate a picture, but thinking of nothing but his beloved, for whose light step he was listening. If his bodily eyes were fixed on the "Cloister Pond" or "Evening," or any other of the tranquil landscapes pictured on the wall, he thought of Elizabeth resting with him under green trees, far from the madding crowd's ignoble strife, absolutely his own, and in a world that (practically) held nobody but him and her. If he looked at autumnal rain slanting fiercely across the canvas, he thought how he would protect and shield her in all the storms that might visit her life—"My plaidie to the angry airt, I'd shelter thee, I'd shelter thee!" And visions of a fair morning in Thuringia, of a lake in the Bavarian mountains, of a glacier in the Engadine, and of Venice in four or five aspects of sunlight and moonlight, suggested his wedding journey and how beautiful the world she had so longed to see—the world that he knew so well—would look henceforth, if—if—

There was a step upon the corridor outside, and he turned sharply from his contemplation of a little picture of an Isle of Wight sunrise to meet her as she came in. She had been walking hurriedly, but in the doorway she paused, seeing him striding towards her, and stood for a moment confused and hesitating, overcome with embarrassment. It was a bright morning, and she had dressed herself in a delicate linen gown, fitting easily to the sweeping curves of her noble figure—a gown over which Mrs. Duff-Scott had spent hours of careful thought and a considerable amount of money, but which was so simple and unpretending in its effects as to suggest the domestic needle and the judicious outlay of a few shillings to those admirable critics of the other sex who have so little knowledge of such matters and so much good taste; and all the details of her costume were in harmony with this central feature—her drooping straw hat, tied with soft Indian muslin under the chin, her Swedish gloves, her neat French shoes, her parasol—and the effect was insidious but impressive. She had got herself up carefully for her lover's eyes, and nobody could have looked less got up than she. Mr. Yelverton thought how much more charming was a homely every-day style than the elaborate dressing of the ball-room and the block, and that it was certainly evident to any sensible person that a woman like Elizabeth needed no arts of the milliner to make her attractive. He took her hand in a strong clasp, and held it in silence for a moment, his left hand laid over her fine unwrinkled glove, while he looked into her downcast face for some sign of the nature of her errand.

"Well, my love," he murmured eagerly, "what is it? Don't keep me in suspense. Is it yes or no, Elizabeth?"

Her embarrassment melted away before the look he bent upon her, as a morning mist before the sun. She lifted her eyes to his—those honest eyes that he could read like a book—and her lips parted in an effort to speak. The next instant, before a word was said, he had her in his arms, and her mouth met his under the red moustache in a long, and close, and breathless kiss; and both of them knew that they were to part no more till their lives' end. While that brief ceremony of betrothal lasted, they might have been in the black grotto where they kissed each other first, so oblivious were they of their surroundings; but they took in presently the meaning of certain sounds in the gallery on the other side of the curtain, and resumed their normal attitudes. "Come and sit down," said Mr. Yelverton, drawing her into the room. "Come and let's have a talk." And he set her down on the velvet ottoman and took a seat beside her—leaning forward with an arm on his knee to barricade her from an invasion of the public as far as possible. His thoughts turned, naturally enough, to their late very important interview in the caves.

"We will go back there," he said, expressing his desire frankly. "When we are married, Elizabeth, we will go to your old home again together, before we set out on longer travels, and you and I will have a picnic to the caves all alone by ourselves, in that little buggy that we drove the other day. Shall we?"

"We might tumble into one of those terrible black holes," she replied, "if we went there again."

"True—we might. And when we are married we must not run any unnecessary risks. We will live together as long as we possibly can, Elizabeth."

She had drawn off her right glove, and now slipped her hand into his. He grasped it fervently, and kneaded it like a lump of stiff dough (excuse the homely simile, dear reader—it has the merit of appropriateness, which is more than you can say for the lilies and jewellery) between his two strong palms. How he did long for that dark cave!—for any nook or corner that would have hidden him and her from sight for the next half hour.

"Why couldn't you have told me a week ago?" he demanded, with a thrill in his deep voice. "You must have known you would take me then, or you would not have come to me like this to-day. Why didn't you give yourself to me at first? Then we should have been together all this time—all these precious days that we have wasted—and we should have been by the sea at this moment, sitting under those big rocks, or wandering away into the bush, where nobody could interfere with us."

As he spoke, a party of ladies strolled into the court, and he leaned back upon his cushioned seat to wait until they were gone again. They looked at the pictures, with one eye on him, dawdled up and down for five minutes, trying to assert their right to be there if they chose; and then, too uncomfortably conscious of being *de trop*, departed. After which the lovers were alone again for a little while. Mr. Yelverton resumed possession of Elizabeth's hand, and repeated his rather cruel question.

"Didn't you know all along that it must come to this?"

"A week ago I did not know what I know now," she replied.

"Ah, my dear, you knew it in your heart, but you would not listen to your heart."

He thought he understood it all, perfectly. He pictured her regret and hungry longing for him after he was gone, how she had fought against it for a time, and how it had precipitately driven her to Melbourne at last, and driven her to summon him in this importunate fashion to her side. It was exactly what he would have done, he thought, had he been in her place.

"Mr. Yelverton—"

She was beginning to speak seriously, but he stopped her. "No," he said, "I am not going to be called Mr. Yelverton by *you*. Never again, remember. My name is Kingscote, if you wish to know. My people at home, when I had any people, called me King. I think you might as well call me King—it will keep your dear name alive in the family when you no longer answer to it yourself. Now"—as she paused, and was looking at him rather strangely—"what were you going to say?"

"I was going to say that I have not wasted this week since you went away. A great deal has happened—a great many changes—and I was helped by something outside myself to make up my mind."

"I don't believe it—I don't believe it, Elizabeth. You know you love me, and you know that, whatever your religious sentiments may be, you would not do violence to them for anything *less* than that. You are taking me because you love me too well to give me up—for any consideration whatever. So don't say you are not."

She touched his shoulder for a moment with her cheek. "Oh, I do love you, I do love you!" she murmured, drawing a long, sighing breath.

He knew it well, and he did not know how to bear to sit there, unable to respond to her touching confession. He could only knead her hand between his palms.

"And you are going to trust me, my love—me and yourself? You are not afraid now?"

"No, I don't think I am afraid." She caught her breath a little, and looked grave and anxious as she said it, haunted still by the feeling that duty meant sacrifice and that happiness meant sin in some more or less insidious shape; a habit of thought in which she, like so many more of us, had been educated until it had taken the likeness of a natural instinct. "I don't think I am afraid. Religion, as you say, is a living thing, independent of the creeds that it is dressed in. And—and—you *must* be a good man!"

"Don't begin by making that an article of faith," he returned promptly. "To set up for being a good man is the last thing I would dream of. Like other men, I am good as far as I was born and have been made so, and neither more nor less. All I can take credit for on my own account is that I try to live up to the light that has been given me."

"What can anyone do more?" she said, eagerly. "It is better than believing at haphazard and not trying at all—which is what so many good people are content with."

"It seems better to me," he said.

"I will trust you—I will trust you," she went on, leaning towards him as he sat beside her. "You are doing more good in the world than I had even thought of until I knew you. It is I who will not be up to the mark—not you. But I will help you as much as you will let me—I am going to give my life to helping you. And at least—at least—you believe in God," she concluded, yearning for some tangible and definite evidence of faith, as she had understood faith, wherewith to comfort her conscientious soul. "We are together in *that*—the chief thing of all—are we not?"

He was a scrupulously truthful man, and he hesitated for a moment. "Yes, my dear," he said, gravely. "I believe in God—that is to say, I *feel* Him—I lean my littleness on a greatness that I know is all around me and upholding me, which is Something that even God seems a word too mean for. I think," he added, "that God, to me, is not what He has been taught to seem to you."

"Never mind," she said, in a low voice, responding to the spirit rather than the letter of his words. "Whatever you believe you are sure to believe thoroughly, and if you believe in God, your God must be a true God. I feel it, though I don't know it."

"You feel that things will all come right for us if we have faith in our own hearts, and love and trust each other. So do I, Elizabeth." There was nobody looking, and he put his arm round her shoulder for a moment. "And we may consider our religious controversy closed then? We need not trouble ourselves about that any more?"

"I would not say 'closed.' Don't you think we ought to talk of *all* our thoughts—and especially those that trouble us—to each other?"

"I do—I do, indeed. And so we shall. Ours is going to be a real marriage. We shall be, not two, but one. Only for the present we may put this topic aside, as being no longer an obstruction in the way of our arrangements, mayn't we?"

"Yes," she said. And the die was cast.

"Very well, then." He seemed to pull himself together at this point, and into his fine frame and his vigorous face a new energy was infused, the force of which seemed to be communicated to the air around her, and made her heart beat more strongly to the quicker pulse of his. "Very well, then. Now tell me, Elizabeth—without any formality, while you and I are here together—when shall we be married?"

The question had a tone of masterful command about it, for, though he knew how spontaneous and straightforward she was, her natural delicacy unspoiled by artificial sentiment, he yet prepared himself to encounter a certain amount of maidenly reluctance to meet a man's reasonable views upon this matter. But she answered him without delay or hesitation, impelled by the terrors that beset her and thinking of Patty's awful warnings and prophesyings—"I will leave you to say when."

"Will you really? Do you mean you will *really?*" His deep-set eyes glowed, and his voice had a thrilling tremor in it as he made this incredulous inquiry. "Then I say we will be married soon—*very* soon—so as not to lose a day more than we can help. Will you agree to that?"

She looked a little frightened, but she stood her ground. "If you wish," she whispered, all the tone shaken out of her voice.

"If *I* wish!" A palpitating silence held them for a moment. Then "What do you say to *to-morrow?*" he suggested.

She looked up at him, blushing violently.

"Ah, you are thinking how forward I am!" she exclaimed, drawing her hand from his.

"Elizabeth," he remonstrated, with swift energy, "did I not ask you, ever so long ago, not to be conventional? Why should I think you forward? How can you be forward—with *me*? You are the most delicate-minded woman I ever knew, and I think you are showing yourself so at this moment—when anything short of perfect truth and candour would have disappointed me. Now, I am quite serious—will you marry me to-morrow? There is no reason why you should not, that I can see. Just think of it, calmly. Mrs. Duff-Scott gave her consent a fortnight ago—yes, she gave it privately, to *me*; and Patty and Nelly, I know, would be delighted. As for you and me, what have we—honestly, what *have* we—to wait for? Each of us is without any tie to be broken by it. Those who look to us will all be better off. I want to get home soon, and you have taken me, Elizabeth—it will be all the same in the end—you know that no probation will prove us unfit or unwilling to marry—the *raison d'être* of an engagement does not exist for us. And I am not young, my love, and life is short and uncertain; while you—"

"I am not young either," she interrupted. "I shall soon be thirty."

"Shall you? I am glad of it. Well, think of it then—*why* should we not do it, so exceptionally circumstanced as we are? We can take the afternoon train to somewhere—say to Macedon, to live up there amongst the mountains for a little while—till we decide what next to do, while our sisters enjoy themselves with Mrs. Duff-Scott. I can make all arrangements to-day, except for wedding cake and bridesmaids—and we would rather be without them. Come here to-morrow morning, my darling, as soon as the place is open, in that same pretty gown that you have got on now; and we will take a cab and go and get married peaceably, without all the town staring at us. I will see Mrs. Duff-Scott and make it all right. She shall meet us at the church, with the girls, and the major to give you away. Will you? Seriously, *will* you?"

She was silent for some time, while he leaned forward and watched her face. He saw, to his surprise, that she was actually thinking over it, and he did not interrupt her. She was, indeed, possessed by the idea that this wild project offered safety to them both in face of the impending catastrophe. If she could not secure him in the possession of his property before he was made aware that he had lost it, she might anticipate his possible refusal to let her be his benefactor, and the hindrances and difficulties that seemed likely to sunder them after having come so near to each other. She lifted her eyes from the carpet presently, and looked into his.

"Do you mean that you *will?*" he exclaimed, the fierceness of his delight tempered by a still evident incredulity.

"I will," she said, "if—"

"Hush—hush! Don't let there be any ifs, Elizabeth!"

"Yes—listen. If Mrs. Duff-Scott will freely consent and approve—"

"You may consider *that* settled, anyhow. I know she will."

"And if you will see Mr. Brion to-night—"

"Mr. Brion? What do we want with Mr. Brion? Settlements?"

"No. But he has something to tell you about me—about my family—something that you *must* know before we can be married."

"What is it? Can't *you* tell me what it is?" He looked surprised and uneasy. "Don't frighten me, Elizabeth—it is nothing to matter, is it?"

"I don't know. I hope not. I cannot tell you myself. He will explain everything if you will see him this evening. He came back to Melbourne with us, and he is waiting to see you."

"Tell me this much, at any rate," said Mr. Yelverton, anxiously; "it is no just cause or impediment to our being married to-morrow, is it?"

"No. At least, I don't think so. I hope you won't."

"*I* shan't if *you* don't, you may depend upon that." He made up his mind on the spot that there were some shady pages in her family history that a sense of honour prompted her to reveal to him before he married her, and congratulated himself that she was not like the conventional heroine, who would have been too proud to make him happy under such circumstances. "I am not afraid of Mr. Brion, if you are not," he repeated. "And we will shunt him for the present, with your permission. Somehow I can't bring myself to think of anybody just now except you and me." The picture galleries were pretty full by this time, and the public was invading the privacy of the German Court rather freely. "Come and let us walk about a little," he said, rising from the ottoman, "and enjoy the sensation of being alone in a crowd." And they sauntered out into the corridor, and down the stairs, and up and down the long nave, side by side—a distinguished and imposing if not strictly handsome couple—passing shoals of people, and bowing now and then to an acquaintance; mixing unsuspected with the common herd, and hugging the delicious consciousness that in secret they were alone and apart from everybody. They talked with more ease and freedom than when *tête-à-tête* on their settee upstairs.

"And so, by this time to-morrow, we shall be man and wife," Mr. Yelverton said, musingly. "Doesn't your head swim a little when you think of that, Elizabeth? *I* feel as if I had been drinking, and I am terribly afraid of finding myself sober presently. No, I am not afraid," he continued, correcting himself. "You have given me your promise, and you won't go back on it, as the Yankees say, will you?"

"If either of us goes back," said Elizabeth, unblushingly; "it won't be me."

"You seem to think it possible that *I* may go back? Don't you flatter yourself, my young friend. When you come here to-morrow, as you will, in that pretty cool gown—I stipulate for that gown remember—"

"Even if it is a cold day?—or pouring with rain?"

"Well, I don't know. Couldn't you put a warm jacket over it? When you come here to-morrow, I say, you will find me waiting for you, the embodiment of relentless fate, with the wedding ring in my pocket. By the way—that reminds me—how am I to know the size of your finger? And you have not got your engagement ring yet! I'll tell you what we'll do, Elizabeth; we'll choose a ring out of the Exhibition, and we'll cheat the customs for once. The small things are smuggled out of the place all day long, and every day, as you may see by taking stock of the show cases occasionally. We'll be smugglers too—it is in a good cause—and I'll go so far as to use bribery and corruption, if necessary, to get possession of that ring to-day. I'll say, 'Let me have it now, or I won't have it at all,' and you will see they'll let me have it. I will then put it on your finger, and you shall wear it for a little while, and then I will borrow it to get the size of your wedding ring from it. By-and-bye, you know, when we are at home at Yelverton—years hence, when we are old people—"

"Oh, don't talk of our being old people!" she interrupted, quickly.

"No, I won't—it will be a long time yet, dear. By-and-bye, when we are at home at Yelverton, you will look at your ring, and think of this day, and of the German picture gallery—of the dear Exhibition which brought us together, and where you gave yourself to me—long after I had given myself to *you*, Elizabeth! It is most appropriate that your engagement ring should be got here. Come along and let us choose it. What stones do you like best?"

They spent nearly an hour amongst the jewellery of all nations before Mr. Yelverton could decide on what he liked. At last he selected from a medley of glittering trinkets a sober ring that did not glitter, and yet was rare and valuable—a broad, plain band of gold set with a lovely cameo carved out of an opal stone. "There is some little originality about it," he said, as he tried it on her finger, which it fitted perfectly, "and, though the intaglio looks so delicate, it will stand wear and tear, and last for ever. That is the chief thing. Do you like it? Or would you rather have diamonds?"

She had no words to say how much she liked it, and how much she preferred it to diamonds. And so, after a few severe struggles, carried on in a foreign tongue, he obtained immediate possession of his purchase, and she carried it away on her finger.

"Now," said he, looking at his watch, "are you in any great hurry to get home?"

She thought of her non-existent trousseau, and the packing of her portmanteau for her wedding journey; nevertheless, she intimated her willingness to stay a little while longer.

"Very well. We will go and have our lunch then. We'll join the *table d'hôte* of the Exhibition, Elizabeth—that will give us a foretaste of our Continental travels. To-morrow we shall have lunch—where? At Mrs. Duff-Scott's, I suppose—it would be too hard upon her to leave her literally at the church door. Yes, we shall have lunch at Mrs. Duff-Scott's, and I suppose the major will insist our drinking our healths in champagne, and making us a pretty speech. Never mind, we will have our dinner in peace. To-morrow evening we shall be at home, Elizabeth, and you and I will dine *tête-à-tête*, without even a single parlourmaid to stand behind our chairs. I don't quite know yet where I shall discover those blessed four walls that we shall dine in, nor what sort of dinner it will be—but I will find out before I sleep to-night."

CHAPTER XL
MRS. DUFF-SCOTT HAS TO
BE RECKONED WITH

Prosaic as were their surroundings and their occupation—sitting at a long table, he at the end and she at the corner on his left hand, amongst a scattered crowd of hungry folk, in the refreshment room of the Exhibition, eating sweetbreads and drinking champagne and soda water—it was like a dream to Elizabeth, this foretaste of Continental travels. In the background of her consciousness she had a sense of having acted madly, if not absurdly, in committing herself to the programme that her audacious lover had drawn out; but the thoughts and fancies floating on the surface of her mind were too absorbing for the present to leave room for serious reflections. Dreaming as she was, she not only enjoyed the homely charm of sitting at meat with him in this informal, independent manner, but she enjoyed her lunch as well, after her rather exhausting emotions. It is commonly supposed, I know, that overpowering happiness takes away the appetite; but experience has taught me that it is not invariably the case. The misery of suspense and dread can make you sicken at the sight of food, but the bliss of rest and security in having got what you want has an invigorating effect, physically as well as spiritually, if you are a healthy person. So I say that Elizabeth was unsentimentally hungry, and enjoyed her sweetbreads. They chatted happily over their meal, like truant children playing on the edge of a precipice. Mr. Yelverton had the lion's share in the conversation, and talked with distracting persistence of the journey to-morrow, and the lighter features of the stupendous scheme that they had so abruptly adopted. Elizabeth smiled and blushed and listened, venturing occasionally upon a gentle repartee. Presently, however, she started a topic on her own account "Tell me," she said, "do you object to first cousins marrying?"

"Dear child, I don't object to anything to-day," he replied. "As long as I am allowed to marry you, I am quite willing to let other men please themselves."

"But tell me seriously—do you?"

"Must I be serious? Well, let me think. No, I don't know that I object—there is so very little that I object to, you see, in the way of things that people want to do—but I think, perhaps, that, all things being equal, a man would not *choose* to marry so near a blood relation."

"You *do* think it wrong, then?"

"I think it not only wrong but utterly preposterous and indefensible," he said, "that it should be lawful and virtuous for a man to marry his first cousin and wicked and indecent to marry his sister-in-law—or his aunt-in-law for the matter of that—or any other free woman who has no connection with him except through other people's marriages. If a legal restriction in such matters can ever be necessary or justifiable, it should be in the way of preventing the union of people of the same blood. Sense and the laws of physiology have something to say to *that*—they have nothing whatever to say to the relations that are of no kin to each other. Them's my sentiments, Miss King, if you particularly wish to know them."

Elizabeth put her knife and fork together on her plate softly. It was a gesture of elaborate caution, meant to cover her conscious agitation. "Then you would not—if it were your own case—marry your cousin?" she asked, after a pause, in a very small and gentle voice. He was studying the *menu* on her behalf, and wondering if the strawberries and cream would be fresh. Consequently he did not notice how pale she had grown, all of a sudden.

"Well," he said, "you see I have no cousin, to begin with. And if I had I could not possibly want to marry her, since I am going to marry you to-morrow, and a man is only allowed to have one wife at a time. So my own case doesn't come in."

"But if *I* had been your cousin?" she urged, breathlessly, but with her eyes on her plate. "Supposing, for the sake of argument, that *I* had been of your blood—would you still have had me?"

"Ah!" he said, laughing, "that is, indeed, a home question."

"*Would* you?" she persisted.

"Would I?" he echoed, putting a hand under the table to touch hers. "I really think I would, Elizabeth. I'm afraid that nothing short of your having been my own full sister could have saved you."

After that she regained her colour and brightness, and was able to enjoy the early strawberries and cream—which did happen to be fresh.

They did not hurry themselves over their lunch, and when they left the refreshment-room they went and sat down on two chairs by the Brinsmead pianos and listened to a little music (in that worst place that ever was for hearing it). Then Mr. Yelverton took his *fiancée* to get a cup of Indian tea. Then he looked at his watch gravely.

"Do you know," he said, "I really have an immense deal of business to get through before night if we are to be married to-morrow morning."

"There is no reason why we should be married to-morrow morning," was her immediate comment "Indeed—indeed, it is far too soon."

"It may be soon, Elizabeth, but I deny that it is too soon, reluctant as I am to contradict you. And, whether or no, the date is fixed, *irrevocably*. We have only to consider"—he broke off, and consulted his watch again, thinking of railway and telegraph arrangements. "Am I obliged to see Mr. Brion to-day?" he asked, abruptly. "Can't I put him off till another time? Because, you know, he may say just whatever he likes, and it won't make the smallest particle of difference."

"Oh," she replied earnestly, "you *must* see him. I can't marry you till he has told you everything. I wish I could!" she added, impulsively.

"Well, if I must I must—though I know it doesn't matter the least bit. Will he keep me long, do you suppose?"

"I think, very likely, he will."

"Then, my darling, we must go. Give me your ring—you shall have it back to-night. Go and pack your portmanteau this afternoon, so that you have a little spare time for Mrs. Duff-Scott. She will be sure to want you in the evening. You need not take much, you know—just enough for a week or two. She will be only too delighted to look after your clothes while you are away, and"—with a smile—"we'll buy the trousseau in Paris on our way home. I am credibly informed that Paris is the proper place to go to for the trousseau of a lady of quality."

"Trousseaus are nonsense," said Elizabeth, who perfectly understood his motives for this proposition, "in these days of rapidly changing fashions, unless the bride cannot trust her husband to give her enough pocket money."

"Precisely. That is just what I think. And I don't want to be deprived of the pleasure of dressing you. But for a week or two, Elizabeth, we are going out of the world just as far as we can get, where you won't want much dressing. Take only what is necessary for comfort, dear, enough for a fortnight—or say three weeks. That will do. And tell me where I shall find Mr. Brion."

They were passing out of the Exhibition building—passing that noble group of listening hounds and huntsman that stood between the front entrance and the gate—and Elizabeth was wondering how she should find Mr. Brion at once and make sure of that evening interview, when she caught sight of the old lawyer himself coming into the flowery enclosure from the street. "Why, there he is!" she exclaimed. "And my sisters are with him."

"We are taking him out for an airing," exclaimed Eleanor, who was glorious in her Cup-day costume, and evidently in an effervescence of good spirits, when she recognised the engaged pair. "Mr. Paul was too busy to attend to him, and he had nobody but us, poor man! So we are going to show him round. Would you believe that he has never seen the Exhibition, Elizabeth?"

They had scarcely exchanged greetings with each other when, out of an open carriage at the gate, stepped Mrs. Duff-Scott, on her way to that extensive kettle-drum which was held in the Exhibition at this hour. When she saw her girls, their festive raiment, and their cavaliers, the fairy godmother's face was a study.

"What!" she exclaimed, with heart-rending reproach, "you are back in Melbourne! You are walking about with—with your friends"—hooking on her eye-glass the better to wither poor Mr. Brion, who wasted upon her a bow that would have done credit to Lord Chesterfield—"and I am not told!"

Patty came forward, radiant with suppressed excitement. "She must be told," exclaimed the girl, breathlessly. "Elizabeth, we are all here now. And it is Mrs. Duff-Scott's *right* to know what we know. And Mr. Yelverton's too."

"You may tell them now," said Elizabeth, who was as white as the muslin round her chin. "Take them all to Mrs. Duff-Scott's house, and explain everything, and get it over—while I go home."

CHAPTER XLI
MR. YELVERTON STATES HIS INTENTIONS

"I don't think you know Mr. Brion," said Mr. Yelverton, first lifting his hat and shaking hands with Mrs. Duff-Scott, and then, with an airy and audacious cheerfulness, introducing the old man (whose name and association with her *protégées* she immediately recalled to mind); "Mr. Brion—Mrs. Duff-Scott."

The fairy godmother bowed frigidly, nearly shutting her eyes as she did so, and for a moment the little group kept an embarrassed silence, while a sort of electric current of intelligence passed between Patty and her new-found cousin. Mr. Yelverton was, as we say, not the same man that he had been a few hours before. Quiet in his manner, as he ever was, there was yet an aspect of glowing energy about him, an air of being at high pressure, that did not escape the immediate notice of the girl's vigilant and sympathetic eyes. I have described him very badly if I have not made the reader understand the virile breadth and strength of his emotional nature, and how it would be affected by his present situation. The hot blue blood and superfine culture of that ardent young aristocrat who became his father at such an early age, and the wholesome physical and moral solidity of the farmer's fair and rustic daughter who was his mother, were blended together in him; with the result that he was a man at all points, having all the strongest human instincts alive and active in him. He was not the orthodox philanthropist, the half-feminine, half-neuter specialist with a hobby, the foot-rule reformer, the prig with a mission to set the world right; his benevolence was simply the natural expression of a sense of sympathy and brotherhood between him and his fellows, and the spirit which produced that was not limited in any direction. From the same source came a passionately quick and keen apprehension of the nature of the closest bond of all, not given to the selfish and narrow-hearted. Amongst his abstract brothers and sisters he had been looking always for his own concrete mate, and having found her and secured her, he was as a king newly anointed, whose crown had just been set upon his head.

"Will you come?" said Patty to him, trying not to look too conscious of the change she saw in him. "It is time to have done with all our secrets now."

"I agree with you," he replied. "And I will come with pleasure." Mrs. Duff-Scott was accordingly made to understand, with some difficulty, that the mystery which puzzled her had a deep significance, and that she was desired to take steps at once whereby she might be made acquainted with it. Much bewildered, but without relaxing her offended air—for she conceived that no explanation would make any difference in the central fact that Mr. Yelverton and Mr. Brion had taken precedence of her in the confidence of her own adopted daughters—she returned to her carriage, all the little party following meekly at her heels. The girls were put in first—even Elizabeth, who, insisting upon detaching herself from the assembling council, had to submit to be conveyed to Myrtle Street; and the two men, lifting their hats to the departing vehicle, were left on the footpath together. The lawyer was very grave, and slightly nervous and embarrassed. To his companion he had all the air of a man with a necessary but disagreeable duty to perform.

"What is all this about?" Mr. Yelverton demanded with a little anxious irritation in his tone. "Nothing of any great consequence, is it?"

"I—I'm afraid you will think it rather a serious matter," the lawyer replied, with hesitation. "Still," he added, earnestly, "if you are their friend, as I believe you are—knowing that they have no responsibility in the matter—you will not let it make any difference in your feeling for them—"

"There is not the *faintest* danger of that," Mr. Yelverton promptly and haughtily interposed.

"I am sure of it—I am sure of it. Well, you shall know all in half an hour. If you will kindly find Major Duff-Scott—he has constituted himself their guardian, in a way, and ought to be present—I will just run round to my lodgings in Myrtle Street."

"Are you going to fetch your son?" asked Mr. Yelverton, quickly. "Don't you think that, under the circumstances—supposing matters have to be talked of that will be painful to the Miss Kings—the fewer present the better?"

"Certainly. I am not going to fetch my son, who, by the way, already knows all there is to know, but some documents relating to the affair, which he keeps in his strong-box for safety. Major Duff-Scott is the only person whose presence we require, since—"

"Since what?"

Mr. Brion was going to say, "Since your solicitors are not at hand," but checked himself. "Never mind," he said, "never mind. I cannot say any more now."

"All right. I'll go and find the major. Thank Heaven, he's no gossip, and I think he is too real a friend of the Miss Kings to care what he hears any more than I do." But Mr. Yelverton got anxious about this point after it occurred to him, and went off thoughtfully to the club, congratulating himself that, thanks to his sweetheart's reasonableness, he was in a position which gave him the privilege of protecting them should the issue of this mysterious business leave them in need of protection.

At the club he found the major, talking desultory politics with other ex-guardians of the State now shelved in luxurious irresponsibility with him; and the little man was quite ready to obey his friend's summons to attend the family council.

"The Miss Kings are back," said Mr. Yelverton, "and old Brion, the lawyer, is with them, and there are some important matters to be talked over this afternoon, and you must come and hear."

The major said that he was at the Miss Kings' service, and got his hat. He asked no questions as he passed through the lobby and down the steps to Mr. Yelverton's cab, which waited in the street. In his own mind he concluded that Elizabeth's engagement had "come off," and this legal consultation had some more or less direct reference to settlements, and the relations of the bride-elect's sisters to her new lot in life. What chiefly occupied his thoughts was the fear that he was going to be asked to give up Patty and Eleanor, and all the way from the club to his house he was wondering how far his and his wife's rights in them extended, and how far his energetic better half might be relied upon to defend and maintain them. At the house they found that Mr. Brion had already arrived, and that Mrs. Duff-Scott was assembling her party in the library, as being an appropriate place for the discussion of business in which men were so largely concerned. It was a spacious, pleasant room; the books ranging all round from the floor to about a third of the way up the wall, like a big dado; the top shelf supporting bric-à-brac of a stately and substantial order, and the deep red walls, which had a Pompeian frieze that was one of the artistic features of the house, bearing those pictures in oils which were the major's special pride as a connoisseur and man of family, and which held their permanent place of honour irrespective of the waves of fashion that ebbed and flowed around them. There was a Turkey carpet on the polished floor, and soft, thick oriental stuffs on the chairs and sofas and in the drapery of the wide bow-window—stuffs of dim but richly-coloured silk and wool, with tints of gold thread where the light fell. There was a many-drawered and amply-furnished writing table in that bow-window, the most comfortable and handy elbow tables by the hearth, and another and substantial one for general use in the centre of the floor. And altogether it was a pleasant place both to use and to look at, and was particularly pleasant in its shadowed coolness this summer afternoon. At the centre table sat the lady of the house, with an air of reproachful patience, talking surface talk with the girls about their country trip. Eleanor stood near her, looking very charming in her pale blue gown, with her flushed cheeks, and brightened eyes. Patty supported Mr. Brion, who was not quite at home in this strange atmosphere, and she watched the door with a face of radiant excitement.

"Where is Elizabeth?" asked the major, having hospitably shaken hands with the lawyer, whom he had never seen before.

"Elizabeth," said Mr. Yelverton, using the name familiarly, as if he had never called her by any other, "is not coming."

"Oh, indeed. Well, I suppose we are to go on without her, eh?"

"Yes, I suppose so." They were all seating themselves at the table, and as he took a chair by Patty's side he looked round and caught a significant glance passing between the major and his wife. "It is not of *my* convening, this meeting," he explained; "whatever business is on hand, I know nothing of it at present."

"*Don't* you?" cried his hostess, opening her eyes.

The major smiled; he, too, was thrown off the scent and puzzled, but did not show it as she did.

"No," said Mr. Brion, clearing his throat and putting his hand into his breast pocket to take out his papers, "what Mr. Yelverton says is true. He knows nothing of it at present. I am very sorry, for his sake, that it is so. I may say I am very sorry for everybody's sake, for it is a very painful thing to—"

Here Mr. Yelverton rose to his feet abruptly, nipping the exordium in the bud. "Allow me one moment," he said with some peremptoriness. "I don't know what Mr. Brion means by saying he is sorry for *my* sake. I don't know whether he alludes to a—a special attachment on my part, but I cannot conceive how any revelation he may make can affect me. As far as I am concerned—"

"My dear sir," interrupted the lawyer in his turn, "if you will wait until I have made my explanation, you will understand what I mean."

"Sit down," said Patty, putting a hand on his arm. "You have no idea what he is going to say. Sit down and listen."

"I do not want to listen, dear," he said, giving her a quick look. "It cannot be anything painful to me unless it is painful to you, and if it is painful to you I would rather not hear it."

The major was watching them all, and ruminating on the situation. "Wait a bit, Yelverton," he said in his soft voice. "If it's their doing there's some good reason for it. Just hear what it is that Mr. Brion has to say. I see he has got some legal papers. We must pay attention to legal papers, you know."

"Oh, for goodness sake, go on!" cried Mrs. Duff-Scott, whose nerves were chafed by this delay. "If anything is the matter, let us know the worst at once."

"Very well. Mr. Brion shall go on. But before he does so," said Mr. Yelverton, still standing, leaning on the table, and looking round on the little group with glowing eyes, "I will ask leave to make a statement. I am so happy—Mrs. Duff-Scott would have known it in an hour or two—I am so happy as to be Miss King's promised husband, and I hope to be her husband actually by this time to-morrow." Patty gave a little hysterical cry, and snatched at her handkerchief, in which her face was immediately buried. Mrs. Duff-Scott leaned back in her chair with a stoical composure, as if inured to thunderbolts, and waited for what would happen next. "I know it is very short notice," he went on, looking at the elder lady with a half-tender, half-defiant smile, "but my available time here is limited, and Elizabeth and I did not begin to care for each other yesterday. I persuaded her this morning to consent to an early and quiet marriage, for various reasons that I do not need to enter into now; and she has given her consent—provided only that Mrs. Duff-Scott has no objection."

"But I have the greatest objection," said that lady, emphatically. "Not to your marrying Elizabeth you know I am quite agreeable to *that*—but to your doing it in such an unreasonable way. To-morrow! you must be joking. It is preposterous, on the face of it."

"You are thinking of clothes, of course."

"No, I am not thinking of clothes. I am thinking of what people will say. You can have no idea of the extraordinary tales that will get about. I must consider Elizabeth."

"*I* consider Elizabeth," he said. "And before Mr. Brion makes his communication, whatever it may be, I should like to have it settled and understood that the arrangements she and I have made will be permitted to stand." He paused, and stood looking at Mrs. Duff-Scott, with an air that impressed her with the hopelessness of attempting to oppose such a man as that.

"I don't know what to say," she said. "We will talk it over presently."

"No, I want it settled now. Elizabeth will do whatever you desire, but I want her to please me." The major chuckled, and, hearing him, Mr. Yelverton laughed for a moment, and then bent his emphatic eyes upon the old man sitting silent before his unopened papers. "I want you and everybody to understand that whatever is to be said concerns my wife and sisters, Mr. Brion."

"Very good, sir," said Mr. Brion. "I am delighted to hear it. At the same time I would suggest that it might be wiser not to hurry things quite so much."

At this point Patty, who had been laughing and crying in her handkerchief, and clinging to Eleanor, who had come round the table and was hanging over her, suddenly broke into the discussion. "Oh, let them, let them, let them!" she exclaimed eagerly, to the bewilderment of the uninitiated, who were quite sure that some social disability was about to be attached to the bride elect, from which her lover was striving to rescue her. "Do let them be married to-morrow, dear Mrs. Duff-Scott, if Mr. Yelverton wishes it. Elizabeth knows why she consents—I know, too—so does Nelly. Give them your permission now, as he says, before Mr. Brion goes on—how can anyone say anything against it if *you* approve? Let it be all settled now—absolutely settled—so that no one can undo it afterwards." She turned and looked at the major with such a peculiar light and earnestness in her face that the little man, utterly adrift himself, determined at once to anchor himself to her. "Look here," he said, in his gentle way, but with no sign of indecision, "I am the head of the house, and if anybody has any authority over Elizabeth here, it is I. Forgive me, my dear"—to his wife at the other end of the table—"if I seem to take too much upon myself, but it appears to me that I ought to act in this emergency. Mr. Yelverton, we have every reason to trust your motives and conduct, and Elizabeth's also; and she is her own mistress in every way. So you may tell her from my wife and me that we hope she will do whatever seems right to herself, and that what makes her happy will make us so."

Mrs. Duff-Scott got up from her chair proudly, as if to leave the room where this outrage had been put upon her; but she sat down again and wept a few tears instead. At the unwonted sight of which Patty flew round to her and took her majestic head into her young arms. "Ah! how ungrateful we *seem* to hurt and vex you," she murmured, in the tone of a mother talking to a suffering child, "but you don't know how it is all going to turn out. If you give them your consent now, you will see how glad you will be in a little while."

"It doesn't seem that anybody cares much whether I give my consent or not," said Mrs. Duff-Scott. But she wiped away her tears, kissed her consoler, and made an effort to be cheerful and business-like. "There, there—we have wasted enough time," she said, brusquely. "Go on, Mr. Brion, or we shall have dinner time here before we begin."

"Shall I go on?" asked Mr. Brion, looking round.

Mr. Yelverton, who was very grave, nodded.

And Mr. Brion went on.

CHAPTER XLII
HER LORD AND MASTER

It was not much after three o'clock when Elizabeth walked slowly upstairs to her room, bearing single-handed her own responsibilities. Now that she was alone and undisturbed, she began to realise how great they were. She sat down on her little bed to think what she was doing—to look back upon the past, and forward into the future—until her head spun round. When she could think no more, she slid down upon her knees and prayed a fervent, wordless prayer—rested her over-weighted soul on the pillars of the universe, which bore up the strange little world in which she was but an infinitesimal atom—and, feeling that there was a strong foundation somewhere, and perhaps even feeling dimly that she had touched her point of contact with it only just now when she touched her true love's lips, she felt less intolerably burdened with the charge of herself. She rose up with her nerves steadied and her brain composed. What was done was done, and it had been done for the best. "We can but do our best, and leave it," he had said; and, thinking of his words, a sense of his robust faith, which she did not call faith, permeated her unsettled mind and comforted her with the feeling that she would have support and strength in him. She could not repent. She could not wish anything to be altered. She loved him and needed him; and he loved and needed her, and had a right to her. Yes, he had a right to her, independently of that fortune which was hers and which she dared not take away from him while he was using it so much better than she could, he was her mate and lord, and she belonged to him. What reason was there against her marrying him? Only one; Mrs. Duff-Scott's reason, which even she had abandoned, apparently—one obligation of duty, which conscience, left to its own delicate sense of good and evil, refused to insist upon as such. And what reason was there against marrying him to-morrow, if he desired it, and by doing which, while they would be made so happy, no one else could be made unhappy? She was unlearned in the social views and customs concerning such matters, and said in her simple heart there was no reason whatever—none, none.

So she set to work on her preparations, her eyes shining and her hands trembling with the overwhelming bliss of her anticipations, which awed and dazzled her; beset at intervals with chill misgivings, and thrills of panic, dread and fear, as to what effect upon her blessed fortune that afternoon's work at Mrs. Duff-Scott's house might have. She took off her pretty gown, which he had sanctified by his approval, and laid it tenderly on the bed; put on a loose wrapper, pulled out drawers and opened cupboards, and proceeded to pack her portmanteau for that wedding journey which she still could not believe was to be taken to-morrow. If such a sudden demand upon the resources of her wardrobe had been made a few months ago, she would have been greatly perplexed to meet it. Now she had, not only a commodious portmanteau (procured for their country visit), but drawers full of fine linen, piles of handkerchiefs, boxes of gloves, everything that she could need for an indefinite sojourn either in the world or out of it. When Mrs. Duff-Scott had gained their consent to be allowed to become a mother to them, she had lost no time in fitting them all out as became her adopted daughters, in defiance of any scruples or protests that they might make. Elizabeth's trousseau, it seemed to her, as she filled one side of the portmanteau with dainty underclothes delicately stitched and embroidered and frilled with lace, had been already provided for her, and while her heart went out in gratitude to her munificent friend, she could not help feeling that one of the dearest privileges of being rich was to have the power to acknowledge that munificence suitably. Only that very day, for the first time, she had seen an indication that tended to confirm her and Patty's instinctive sense that they had made a mistake in permitting themselves to accept so many favours. Eleanor, feeling herself already rich and the potential possessor of unlimited fine clothes, had put on her Cup dress and bonnet to walk out with Mr. Brion; and Mrs. Duff-Scott, when she met her in the Exhibition grounds, and while thrown for a moment off her usual even balance, had looked at the girl with a disapproving eye, which plainly accused her of extravagance—in other words, of wasting her (Mrs. Duff-Scott's) substance in riotous living. That little incident, so slight and momentary as it was, would have been as terrible a blow to them as was Paul Brion's refusal of their invitation to tea, had it not been that they were no longer poor, but in a position to discharge their obligations. She thought how Mrs. Duff-Scott would come to Yelverton by-and-bye, and to the London house, and how she (Elizabeth) would lavish the best of everything upon her. It was a delightful thought.

While she was building air castles, she sorted and folded her clothes methodically, and with motherly care turned over those belonging to her sisters, to see that they were well provided for and in need of nothing for the time of her brief absence. While investigating Patty's wardrobe, she thought much of her dear companion and that next-door neighbour, still in their unreconciled trouble, and still so far from the safe haven to which she was drawing nigh; and she was not too selfish in her own happiness to be unable to concern herself anxiously about theirs. Well, even this was to be set right now. She and Kingscote, with their mutually augmented wisdom and power, would be able to settle that matter, one way or another, when they returned from their wedding journey. Kingscote, who was never daunted by any difficulties, would find a way to solve this one, and to do what was best for Patty. Then it occurred to her that if Patty and Paul were married, Paul might want to keep his wife in Australia, and the sisters, who had never been away from each other, might be doomed to live apart. But she persuaded herself that this also would be prevented, and that Paul, stiff-necked as he was, would not let Patty be unhappy, as she certainly would be if separated by the width of the world from herself—not if Kingscote were at hand, to point it out to him in his authoritative and convincing manner. As for Nelly, she was to comfort Mrs. Duff-Scott for awhile, and then she was to come, bringing the fairy godmother with her, to Yelverton, to live under her brother-cousin's protection until she, too, was married—to someone better, far better, than Mr. Westmoreland. Perhaps the Duff-Scotts themselves would be tempted (by the charms of West-End and Whitechapel society, respectively) to settle in England too. In which case there would be nothing left to wish for.

At five o'clock she had finished her packing, put on her dress—not the wedding dress, which was laid smoothly on a cupboard shelf—and sat down by the sitting-room window to wait for her sisters, or for somebody, to come to her. This half-hour of unoccupied suspense was a very trying time; all her tremulous elation died down, all her blissful anticipations became overcast with chill forebodings, as a sunny sky with creeping clouds, while she bent strained eyes and ears upon the street, watching for the news that did not come. In uncontrollable excitement and restlessness, she abandoned her post towards six o'clock, and set herself to prepare tea in the expectation of her sisters' return. She spread the cloth and set out the cups and saucers, the bread and butter, the modest tin of sardines. As the warm day was manifestly about to close with a keen south wind, she thought she would light a fire in the sitting-room and make some toast. It was better to have something to do to distract her from her fierce anxieties, and, moreover, she wished the little home nest to be as cosy and comfortable as possible to-night, which might be the last night that the sisters would be there together—the closing scene of their independent life. So she turned up her cuffs, put on gloves and apron, and fetched wood and coals from their small store in the back-yard; and then she laid and lit a fire, blew it into as cheerful a blaze as the unsatisfactory nature of city fuel and a city grate permitted, and, having shaken down her neat dress and washed her hands, proceeded to make the toast. She was at this work, kneeling on the hearthrug, and staring intently into the fire over a newly-cut slice of bread that she had just put upon the fork, when she heard a sound that made her heart stand still. It was the sound of a cab rattling into the street and bumping against the kerb at her own gate. Springing to her feet and listening breathlessly, she heard the gate open to a quiet, strong hand that belonged to neither of her sisters, and a solid tread on the flags that paved a footpath through the little garden to the door. At the door a quick rapping, at once light and powerful, brought the servant from her underground kitchen, and a sonorous, low voice spoke in the hall and echoed up the stairs—the well-known voice of Kingscote Yelverton. Kingscote Yelverton, unaccompanied by anybody else—paying his first visit to this virgin retreat, where, as he knew very well, his sweetheart at this moment was alone, and where, as he also knew, the unchaperoned male had no business to be. Evidently his presence announced a crisis that transcended all the circumstances and conventionalities of every-day life.

He walked upstairs to her sitting-room, and rapped at the door. She could not tell him to come in, for her heart seemed to be beating in her throat, and she felt too suffocated to speak; she stumbled across to the door, and, opening it, looked at him dumbly, with a face as white as the white frills of her gown. He, for his part, neither spoke to her nor kissed her; his whole aspect indicated strong emotion, but he was so portentously grave, and almost stern, that her heart, which had fluttered so wildly at the sight of him, collapsed and sank. Taking her hand gently, he shut the door, led her across the room to the hearthrug, and stood, her embodied fate, before her. She was so overwhelmed with fear of what he might be going to say that she turned and hid her face in her hands against the edge of the mantelpiece, that she might brace herself to bear it without showing him how stricken she was.

"Well," he said, after a little pause, "I have been having a great surprise, Elizabeth. I little thought what you were letting me in for when you arranged that interview with Mr. Brion. I never was so utterly out of my reckoning as I have found myself to-day."

She did not speak, but waited in breathless anguish for the sentence that she foreboded was to be passed upon her—condemning her to keep that miserable money in exchange for him.

"I know all about the great discovery now," he went on. "I have read all the papers. I can testify that they are perfectly genuine. I have seen the marriage register that that one was copied from—I can verify all those dates, and names, and places—there is not a flaw anywhere in Mr. Brion's case. You are really my cousins, and you—*you*, Elizabeth—are the head of the family now. There was no entail—it was cut off before my uncle Patrick's time, and he died before he made a will: so everything is yours." After a pause, he added, brokenly, "I wish you joy, my dear. I should be a hypocrite if I said I was glad, but—but I wish you joy all the same."

She gave a short, dry sob, keeping her face hidden; evidently, even to him, she was not having much joy in her good fortune just now. He moved closer to her, and laid his hand on her shoulder.

"I have come now to fetch you," he said, in a low, grave tone, that was still unsteady. "Mrs. Duff-Scott wanted to come herself, but I asked her to let me come alone, because I have something to say to you that is only between ourselves."

Then her nervous terrors found voice. "Oh, tell me what it is!" she cried, trembling like a leaf. "Don't keep me in suspense. If you have anything cruel to say, say it quickly."

"Anything cruel?" he repeated. "I don't think you are really afraid of that—from me. No, I haven't anything cruel to say—only a simple question to ask—which you will have to answer me honestly, Elizabeth."

She waited in silence, and he went on. "Didn't you tell me"—emphasising each word heavily—"that you had been induced by something outside yourself to decide in my favour?"

"Not altogether induced," she protested; "helped perhaps."

"Helped, then—influenced—by outside considerations?"

"Yes," she assented, with heroic truthfulness.

"You were alluding to this discovery, of course?"

"Yes."

"And you have consented to marry me in order that I may not be deprived of my property?" She did not speak immediately, from purely physical incapacity, and he went on with a hardening voice. "I will not be married on those grounds, Elizabeth. You must have *known* that I would not."

For a moment she stood with her face hidden, struggling with a rising tide of tears that, when these terrible words were spoken, would not be kept in check; then she lifted her head, and flung out her arms, and clasped him round his great shoulders. (It is not, I own, what a heroine should have done, whose duty was to carry a difficulty of this sort through half a volume at least, but I am nevertheless convinced that my real Elizabeth did it, though I was not there to see—standing, as she did, within a few inches of her lover, and with nothing to prevent their coming to a reasonable understanding.) "Oh," she cried, between her long-drawn sobs, "*don't* cast me off because of that horrid money! I could not bear it *now!*"

"What!" he responded, stooping over her and holding her to his breast, speaking in a voice as shaken as her own, "is it really so? Is it for love of me only, my darling, my darling?"—pouring his long pent-up passion over her with a force that seemed to carry her off her feet and make the room spin round. "Would you have me if there was no property in the question, simply because you feel, as I do, that we could not do without each other? Then we will be married to-morrow, Elizabeth, and all the world shall be welcome to brand me a schemer and fortune-hunter if it likes."

She got her breath in a few seconds, and recovered sufficient consciousness to grasp the vanishing tail of those last words.

"A fortune-hunter! Oh, how *preposterous!* A fortune-hunter!"

"That is what I shall seem," he insisted, with a smile, "to that worthy public for whose opinion some people care so much."

"But you don't care?"

"No; I don't care."

She considered a moment, with her tall head at rest on his tall shoulder; then new lights dawned on her. "But I must care for you," she said, straightening herself. "I must not allow anything so unjust—so outrageous—to be said of you—of *you*, and through my fault. Look here"—very seriously—"let us put off our marriage for a while—for just so long as may enable me to show the world, as I very easily can, that it is *I* who am seeking *you*—"

"Like a queen selecting her prince consort?"

"No, like Esther—seeking favour of her king. I would not be too proud to run after you—" She broke off, with a hysterical laugh, as she realised the nature of her proposal.

"Ah, my darling, that would be very sweet," said he, drowning her once more in ineffable caresses, "but to be married to-morrow will be sweeter still. No, we won't wait—I *can't*—unless there is an absolute necessity for it. That game would certainly not be worth the candle. What is the world to me if I have got you? I said we would be married to-morrow; I told Mrs. Duff-Scott so, and got her consent—not without some difficulty, I must own—before Mr. Brion opened his budget. I would not hear what he had to say—little thinking what it was I was going to hear!—until I had announced my intentions and the date of our wedding. Think of my cheek! Conceive of such unparalleled impudence! But now that everything is square between us, that date shall be kept—it shall be faithfully kept. Come, then, I must take you away. Have you done your packing? Mrs. Duff-Scott says we are to bring that portmanteau with us, that she may see for herself if you have furnished it properly. And you are not to come back here—you are not to come to me to the Exhibition to-morrow. She was terribly scandalised at that item in our programme."

"In yours," said Elizabeth, ungenerously.

"In mine. I accept it cheerfully. So she is going to take charge of you from this hour until you are Mrs. Yelverton, and in my sole care for the rest of your life—or mine. Poor woman, she is greatly cut up by the loss of that grand wedding that she would have had if we had let her."

"I am sure she must be cut up," said Elizabeth, whose face was suffused with blushes, and whose eyes looked troubled. "She must be shocked and vexed at such—such precipitancy. It really does not seem decorous," she confessed, with tardy scrupulousness; "do you think it does?"

"Oh, yes, I think it is quite decorous. It may not be conventional, but that is quite another thing."

"It is like a clandestine marriage—almost like an elopement. It *must* vex her to see me acting so—so—"

"So what? No, I don't think it does. She *was* a little vexed at first, but she has got over it. In her heart of hearts I believe she would be disappointed now if we didn't do it. She likes a little bit of innocent unconventionalism as well as anybody, and the romance of the whole thing has taken hold of her. Besides," added Mr. Yelverton, "you know she intended us for each other, sooner or later."

"You have said as much before, but *I* don't know anything about it," laughed Elizabeth.

"Yes, she told me I might have you—weeks ago."

"She was very generous."

"She was. She was more generous than she knew. Well"—catching himself up suddenly—"we really must go to her now, Elizabeth. I told her I would only come in here, where I have no business to be to-day, for half a minute, and I have stayed more than half an hour. It is nearly dinner time, and I have a great deal to do this evening. I have more to do even than I bargained for."

"Why more?" she asked, apprehensively.

"I am going to have some papers prepared by Mr. Brion and the major's lawyers, which you will have to sign before you surrender your independence to-morrow."

"I won't sign anything," said Elizabeth.

"Oh, won't you! We'll see about that."

"I know what it means. You will make me sign away your freedom to use that money as your own—and I won't do it."

"We'll see," he repeated, smiling with an air which said plainly that if she thought herself a free agent she was very much mistaken.

CHAPTER XLIII
THE EVENING BEFORE THE WEDDING

"Now, where is that portmanteau?"

"It is in my room."

"Strapped up?"

"Yes."

"Let me take it down to the cab. Have you anything else to do?"

"Only to change my dress."

"Don't be long about it; it is seven o'clock. I will wait for you downstairs."

Mr. Yelverton walked into the passage, possessed himself of the portmanteau, and descended the stairs to the little hall below. The wide-eyed maid-of-all-work hastened to offer her services. She had never volunteered to carry luggage for the Miss Kings, but she seemed horrified at the sight of this stalwart gentleman making a porter of himself. "Allow me, sir," she said, sweetly, with her most engaging smile.

"Thank you, my girl; I think I am better able to carry it than you are," he said, pleasantly. But he scrutinised her face with his keen eyes for a moment, and then took a sovereign from his pocket and slipped it into her hand. "Go and see if you can help Miss King," he said. "And ask her if there is anything you can do for her while she is away from home."

"Oh, sir" —simpering and blushing—"I'm sure—*anything*—" and she rushed upstairs and offered her services to Elizabeth in such acceptable fashion that the bride-elect was touched almost to tears, as by the discovery of a new friend. It seemed to her that she had never properly appreciated Mary Ann before.

Mr. Yelverton meanwhile paced a few steps to and fro on the footpath outside the gate, looking at his watch frequently. Paul Brion was at home, listening to his father's account of the afternoon's events and the news of the imminent marriage, with moody brow and heavy heart; it was the end of the romance for *him*, he felt, and he was realising what a stale and flat residuum remained in his cup of life. He had seen Mr. Yelverton go to No. 6 with fierce resentment of the liberty that the fortunate lover permitted himself to take with those sacred rights of single womanhood which he, Paul, had been so scrupulous to observe; now he watched the tall man pacing to and fro in the street below, waiting for his bride, with a sense of the inequalities of fortune that made him almost bloodthirsty. He saw the portmanteau set on end by the cabdriver's seat; he saw Elizabeth come forth with a bag in one hand and an umbrella in the other, followed by the servant with an ulster and a bonnet-box. He watched the dispossessed master of Yelverton, who, after all, had lost nothing, and had gained so much, and the great heiress who was to know Myrtle Street and obscurity no more, as they took their seats in the vehicle, she handed in by him with such tender and yet masterful care. He had an impulse to go out upon the balcony to bid her good-bye and God-speed, but he checked it proudly; and, surveying her departure from the window of his sitting-room, convinced himself that she was too much taken up with her own happiness to so much as remember his existence. It was the closing scene of the Myrtle Street drama—the last chapter of the charming little homely story which had been the romance of his life. No more would he see the girls going in and out of the gate of No. 7, nor meet them in the gardens and the street, nor be privileged to offer them his assistance and advice. No more would he sit on his balcony of nights to listen to Beethoven sonatas and Schubert serenades. The sponge had been passed over all those pleasant things, and had wiped them out as if they had never been. There were no longer any Miss Kings. And for Paul there was no longer anything left in life but arid and flavourless newspaper work—the ceaseless grinding of his brains in the great mill of the Press, which gave to the world its daily bread of wisdom, but had no guerdon for the producers of that invaluable grist.

In truth, Elizabeth *did* forget all about him. She did not lift her eyes to the window where he sat; she could see and think of nothing but herself and her lover, and the wonderful circumstances that immediately surrounded them. When the cabman closed the door upon them, and they rattled away down the quiet street, it was borne in upon her that she really *was* going to be married on the morrow; and that circumstance was far more than enough to absorb her whole attention. In the suburbs through which they passed it was growing dusk, and the lamps were lighted. A few carriages were taking people out to dinner. It was already evening—the day was over. Mrs. Duff-Scott was standing on her doorstep as they drove up to the house, anxiously looking out for them. She had not changed her morning dress; nor had Patty, who stood beside her. All the rules of daily life were suspended at this crisis. A grave footman came to the door of the cab, out of which Mr. Yelverton helped Elizabeth, and then led her into the hall, where she was received in the fairy godmother's open arms.

"Take care of her," he said to Patty, "and make her rest herself. I will come back about nine or ten o'clock."

Patty nodded. Mrs. Duff-Scott tried to keep him to dinner, but he said he had no time to stay. So the cab departed with him, and his betrothed was hurried upstairs to her bedroom, where there ensued a great commotion. Even Mrs. Duff-Scott, who had tried to stand upon her dignity a little, was unable to do so, and shared the feverish excitement that possessed the younger sisters. They were all a little off their heads—as, indeed, they must have been more than women not to be. The explanations and counter-explanations, the fervid congratulations, the irrepressible astonishment, the loving curiosity, the tearful raptures, the wild confusion of tongues and miscellaneous caresses, were very bewildering and upsetting. They did, in fact, bring on that attack of hysterics, the first and last in Elizabeth's life, which had been slowly generating in her healthy nervous system under the severe and various trials of the day. This little accident sobered them down, and reminded them of Mr. Yelverton's command that Elizabeth was to be made to rest herself. The heiress was accordingly laid upon a sofa, much against her wish, and composed with sal-volatile, and eau-de-cologne, and tea, and fans, and a great deal of kissing and petting.

"But I *cannot* understand this excessive, this abnormal haste," Mrs. Duff-Scott said, when the girl seemed strong enough to bear being mildly argued with. "Mr. Yelverton explains it very plausibly, but still I can't understand it, from *your* point of view. Patty's theory is altogether untenable."

"I don't understand it either," the bride-elect replied. "I think I had an idea that it might prevent him from knowing or realising that I was giving him the money instead of his giving it to me—I wanted to be beforehand with Mr. Brion. But of course that was absurd. And if you can persuade him to put it off for a few weeks—"

"O dear no!—I know him too well. He is not a man to be persuaded. Well, I am thankful he is going to let you be married in church. I expected he would insist on the registry office. And he has promised to bring you back to me at the end of a fortnight or so, to stay here all the time till you go home. That is something." The fairy godmother was certainly a little huffy— for all these wonderful things had come to pass without her permission or assistance—but in her heart of hearts, as Mr. Yelverton had suspected, she was charmed with the situation, and as brimful of sympathy for the girl in her extraordinary circumstances as her own mother could have been.

They had a quiet dinner at eight o'clock, for which the major, who had been despatched to his solicitors (to see about the drawing up of that "instrument" which Miss Yelverton's *fiancé* and cousin required her to sign on her own behalf before her individuality was irrevocably merged in his), returned too late to dress, creeping into the house gently as if he had no business to be there; and Elizabeth sat at her host's right hand, the recipient of the tenderest attentions and tit-bits. The little man, whose twinkling eye had lost its wonted humour, was profoundly touched by the events that had transpired, and saddened by the prospect of losing that sister of the three whom he had made his own particular chum, and with the presentiment that her departure would mean the loss of the others also. He could not even concern himself about the consequences to his wife of their removal from the circle of her activities, so possessed was he by the sad vision of his house left desolate. Perhaps the major felt himself getting old at last, and realised that cakes and ale could not be heaped upon his board for ever. He was certainly conscious of a check in his prosperous career, by the translation of the Miss Kings, and a feeling of injury in that Providence had not given him children that he *could* have kept around him for the solace of his declining years. It was hard to have just learned what it was to have charming daughters, and then to be bereaved of them like this, at a moment's notice. Yet he bore his disappointment with admirable grace; for the little major, despite all the traditions of his long-protracted youth, was the most unselfish of mortals, and a gentleman to the marrow of his bones.

In the evening he went to town again, to find Mr. Yelverton. Mrs. Duff-Scott, when dinner was over, had a consultation with her cook, and made arrangements for a festive luncheon for the following day. The girls went upstairs again, and thither their adopted mother presently followed them, and they spent an hour together in Elizabeth's bedroom, absorbed in the sad but delightful business of overhauling her portmanteau. By this time they were able to discuss the situation with sobriety—a sobriety infused with much chastened emotion, to be sure, but still far removed from the ferment of hysterics. Patty, in particular, had a very bracing air about her.

"Now I call this *life*," she said, flourishing open the skirt of one of Elizabeth's dresses to see if it was fit to be worn on a wedding journey; "I call this really *living*. One feels as if one's faculties were given for some purpose. After all, it is not necessary to go to Europe to see the world. It is not necessary to travel to gain experience and to have adventures. Is not this frock too shabby, Mrs. Duff-Scott—all things considered?"

"Certainly," assented that lady, promptly. "Put in her new cashmere and the Indian silk, and throw away those old things now."

"Go and get the Indian silk, Nelly. It is in the wardrobe. And don't hang over Elizabeth in that doleful manner, as if she were going to have her head cut off, like Lady Jane Grey. She is one of the happiest women on the face of the earth—or, if she isn't, she ought to be—with such a prospect before her. Think of it! It is enough to make one gnash one's teeth with envy."

"Let us hope she will indeed realise her prospects," said Mrs. Duff-Scott, feeling called upon to reprove and moderate the pagan spirit that breathed in Patty's words. "Let us hope she will be as happy in the future as she is now."

"Oh, she will—she will! Let us hope she will have enough troubles to keep her from being *too* happy—too happy to last," said the girl audaciously; "that is the danger she will want preserving from."

"You may say what you like, but it is a rash venture," persisted the matron, shaking her head. "She has known him but for such a *very* short time. Really, I feel that I am much to blame to let her run into it like this—with so little knowledge of what she is undertaking. And he *has* a difficult temperament, Elizabeth. There is no denying it—good and nice as he is, he is terribly obstinate about getting his own way. And if he is so *now*, what will he be, do you suppose, presently?"

Patty, sitting on her heels on the floor, with her sister's clothes spread around her, looked up and laughed.

"Ah! that is one safeguard against too much happiness, perhaps. I do think, with Mrs. Duff-Scott, that you have met your master, my dear."

"I don't think it," replied Elizabeth, serenely. "I know I have."

"And you are quite content to be mastered?"

"Yes—by him."

"Of course you are. Who would marry a chicken-hearted milksop if she could get a splendid tyrant like that?" exclaimed Patty, fervently, for the moment forgetting there were such things as woman's rights in the world. "I wouldn't give a straw for a man who let you have your own way—unless, of course, he was no wiser than you. A man who sets up to domineer when he can't carry it out thoroughly is the most detestable and contemptible of created beings, but there is no want of thoroughness about *him*. To see him standing up at the table in the library this afternoon and defying Mrs. Duff-Scott to prevent him from marrying you to-morrow did one's heart good. It did indeed."

"I daresay," said the fairy godmother. "But I should like to see *you* with a man like that to deal with. It is really a pity he did not take to you instead of Elizabeth. I should have liked to see what would have happened. The 'Taming of the Shrew' would have been a trifle to it."

"Well," said Patty, "he will be my brother and lawful guardian to-morrow, and I suppose I shall have to accept his authority to a certain extent. Then you will see what will happen." She was silent for a few minutes, folding the Indian silk into the portmanteau, and a slow smile spread over her face. "We shall have some fights," she said, laughing softly. "But it will be worth while to fight with him."

"Elizabeth will never fight with him," said Eleanor.

"Elizabeth!" echoed Patty. "She will be wax—she will be butter— simply. She would spoil him if he could be spoiled. But I don't think he is spoilable. He is too tough. He is what we may call an ash tree man. And what isn't ash-tree is leather."

"You are not complimentary," said Nelly, fearing that Elizabeth's feelings might be hurt by what seemed an allusion to the bridegroom's complexion.

"Pooh! He is not the sort of man to compliment. Elizabeth knows what I mean. I feel inclined to puff myself out when I think of his being our own kith and kin—a man like that. I shall have ever so much more confidence in myself now that I know I have his blood in my veins; one can't be so near a relation without sharing some of the virtue of it—and a little of that sort ought to go a long way. Ha!"—lifting her finger for silence as she heard a sound in the hall below—"there he is."

Mrs. Duff-Scott's maid came running upstairs to say, "Please'm, could you and the young ladies come down to the library for a few minutes?" She was breathless and fluttered, scenting mystery in the air, and she looked at Elizabeth with intense interest. "The major and Mr. Yelverton is 'ome," she added, "and some other gentlemen 'ave come. Shall I just put your 'air straight, Miss?"

She was a little Cockney who had waited on fine ladies in London, and was one of Mrs. Duff-Scott's household treasures. In a twinkling she had "settled up" Elizabeth's rather dishevelled braids and twitched her frills and draperies into trim order; then, without offering to straighten any one else, she withdrew into the background until she could safely watch them go downstairs to the hall, where she knew Mr. Yelverton was waiting. Looking over the balustrade presently, she saw the four ladies join him; three of them were passing on to the library, as feeling themselves *de trop*, but were called back. She could not hear what was said, but she saw what was done, to the very best advantage. Mr. Yelverton fitted a substantial wedding-ring upon Miss King's finger, and then, removing it, put another ring in its place; a deeply-interested and sympathetic trio standing by to witness the little ceremony. The maid slipped down by the back-stairs to the servants' hall, and communicated the result of her observations to her fellow-servants. Mr. Yelverton meanwhile led Elizabeth into the library, where were seated at the same table where Mr. Brion had read his documents earlier in the day, three sedate gentlemen, Mr. Brion being one of them, with other documents spread out before them. The major was languidly fetching pens and ink from the writing-table in the window, and smiling furtively. He seemed to be amused by this latest phase of the Yelverton affair. His eyes twinkled with sagacious humour politely repressed, when he saw the betrothed couple enter the room together.

He hastened forward to put a chair for the interesting "client," for this one night his ward, at the head of the table; the girls and Mrs. Duff-Scott grouped themselves before the hearth to watch the proceedings, and whisper their comments thereupon. The bridegroom took his stand at Elizabeth's elbow, and intimated that it was his part to direct her what to do.

"Why should I do anything?" she inquired, looking round her from face to face with a vague idea of seeking protection in legal quarters. "It cannot make the least difference. I know that a woman's property, if you don't meddle with it, is her husband's when she is married" — this was before the late amendment of the law on this matter, and she was, as one of the lawyers advised her, correctly informed — "and if ever it should be so, it should be so in *our* case. I cannot, I will not, have any separate rights. No"—as Mr. Yelverton laid a paper before her—"I don't want to read it."

"Well, you need not read it," he said, laughing. "Mr. Brion does that for you. But I want you to sign. It is nothing to what you will have to do before we get this business settled."

"Mr. Yelverton is an honourable man, my dear," said Mr. Brion, with some energy—and his brother lawyers nodded in acquiescence—as he gave her a pen.

"You need not tell me that," she replied, superbly. And, seeing no help for it, she took the pen and signed "Elizabeth Yelverton" (having to be reminded of her true name on each occasion) with the most reckless unconcern, determined that if she had signed away her husband's liberty to use her property as he liked, she would sign it back again when she had married him.

And this was the last event of that eventful day. At midnight, lawyers and lover went away, and the tired girls to bed, and Elizabeth and Patty spent their last night together in each other's arms.

CHAPTER XLIV
THE WEDDING DAY

After all, Elizabeth's wedding ceremonies, though shorn of much customary state, were not so wildly unconventional as to shock the feelings of society. Save in the matter of that excessive haste—which Mr. Yelverton took pains to show was not haste at all, seeing that, on the one hand, his time was limited, and that, on the other, there was absolutely nothing to wait for—all things were done decently and in order; and Mrs. Duff-Scott even went so far as to confess, when the bride and bridegroom had departed, that the fashion of their nuptials was "good art;" and that these were not the days to follow stereotyped customs blindfold. There was no unnecessary secrecy about it. Overnight, just, and only just, before she went to bed, the mistress of the house had explained the main facts of the case to her head servants, who, she knew, would not be able to repeat the story until too late for the publication of it to cause any inconvenience. She told them how the three Miss Kings—who had never been Miss Kings after all—had come in for large fortunes, under a will that had been long mislaid and accidentally recovered; and how Miss Elizabeth, who had been engaged for some considerable time (O, mendacious matron!), was to be married to her cousin, Mr. Yelverton, in the morning—very quietly, because both of them had a dislike to publicity and fuss. And in the morning the little Cockney lady's-maid, bringing them their tea, brought a first instalment of congratulations to the bride and her sisters, who had to hold a *levée* in the servants' hall as soon as they went downstairs. The household, if not boiling over with the excitement inseparable from a marriage *à la mode*, was in a pleasant simmer of decorous enjoyment; and the arrangements for the domestic celebration of the event lacked nothing in either completeness or taste. The gardener brought his choicest flowers for the table and for the bride's bouquet, which was kept in water until her return from church; and the cook surpassed himself in his efforts to provide a wedding breakfast that should be both faultless and unique. The men servants wore bits of strong-scented orange blossom in their button-holes, and the women white ribbons in their caps. They did what they could, in short, to honour the occasion and the young lady who had won their affection before she came into her inheritance of wealth, and the result to themselves and the family was quite satisfactory.

There was a great deal of cold weather in the last month of 1880, summer time though it was, and this special morning was very cold. Elizabeth had not the face to come down to the early breakfast and a blazing fire in the gown she had worn the day before, and Mrs. Duff-Scott would not hear of her going to church in it. "Do you suppose he is quite an idiot?" she indignantly demanded (forgetting the absolute indifference to weather shown in the conventional bridal costume), when the bride gave an excuse for her own unreasonableness. "Do you suppose he wants you to catch your death of cold on your wedding day?"

"What does it matter?" said Patty. "He won't care what you have on. Put it in the portmanteau and wear it at dinner every night, if he likes to see you in it. This morning you had better make yourself warm. He never expected the day to turn out so cold as this."

And while they were talking of it Mr. Yelverton himself appeared, contrary to etiquette and his own arrangements. "Good morning," he said, shaking hands impartially all round. "I just came in to tell you that it is exceedingly cold, and that Elizabeth had better put a warm dress on. One would think it was an English December day by the feel of the wind."

She got up from the breakfast-table and went out of the room, hurried away by Mrs. Duff-Scott; but in a minute she came back again.

"Did you come for anything in particular?" she asked, anxiously.

"No," he said, "only to take care that you did not put on that thin dress. And to see that you were alive," he added, dropping his voice.

"And we really are to be married this morning?"

"We really are, Elizabeth. In three quarters of an hour, if you can be at the church so soon. I am on my way there now. I am just going round to Myrtle Street to pick up old Brion."

"Pick up young Brion, too," she urged earnestly, thinking of Patty. "Tell him I specially wished it."

"He won't come," said Mr. Yelverton; "I asked him yesterday. His father says his liver must be out of order, he has grown so perverse and irritable lately. He won't do anything that he is wanted to do."

"Ah, poor boy! We must look after him, you and I, when we come back. Where are we going, Kingscote?"

"My darling, I fear you will think my plans very prosaic. I think we are just going to Geelong—till to-morrow or next day. You see it is so cold, and I don't want you to be fagged with a long journey. Mount Macedon would have been charming, but I could not get accommodation. At Geelong, where we are both strangers, we shall be practically to ourselves, and it is better to make sure of a good hotel than of romantic scenery, if you have to choose between the two—for the present, at any rate—vulgar and sordid as that sentiment may appear. We can go where we like afterwards. I have just got a telegram to say that things will be ready for us. You left it to me, you know."

"I am only too happy to leave everything to you," she said, at once. "And I don't care where we go—-it will be the same everywhere."

"I think it will, Elizabeth—I think we shall be more independent of our circumstances than most people. Still I am glad to have made sure of a warm fire and a good dinner for you at your journey's end. We start at twenty minutes past four, I may tell you, and we are to get home—*home*, my dear, which will be wherever you and I can be together, henceforth—at about half-past six. That will give you time to rest before dinner. And you will not be very tired, after such a little journey, will you?"

"Elizabeth!" called a voice from the corridor above their heads, "send Mr. Yelverton away, and come upstairs at once."

So Mr. Yelverton departed in his cab, to pick up old Brion and await his bride at the nearest church; and he was presently followed by the major in his brougham, and a little later by Mrs. Duff-Scott's capacious open carriage, containing herself and the three sisters, all in woollen walking dresses and furs. And Elizabeth really was married, still to her own great surprise. She stood in the cold and silent church, and took Kingscote, her lover, to be her lawful husband, and legally ratified that irrevocable contract in the clearest handwriting. He led her out into the windy road, when it was over, and put her into the brougham—the major taking her place in the other carriage, and on their way back both bride and bridegroom were very serious over their exploit.

"You have the most wonderful trust in me," he said to her, holding her still ungloved hand, and slipping the wedding ring round on her finger—"the most amazing trust."

"I have," she assented, simply.

"It rather frightens me," he went on, "to see you taking me so absolutely for granted. Do you really think I am quite perfect, Elizabeth?"

"No," she replied, promptly.

"Well, I am glad of that. For I am far from it, I assure you." Then he added, after a pause, "What are the faults you have to find with me, then?"

"None—none," she responded fervently. "Your faults are no faults to me, for they are part of you. I don't want you perfect—I only want you to be always as I know you now."

"I think I am rather a tyrant," he said, beginning to criticise himself freely, now that she showed no disposition to do it, "and perhaps I shall bully you if you allow me too much latitude. I am too fond of driving straight at everything I want, Elizabeth—I might drive over you, without thinking, some day, if you give me my own way always."

"You may drive over me, if you like, and welcome," she said, smiling.

"You have no consideration for your rights as a woman and a matron?—no proper pride?—no respect for your dignity, at all?"

"None whatever—now."

"Ah, well, after all, I think it is a good thing for you that I have got you. You might have fallen into worse hands. You are just made to be a victim. And you will be better off as my victim than you might have been as another man's victim."

"Much better," she said. "But I don't think I should have been another man's victim."

When they reached Mrs. Duff-Scott's house, Patty and Eleanor, who had arrived a few minutes earlier, met their brother and sister, kissed them both, and took Elizabeth upstairs, where they tenderly drew off her furs and her bonnet, and waited upon her with a reverential recognition of her new and high estate. During their absence, Mr. Yelverton, Mr. Brion, and their host and hostess stood round the drawing-room fire, talking over a plan they had hatched between them, prior to taking leave of the old lawyer, who had to depart for his country home and business by an afternoon boat. This plan provided for a temporary disposal of that home and business at an early date, in order that Mr. Brion might accompany the entire party—the major and his wife, Mr. Yelverton and the three sisters—to England as the legal adviser of the latter, it having been deemed expedient to take these measures to facilitate the conveyance and distribution of the great Yelverton property. The old man was delighted at the prospect of his trip, which it was intended should be made both profitable and pleasant to him, and at the certainty of being identified for some time longer with the welfare of his young friends. Mrs. Duff-Scott was also ardent in her anticipation of seeing Elizabeth installed at Yelverton, of investigating the philanthropical enterprises of Elizabeth's husband, and of keeping, during the most critical and most interesting period of their career, the two unappropriated heiresses under her wing. The major was pleased to join this family party, and looked forward with some avidity to the enjoyment of certain London experiences that he had missed from his cup of blessings of late years.

"And the dear girls will not be separated, except for this little week or two," said the fairy godmother, wiping away a surreptitious tear. "How happy that will make them!"

They entered the room as she spoke, clinging together; and they sat down round the hearthrug, and were drawn into the discussion. Yes, it did make them happy, they said; it was the sweetest and brightest of plans and prospects. Only Patty, thinking of Elizabeth and Nelly going and Paul Brion left behind, felt her heart torn in two.

The wedding breakfast was the mid-day lunch, to which they were summoned by the butler with his bridal favour in his button-hole. The little party of seven, when they went into the dining-room, found that apartment decorated with flowers and evergreens in a manner wonderful to behold, considering the short notice that had been given. The table was glorious with white blossoms of every description, the orange predominating and saturating the air with its almost too strong fragrance; and the dishes and the wines would have done honour to the bridal banquet of a princess. Little did anyone care for dishes and wines, except the host and hostess, who would have been less than mortal had they not felt interested therein; and most of them were glad to get the meal over. Some healths were drunk in the major's best dry champagne, and three little speeches were delivered; and then Mr. Brion respectfully begged to be excused, said good-bye all round, made his Grandisonian bow, and departed.

"Tell Paul," said Elizabeth (she could call him Paul now), "that we have missed him to-day."

"I will, my dear, I will," said the old man. And when he delivered that message half-an-hour later, he was hurt to see in what a bad spirit it was received. "I daresay!" was Paul's cynical comment.

When Mr. Brion was gone, the little family returned to the drawing-room, and again sat round the bright fire, and behaved themselves as if nothing had happened. Elizabeth spread out her hands to the warmth, and gazed at her thick wedding ring meditatively: and the girls, who hung about her, gazed at it also with fascinated eyes. Mr. Yelverton sat a little apart, and watched his wife furtively. Mrs. Duff-Scott chatted, recalling the topography and notable features of Geelong. They had afternoon tea, as usual (only earlier than usual), in the familiar precious teacups, out of the familiar Queen Anne teapot. There was an every-day homeliness about this quiet hour, and yet it seemed that years had come and gone since yesterday. Presently Mr. Yelverton's watch-case was heard to shut with a sharp click, and the bride turned her head quickly and looked at him. He nodded. And as she rose from her low chair, holding out her hand to the faithful Patty, the wheels of the brougham crunched over the gravel in front of the windows. It was time to go.

And in ten minutes more they were gone. Like that monarch who went into his own kingdom and shut the door, Elizabeth went into hers—to assume the crown and sceptre of a sovereignty than which no woman can boast a greater, let her be who she may—passing wholly into her strong husband's keeping without one shadow of regret or mistrust left in her heart, either for herself or him. They were driven to Spencer Street, where, while they waited a few minutes for their train, people who knew them stared at them, recognising the situation. They paced up and down the platform, side by side, she in her modest cloth dress and furs; and, far from avoiding observation, they rather courted it unconsciously, in a quiet way. They were so proud of belonging to each other, and from the enclosure of their own kingdom the outside world seemed such an enormous distance off. They went to Geelong in a saloon car full of people—what did it matter to them?—and at the seaside station found a carriage waiting for them. And by half-past six, as her husband said, Elizabeth reached home. There was a bright and cosy sitting-room, with a table prettily set for their *tête-à-tête* dinner, and a bright fire (of wood and not coal—a real bush fire) crackling on the hearth. In an inner room there was a fire too; and here, when her portmanteau had been unstrapped, and while Kingscote was consulting with the landlord, she hastily threw off her wraps and travelling dress, twisted up her fine hair afresh, put on that delicate gown that she had worn yesterday morning—could it possibly, she asked herself, have been *only* yesterday morning?—and made herself as fair to look upon as she knew how. And, when she opened the door softly, trembling with excitement and happiness, he was waiting for her, standing on the hearthrug, with his back to the fire—looking at her as he had looked that day, not so very long ago, when they were in the cave together, he on one side of the gulf and she on the other. He held out his arms again, and this time she sprang into them, and lifted her own to clasp his neck. And so they stood, without moving or speaking—"resting before dinner"—until the waiter, heralding his approach by a discreet tap at the door, came in with the soup-tureen.

CHAPTER XLV
IN SILK ATTIRE

The bride and bridegroom did not return to Melbourne until the day before Christmas—Friday the 24th, which was a warm, and bright, and proper summer day, but working up for a spell of north winds and bush fires before the year ran out. They had been wandering happily amongst the lovely vales and mountains of that sequestered district of Victoria which has become vaguely known as the "Kelly Country," and finding out before they left it, to their great satisfaction, that Australia could show them scenery so variously romantic as to put the charms of the best hotels into the shade. Even that terrestrial paradise on the ferny slopes of Upper Macedon was, if not eclipsed, forgotten, in the beauty of the wilder woodland of the far Upper Murray, which was beyond the reach of railways. They had also been again to visit the old house by the sea and Mr. Brion; had dawdled along the familiar shore in twilight and moonlight; had driven to the caves and eaten lunch once more in the green dell among the bracken fronds; had visited the graves of that other pair of married lovers—that Kingscote and Elizabeth of the last generation—and made arrangements for the perpetual protection from disturbance and desecration of that sadly sacred spot. And it was only on receipt of an urgent telegram from Mrs. Duff-Scott, to remind them that Christmas was approaching, and that she had devised festivities which were to be more in honour of them than of the season, that they remembered how long they had been away, and that it had become time to return to their anxious relatives.

They arrived in Melbourne by the 3.41 train from Ballarat, where they had broken a long journey the evening before, and found Patty and Eleanor and the major's servants waiting for them at Spencer Street. The meeting between the sisters, after their first separation, was silent, but intensely impressive. On the platform though they were, they held each other's hands and gazed into each other's eyes, unconscious of the attention they attracted, unable to find words to express how much they had missed each other and how glad they were to be reunited. They drove home together in a state of absolute happiness; and at home Mrs. Duff-Scott and the major were standing on their doorstep as the carriage swept up the broad drive to the house, as full of tender welcomes for the bride as any father or mother could have been, rejoicing over a recovered child. Elizabeth thought of the last Christmas Eve which she and her sisters, newly orphaned and alone in the world, poor in purse and destitute of kith and kin, spent in that humble little bark-roofed cottage on the solitary cliff; and she marvelled at the wonderful and dazzling changes that the year had brought. Only one year out of twenty-nine!—and yet it seemed to have held the whole history of her life. She was taken into the drawing-room and put into a downy chair, and fed with bread and butter and tea and choice morsels of news, while Patty knelt on the floor beside her, and her husband stood on the hearthrug watching her, with, his air of quiet but proud proprietorship, as he chatted of their travels to the major. It was very delightful. She wondered if it were really herself—Elizabeth King that used to be—whose lines had fallen on these pleasant places.

While the afternoon tea was in progress, Eleanor fidgetted impatiently about the room. She was so graceful and undulating in her movements that her fidgetting was only perceived to be such by those who knew her ways; but Elizabeth marked her gentle restlessness, in spite of personal preoccupations.

"Do you want me to go upstairs with you?" she inquired with her kind eyes, setting down her teacup; and Nelly almost flew to escort her out of the room. There was to be a large dinner party at Mrs. Duff-Scott's to-night, to "meet Mr. and Mrs. Yelverton on their return," all Melbourne having been made acquainted with the romance of their cousinship and marriage, and the extent of their worldly possessions, during their absence.

"It is to be so large," said Patty, as her brother-in-law shut the drawing-room door upon the trio, "that even Mrs. Aarons will be included in it."

"Mrs. Aarons!" echoed Elizabeth, who knew that the fairy godmother had repaid that lady's hospitality and attentions with her second-best bit of sang-de-boeuf crackle and her sole specimen of genuine Rose du Barry—dear and precious treasures sacrificed to the demands of conscience which proclaimed Mrs. Aarons wronged and insulted by being excluded from the Duff-Scott dinner list. "And she is really coming?"

"She really is—though it is her own right to receive, as I think Mrs. Duff-Scott perfectly remembered when she sent her invitation—accompanied, of course, by Mr. Aarons."

"And now," said Nelly, looking back, "Patty has got her old wish—she really *is* in a position to turn up her nose, at last."

"Oh," said Patty, vehemently, "don't remind me of that wicked, vulgar, indecent speech! Poor woman, who am I that I should turn up my nose at her? I am very glad she is coming—I think she ought to have been asked long ago. Why not? She is just as good as we are, every bit."

Eleanor laughed softly. "Ah, what a difference in one's sentiments does a large fortune make—doesn't it, Elizabeth? Patty doesn't want to turn up her nose at Mrs. Aarons, because, don't you see, she knows she can crush her quite naturally and comfortably by keeping it down. And, besides, when one has got one's revenge—when one has paid off one's old score—one doesn't want to be mean and barbarous. Oh," exclaimed Nelly, rapturously, "I never thought that being rich was so delicious as it is!"

"I hope it won't spoil you," said Elizabeth.

"I hope it won't spoil *you*," retorted the girl, saucily. "You are in far greater danger than I am."

By this time they had reached the top of the stairs, and Eleanor, who had led the way, opened the door, not of Elizabeth's old bedroom, but of the state guest-chamber of the house; and she motioned the bride to enter with a low bow. Here was the explanation of that impatience to get her upstairs. Elizabeth took a few steps over the threshold and then stood still, while the tears rushed into her eyes. The room had been elaborately dressed in white lace and white ribbons; the dressing-table was decorated with white flowers; the bed was covered with an æsthetic satin quilt, and on the bed was spread out a bridal robe—white brocade, the bodice frilled with Brussels lace—with white shoes, white gloves, white silk stockings, white feather fan, white everything *en suite*.

"This is your dress for to-night," said Patty, coaxing it with soft hands. "And you will find lots more in the wardrobe. Mrs. Duff-Scott has been fitting you up while you have been away."

Upon which Nelly threw open the doors of the wardrobe and pulled out the drawers, and displayed with great pride the piles and layers of new clothes that the fairy godmother had laboriously gathered together; the cream, or, to speak more correctly (if less poetically), the butter, churned from the finest material that the Melbourne shops could produce, and "made up" by a Collins Street mademoiselle, whose handiwork was as recognisable to the local initiated as that of Elise herself. The bride had been allowed no choice in the matter of her own trousseau, but she did not feel that she had missed anything by that. She stood and gazed at the beautiful garments, which were all dim and misty as seen through her tears, with lips and hands trembling, and a sense of misgiving lest such extravagant indulgence of all a woman's possible desires should tempt Fate to lay hands prematurely upon her. Then she went to find her friend—who had had so much enjoyment in the preparation of her surprise—and did what she could by dumb caresses to express her inexpressible sentiments.

Then in course of time these upsetting incidents were got over, and cheerful calmness supervened. As the night drew on, Mrs. Duff-Scott retired to put on her war paint. Nelly also departed to arrange her own toilet, which was a matter of considerable importance to her in these days. The girl who had worn cotton gloves to keep the sun from her hands, a year ago, had developed a great faculty for taking care of her beauty and taking pains with her clothes. Patty lingered behind to wait on Elizabeth. And in the interval before the bridegroom came up, these two had a little confidential chat. "What have you been doing, my darling," said the elder sister, "while I have been away?"

"Oh, nothing much," said Patty, rather drearily. "Shopping about your things most of the time, and getting ready for our voyage. They say we are to go as far as Italy next month, because January is the best time for the Red Sea. And they want the law business settled. It is dreadfully soon, isn't it?" This was not the tone of voice in which Italy was talked of a year ago.

"And you haven't—seen anybody?"

"No, I haven't seen anybody. Except once—and then he took off his hat without looking at me."

Elizabeth sighed. She was herself so safe and happy with her beloved that she could not bear to think of this other pair estranged and apart, making themselves so miserable.

"And what about Nelly and Mr. Westmoreland?" she inquired presently.

"Nelly is a baby," said Patty, with lofty scorn, "and Mr. Westmoreland is a great lout. You have no idea what a spectacle they are making of themselves."

"What—is it going on again?"

"Yes, it is going on—but not in the old style. Mr. Westmoreland has fallen in love with her really now—as far as such a brainless hippopotamus is capable of falling in love, that is to say. I suppose, the fact of her having a great fortune and high connections makes all the difference. And she is really uncommonly pretty. It is only in these last weeks that I have fully understood how much prettier she is than other girls, and I believe he, to do him justice, has always understood it in his stupid, coarse way."

"And Nelly?"

"Nelly," said Patty, "has been finding out a great deal lately. She knows well enough how pretty she is, and she knows what money and all the other things are worth. She is tasting the sweets of power, and she likes it—she likes it too much, I think—she will grow into a bit of a snob, if she doesn't mind. She is 'coming the swell' over Mr. Westmoreland, to use one of his own choice idioms—not exactly rudely, because she has such pretty manners, but with the most superb impertinence, all the same—and practising coquetry as if she had been beset with abject lovers all her life. She sits upon him and teases him and aggravates him till he doesn't know how to contain himself. It is *too* ridiculous."

"I should have thought he was the last man to let himself be sat upon."

"So should I. But he courts it—he obtrudes his infatuated servility—he goes and asks her, as it were, to sit upon him. It has the charm of novelty and difficulty, I suppose. People must get tired of having their own way always."

"But I can't understand Nelly."

"You soon will. You will see to-night how she goes on, for he is coming to dinner. She will tantalise him till he will forget where he is, and lose all sense of decency, and be fit to stamp and roar like a great buffalo. She says it is 'taking it out of him.' And she will look at the time so sweet and serene and unconscious—bah! I could box her ears," concluded Patty.

"And Mrs. Duff-Scott encourages him still, then?"

"No. That is another change. Mrs. Duff-Scott has withdrawn her gracious favour. She doesn't want him now. She thinks she will make a pair of duchesses of us when she gets us to London, don't you see? Dear woman, I'm afraid she will be grievously disappointed, so far as I am concerned. No, ever since the day you went away—which was the very day that Mr. Westmoreland began to come back—she has given him the cold shoulder. You know *what* a cold shoulder it can be! There is not a man alive who could stand up against it, except him. But he doesn't care. He can't, or won't, see that he is not wanted. I suppose it doesn't occur to him that *he* can possibly be unwelcome anywhere. He loafs about the house—he drops on us at Alston and Brown's—he turns up at the theatre—at the Exhibition—at Mullen's—everywhere. We can't escape him. Nelly likes it. If a day passes without her seeing him, she gets quite restless. She is like a horrid schoolboy with a cockroach on a pin—it is her great amusement in life to see him kicking and struggling."

"Perhaps she really does care about him, Patty."

"Not she. She is just having her revenge—heartless little monkey! I believe she will be a duchess, after all, with a miserable old toothless creature for her husband. It would be no more than she deserves. Oh, Elizabeth!"—suddenly changing her voice from sharps to flats—"how *beautiful* you do look! Nelly may be a duchess, and so might I, and neither of us would ever beat you for *presence*. I heard Mrs. Duff-Scott the other day congratulating herself that the prettiest of her three daughters were still left to dispose of. I don't believe we are the prettiest, but, if we are, what is mere prettiness compared with having a head set on like yours and a figure like a Greek statue?"

Elizabeth had been proceeding with her toilet, in order to have leisure to gossip with her husband when he came up; and now she stood before her long glass in her bridal dress, which had been composed by Mrs. Duff-Scott with an unlimited expenditure of taste and care. The material of it was exceptionally, if not obtrusively, rich—like a thick, dull, soft silk cloth, covered all over with a running pattern of flowers severely conventionalised; and it was made as plain as plain could be, falling straight to her feet in front, and sweeping back in great heavy folds behind, and fitting like a pliant glove to the curves of her lovely shape. Only round the bodice, cut neither low nor high, and round her rather massive elbows, had full ruffles of the lace that was its sole trimming been allowed; and altogether Mrs. Yelverton's strong points were brought out by her costume in a marvellously effective manner.

There was a sound at this moment in the adjoining room, on hearing which Patty abruptly departed; and the bride stood listening to her lord's footsteps, and still looking at herself in the glass. He entered her room, and she did not turn or raise her eyes, but a soft smile spread over her face as if a sun had risen and covered her with sudden light and warmth. She tried to see if the waist of her gown was wrinkled, or the set of it awry, but it was no use. When he came close to her and stooped to kiss her white neck, she lost all recollection of details.

"You want," he said, about ten minutes afterwards, when he had himself turned her round and round, and fingered the thick brocade and the lace critically, "you want diamonds with such a stately dress."

"Oh, no," she said; "I won't have any diamonds."

"You *won't*, did you say? This language to *me*, Elizabeth!"

"The diamonds shall go in beer and tobacco, Kingscote."

"My dear, they can't."

"Why not?"

"Because the Yelverton diamonds are heirlooms."

"Oh, dear me! Are there Yelverton diamonds too?"

"There are, I grieve to say. They have been laid up under lock and key for about forty years, and they must be very old-fashioned. But they are considered rather fine, and they are yours for the present, and as you can't make any use of them they may as well fulfil their purpose of being ornamental. You must wear them by-and-by, you know, when you go to Court."

"To Court?" reproachfully. "Is that the kind of life we are going to lead?"

"Just occasionally. We are going to combine things, and our duties to ourselves and to society. It is not going to be all Buckingham Palace, nor yet all Whitechapel, but a judicious blending of the two."

"And Yelverton?"

"And Yelverton of course. Yelverton is to be always there—our place of rest—our base of operations—our workshop—our fortress—our home with a capital H."

"Oh," she said, "we seem to have the shares of so many poor people besides our own. It overwhelms me to think of it."

"Don't think of it," he said, as she laid her head on his shoulder, and he smoothed her fine brown hair with his big palm. "Don't be afraid that we are destined to be too happy. We shall be handicapped yet."

They did not go down until the carriages had begun to arrive, and then they descended the wide stairs dawdlingly, she leaning on him, with her two white gloved hands clasped round his coat sleeve, and he bending his tall head towards her—talking still of their own affairs, and quite indifferent to the sensation they were about to make. When they entered the dim-coloured drawing-room, which was suffused with a low murmur of conversation, and by the mild radiance of many wax candles and coloured lamps, Elizabeth was made to understand by hostess and guests the exceptional position of Mrs. Yelverton of Yelverton, and wherein and how enormously it differed from that of Elizabeth King. But she was not so much taken up with her own state and circumstance as to forget those two who had been her charge for so many years. She searched for Nelly first. And Nelly was in the music-room, sitting at the piano, and looking dazzlingly fair under the gaslight in the white dress that she had worn at the club ball, and with dark red roses at her throat and in her yellow hair. She was playing Schubert's A Minor Sonata ravishingly—for the benefit of Mr. Smith, apparently, who sat, the recipient of smiles and whispers, beside her, rapt in ecstasies of appreciation; and she was taking not the slightest notice of Mr. Westmoreland, who, leaning over the other end of the piano on his folded arms, was openly sighing his soul into his lady's face. Then Elizabeth looked for Patty. And Patty she found on that settee within the alcove at the opposite end of the big room—also in her white ball dress, and also looking charming—engaged in what appeared to be an interesting and animated dialogue with the voluble Mrs. Aarons.

The young matron sighed as she contrasted her own blessed lot with theirs—with Nelly's, ignorant of what love was, and with Patty's, knowing it, and yet having no comfort in the knowing. She did not know which to pity most.

CHAPTER XLVI
PATTY CHOOSES HER CAREER

The dinner party on Christmas Eve was the first of a series of brilliant festivities, extending all through the hot last week of 1880, and over the cool new year (for which fires were lighted and furs brought out again), and into the sultry middle of January, and up to the memorable anniversary of the day on which the three Miss Kings had first arrived in Melbourne; and when they were over this was the state of the sisters' affairs:—Elizabeth a little tired with so much dissipation, but content to do all that was asked of her, since she was not asked to leave her husband's side; Eleanor, still revelling in the delights of wealth and power, and in Mr. Westmoreland's accumulating torments; and Patty worn and pale with sleepless nights and heart-sick with hope deferred, longing to set herself straight with Paul Brion before she left Australia, and seeing her chances of doing so dwindling and fading day by day. And now they were beginning to prepare for their voyage to a world yet larger and fuller than the one in which they had lived and learned so much.

One afternoon, while Mrs. Duff-Scott and Eleanor paid calls, Elizabeth and Patty went for the last time to Myrtle Street, to pack up the bureau and some of their smaller household effects in preparation for the men who were to clear the rooms on the morrow. Mr. Yelverton accompanied them, and lingered in the small sitting-room for awhile, helping here and there, or pretending to do so. For his entertainment they boiled the kettle and set out the cheap cups and saucers, and they had afternoon tea together, and Patty played the Moonlight Sonata; and then Elizabeth bade her husband go and amuse himself at his club and come back to them in an hour's time. He went, accordingly; and the two sisters pinned up their skirts and tucked up their sleeves, and worked with great diligence when he was no longer there to distract them. They worked so well that at the end of half an hour they had nothing left to do, except a little sorting of house linen and books. Elizabeth undertaking this business, Patty pulled down her sleeves and walked to the window; and she stood there for a little while, leaning her arm on the frame and her head on her arm.

"Paul Brion is at home, Elizabeth," she said, presently.

"Is he, dear?" responded the elder sister, who had begun to think (because her husband thought it) that it was a pity Paul Brion, being so hopelessly cantankerous, should be allowed to bother them any more.

"Yes. And, Elizabeth, I hope you won't mind—it is very improper, I know—but *I shall go and see him*. It is my last chance. I will go and say good-bye to Mrs. M'Intyre, and then I will run up to his room and speak to him—just for one minute. It is my last chance," she repeated; "I shall never have another."

"But, my darling—"

"Oh, don't be afraid"—drawing herself up haughtily—"I am not going to be *quite* a fool. I shall not throw myself into his arms. I am simply going to apologise for cutting him on Cup Day. I am simply going to set myself right with him before I go away—for his father's sake."

"It is a risky experiment, my dear, whichever way you look at it. I think you had better write."

"No. I have no faith in writing. You cannot make a letter say what you mean. And he will not come to us—he will not share his father's friendship for Kingscote—he was not at home when you and Kingscote called on him—he was not even at Mrs. Aarons's on Friday. There is no way to get at him but to go and see him now. I hear him in his room, and he is alone. I will not trouble him long—I will let him see that I can do without him quite as well as he can do without me—but I must and will explain the horrible mistake that I know he has fallen into about me, before I lose the chance for the rest of my life."

"My dear, how can you? How can you tell him your true reason for cutting him? How can you do it at all, without implying more than you would like to imply? You had better leave it, Patty. Or let me go for you, my darling."

But Patty insisted upon going herself, conscientiously assuring her sister that she would do it in ten minutes, without saying anything improper about Mrs. Aarons, and without giving the young man the smallest reason to suppose that she cared for him any more than she cared for his father, or was in the least degree desirous of being cared for by him. And this was how she did it.

Paul was sitting at his table, with papers strewn before him. He had been writing since his mid-day breakfast, and was half way through a brilliant article on "Patronage in the Railway Department," when the sound of the piano next door, heard for the first time after a long interval, scattered his political ideas and set him dreaming and meditating for the rest of the afternoon. He was leaning back in his chair, with his pipe in his mouth, his hands in his pockets, and his legs stretched out rigidly under the table, when he heard a tap at the door. He said "Come in," listlessly, expecting Betsy's familiar face; and when, instead of an uninteresting housemaid, he saw the beautiful form of his beloved standing on the threshold, he was so stunned with astonishment that at first he could not speak.

"Miss—Miss Yelverton!" he exclaimed, flinging his pipe aside and struggling to his feet.

"I hope I am not disturbing you," said Patty, very stiffly. "I have only come for a moment—because we are going away, and—and—and I had something to say to you before we went. We have been so unfortunate—my sister and brother-in-law were so unfortunate—as to miss seeing you the other day. I—we have come this afternoon to do some packing, because we are giving up our old rooms, and I thought—I thought—"

She was stammering fearfully, and her face was scarlet with confusion and embarrassment. She was beginning already to realise the difficulty of her undertaking.

"Won't you sit down?" he said, wheeling his tobacco-scented arm-chair out of its corner. He, too, was very much off his balance and bewildered by the situation, and his voice, though grave, was shaken.

"No, thank you," she replied, with what she intended to be a haughty and distant bow. "I only came for a moment—as I happened to be saying good-bye to Mrs. M'Intyre. My sister is waiting for me. We are going home directly. I just wanted—I only wanted"—she lifted her eyes, full of wistful appeal, suddenly to his—"I wanted just to beg your pardon, that's all. I was very rude to you one day, and you have never forgiven me for it. I wanted to tell you that—that it was not what you thought it was—that I had a reason you did not know of for doing it, and that the moment after I was sorry—I have been sorry every hour of my life since, because I knew I had given you a wrong impression, and I have not been able to rectify it."

"I don't quite understand—" he began.

"No, I know—I know. And I can't explain. Don't ask me to explain. Only *believe*," she said earnestly, standing before him and leaning on the table, "that I have never, never been ungrateful for all the kindness you showed us when we came here a year ago—I have always been the same. It was not because I forgot that you were our best friend—the best friend we ever had—that I—that I"—her voice was breaking, and she was searching for her pocket-handkerchief—"that I behaved to you as I did."

The Three Miss Kings | 283

"Can't you tell me how it was?" he asked, anxiously. "You have nothing to be grateful for, Miss Patty—Miss Yelverton, I ought to say—and I cannot feel that I have anything to forgive. But I should like to know—yes, now that you have spoken of it, I think you ought to tell me—why you did it."

"I cannot—I cannot. It was something that had been said of you. I believed it for a moment, because—because it looked as if it were true—but only for a moment. When I came to think of it I knew it was impossible."

Paul Brion's keen face, that had been pale and strained, cleared suddenly, and his dark eyes brightened. He was quite satisfied with this explanation. He knew what Patty meant as well as if there had been but one word for a spade, and she had used it—as well, and even better than she could have imagined; for she forgot that she had no right or reason to resent his shortcomings, save on the ground of a special interest in him, and he was quick to remember it.

"Oh, do sit down a moment," he said, pushing the arm-chair a few inches forward. He was trying to think what he might dare to say to her to show how thankful he was. It was impossible for her to help seeing the change in him.

"No," she replied, hastily pulling herself together. "I must go now. I had no business to come here at all—it was only because it seemed the last chance of speaking to you. I have said what I came to say, and now I must go back to my sister." She looked all round the well-remembered room—at the green rep suite, and the flowery carpet, and the cedar chiffonnier, and the Cenci over the fire-place—at Paul's bookshelves and littered writing-table, and his pipes and letters on the chimney-piece, and his newspapers on the floor; and then she looked at him with eyes that *would* cry, though she did her very best to help it. "Good-bye," she said, turning towards the door.

He took her outstretched hand and held it "Good-bye—if it must be so," he said. "You are really going away by the next mail?"

"Yes."

"And not coming back again?"

"I don't know."

"Well," he said, "you are rich, and a great lady now. I can only wish with all my heart for your happiness—I cannot hope that I shall ever be privileged to contribute to it again. I am out of it now, Miss Patty."

She left her right hand in his, and with the other put her handkerchief to her eyes. "Why should you be out of it?" she sobbed. "Your father is not out of it. It is you who have deserted us—we should never have deserted you."

"I thought you threw me over that day on the racecourse, and I have only tried to keep my place."

"But I have told you I never meant that."

"Yes, thank God! Whatever happens, I shall have this day to remember— that you came to me voluntarily to tell me that you had never been unworthy of yourself. You have asked me to forgive you, but it is I that want to be forgiven—for insulting you by thinking that money and grandeur and fine clothes could change you."

"They will never change me," said Patty, who had broken down altogether, and was making no secret of her tears. In fact, they were past making a secret of. She had determined to have no tender sentiment when she sought this interview, but she found herself powerless to resist the pathos of the situation. To be parting from Paul Brion—and it seemed as if it were really going to be a parting—was too heartbreaking to bear as she would have liked to bear it.

"When you were poor," he said, hurried along by a very strong current of emotions of various kinds, "when you lived here on the other side of the wall—if you had come to me—if you had spoken to me, and treated me like this *then*—"

She drew her hand from his grasp, and tried to collect herself. "Hush— we must not go on talking," she said, with a flurried air; "you must not keep me here now."

"No, I will not keep you—I will not take advantage of you now," he replied, "though I am horribly tempted. But if it had been as it used to be—if we were both poor alike, as we were then—if you were Patty King instead of Miss Yelverton—I would not let you out of this room without telling me something more. Oh, why did you come at all?" he burst out, in a sudden rage of passion, quivering all over as he looked at her with the desire to seize her and kiss her and satisfy his starving heart.

"You have been hard to me always—from first to last—but this is the very cruellest thing you have ever done. To come here and drive me wild like this, and then go and leave me us if I were Mrs. M'Intyre or the landlord you were paying off next door. I wonder what you think I am made of? I have stood everything—I have stood all your snubs, and slights, and hard usage of me—I have been humble and patient as I never was to anybody who treated me so in my life before—but that doesn't mean that I am made of wood or stone. There are limits to one's powers of endurance, and though I have borne so much, I *can't* bear *this*. I tell you fairly it is trying me too far." He stood at the table fluttering his papers with a hand as unsteady as that of a drunkard, and glaring at her, not straight into her eyes—which, indeed, were cast abjectly on the floor—but all over her pretty, forlorn figure, shrinking and cowering before him. "You are kind enough to everybody else," he went on; "you might at least show some common humanity to me. I am not a coxcomb, I hope, but I know you can't have helped knowing what I have felt for you—no woman can help knowing when a man cares for her, though he never says a word about it. A dog who loves you will get some consideration for it, but you are having no consideration for me. I hope I am not rude—I'm afraid I am forgetting my manners, Miss Patty—but a man can't think of manners when he is driven out of his senses. Forgive me, I am speaking to you too roughly. It was kind of you to come and tell me what you have told me—I am not ungrateful for that—but it was a cruel kindness. Why didn't you send me a note—a little, cold, formal note? or why did you not send Mrs. Yelverton to explain things? That would have done just as well. You have paid me a great honour, I know; but I can't look at it like that. After all, I was making up my mind to lose you, and I think I could have borne it, and got on somehow, and got something out of life in spite of it. But now how can I bear it?—how can I bear it *now?*"

Patty bowed like a reed to this unexpected storm, which, nevertheless, thrilled her with wild elation and rapture, through and through. She had no sense of either pride or shame; she never for a moment regretted that she had not written a note, or sent Mrs. Yelverton in her place. But what she said and what she did I will leave the reader to conjecture. There has been too much love-making in these pages of late. Tableau. We will ring the curtain down.

Meanwhile Elizabeth sat alone when her work was done, wondering what was happening at Mrs. M'Intyre's, until her husband came to tell her that it was past six o'clock, and time to go home to dress for dinner. "The child can't possibly be with *him*," said Mr. Yelverton, rather severely. "She must be gossiping with the landlady."

"I think I will go and fetch her," said Elizabeth. But as she was patting on her bonnet, Patty came upstairs, smiling and preening her feathers, so to speak—bringing Paul with her.

CHAPTER XLVII
A FAIR FIELD AND NO FAVOUR

When Mrs. Duff-Scott came to hear of all this, she was terribly vexed with Patty. Indeed, no one dared to tell her the whole truth, and to this day she does not know that the engagement was made in the young bachelor's sitting-room, whither Patty had sought him because he would not seek her. She thinks the pair met at No. 6, under the lax and injudicious chaperonage of Elizabeth; and, in the first blush of her disappointment and indignation, she was firmly convinced, though too well bred to express her conviction, that the son had taken advantage of the father's privileged position to entrap the young heiress for the sake of her thirty thousand pounds. Things did not go smoothly with Patty, as they had done with her sister. Elizabeth herself was a rock of shelter and a storehouse of consolation from the moment that the pair came up to the dismantled room where she and her husband were having a lovers' *tête-à-tête* of their own, and she saw that the long misunderstanding was at an end; but no one else except Mrs. M'Intyre (who, poor woman, was held of no account), took kindly to the alliance so unexpectedly proposed. Quite the contrary, in fact. Mr. Yelverton, notwithstanding his late experiences, had no sympathy whatever for the young fellow who had flattered him by following his example. The philanthropist, with all his full-blown modern radicalism, was also a man of long descent and great connections, and some subtle instinct of race and habit rose up in opposition to the claims of an obscure press writer to enter his distinguished family. It was one thing for a Yelverton man to marry a humbly-circumstanced woman, as he had himself been prepared to do, but quite another thing for a humbly-circumstanced man to aspire to the hand of a Yelverton woman, and that woman rich and beautiful, his own ward and sister. He was not aware of this strong sentiment, but believed his objections arose from a proper solicitude for Patty's welfare. Paul had been rude and impertinent, wanting in respect for her and hers; he had an ill-conditioned, sulky temper; he lived an irregular life, from hand to mouth; he had no money; he had no reputable friends. Therefore, when Paul (with some defiance of mien, as one who knew that it was a merely formal courtesy) requested the consent of the head of the house to his union with the lady of his choice, the head of the house, though elaborately polite, was very high and mighty, and—Patty and Elizabeth being out of the way, shut up together to kiss in comfort in one of the little bedrooms at the back—made some very plain statements of his views to the ineligible suitor, which fanned the vital spark in that young man's ardent spirit to a white heat of wrath. By-and-by Mr. Yelverton modified those views, like the just and large-hearted student of humanity that he was, and was brought to see that a man can do no more for a woman than love her, be he who he may, and that a woman, whether queen or peasant, millionaire or pauper, can never give more than value for that "value received." And by-and-by Paul learned to respect his brother-in-law for a man whose manhood was his own, and to trust his motives absolutely, even when he did not understand his actions. But just at first things were unpleasant. Mr. Yelverton touched the young man's sensitive pride, already morbidly exercised by his consciousness of the disparity between Patty's social position and fortunes and his own, by some indirect allusion to that painful circumstance, and brought upon himself a revengeful reminder that his (Mr. Yelverton's) marriage with Elizabeth might not be considered by superficial persons to be entirely above suspicion. Things were, indeed, very unpleasant. Paul, irritated in the first rapture of happiness, used more bad language (in thought if not in speech) than he had done since Cup Day, when he went back to his unfinished article on Political Patronage; Patty drove home with a burning sense of being of age and her own mistress; and Elizabeth sat in the carriage beside her, silent and thoughtful, feeling that the first little cloud (that first one which, however faint and small, is so incredible and so terrible) had made its appearance on the hitherto stainless horizon of her married life.

Mrs. Duff-Scott, when they got home, received the blow with a stern fortitude that was almost worse than Mr. Yelverton's prompt resistance, and much worse than the mild but equally decided opposition of that punctilious old gentleman at Seaview Villa, who, by-and-by, used all his influence to keep the pair apart whom he would have given his heart's blood to see united, out of a fastidious sense of what he conceived to be his social and professional duty. Between them all, they nearly drove the two high-spirited victims into further following the example of the head of the house—the imminent danger of which became apparent to Patty's confidante Elizabeth, who gave timely warning of it to her husband. This latter pair, who had themselves carried matters with such a very high hand, were far from desiring that Paul and Patty should make assignations at the Exhibition with a view to circumventing their adversaries by a clandestine or otherwise untimely marriage (such divergence of opinion with respect to one's own affairs and other people's being very common in this world, the gentle reader may observe, even in the case of the most high-minded people).

"Kingscote," said Elizabeth, when one night she sat brushing her hair before the looking-glass, and he, still in his evening dress, lounged in an arm-chair by the dressing-table, talking to her, "Kingscote, I am afraid you are too hard on Patty—you and the Duff-Scotts—keeping her from Paul still, though she has but three days left, and I don't believe she will stand it."

"My dear, we are not hard upon her, are we? It is for her sake. If we can tide over these few days and get her away all right, a year or two of absence, and all the new interests that she will find in Europe and in her changed position, will probably cure her of her fancy for a fellow who is not good enough for her."

"That shows how little you know her," said Elizabeth, with a melancholy smile. "She is not a girl to take 'fancies' in that direction, and having given her heart—and she has not given it so easily as you imagine—she will be as faithful to him—as faithful"—casting about for an adequate illustration—"as I should have been to you, Kingscote."

"Perhaps so, dear. I myself think it very likely. And in such a case no harm is done. They will test each other, and if they both stand the test it will be better and happier for them to have borne it, and we shall feel then that we are justified in letting them marry. But at present they know so little of each other—she has had no fair choice of a husband—and she is too good to be thrown away. I feel responsible for her, don't you see? And I only want her to have all her chances. I will be the last to hinder the course of true love when once it proves itself to *be* true love."

"*We* did not think it necessary to prove *our* love—and I don't think we should have allowed anybody else to prove it—by a long probation, Kingscote."

"My darling, we were different," he said, promptly.

She did not ask him to explain wherein they were different, he and she, who had met for the first time less than four months ago; she shared the usual unconscious prejudice that we all have in favour of our own sincerity and trustworthiness, and wisdom and foresight, and assumed as a matter of course that their case was an exceptional one. Still she had faith in others as well as in herself and her second self.

"I know Patty," she said, laying her hair brush on her knee and looking with solemn earnestness into her husband's rough-hewn but impressive face—a face that seemed to her to contain every element of noble manhood, and that would have been weakened and spoiled by mere superficial beauty—"I know Patty, Kingscote, better than anyone knows her except herself. She is like a little briar rose—sweet and tender if you are gentle and sympathetic with her, but certain to prick if you handle her roughly. And so strong in the stem—so tough and strong—that you cannot root her out or twist her any way that she doesn't feel naturally inclined to grow—not if you use all your power to make her."

"Poor little Patty!" he said, smiling. "That is a very pathetic image of her. But I don't like to figure in your parable as the blind genius of brute force—a horny-handed hedger and ditcher with a smock frock and a bill-hook. I am quite capable of feeling the beauty, and understanding the moral qualities of a wild rose—at least, I thought I was. Perhaps I am mistaken. Tell me what you would do, if you were in my place?"

Elizabeth slipped from her chair and down upon her knees beside him, with her long hair and her long dressing-gown flowing about her, and laid her head where it was glad of any excuse to be laid—a locality at this moment indicated by the polished and unyielding surface of his starched shirt front. "You know I never likened you to a hedger and ditcher," she said, fondly. "No one is so wise and thoughtful and far-sighted as you. It is only that you don't know Patty quite yet—you will do soon—and what might be the perfect management of such a crisis in another girl's affairs is likely not to succeed with her—just simply and only for the reason that she is a little peculiar, and you have not yet had time to learn that."

"It is time that I should learn," he said, lifting her into a restful position and settling himself for a comfortable talk. "Tell me what you think and know yourself, and what, in your judgment, it would be best to do."

"In my judgment, then, it would be best," said Elizabeth, brief interval given up to the enjoyment of a wordless *tête-à-tête*, "to let Patty and Paul be together a little before they part. For this reason—that they *will* be together, whether they are let or not. Isn't it preferable to make concessions before they are ignominiously extorted from you? And if Patty has much longer to bear seeing her lover, as she thinks, humiliated and insulted, by being ignored as her lover in this house, she will go to the other extreme—she will go away from us to him—by way of making up to him for it. It is like what you say of the smouldering, poverty-bred anarchy in your European national life—that if you don't find a vent for the accumulating electricity generating in the human sewer—how do you put it?—it is no use to try to draw it off after the storm has burst."

"Elizabeth," said her husband, reproachfully, "that is worse than being called a hedger and ditcher."

"Well, you know what I mean."

"Tell me what you mean in the vulgar tongue, my dear. Do you want me to go and call on Mr. Paul Brion and tell him that we have thought better of it?"

"Not exactly that. But if you would persuade Mrs. Duff-Scott to be nice about it—no one can be more enchantingly nice than she, when she likes, but when she doesn't like she is enough to drive a man—a proud man like Paul Brion—simply frantic. And Patty will never stand it—she will not hold out—she will not go away leaving things as they are now. We could not expect it of her."

"Well? And how should Mrs. Duff-Scott show herself nice to Mr. Brion?"

"She might treat him as—as she did you, Kingscote, when you were wanting me."

"But she approved of me, you see. She doesn't approve of him."

"You are both gentlemen, anyhow—though he is poor. I would have been the more tender and considerate to him, because he is poor. He is not too poor for Patty—nor would he have been if she had no fortune herself. As it is, there is abundance. And, Kingscote, though I don't mean for a moment to disparage you—"

"I should hope not, Elizabeth."

"Still I can't help thinking that to have brains as he has is to be essentially a rich and distinguished man. And to be a writer for a high-class newspaper, which you say yourself is the greatest and best educator in the world—to spend himself in making other men see what is right and useful—in spreading light and knowledge that no money could pay for, and all the time effacing himself, and taking no reward of honour or credit for it—surely that must be the noblest profession, and one that should make a man anybody's equal—even yours, my love!"

She lifted herself up to make this eloquent appeal, and dropped back on his shoulder again, and wound her arm about his neck and his bent head with tender deprecation. He was deeply touched and stirred, and did not speak for a moment. Then he said gruffly, "I shall go and see him in the morning, Elizabeth. Tell me what I shall say to him, my dear."

"Say," said Elizabeth, "that you would rather not have a fixed engagement at first, in order that Patty may be unhampered during the time she is away—in order that she may be free to make other matrimonial arrangements when she gets into the great world, if she *likes*—but that you will leave that to him. Tell him that if love is not to be kept faithful without vows and promises, it is not love nor worth keeping—but I daresay he knows that. Tell him that, except for being obliged to go to England just now on the family affairs, Patty is free to do exactly as she likes—which she is by law, you know, for she is over three-and-twenty—and that we will be happy to see her happy, whatever way she chooses. And then let him come here and see her. Ask Mrs. Duff-Scott to be nice and kind, and to give him an invitation—she will do anything for you—and then treat them both as if they were engaged for just this little time until we leave. It will comfort them so much, poor things! It will put them on their honour. It will draw off the electricity, you know, and prevent catastrophes. And it will make not the slightest difference in the final issue. But, oh," she added impulsively, "you don't want me to tell you what to do, you are so much wiser than I am."

"I told you we should give and take," he responded; "I told you we should teach and lead each other—sometimes I and sometimes you. That is what we are doing already—it is as it should be. I shall go and see Paul Brion in the morning. Confound him!" he added, as he got up out of his chair to go to his dressing-room.

And so it came to pass that the young press writer, newly risen from his bed, and meditating desperate things over his coffee and cutlet, received a friendly embassy from the great powers that had taken up arms against him. Mr. Yelverton was the bearer of despatches from his sovereign, Mrs. Duff-Scott, in the shape of a gracious note of invitation to dinner, which—after a long discussion of the situation with her envoy—Mr. Paul Brion permitted himself to accept politely. The interview between the two men was productive of a strong sense of relief and satisfaction on both sides, and it brought about the cessation of all open hostilities.

CHAPTER XLVIII
PROBATION

Mr. Yelverton did not return home from his mission until Mrs. Duff-Scott's farewell kettle-drum was in full blast. He found the two drawing-rooms filled with a fashionable crowd; and the hum of sprightly conversation, the tinkle of teaspoons, the rustle of crisp draperies, the all-pervading clamour of soft feminine voices, raised in staccato exclamations and laughter, were such that he did not see his way to getting a word in edgeways. Round each of the Yelverton sisters the press of bland and attentive visitors was noticeably great. They were swallowed up in the compact groups around them. This I am tempted to impute to the fact of their recent elevation to rank and wealth, and to a certain extent it may be admitted that that fact was influential. And why not? But in justice I must state that the three pretty Miss Kings had become favourites in Melbourne society while the utmost ignorance prevailed as to their birth and antecedents, in conjunction with the most exact knowledge as to the narrowness of their incomes. Melbourne society, if a little too loosely constituted to please the tastes of a British prig, born and bred to class exclusiveness, is, I honestly believe, as free as may be from the elaborate snobbishness with which that typical individual (though rather as his misfortune than his fault) must be credited.

In Mrs. Duff-Scott's drawing-room were numerous representatives of this society—its most select circle, in fact—numbering amongst them women of all sorts; women like Mrs. Duff-Scott herself, who busied themselves with hospitals and benevolent schemes, conscious of natural aspirations and abilities for better things than dressing and gossiping and intriguing for social triumphs; women like Mrs. Aarons, who had had to struggle desperately to rise with the "cream" to the top of the cup, and whose every nerve was strained to retain the advantages so hardly won; women to whom scandal was the breath of their nostrils, and the dissemination thereof the occupation of their lives; women whose highest ambition was to make a large waist into a small one; women with the still higher ambition to have a house that was more pleasant and popular than anybody else's. All sorts and conditions of women, indeed; including a good proportion of those whose womanhood was unspoiled and unspoilable even by the deteriorating influences of luxury and idleness, and whose intellect and mental culture and charming qualities generally were such as one would need to hunt well to find anything better in the same line elsewhere. These people had all accepted the Miss Kings cordially when Mrs. Duff-Scott brought them into their circle and enabled the girls to do their duty therein by dressing well, and looking pretty, and contributing a graceful element to fashionable gatherings by their very attractive manners. That was all that was demanded of them, and, as Miss Kings only, they would doubtless have had a brilliant career and never been made to feel the want of either pedigree or fortune. Now, as representatives of a great family and possessors of independent wealth, they were overwhelmed with attentions; but this, I maintain, was due to the interesting nature of the situation rather than to that worship of worldly prosperity which (because he has plenty of it) is supposed to characterise the successful colonist.

Mr. Yelverton looked round, and dropped into a chair near the door, to talk to a group of ladies with whom he had friendly relations until he could find an opportunity to rejoin his family. The hostess was dispensing tea, with Nelly's assistance—Nelly being herself attended by Mr. Westmoreland, who dogged her footsteps with patient and abject assiduity—other men straying about amongst the crowd with the precious little fragile cups and saucers in their hands. Elizabeth was surrounded by young matrons fervently interested in her new condition, and pouring out upon her their several experiences of European life, in the form of information and advice for her own guidance. The best shops, the best dressmakers, the best hotels, the best travelling routes, and generally the best things to do and see, were emphatically and at great length impressed upon her, and she made notes of them on the back of an envelope with polite gratitude, invariably convinced that her husband knew all about such things far better than anybody else could do. Patty was in the music-room, not playing, but sitting at the piano, and when Kingscote turned his head in her direction he met a full and glowing look of inquiry from her bright eyes that told him she knew or guessed the nature of his recent errand. There was such an invitation in her face that he found himself drawn from his chair as by a strong magnet. He and she had already had those "fights" which she had prophetically anticipated. Lately their relations had been such that he had permitted himself to call her a "spitfire" in speaking of her to her own sister. But they were friends, tacitly trusting each other at heart even when most openly at war, and the force that drew them apart was always returned in the rebound that united them when their quarrels were over. They seemed to be all over for the present. As he approached her she resumed her talk with the ladies beside her, and dropped her eyes as if taking no notice of him; but she had the greatest difficulty to keep herself down on the music-stool and resist an inclination to kiss him that for the first time beset her. She did, indeed, suddenly put out her hand to him—her left hand—with a vigour of intention that called faint smiles to the faces of the fair spectators; who concluded that Mr. Yelverton had been out of town and was receiving a welcome home after a too long absence. Then Patty was seized with an ungovernable restlessness. She quivered all over; she fidgetted in her seat; she did not know who spoke to her or what she was talking about; her fingers went fluttering up and down the keyboard.

"Play us something, dear Miss Yelverton," said a lady sitting by. "Let us hear your lovely touch once more."

"I don't think I can," said Patty, falteringly—the first time she had ever made such a reply to such a demand. She got up and began to turn over some loose music that lay about on the piano. Her brother-in-law essayed to help her; he saw what an agony of suspense and expectation she was in.

"You know where I have been?" he inquired in a careless tone, speaking low, so that only she could hear.

"Yes"—breathlessly—"I think so."

"I went to take an invitation from Mrs. Duff-Scott."

"Yes?"

"I had a pleasant talk. I am very glad I went. He is coming to dine here to-night."

"Is he?"

"Mrs. Duff-Scott thought you would all like to see him before you went away. Let us have the 'Moonlight Sonata,' shall we? Beauty fades and mere goodness is apt to pall, as Mrs. Ponsonby de Tompkins would say, but one never gets tired of the 'Moonlight Sonata,' when it is played as you play it. Don't you agree with me, Mrs. Aarons?"

"I do, indeed," responded that lady, fervently. She agreed with everybody in his rank of life. And she implored Patty to give them the "Moonlight Sonata."

Patty did—disdaining "notes," and sitting at the piano like a young queen upon her throne. She laid her fingers on the keyboard with a touch as light as thistle-down, but only so light because it was so strong, and played with a hushed passion and subdued power that testified to the effect on her of her brother-in-law's communication—her face set and calm, but radiant in its sudden peacefulness. Her way, too, as well as Elizabeth's, was opening before her now. She lost sight of the gorgeous ladies around her for a little while, and saw only the comfortable path which she and Paul would tread together thenceforth. She played the "Moonlight Sonata" to *him*, sitting in his own chamber corner, with his pipe, resting himself after his work. "I will never," she said to herself, with a little remote smile that nobody saw, "I will never have a room in my house that he shall not smoke in, if he likes. When he is with me, he shall enjoy himself." In those sweet few minutes she sketched the entire programme of her married life.

The crowd thinned by degrees, and filtered away; the drawing-rooms were deserted, save for the soft-footed servants who came in to set them in order, and light the wax candles and rosy lamps, and the great gas-burner over the piano, which was as the sun amongst his planet family. Night came, and the ladies returned in their pretty dinner costumes; and the major stole downstairs after them, and smiled and chuckled silently over the new affair as he had done over the old—looking on like a benevolent, superannuated Jove upon these simple little romances from the high Olympus of his own brilliant past; and then (preceded by no carriage wheels) there was a step on the gravel and a ring at the door bell, and the guest of the evening was announced.

When Paul came in, correctly appointed, and looking so fierce and commanding that Patty's heart swelled with pride as she gazed at him, seeing how well—how almost too well, indeed—he upheld his dignity and hers, which had been subjected to so many trials, he found himself received with a cordiality that left him nothing to find fault with. Mrs. Duff-Scott was an impulsive, and generous, and well-bred woman, not given to do things by halves. She still hoped that Patty would not marry this young man, and did not mean to let her if she could help it; but, having gone the length of inviting him to her house, she treated him accordingly. She greeted him as if he were an old friend, and she chatted to him pleasantly while they waited for dinner, questioning him with subtle flattery about his professional affairs, and implying that reverence for the majesty of the press which is so gratifying to all enlightened people. Then she took his arm into dinner, and continued to talk to him throughout the meal as only one hostess in a hundred, really nice and clever, with a hospitable soul, and a warm heart, and abundant tact and good taste, can talk, and was surprised herself to find how much she appreciated it. She intended to make the poor young fellow enjoy his brief taste of Paradise, since she had given herself leave to do so, and Paul responded by shining for her entertainment with a mental effulgence that astonished and charmed her. He put forth his very best wares for her inspection, and at the same time, in a difficult position, conducted himself with irreproachable propriety. By the time she left the table she was ready to own herself heartily sorry that fickle fortune had not endowed him according to his deserts.

"I *do* so like really interesting and intellectual young men, who don't give themselves any airs about it," she said to nobody in particular, when she strolled back to the drawing-room with her three girls; "and one does so *very* seldom meet with them!" She threw herself into a low chair, snatched up a fan, and began to fan herself vigorously. The discovery that a press writer of Paul Brion's standing meant a cultured man of the world impressed her strongly; the thought of him as a new son for herself, clever, enterprising, active-minded as she was—a man to be governed, perhaps, in a motherly way, and to be proud of whether he let himself be governed or not—danced tantalisingly through her brain. She felt it necessary to put a very strong check upon herself to keep her from being foolish.

She escaped that danger, however. A high sense of duty to Patty held her back from foolishness. Still she could not help being kind to the young couple while she had the opportunity; turning her head when they strolled into the conservatory after the men came in from the dining-room, and otherwise shutting her eyes to their joint proceedings. And they had a peaceful and sad and happy time, by her gracious favour, for two days and a half—until the mail ship carried one of them to England, and left the other behind.

CHAPTER XLIX
YELVERTON

Patty went "home," and stayed there for two years; but it was never home to her, though all her friends and connections, save one, were with her—because that one was absent. She saw "the great Alps and the Doge's palace," and all the beauty and glory of that great world that she had so ardently dreamed of and longed for; travelling in comfort and luxury, and enjoying herself thoroughly all the while. She was presented at Court— "Miss Yelverton, by her sister, Mrs. Kingscote Yelverton"—and held a distinguished place in the *Court Journal* and in the gossip of London society for the better part of two seasons. She was taught to know that she was a beauty, if she had never known it before; she was made to understand the value of a high social position and the inestimable advantage of large means (and she did understand it perfectly, being a young person abundantly gifted with common sense); and she was offered these good things for the rest of her life, and a coronet into the bargain. Nevertheless, she chose to abide by her first choice, and to remain faithful to her penniless press writer under all temptations. She passed through the fire of every trying ordeal that the ingenuity of Mrs. Duff-Scott could devise; her unpledged constancy underwent the severest tests that, in the case of a girl of her tastes and character, it could possibly be subjected to; and at the end of a year and a half, when the owner of the coronet above-mentioned raised the question of her matrimonial prospects, she announced to him, and subsequently to her family, that they had been irrevocably settled long ago; that she was entirely unchanged in her sentiments and relations towards Paul Brion; and that she intended, moreover, if they had no objection, to return to Australia to marry him.

It was in September when she thus declared herself—after keeping a hopeful silence, for the most part, concerning her love affairs, since she disgraced herself before a crowd of people by weeping in her sweetheart's arms on the deck of the mail steamer at the moment when she was bidden by a cruel fate to part from him. The Yelverton family had spent the previous winter in the South of Europe, "doing" the palaces, and churches, and picture galleries that were such an old story to most people of their class, but to the unsophisticated sisters so fresh and wonderful an experience—an experience that fulfilled all expectations, moreover, which such realisations of young dreams so seldom do. Generally, when at last one has one's wish of this sort, the spirit that conceived the charms and pleasures of it is quenched by bodily wearinesses and vexations and the thousand and one petty accidents that circumvent one's schemes. One is burdened and fretted with uncongenial companions, perhaps, or one is worried and hampered for want of money; or one is nervous or bilious, or one is too old and careworn to enjoy as one might once have done; in some way or other one's heart's desire comes to one as if only to show the "leanness withal" in the soul that seemed (until thus proved) to have such power to assimilate happiness and enrich itself thereby. But with the Yelverton sisters there was no disillusionment of this sort. They had their little drawbacks, of course. Elizabeth was not always in good health; Patty pined for her Paul; Eleanor sprained her ankle and had to lie on Roman sofas while the others were exploring Roman ruins out of doors; and there were features about the winter, even in those famous climes, which gave them sensible discomfort and occasionally set them on the verge of discontent. But, looking back upon their travels, they have no recollection of these things. Young, and strong, and rich, with no troubles to speak of and the keenest appetites to see and learn, they had as good a time as pleasure-seeking mortals can hope for in this world; the memories of it, tenderly stored up to the smallest detail, will be a joy for ever to all of them. On their return to England they took up their abode in the London house, and for some weeks they revelled delightedly in balls, drums, garden parties, concerts, and so on, under the supervision and generalship of Mrs. Duff-Scott; and they also made acquaintance with the widely-ramifying Whitechapel institutions. Early in the summer Elizabeth and her husband went to Yelverton, which in their absence had been prepared for "the family" to live in again. A neighbouring country house and several cottages had been rented and fitted up for the waifs and strays, where they had been made as comfortable as before, and were still under the eye of their protector; and the ancestral furniture that had been removed for their convenience and its own safety was put back in its place, and bright (no, not bright—Mrs. Duff-Scott undertook the task of fitting them up—but eminently artistic and charming) rooms were newly decorated and made ready for Elizabeth's occupation.

She went there early in June—she and her husband alone, leaving Mrs. Duff-Scott and the girls in London. Mr. Yelverton had always a little jealousy about keeping his wife to himself on these specially sacred occasions, and he invited no one to join them during their first days at home, and instructed Mr. Le Breton to repress any tendency that might be apparent in tenants or *protégés* to make a public festival of their arrival there. The *rôle* of squire was in no way to his taste, nor that of Lady Bountiful to hers. And yet he had planned for their home-coming with the utmost care and forethought, that nothing should be wanting to make it satisfying and complete—as he had planned for their wedding journey on the eve of their hurried marriage.

It is too late in my story to say much about Yelverton. It merits a description, but a description would be out of place, and serve no purpose now. Those who are familiar with old Elizabethan country seats, and the general environment of a hereditary dweller therein, will have a sufficient idea of Elizabeth's home; and those who have never seen such things—who have not grown up in personal association with the traditions of an "old family"—will not care to be told about it. In the near future (for, though his brother magnates of the county, hearing of the restoration of the house, congratulated themselves that Yelverton's marriage had cured him of his crack-brained fads, he only delivered her property intact to his wife in order that they might be crack-brained together, at her instance and with her legal permission in new and worse directions afterwards) Yelverton will lose many of its time-honoured aristocratic distinctions; oxen and sheep will take the place of its antlered herds, and the vulgar plough and ploughman will break up the broad park lawns, where now the pheasant walks in the evening, and the fox, stealing out from his cover, haunts for his dainty meal. But when Elizabeth saw it that tender June night, just when the sun was setting, as in England it only sets in June, all its old-world charm of feudal state and beauty, jealously walled off from the common herd outside as one man's heritage by divine right and for his exclusive enjoyment, lay about it, as it had lain for generations past. Will she ever forget that drive in the summer evening from the little country railway station to her ancestral home?—the silent road, with the great trees almost meeting overhead; the snug farm-houses, old and picturesque, and standing behind their white gates amongst their hollyhocks and bee-hives; the thatched cottages by the roadside, with groups of wide-eyed children standing at the doors to see the carriage pass; the smell of the hay and the red clover in the fields, and the honeysuckle and the sweet-briar in the hedges; the sound of the wood pigeons cooing in the plantations; the first sight of her own lodge gates, with their great ramping griffins stonily pawing the air, and of those miles and miles of shadow-dappled sward within, those mysterious dark coverts, whence now and then a stag looked out at her and went crashing back to his ferny lair, and those odorous avenues of beech and lime, still haunted by belated bees and buzzing cockchafers, under which she passed to the inner enclosure of lawns and gardens where the old house stood, with open doors of welcome, awaiting her. What an old house! She had seen such in pictures—in the little prints that adorned old-fashioned pocket-books of her mother's time—-but the reality, as in the case of the Continental palaces, transcended all her dreams. White smoke curled up to the sky from the fluted chimney-stacks; the diamond-paned casements—little sections of the enormous mullioned windows—were set wide to the evening breezes and sunshine; on the steps before the porch a group of servants, respectful but not obsequious, stood ready to receive their new mistress, and to efface themselves as soon as they had made her welcome.

"It is more than my share," she said, almost oppressed by all these evidences of her prosperity, and thinking of her mother's different lot. "It doesn't seem fair, Kingscote."

"It is not fair," he replied. "But that is not your fault, nor mine. We are not going to keep it all to ourselves, you and I—because a king happened to fall in love with one of our grandmothers, who was no better than she should be—which is our title to be great folks, I believe. We are going to let other people have a share. But just for a little while we'll be selfish, Elizabeth; it's a luxury we don't indulge in often."

So he led her into the beautiful house, after giving her a solemn kiss upon the threshold; and passing through the great hall, she was taken to a vast but charming bedroom that had been newly fitted up for her on the ground floor, and thence to an adjoining sitting-room, looking out upon a shady lawn—a homely, cosy little room that he had himself arranged for her private use, and which no one was to be allowed to have the run of, he told her, except him.

"I want to feel that there is one place where we can be together," he said, "whenever we want to be together, sure of being always undisturbed. It won't matter how full the house is, nor how much bustle and business goes on, if we can keep this nest for ourselves, to come to when we are tired and when we want to talk. It is not your boudoir, you know—that is in another place—and it is not your morning room; it is a little sanctuary apart, where nobody is to be allowed to set foot, save our own two selves and the housemaid."

"It shall be," said his wife, with kindling eyes. "I will take care of that."

"Very well. That is a bargain. We will take possession to-night. We will inaugurate our occupation by having our tea here. You shall not be fatigued by sitting up to dinner—you shall have a Myrtle Street tea, and I will wait on you."

She was placed in a deep arm-chair, beside a hearth whereon burned the first wood fire that she had seen since she left Australia—billets of elm-wood split from the butts of dead and felled giants that had lived their life out on the Yelverton acres—with her feet on a rug of Tasmanian opossum skins, and a bouquet of golden wattle blossoms (procured with as much difficulty in England as the lilies of the valley had been in Australia) on a table beside her, scenting the room with its sweet and familiar fragrance. And here tea was brought in—a dainty little nondescript meal, with very little about it to remind her of Myrtle Street, save its comfortable informality; and the servant was dismissed, and the husband waited upon his wife—helping her from the little savoury dishes that she did not know, nor care to ask, the name of—pouring the cream into the cup that for so many years had held her strongest beverage, dusting the sugar over her strawberries—all the time keeping her at rest in her soft chair, with the sense of being at home and in peace and safety under his protection working like a delicious opiate on her tired nerves and brain.

This was how they came to Yelverton. And for some days thereafter they indulged in the luxury of selfishness—they took their happiness in both hands, and made all they could of it, conscious they were well within their just rights and privileges—gaining experiences that all the rest of their lives would be the better for, and putting off from day to day, and from week to week, that summons to join them, which the matron and girls in London were ready to obey at a moment's notice. Husband and wife sat in their gable room, reading, resting, talking, love-making. They explored all the nooks and corners of their old house, investigated its multifarious antiquities, studied its bygone history, exhumed the pathetic memorials of the Kingscote and Elizabeth whose inheritance had come to them in so strange a way. They rambled in the beautiful summer woods, she with her needlework, he with his book—sometimes with a luncheon basket, when they would stay out all day; and they took quiet drives, all by themselves in a light buggy, as if they were in Australia still—apparently with no consciousness of that toiling and moiling world outside their park-gates which had once been of so much importance to them. And then one day Elizabeth complained of feeling unusually tired. The walks and drives came to an end, and the sitting-room was left empty. There was a breathless hush all over the great house for a little while; whispers and rustlings to and fro; and then a little cry—which, weak and small as it was, and shut in with double doors and curtains, somehow managed to make itself heard from the attic to the basement—announced that a new generation of Yelvertons of Yelverton had come into the world.

Mrs. Duff-Scott returned home from a series of Belgravian entertainments, with that coronet of Patty's capture on her mind, in the small hours of the morning following this eventful day; and she found a telegram on her hall table, and learned, to her intense indignation, that Elizabeth had dared to have a baby without her (Mrs. Duff-Scott) being there to assist at the all-important ceremony.

"It's just like him," she exclaimed to the much-excited sisters, who were ready to melt into tears over the good news. "It is just what I expected he would do when he took her off by herself in that way. It is the marriage over again. He wants to manage everything in his own fashion, and to have no interference from anybody. But this is really carrying independence too far. Supposing anything had gone wrong with Elizabeth? And how am I to know that her nurse is an efficient person?—and that the poor dear infant will be properly looked after?"

"You may depend," said Patty, who did not grudge her sister her new happiness, but envied it from the bottom of her honest woman's heart, "You may depend he has taken every care of that. He is not a man to leave things to chance—at any rate, not where *she* is concerned."

"Rubbish!" retorted the disappointed matron, who, though she had had no children of her own—perhaps because she had had none—had looked forward to a vicarious participation in Elizabeth's experiences at this time with the strongest interest and eagerness; "as if a man has any business to take upon himself to meddle at all in such matters! It is not fair to Elizabeth. She has a right to have us with her. I gave way about the wedding, but here I must draw the line. She is in her own house, and I shall go to her at once. Tell your maid to pack up, dears—we will start to-morrow."

But they did not. They stayed in London, with what patience they could, subsisting on daily letters and telegrams, until the season there was over, and the baby at Yelverton was three weeks old. Then, though no explanations were made, they became aware that they would be no longer considered *de trop* by the baby's father, and rushed from the town to the country house with all possible haste.

"You are a tyrant," said Mrs. Duff-Scott, when the master came forth to meet her. "I always said so, and now I know it."

"I was afraid she would get talking and exerting herself too much if she had you all about her," he replied, with his imperturbable smile.

"And you didn't think that *we* might possibly have a grain of sense, as well as you?"

"I didn't think of anything," he said coolly, "except to make sure of her safety as far as possible."

"O yes, I know"—laughing and brushing past him—"all you think of is to get your own way. Well, let us see the poor dear girl now we are here. I know how she must have been pining to show her baby to her sisters all this while, when you wouldn't let her."

The next time he found himself alone with his wife, Mr. Yelverton asked her, with some conscientious misgiving, whether she *had* been pining for this forbidden pleasure, and whether he really was a tyrant. Of course, Elizabeth scouted any suggestion of such an idea as most horrible and preposterous, but the fact was—

Never mind. We all have our little failings, and the intelligent reader will not expect to find the perfect man any more than the perfect woman in this present world. And if he—or, I should say, she—*could* find him, no doubt she would be dreadfully disappointed, and not like him half so well as the imperfect ones. Elizabeth, who, as Patty had predicted, was "butter" in his hands, would not have had her husband less fond of his own way on any account.

For some time everybody was taken up with the baby, who was felt to be the realisation of that ideal which Dan and the magpies had faintly typified in the past. Dan himself lay humbly on the hem of the mother's skirts, or under her chair, resting his disjointed nose on his paws, and blinking meditatively at the rival who had for ever superseded him. Like a philosophical dog as he was, he accepted superannuation without a protest as the inevitable and universal lot, and, when no one took any notice of him, coiled himself on the softest thing he could find and went to sleep, or if he couldn't go to sleep, amused himself snapping at the English flies. The girls forgot, or temporarily laid aside, their own affairs, in the excitement of a constant struggle for possession of the person of the little heir, whom they regarded with passionate solicitude or devouring envy and jealousy according as they were successful or otherwise. The nurse's post was a sinecure at this time. The aunts hushed the infant to sleep, and kept watch by his cradle, and carried him up and down the garden terraces with a parasol over his head. The mother insisted upon performing his toilet, and generally taking a much larger share of him than was proper for a mother in her rank of life; and even Mrs. Duff-Scott, for whom china had lost its remaining charms, assumed privileges as a deputy grandmother which it was found expedient to respect. In this absorbing domesticity the summer passed away. The harvest of field and orchard was by-and-by gathered in;

the dark-green woods and avenues turned red, and brown, and orange under the mellow autumn sun; the wild fruits in the hedgerows ripened; the swallows took wing. To Yelverton came a party of guests—country neighbours and distinguished public men, of a class that had not been there a-visiting for years past; who shot the well-stocked covers, and otherwise disported themselves after the manner of their kind. And amongst the nobilities was that coronet, that incarnation of dignity and magnificence, which had been singled out as an appropriate mate for Patty. It, or he, was offered in form, and with circumstances of state and ceremony befitting the great occasion; and Patty was summoned to a consultation with her family—every member of which, not even excepting Elizabeth herself, was anxious to see the coronet on Patty's brow (which shows how hereditary superstitions and social prejudices linger in the blood, even after they seem to be eradicated from the brain)—for the purpose of receiving their advice, and stating her own intentions.

"My intention," said Patty, firmly, with her little nose uplifted, and a high colour in her face, "is to put an end to this useless and culpable waste of time. The man I love and am *engaged to* is working, and slaving, and waiting for me; and I, like the rest of you, am neglecting him, and sacrificing him, as if he were of no consequence whatever. *This* shows me how I have been treating him. I will not do it any more. I did not become Miss Yelverton to repudiate all I undertook when I was only Patty King. I am Yelverton by name, but I am King by nature, still. I don't want to be a great swell. I have seen the world, and I am satisfied. Now I want to go home to Paul—as I ought to have done before. I will ask you, if you please, Kingscote, to take my passage for me at once. I shall go back next month, and I shall marry Paul Brion as soon as the steamer gets to Melbourne."

Her brother-in-law put out his hand, and drew her to him, and kissed her. "Well done," he said, speaking boldly from his honest heart. "So you shall."

CHAPTER L
"THY PEOPLE SHALL BE MY PEOPLE"

Patty softened down the terms in which she made her declaration of independence, when she found that it was received in so proper a spirit. She asked them if they had *any objection*—which, after telling them that it didn't matter whether they had or not, was a graceful act, tending to make things pleasant without committing anybody. But if they had objections (as of course they had) they abandoned them at this crisis. It was no use to fight against Paul Brion, so they accepted him, and made the best of him. The head of the family suddenly and forcibly realised that he should have been disappointed in his little sister-in law if she had acted otherwise; and even Mrs. Duff-Scott, who would always so much rather help than hinder a generous project, no matter how opposed to the ethics of her class, was surprised herself by the readiness with which she turned her back on faded old lords and dissipated young baronets, and gave herself up to the pleasant task of making true lovers happy. Elizabeth repented swiftly of her own disloyalty to plighted love, temporary and shadowy as it was; and, seeing how matters really stood, acquiesced in the situation with a sense of great thankfulness that her Patty was proved so incorruptible by the tests she had gone through. Mrs. Yelverton's only trouble was the fear of separation in the family, which the ratification of the engagement seemed likely to bring about.

But Patty was dissuaded from her daring enterprise, as first proposed; and Paul was written to by her brother and guardian, and adjured to detach himself from his newspaper for a while and come to England for a holiday— which, it was delicately hinted, might take the form of a bridal tour. And in that little sitting-room, sacred to the private interviews of the master and mistress of the house, great schemes were conceived and elaborated for the purpose of seducing Mrs. Brion's husband to remain in England for good and all. They settled his future for him in what seemed to them an irresistibly attractive way. He was to rent a certain picturesque manor-house in the Yelverton neighbourhood, and there, keeping Patty within her sister's reach, take up that wholesome, out-door country life which they were sure would be so good for his health and his temper. He could do a little high farming, and "whiles" write famous books; or, if his tastes and habits unfitted him for such a humdrum career, he could live in the world of London art and intellect, and be a "power" on behalf of those social reforms for which his brother-in-law so ardently laboured. Mr. Brion, senior, who had long ago returned to Seaview Villa, was, of course, to be sent for back again, to shelter himself under the broad Yelverton wing. The plan was all arranged in the most harmonious manner, and Elizabeth's heart grew more light and confident every time she discussed it.

Paul received his pressing invitation—which he understood to mean, as it did, a permission to go and marry Patty from her sister's house—just after having been informed by Mrs. Aarons, "as a positive fact," that Miss Yelverton was shortly to be made a countess. He did not believe this piece of news, though Mrs. Aarons, who had an unaccountably large number of friends in the highest circles of London society, was ready to vouch for its authenticity with her life, if necessary; but, all the same, it made him feel moody, and surly, and ill-used, and miserable. It was his dark hour before the dawn. In Australia the summer was coming on. It was the middle of November. The "Cup" carnival was over for another year. The war in Egypt was also over, and the campaign of Murdoch's cricketers in England—two events which it seemed somehow natural to bracket together. The Honourable Ivo Bligh and his team had just arrived in Melbourne. The Austral had just been sunk in Sydney Harbour. It was early summer with us here, the brightest and gayest time of the whole year. In England the bitter winter was at hand—that dreaded English winter which the Australian shudders to think of, but which the Yelverton family had agreed to spend in their ancestral house, in order to naturalise and acclimatise the sisters, and that duty might be done in respect of those who had to bear the full extent of its bitterness, in hunger, and cold, and want. When Mr. Yelverton wrote to Paul to ask him to visit them, Patty wrote also to suggest that his precious health might suffer by coming over at such a season, and to advise him to wait until February or March. But the moment her lover had read those letters, he put on his hat and went forth to his office to demand leave for six months, and in a few days was on board the returning mail steamer on his way to England. He did not feel like waiting now—after waiting for two years—and she was not in the least afraid that he would accept her advice.

Paul's answers arrived by post, as he was himself speeding through Europe—not so much absorbed in his mission as to neglect note-making by the way, and able to write brilliant articles on Gambetta's death, and other affairs of the moment, while waiting for boat or train to carry him to his beloved; and it was still only the first week in January when they received a telegram at Yelverton announcing his imminent arrival. Mr. Yelverton himself went to London to meet him, and Elizabeth rolled herself in furs and an opossum rug in her snug brougham and drove to the country railway station to meet them both, leaving Patty sitting by the wood fire in the hall. Mrs. Duff-Scott was in town, and Eleanor with her, trying to see Rossetti's pictures through the murky darkness of the winter days, but in reality bent on giving the long-divided lovers as much as possible of their own society for a little while. The carriage went forth early in the afternoon, with its lamps lighted, and it returned when the cold night had settled down on the dreary landscape at five o'clock. Paul, ulstered and comfortered, walked into the dimly-lighted, warm, vast space, hung round with ghostly banners and antlers, and coats of mail, and pictures whereof little was visible but the frames, and marched straight into the ruddy circle of the firelight, where the small figure awaited him by the twinkling tea-table, herself only an outline against the dusk behind her; and the pair stood on the hearthrug and kissed each other silently, while Elizabeth, accompanied by her husband, went to take her bonnet off, and to see how Kingscote junior was getting on.

After that Paul and Patty parted no more. They had a few peaceful weeks at Yelverton, during which the newspaper in Melbourne got nothing whatever from the fertile brain of its brilliant contributor (which, Patty thought, must certainly be a most serious matter for the proprietors); and in which interval they made compensation for all past shortcomings as far as their opportunities, which were profuse and various, allowed. It delighted Paul to cast up at Patty the several slights and snubs that she had inflicted on him in the old Myrtle Street days, and it was her great luxury in life to make atonement for them all—to pay him back a hundredfold for all that he had suffered on her account. The number of "soft things" that she played upon the piano from morning till night would alone have set him up in "Fridays" for the two years that he had been driven to Mrs. Aarons for entertainment; and the abject meekness of the little spitfire that he used to know was enough to provoke him to bully her, if he had had anything of the bully in him. The butter-like consistency to which she melted in this freezing English winter time was such as to disqualify her for ever from sitting in judgment upon Elizabeth's conjugal attitude. She fell so low, indeed, that she became, in her turn, a mark for Eleanor's scoffing criticism.

"Well, I never thought to see you grovel to any living being—let alone a *man*—as you do to him," said that young lady on one occasion, with an impudent smile. "The citizens of Calais on their knees to Edward the Third were truculent swaggerers by comparison."

"You mind your own business," retorted Patty, with a flash of her ancient spirit.

Whereat Nelly rejoined that she would mind it by keeping her *fiancé* in his proper place when *her* time came to have a *fiancé*. *She* would not let him put a rope round her neck and tie it to his button-hole like a hat-string. She'd see him farther first.

February came, and Mrs. Duff-Scott returned, and preparations for the wedding were set going. The fairy godmother was determined to make up for the disappointment she had suffered in Elizabeth's case by making a great festival of the second marriage of the family, and they let her have her wish, the result being that the bride of the poor press-writer had a *trousseau* worthy of that coronet which she had extravagantly thrown away, and presents the list and description of which filled a whole column of the *Yelverton Advertiser*, and made the hearts of all the local maidens to burn with envy. In March they were married in Yelverton village church. They went to London for a week, and came back for a fortnight; and in April they crossed the sea again, bound for their Melbourne home.

For all the beautiful arrangements that had been planned for them fell through. The Yelvertons had reckoned without their host—as is the incurable habit of sanguine human nature—with the usual result. Paul had no mind to abandon his chosen career and the country that, as a true Australian, he loved and served as he could never love and serve another, because he had married into a great English family; and Patty would not allow him to be persuaded. Though her heart was torn in two at the thought of parting with Elizabeth, and with that precious baby who was Elizabeth's rival in her affections, she promptly and uncomplainingly tore herself from both of them to follow her husband whithersoever it seemed good to him to go.

"One cannot have everything in this world," said Patty philosophically, "and you and I, Elizabeth, have considerably more than our fair share. If we hadn't to pay something for our happiness, how could we expect it to last?"

CHAPTER LI
PATIENCE REWARDED

Eleanor, like Patty, withstood the seductions of English life and miscellaneous English admirers, and lived to be Miss Yelverton in her turn, unappropriated and independent. And, like both her sisters, though more by accident than of deliberate intention, she remained true to her first love, and, after seeing the world and supping full of pleasure and luxury, returned to Melbourne and married Mr. Westmoreland. That is to say, Mr. Westmoreland followed her to England, and followed her all over Europe—dogging her from place to place with a steadfast persistence that certainly deserved reward—until the major and Mrs. Duff-Scott, returning home almost immediately after Patty's marriage and departure, brought their one ewe lamb, which the Yelvertons had not the conscience to immediately deprive them of, back to Australia with them; when her persevering suitor promptly took his passage in the same ship. All this time Mr. Westmoreland had been as much in love as his capacity for the tender passion—much larger than was generally supposed—permitted. Whether it was that she was the only woman who dared to bully him and trample on him, and thereby won his admiration and respect—or whether his passion required that the object of it should be difficult of attainment—or whether her grace and beauty were literally irresistible to him—or whether he was merely the sport of that unaccountable fate which seems to govern or misgovern these affairs, it is not necessary to conjecture. No one asks for reasons when a man or woman falls a victim to this sort of infatuation. Some said it was because she had become rich and grand, but that was not the case—except in so far as the change in her social circumstances had made her tyrannical and impudent, in which sense wealth and consequence had certainly enhanced her attractions in his eyes. Thirty thousand pounds, though a very respectable marriage portion in England, is not sufficient to make a fortune-hunter of an Australian suitor in his position; and let me do the Australian suitor of all ranks justice and here state that fortune hunting, through the medium of matrimony, is a weakness that his worst enemy cannot accuse him of—whatever his other faults may be. Mr. Westmoreland, being fond of money, as a constitutional and hereditary peculiarity—if you can call that a peculiarity—was tempted to marry it once, when that stout and swarthy person in the satin gown and diamonds exercised her fascinations on him at the club ball, and he could have married it at any time of his bachelor life, the above possessor of it being, like Barkis, "willin'", and even more than "willin'". Her fortune was such that Eleanor's thirty thousand was but a drop in the bucket compared with it, and yet even he did not value it in comparison with the favour of that capricious young lady. So he followed her about from day to day and from place to place, as if he had no other aim in life than to keep her within sight, making himself an insufferable nuisance to her friends very often, but apparently not offending her by his open and inveterate pursuit. She was not kind, but she was not cruel, and yet she was both in turn to a distracting degree. She made his life an ecstasy of miserable longing for her, keeping him by her side like a big dog on a chain, and feeding him with stones (in the prettiest manner) when he asked for bread. But she grew very partial to her big dog in the process of tormenting him and witnessing his touching patience under it. She was "used to him," she said; and when, from some untoward circumstance over which he had no control, he was for a little while absent from her, she felt the gap he left. She sensibly missed him. Moreover, though she trampled on him herself, it hurt her to see others do it; and when Mrs. Duff-Scott and Kingscote Yelverton respectively aired their opinions of his character and conduct, she instantly went over to his side, and protested in her heart, if not in words, against the injustice and opprobrium that he incurred for her sake. So, when Elizabeth became the much-occupied mother of a family, and when Patty was married and gone off into the world with her Paul, Eleanor, left alone in her independence, began to reckon up what it was worth. The spectacle of her sisters' wedded lives gave her pleasant notions of matrimony, and the state of single blessedness, as such, never had any particular charms for her. Was it worth while, she asked herself, to be cruel any more?—and might she not just as well have a house and home of her own as Elizabeth and Patty? Her lover was only a big dog upon a chain, but then why shouldn't he be? Husbands were not required to be all of the same pattern. She didn't want to be domineered over. And she didn't see anybody she liked better. She might go farther and fare worse. And—she was getting older every day.

Mrs. Duff-Scott broke in upon these meditations with the demand that she (Eleanor) should return with her to Melbourne, if only for a year or two, so that she should not be entirely bereft and desolate.

"I must start at once," said the energetic woman, suddenly seized with a paroxysm of home sickness and a sense of the necessity to be doing something now that at Yelverton there seemed nothing more to do, and in order to shake off the depressing effect of the first break in their little circle. "I have been away too long—it is time to be looking after my own business. Besides, I can't allow Patty to remain in that young man's lodgings—full of dusty papers and tobacco smoke, and where, I daresay, she hasn't so much as a peg to hang her dresses on. She must get a house at once, and I must be there to see about it, and to help her to choose the furniture. Elizabeth, my darling, you have your husband and child—I am leaving you happy and comfortable—and I will come and see you again in a year or two, or perhaps you and Kingscote will take a trip over yourselves and spend a winter with us. But I must go now. And do, do—oh, *do* let me keep Nelly for a little while longer! You know I will take care of her, and I couldn't bear the sight of my house with none of you in it!"

So she went, and of course she took Eleanor, who secretly longed for the land of sunshine after her full dose of "that horrid English climate," and who, with a sister at either end of the world, perhaps missed Patty, who had been her companion by night as well as by day, more than she would miss Elizabeth. The girl was very ready to go. She wept bitterly when the actual parting came, but she got over it in a way that gave great satisfaction to Mrs. Duff-Scott and the major, and relieved them of all fear that they had been selfish about bringing her away. They joined the mail steamer at Venice, and there found Mr. Westmoreland on board. He had been summoned by his agent at home he explained; one of his partners wanted to retire, and he had to be there to sign papers. And since it had so happened that he was obliged to go back by this particular boat, he hoped the ladies would make him useful, and let him look after their luggage and things. Eleanor was properly and conventionally astonished by the curious coincidence, but had known that it would happen just as well as he. The chaperon, for her part, was indignant and annoyed by it—for a little while; afterwards she, too, reflected that Eleanor had spent two unproductive years in England and was growing older every day. Also that she might certainly go farther and fare worse. So Mr. Westmoreland was accepted as a member of the travelling party. All the heavy duties of escort were relegated to him by the major, and

Mrs. Duff-Scott sent him hither and thither in a way that he had never been accustomed to. But he was meek and biddable in these days, and did not mind what uses he put his noble self to for his lady's sake. And she was very gracious. The conditions of ship life, at once so favourable and so very unfavourable for the growth of tender relations, suited his requirements in every way. She could not snub him under the ever-watchful eyes of their fellow-passengers. She could not send him away from her. She was even a little tempted, by that ingrained vanity of the female heart, to make a display before the other and less favoured ladies of the subject-like homage which she, queen-like, received. Altogether, things went on in a very promising manner. So that when, no farther than the Red Sea—while life seemed, as it does in that charming locality, reduced to its simple elements, and the pleasure of having a man to fan her was a comparatively strong sensation—when at this propitious juncture, Mr. Westmoreland bewailed his hard fate for the thousandth time, and wondered whether he should ever have the good fortune to find a little favour in her sight, it seemed to her that this sort of thing had gone on long enough, and that she might as well pacify him and have done with it. So she said, looking at him languidly with her sentimental blue eyes—"Well, if you'll promise not to bother me any more, I'll think about it."

He promised faithfully not to bother her any more, and he did not. But he asked her presently, after fanning her in silence for some minutes, what colour she would like her carriage painted, and she answered promptly, "Dark green."

While they were yet upon the sea, a letter—three letters, in fact—were despatched to Yelverton, to ask the consent of the head of the family to the newly-formed engagement, and not long after the party arrived in Melbourne the desired permission was received, Mr. and Mrs. Yelverton having learned the futility of opposition in these matters, and having no serious objection to Nelly's choice. And then again Mrs. Duff-Scott plunged into the delight of preparation for trousseau and wedding festivities—quite willing that the "poor dear fellow," as she now called him (having taken him to her capacious heart), should receive the reward of his devotion without unnecessary delay. The house was already there, a spick and span family mansion in Toorak, built by Mr. Westmoreland's father, and inherited by himself ere the first gloss was off the furniture; there was nothing to do to that but to arrange the chairs and sofas, and scatter Eleanor's wedding presents over the tables. There was nothing more *possible*. It was "hopeless,"

Mrs. Duff-Scott said, surveying the bright and shining rooms through her double eye-glass. Unless it were entirely cleared out, and you started afresh from the beginning, she would defy you to make anything of it. So, as the bridegroom was particularly proud of his furniture, which was both new and costly, and would have scouted with indignation any suggestion of replacing it, Mrs. Duff-Scott abandoned Eleanor æsthetically to her fate. There was nothing to wait for, so the pair were made one with great pomp and ceremony not long after their return to Australia. Eleanor had the grandest wedding of them all, and really did wear "woven dew" on the occasion—with any quantity of lace about it of extravagant delicacy and preciousness. And now she has settled herself in her great, gay-coloured, handsome house, and is already a very fashionable and much-admired and much-sought-after lady—so overwhelmed with her social engagements and responsibilities sometimes that she says she doesn't know what she should do if she hadn't Patty's quiet little house to slip into now and then. But she enjoys it. And she enjoys leading her infatuated husband about with her, like a tame bear on a string, to show people how very, very infatuated he is. It is her idea of married happiness—at present.

CHAPTER LII
CONCLUSION

While Mrs. Westmoreland thus disports herself in the gay world, Mrs. Brion pursues her less brilliant career in much peace and quietness. When she and Paul came back to Australia, a bride and bridegroom, free to follow their own devices unhampered by any necessity to consider the feelings of relatives and friends, nothing would satisfy her but to go straight from the ship to Mrs. M'Intyre's, and there temporarily abide in those tobacco-perfumed rooms which had once been such forbidden ground to her. She scoffed at the Oriental; she turned up her nose at the Esplanade; she would not hear of any suites of apartments, no matter how superior they might be. Her idea of perfect luxury was to go and live as Paul had lived, to find out all the little details of his old solitary life which aforetime she had not dared to inquire into, to rummage boldly over his bookshelves and desk and cupboards, which once it would have been indelicate for her to so much as look at, to revel in the sense that it was improper no longer for her to make just as free as she liked with his defunct bachelorhood, the existing conditions of which had had so many terrors for her. When Paul represented that it was not a fit place for her to go into, she told him that there was no place in the world so fit, and begged so hard to be taken there, if only for a week or two, that he let her have her way. And a very happy time they spent at No. 7, notwithstanding many little inconveniences. And even the inconveniences had their charm. Then Mrs. Duff-Scott and Eleanor came out, when it was felt to be time to say good-bye to these humble circumstances—to leave the flowery carpet, now faded and threadbare, the dingy rep suite, and the smirking Cenci over the mantelpiece, for the delectation of lodgers to whom such things were appropriate; and to select a house and furnish it as befitted the occupation of Miss Yelverton that was and her (now) distinguished husband.

By good fortune (they did not say it was good fortune, but they thought it), the old landlord next door saw fit to die at this particular juncture, and No. 6 was advertised to be let. Mr. and Mrs. Brion at once pounced upon the opportunity to secure the old house, which, it seemed to them, was admirably suited to their present modest requirements; and, by the joint exercise of Mrs. Duff-Scott's and Patty's own excellent taste, educated in England to the last degree of modern perfectibility, the purveyors of art furniture in our enlightened city transformed the humble dwelling of less than a dozen rooms into a little palace of esoteric delights. Such a subdued, harmonious brightness, such a refined simplicity, such an unpretentious air of comfort pervades it from top to bottom; and as a study of colour, Mrs. Duff-Scott will tell you, it is unique in the Australian colonies. It does her good—even her—to go and rest her eyes and her soul in the contemplation of it. Paul has the bureau in his study (and finds it very useful), and Patty has the piano in her drawing-room, its keyboard to a retired corner behind a portière (draped where once was a partition of folding doors), and its back, turned outwards, covered with a piece of South Kensington needlework. In this cosy nest of theirs, where Paul, with a new spur to his energies, works his special lever of the great machine that makes the world go on (when it would fain be lazy and sit down), doing great things for other men if gaining little glory for himself—and where Patty has afternoon teas and evenings that gather together whatever genuine exponents of intellectual culture may be going about, totally eclipsing the attractions of Mrs. Aarons's Fridays to serious workers in the fields of art and thought, without in any way dimming the brilliancy of those entertainments—the married pair seem likely to lead as happy a life as can be looked for in this world of compromises. It will not be all cakes and ale, by any means. The very happiest lives are rarely surfeited with these, perhaps, unwholesome delicacies, and I doubt if theirs will even be amongst the happiest. They are too much alike to be the ideal match. Patty is thin-skinned and passionate, too ready to be hurt to the heart by the mere little pin-pricks and mosquito bites of life; and Paul is proud and crotchety, and, like the great Napoleon, given to kick the fire with his boots when he is put out. There will be many little gusts of temper, little clouds of misunderstanding, disappointments, and bereavements, and sickness of mind and body; but, with all this, they will find their lot so blessed, by reason of the mutual love and sympathy that, through all vicissitudes, will surely grow deeper and stronger every day they live together, that they will not know how to conceive a better one. And, after all, that is the most one can ask or wish for in this world.

Mrs. Duff-Scott, being thus deprived of all her children, and finding china no longer the substantial comfort to her that it used to be, has fulfilled her husband's darkest predictions and "gone in" for philanthropy. In London she served a short but severe apprenticeship to that noble cause which seeks to remove the curse of past ignorance and cruelty from those to whom it has come down in hereditary entail—those on whose unhappy and degraded lives all the powers of evil held mortgages (to quote a thoughtful writer) before ever the deeds were put into their hands—and who are now preached at and punished for the crimes that, not they, but their tyrants of the past committed. She took a lesson in that new political economy which is to the old science what the spirit of modern religion is to the ecclesiasticism which has been its unwilling mother, and has learned that the rich *are* responsible for the poor—that, let these interesting debating clubs that call themselves the people's parliaments say what they like, the moral of the great social problem is that the selfishness of the past must be met by unselfishness in the present, if any of us would hope to see good days in the future.

"It will not do," says Mrs. Duff-Scott to her clergyman, who deplores the dangerous opinions that she has imbibed, "to leave these matters to legislation. Of what use is legislation? Here are a lot of ignorant, vain men who know nothing about it, fighting with one another for what they can get, and the handful amongst them who are really anxious for the public good are left nowhere in the scrimmage. It is *we* who must put our shoulders to the wheel, my dear sir—and the sooner we set about it the better. Look at the state of Europe"—she waves her hand abroad—"and see what things are coming to! The very heart of those countries is being eaten out by the cancer-growths of Nihilism and all sorts of dreadful isms, because the poor are getting educated to understand *why* they are so poor. Look at wealthy England, with more than a million paupers, and millions and millions that are worse than paupers—England is comparatively quiet and orderly under it, and why? Because a number of good people like Mr. Yelverton"—the clergyman shakes his head at the mention of this wicked sinner's name—"have given themselves up to struggle honestly and face to face with the evils that nothing but a self-sacrificing and independent philanthropy can touch. I believe that if England escapes the explosion of this fermenting democracy, which is brewing such a revolution as the world has never seen, it will be owing to neither Church nor State—unless Church and State both mend their ways considerably—but to the self-denying work that is being done outside of them by those who have a single-hearted desire to help, to *really* help, their wronged and wretched fellow-creatures."

Thus this energetic woman, in the headlong ardour of her new conversion. And (if a woman, ready to admit her disabilities as such, may say so) it is surely better to be generous in the cause of a possibly mistaken conviction of your own, than to be selfish in deference to the opinions of other people, which, though they be the product of the combined wisdom of all the legislatures of the world, find no response in the instincts of your human heart. At any rate, I believe we shall be brought to think so some day—that great Someday which looms not far ahead of us, when, as a Cornish proverb puts it, if we have not ruled ourselves by the rudder we shall be ruled by the rock. And so Mrs. Duff-Scott works, and thinks, and writes and (of course) talks, and bothers her husband and her acquaintances for the public weal, and leads her clergyman a life that makes him wish sometimes that he had chosen a less harassing profession; economising her money, and her time, and all she has of this world's goods, that she may fulfil her sacred obligations to her fellow-creatures and help the fortunate new country in which she lives to keep itself from the evil ways that have wrought such trouble and danger to the old ones.

And the man who set her to this good work pursues it himself, not in haste or under fitful and feverish impulses of what we call enthusiasm, but with refreshed energy and redoubled power, by reason of the great "means" that are now at his disposal, the faithful companionship that at once lightens and strengthens the labour of his hands and brain, and the deep passion of love for wife and home which keeps his heart warm with vital benevolence for all the world. Mr. Yelverton has not become more orthodox since his marriage; but that was not to be expected. In these days orthodoxy and goodness are not synonymous terms. It is doubtful, indeed, if orthodoxy has not rather become the synonym for the opposite of goodness, in the eyes of those who judge trees by their fruits and whose ideal of goodness is to love one's neighbour as one's self. While it is patent to the candid observer that the men who have studied the new book of Genesis which latter-day science has written for us, and have known that Exodus from the land of bondage which is the inevitable result of such study, conscientiously pursued, are, as a rule, distinguished by a large-minded justice and charity, sympathy and self-abnegation, a regard for the sacred ties of brotherhood binding man with man, which, being incompatible with the petty meannesses and cruelties so largely practised in sectarian circles, make their unostentatious influence to be felt like sweet and wholesome leaven all around them. Such a man is Elizabeth's husband, and as time goes on she ceases to wish for any change in him save that which means progression in his self-determined course. It was not lightly that he flew in the face of the religious traditions of his youth; rather did he crawl heavily and unwillingly away from them, in irresistible obedience to a conscience so sensitive and well-balanced that it ever pointed in the direction of the truth, like the magnetic needle to the pole, and in which he dared to trust absolutely, no matter how dark the outlook seemed. And now that, after much search, he has found his way, as far as he may hope to find it in this world, he is too intently concerned to discover what may be ahead of him, and in store for those who will follow him, to trouble himself and others with irrelevant trifles—to indulge in spites and jealousies, in ambitions that lead nowhere, in quarrels and controversies about nothing—to waste his precious strength and faculties in the child's play that with so many of us is the occupation of life, and like other child's play, full of pinches and scratches and selfish squabbling over trumpery toys. To one who has learned that "the hope of nature is in man," and something of what great nature is, and what man should be, there no longer exists much temptation to envy, hatred, malice, and uncharitableness, or any other of the vulgar vices of predatory humanity, not yet cured of its self-seeking propensities. He is educated above that level. His recognition of the brotherhood of men, and their common interests and high destiny, makes him feel for others in their differences with him, and patient and forbearing with those whose privileges have been fewer and whose light is less than his. He takes so wide an outlook over life that the little features of the foreground, which loom so large to those who cannot or will not look beyond them, are dwarfed to insignificance; or, rather, he can fix their just relation to the general design in human affairs, and so reads them with their context, as it were, and by the light of truth and justice spread abroad in his own heart—thus proving how different they are in essential value from what they superficially appear. So Mr. Yelverton, despite his constitutional imperiousness, is one of the most tolerant, fine-tempered, and generous of men; and he goes on his way steadily, bending circumstances to his will, but hurting no one in the process—rather lifting up and steadying and strengthening those with whom he comes in contact by the contagion of his bold spirit and his inflexible and incorruptible honesty; and proving himself in private life, as such men mostly do, a faithful exponent and practical illustration of all the domestic virtues.

Elizabeth is a happy woman, and she knows it well. It seems to her that all the prosperity and comfort that should have been her mother's has, like the enormous wealth that she inherits, been accumulating at compound interest, through the long years representing the lapsed generation, for her sole profit and enjoyment. She strolls often through the old plantation, where, in a remote nook, a moss-grown column stands to mark the spot where a little twig, a hair's breadth lack of space, was enough to destroy one strong life and ruin another, and to entail such tremendous consequences upon so many people, living and unborn; and she frequently drives to

Bradenham Abbey to call on or to dine with her step-uncle's wife, and sees the stately environment of her mother's girlhood—the "beautiful rooms with the gold Spanish leather on the walls," the "long gallery with the painted windows and the slippery oak floor and the thirty-seven family portraits all in a row"—which she contrasts with the bark-roofed cottage on the sea-cliff within whose narrow walls that beautiful and beloved woman afterwards lived and died. And then she goes home to Yelverton to her husband and baby, and asks what she has done to deserve to be so much better off than those who went before her?

And yet, perhaps, if all accounts were added up, the sum total of loss and profit on those respective investments that we make, or that are made for us, of our property in life, would not be found to differ so very much, one case with another. We can neither suffer nor enjoy beyond a certain point. Elizabeth is rich beyond the dreams of avarice in all that to such a woman is precious and desirable, and happy in her choice and lot beyond her utmost expectations. Yet not so happy as to have nothing to wish for— which we know, as well as Patty, means "too happy to last." There is that hunger for her absent sisters, which tries in vain to satisfy itself in weekly letters of prodigious length, left as a sort of hostage to fortune, a valuable if not altogether trustworthy security for the safety of her dearest possessions.